Passing Stranger

Passing Stranger

A Historical Civil War Novel about
General John B. Turchin

by

LOUIS S. RUBIN

iUniverse®

PASSING STRANGER
A HISTORICAL CIVIL WAR NOVEL ABOUT GENERAL JOHN B. TURCHIN

iUniverse books may be ordered through booksellers or by contacting:

iUniverse
1663 Liberty Drive
Bloomington, IN 47403
www.iuniverse.com
1-800-Authors (1-800-288-4677)

ISBN: 978-1-4917-9124-0 (sc)
ISBN: 978-1-4917-9125-7 (e)

Library of Congress Control Number: 2016903327

Print information available on the last page.

iUniverse rev. date: 11/14/2016

PREFACE AND ACKNOWLEDGEMENTS

The genesis of this book began many years ago, in 1938. At the time, I was a young man of 27, having come to this country some 10 years earlier from my home and friends in the Soviet Union. During those 10 years, I had developed an interest in President Abraham Lincoln, the "GREAT EMANCIPATOR" and especially in the Civil War years of 1860 - 1865 which had so devastated this country and yet at the same time, given it so much promise for renewal. Having always had a voracious appetite for the written word, my appetite became even more whetted when I became aware of a certain Russian military officer, Colonel Ivan Vasilevich Turchaninoff who had immigrated to the United States and who had played a significant role in the, "War between the States". This seemed to me most unusual. Why would a Russian officer give up the obvious security and prestige of his rank and position in the Russian Imperial Army to endure the severe hardships of starting a new life in America? And what role did he actually play in the Civil War? I searched for a reference book about Colonel Turchaninoff but found none. And so began my quest. I began to collect bits and pieces of information about Colonel Turchaninoff. And the more information I learned about this extraordinary man, the more I came to believe that he deserved more than just a "footnote" in history.

Over the next few years, I amassed thousands of bits and pieces of information about Colonel Turchaninoff. This information was gleaned from libraries and historical societies and from the biographies of Colonel Turchaninoff's contemporaries. I did extensive research in the Official Records of the Civil War and obtained every bit of information that was available from the extant newspapers that covered the Civil War era. I poured over much of Colonel Turchaninoff's correspondence with his senior officers during the War years and even found some valuable papers of Colonel Turchaninoff in the attic of a church in Radom, Illinois, a small town where the colonel had spent the last years of his life.

By 1950, I was ready to put all of my research together in manuscript form. This was, to say the least, a prodigious task. And for someone whose native tongue was not English, the task was even more difficult. Fortunately, for me and for the book, I had a very good friend, Mrs. Bess Kubicek, of Cleveland, Ohio, who came to my aid. Bess very graciously contributed to my efforts through her excellent command of the English language, helping me to reword, rephrase and rewrite the manuscript numerous times. Bess' efforts consumed the better part of 2 years during which time she labored without complaint and without thought of recompense. Without Bess' extraordinary fund of words and expressions and her ability to put my thoughts into meaningful sentences, this novel might never have come to fruition.

And I would be remiss if I did not also give significant recognition to my wonderful wife, Betty. As the "TURCHIN" manuscript developed, as a scene was moved from one place to another, as a phrase was changed here and a thought there, as the novel was restructured bit by bit, it was my dear wife who time and time again typed and retyped the text. Thus, I was able to read and make sense of the countless changes being made, so that I might always have at hand a pristine copy to work from. Her steadfast dedication to my efforts and her constant willingness to "once again" retype the manuscript, are a source of wonder to me. I am eternally indebted to her.

I would also like to extend my sincere appreciation to my son, Joe. Twenty years ago, I put the finishing touches to the manuscript of this book and set it aside for a short time. Unfortunately, the short time became months and then years. Recently, Joe came across a copy of the manuscript and graciously offered his assistance. He proofread the "final" version of the manuscript, made many necessary corrections, had the corrected manuscript typed into a computer, and put it into a form appropriate for publication. For these efforts, I am profoundly grateful.

LOUIS S. RUBIN
November, 1993

ADDENDEUM TO PREFACE AND ACKNOWLEDGEMENTS

Just as it took the Israelites forty years to get from Egypt to Canaan, so too did my father's manuscript take forty years to evolve and maturate.

And so it seems that I am truly my father's son. From the time my father had completed his work in 1993, it has taken me an additional 23 years to prepare the manuscript for publication. It has been a long and tedious journey but well worth the effort.

Joseph L. Rubin
January 2017

CHAPTER I

In 1855, the Crimean War between Russia and Turkey was raging along the shores of the Black Sea. England, France and Sardinia were Turkey's allies and the whole world, including the United States threw concerned apprehensive glances in the direction of Sevastopol and toward the Straits of Bosporus and Dardanelles.

Within Russia itself there were many people who were discontented with the war, not only its prosecution but also its motive. The ostensible reason fooled only the simple and set the mighty Czar in the role of a temperamental tyrant. The Russian people were fighting the Crimean War in the name of the Holy Church in order to protect the Christian population of the Ottoman Empire. On the other hand the Russian rulers (in the name of religious fervor) fought for the control of the straits which led to the outer seas. And so, men trekked across the vast plains of mother Russia until they came at last to die of fever and malaria in the marshlands of semi-tropical Crimea Russia. Their adversaries came in tall masted ships, driven by steam. They waved the tri-colored flag and the Union Jack, but succumbed as did the Russians and the Ukrainians to the southern climate. The diplomats in Vienna sat and pondered a Peace while the guns blasted the fortifications of Sevastopol and men continued to die - and a few to think.

Such a few existed even among the officers of the Czar. They were the younger men of the generation which had been ushered in by the spirited uprising in December, 1825, known as the First Russian Revolution, which, though quickly quelled, served to create a body of dissidents whose influence was far reaching. One such man was a young colonel on the Imperial Staff of the Crown Prince. His name was Ivan Vasilevich Turchaninoff. Since his school days in St. Petersburg, Colonel Turchaninoff had imbibed the dreams of the exiled poets and philosophers and he had become one of those who dared (albeit secretly) to oppose the Crimean War and the follies and foibles of the Czar.

He was a brilliant and handsome fellow, this Turchaninoff, with a fine sense of the ridiculous which enabled him to pursue his course as a field officer in the army without betraying his intransigent differences with the inception and conduct of the war. However, his disaffection with the campaign ran like a dark thread through all his days and added sharpness to his high ranking position. A certain asperity of tongue was even desirable, which bothered the young colonel, feeling as he did that in his vent of passion he merely tightened the rigid bars of his prison and proved a loyalty to a system he abhorred.

What he hated with a fierce passion was autocracy built upon and sustained by a system of serfdom so deeply rooted that the serfs themselves were its best protagonists. As for the Czar, Turchaninoff pitied him more than he hated him, seeing in him the symbol for the ambitions of power-hungry noblemen unashamed to resort to the doctrines of the Church in order to convince the Czar that what he and they sought were not mere personal gain, but holy claims of Justice and Right, the preservation of the Faith of some sixteen thousand Greeks living under Turkish rule.

"They make it sound plausible," Turchaninoff uttered discontentedly to himself. "My poor lads, in shooting Turks, avow their love of God and His word. Bah! It's disgusting."

He was sitting in his field hut which was in good order, maps and charts neatly tacked upon the walls. A case of instruments lay near his elbow beside a carafe of sparkling liquor whose musty fruit essence permeated the room. He was formerly attired in his full dress uniform with his medals and citation ribbons prominently displayed on his chest. A golden eagle on his neckband pressed into his flesh with one metal wing and caused the colonel to hold his head imposingly high, a fact he did not deplore just then as he awaited the appearance of the American Commission in whose honor he was thus arrayed.

To him was assigned the task of interviewing the semiofficial military commission from the United States whose War department showed an unwonted curiosity in the military operations here in this remote peninsula of southern Russia. In the first place, he was the officer on the spot. Secondly, he was one of the few field men with not only knowledge of the English tongue, but an easy facility with it. Thirdly and most importantly, he was an expert in those very matters upon which the commission was bent; no one more than he, in this area, could discourse on military fortifications and installations of defense. (He was the man credited with the brilliant planning for the construction of the Dronstadt project in the Gulf of Finland.) The American Commission thought itself fortunate in being received by Colonel Turchaninoff of the Imperial Staff. This was especially true of the chief of the Commission, one George Brinton McClellan. He was the first, upon being ushered into the presence of the Russian colonel, to give him a dignified salute and to hold out his hand with a frankness that Turchaninoff liked immensely.

"Your country, gentlemen," the Russian colonel began, "surprises us by evidencing an interest in the military doings of Europe. Your country is distant from the problems of Europe and Asia and neither continent can conceivably contain a potential enemy to your Republic. Your geographical position ensures you a safety from aggressors and secures you this permission of our gracious Majesty to inspect at will our activities here."

Beneath his words lay an indefinable irony which McClellan, still young and apologetic for his own and his country's youth, detected and bristled against. He remained perfectly controlled, however and save for erect posture and a small white line at the corner of his mouth, would have appeared indifferent to the colonel's reflection.

"Be seated, gentlemen," the colonel invited with a motion about the room. He, himself returned to the seat behind the massive table he used for a desk. He surveyed his visitors keenly, and then offered to pour them drinks, which they refused.

"You will undoubtedly consider it a Russian whim, our granting permission for your inspection tour," the colonel resumed pleasantly when all were puffing on the cigars he had supplied.

"We hope you will, in turn, avail yourselves of the same courtesy should the occasion arise," Captain McClellan retorted with a smile.

"We are at war with powerful enemies," Turchaninoff persisted, "while you have little to fear, protected as you are by two oceans."

McClellan moved restlessly, eager to begin his inspection, not quite following the Russian's playfulness.

"Perhaps we feel friendly toward a young country which has, before us, defied the strength of the British. You will remember, no doubt, Captain McClellan, that our great Catherine expressed deep sympathies for your young country during its revolutionary days. We professed a friendship for you then which is not altered now as we fight your ancient enemy." He added a winning smile to these words and left it to Captain McClellan to decide what whim lay behind them.

The minutes ticked by while the two officers studied each other. Both enjoyed measuring men's inner stature and each found in the other enough for speculation. They were handsome men each in his own way, each in the uniform of his country. The American was slightly younger than Turchaninoff, but possessed a self assurance to which he lent a dignity. This dignity was impressive in its cool aristocratic poise and surprising in a man from a country whose inhabitants were still believed to be mainly savages. No surface polish was this which the Russian perceived in the American officer. Had it been so, he should have detected its superficial quality at once. It was a genuine refinement and culture bespeaking long training and gentle nurture, that the colonel saw and it drew him inexorably closer to McClellan. "You come at the bequest of your President?" he inquired smoothly.

"With his full cognizance, but primarily at the wish of our Secretary of War, Mr. Jefferson Davis," McClellan answered. In his turn he was impressed favorably by the Russian on whose finely drawn face he read a deliberation not unmixed with raillery, which was pleasant and affable. In the chiseled nose and mouth, he saw traits of an aristocracy greatly to his disliking. But the arrogance he attributed to these traits was complimentary to the man and lent distinction to the friendliness of the colonel's attitude.

This first interview was necessarily brief, but it invited further colloquies between the two men who grew to admire one another the more they met and talked. That they must meet frequently in the limited environs of the camp, was a foregone conclusion; but that they met with pleasure was a happy coincidence, taken perhaps more seriously to heart by the Russian colonel than by the American Captain. Since Captain McClellan and his associates were the first Americans he had ever personally known, he was prone to identify these men with the entire body of the American people of whom he assumed them to be representative. He saw in them a species of man not often encountered in Russia, or for that matter in other countries he had seen. They stood easily and self-confident amidst the appurtenances of war, as levelheaded and intelligent, as full of pointed questions as their own military scientists. The captain, perhaps, seemed somewhat more responsive to the accumulation of foreign nobility still resident in the towns than were his American conferees. They, notwithstanding the glamour, beauty, wealth, and tradition encountered everywhere among the attachés, maintained an independent, sturdy self-respect which gave little obsequiousness to rank and title. This pleased the colonel who often appeared with his lady in the midst of these festivities.

"I admire these independent Americans," he told his wife when first she met with the Americans. "See how well dressed they are without ostentation. Notice how their uniforms are plain, not gilded rags of glorified war. It is pleasant to meet people for whom war is not a business nor a profession. They are men trained in their West Point Academy," he explained, "But how alien our tradition must seem to them who are always citizens first and then soldiers if the need arises."

"How do you know so much about them?" his wife laughed. "They look like pious missionaries to me and surely their interest in warfare is a shade beyond the academic if they travel thousands of miles to study its technique."

"They study for a purpose," he replied, unshaken in his belief that something superior to mere warlike propensities dictated the presence of the American Commission. "Let them study us, we who are ancient in our stupidities and they will learn to avoid our follies."

His wife had even less charitable ideas concerning Captain McClellan. The pleasure he displayed after his day's serious study in the camp, attested in her sight to less idealism than Turchaninoff ascribed to him. At that moment Captain McClellan caught sight of them and moved in their direction.

The colonel presented his wife, to whom the Captain bowed graciously. Turchaninoff then inquired, "Have you made all necessary military observations, Captain?" His friendly smile asked the assurance that no obstacles had been placed in his way.

"Yes, Sir," McClellan replied. "Soon we shall be able to leave with our mission accomplished, thanks to your Sovereign and to yourself. You know, colonel," he continued, "the United States cannot help but be concerned with the problems confronting her sister nations overseas."

"Ah, with one difference," the colonel laughed indulgently. "You are a young country, not spoiled by crossed ambitions for power. You are secure in your isolation and endowed with size. That is the important thing, size, land, room to move, and freedom to move!" He glanced quickly into his companion's eyes as he spoke. "Freedom to move, Sir, that's a wonderful prescription for health, in a nation as in a man."

"You are mistaken, Sir," Captain McClellan ventured to disagree, "if you assume that because of our youthfulness as a nation we are unaffected by the conditions among European nations. We are greatly affected even in our internal economies. Our isolation is purely geographic!"

"That is enough to enable you young Republicans to make the greatest nation under God obtain," said the colonel. "I am somewhat of a cartographer. I know how great are your expanses of land, how long your rivers which knife through your arable lowlands. I am especially aware how progressive is the bent of your national mind. I know that from reports of your addiction to lights. I hear you have millions of gas lights in your great cities. You have no Royal head, Captain. You can well afford lighted streets!"

McClellan was embarrassed though not unflattered by this outspoken candor of the Russian. "We have an aristocracy, too," he defended. "Ours is the aristocracy of achievement. Also we have evils, Colonel. We have freedom and much room; we have great resources and greater advantages with our magnificent coastline and our inland cities; but we have the problems of slavery which are not easy to solve."

"In such a progressive atmosphere, slavery will not long endure," said Turchaninoff as he dismissed the American problems. "If Russia moved forward progressively, our serfdom would drop from us despite its deep-seated entrenchment. Slavery and serfdom can live only where ignorance engenders and supports unlimited greed."

Captain McClellan only smiled at these words. He was not given to discuss his country's sore spot, nor to be honest, could it be said of him that he considered the problem of American slavery as important as certain hotheads in his country were shouting that it was. There were to his mind certain advantages for lowly persons in a state of servitude, which freed them from responsibilities they were inadequate to assume. Russian serfdom he did not see as a blight to that country's wealth or power. American slavery he took for granted as acceptable in an area devoted to the growing of cotton crops. He had a vague idea of the dark primeval tropics out of whose steaming jungles the blacks were rescued and transported to more civilized lands. He could recall several Negroes he had seen in Washington and Philadelphia and remembered them as lazy creatures doing the least amount of work they could for their keep. He continued to smile but with a tinge of acidulous humor as Turchaninoff expatiated on the subject of slavery versus freedom and what evils derived of the former, what perils it offered to the latter.

"You are, if I may be permitted the temerity, colonel, rather sentimental for a Russian officer! Things are not always as black as they are painted, except our blacks who are even blacker!" He laughed at his own joke while the Russian eyed him speculatively. "All things have a certain orderliness if placed in their proper light. In my country, the light is focused upon progress and national development. Slavery is not the subject of first consideration with us who are the descendants of rational men, the founders of our country. They left their slaves to harvest the crops while they rode to battle against the insurmountable odds which the British gave them. Many of their great-grandchildren dismiss their slaves. Many do not see fit to do so. We have an instrument of law governing such matters and our real trouble lies with those who would tamper with our laws. It is easy, I am afraid, Colonel Turchaninoff, to invent a political hobby horse on which one can ride a specious compassion for our African subjects in order to disguise the subterfuge one wishes to employ. Such subterfuge is perfect for those who can grasp power by no traditional forms."

Turchaninoff said not a word.

"We uphold our law, the Constitution," McClellan spoke again, warming to his subject. "Always we, who are conscientious citizens, act subject to that body of law under which we govern ourselves. It is the will of our people which supports the institution of Negro slavery and when our will changes, our black subjects will be absorbed in the life of the country. American slavery is not a threat to American freedom!" he concluded, satisfied with his exposition.

"I should wish to see for myself this American Freedom," Turchaninoff said, remembering his official manners and accompanying his remark with a charming gesture.

"Come and visit us," the Captain laughed good-naturedly. Then, with a grave playfulness he extracted a card from a small leather case and handed it to the colonel. "At this address you will always be able to reach me," he smiled. "It will be my privilege and honor to be your host, to extend to you in the name of my fellow countrymen a small return of the kindness you have accorded to us here." There was no doubt about it. Captain McClellan was a man of breeding and charm. He had a profound effect upon Turchaninoff who thought long about him and about all he had said. Carefully he placed the American's card in his purse.

CHAPTER II

If an idea had been born to Turchaninoff while the Americans were in Russia, he at least was not aware of its visibility until after they had departed. Then it was that Colonel Turchaninoff, his disaffection with the war aggravated, realized that in the idea of the United States, a door had been flung open whereby he could make his escape.

At first, this realization that the United States offered harbor to him, was purely philosophical in implication, however it grew with astonishing rapidity to a maturity of decision and before the year 1855 was out, the idea was clamoring and insistent. And it was there to stay, this resolve to depart from Russian when chance offered him a way.

No simple matter was this decision on the part of a man as highly placed as Colonel Turchaninoff. He was thirty-three when he met Captain McClellan, married, established, and firmly fixed in the career he had followed since his academy days at St. Petersburg. To tear himself up by the roots in the manner his immigration to the United States would necessitate, was no light matter, nothing to plunge into on the impulse of the moment. A man had to have very good cause to justify to himself, why he must break the ties he had developed and nurtured over the years; ties which were very dear to him in spite of certain flaws which he tried to excoriate. Above all there was his beloved wife, Nadine who would have to sever relationships she loved, should she choose to follow him out of Russia, into the unknown, into the perilous prospects of a future where they should have nothing with which to begin their new life except their health, their love, and their high hopes.

Many weeks passed before he could bring himself to mention his determination to Nadine. During these weeks he culled and culled again all his knowledge and experience, all his past life as though hoping among the miscellany of fact and fancy to find something solid enough to withstand his resolve to leave Russia. Among the strong sentiments which bound him to his native land was the abiding love he bore to its physical reality; the flow of its mighty rivers; the countless miles of its dark soil; the mystery that loam presented to his imagination and his ardent sympathies for the people who labored upon it.

He came by his love of the land quite naturally, having been born and brought up close to it in a concrete sense until the day his autocratic father, a retired military man, sent him off at the age of fourteen to the military academy where he was prepared for the College at St. Petersburg.

But in spite of the years of travel and separation from the land on which he had frolicked as a young lad, he never forgot the enchantments which the Don Valley had spelled out for him during his early years. He was willing to forget the dreary mansion in which the family dwelt in stately gloom, the more dark for the air of deathlike piety his mother preserved. She dominated the home with the same determination that she used to push her husband's ambition to reach the peerage, which he did when his son Ivan was granted his Commission. The house held no happy associations for the colonel, but the land which it controlled, held an unending series of delights.

First among these was the Don River which flowed through his father's estate like a huge blood vessel bringing sustenance to both man and beast dwelling on the undulating plains of the estate. To this river the young Ivan brought his problems, his confessions, his rebellions. Into its blue swirling waters he flung his lithe young body and out of its cool perfection he drew strength, courage, and wisdom which sat oddly upon his young brow until the unfolding years brought correlations which explained what as a child had seemed inexplicable, mysterious.

In its inscrutable manner, this great river had forged for the man to be, an indestructible fabric of worship which lay far afield from the dogmas of faith he received at the hands of the family priest, a kindly old fat monk constantly in awe of the mistress, Madame Turchaninoff. The river became a fluid testament of a God who was different from the prescribed delineations of the God of the Faithful. Ivan's God was a great titan, stalking the heavens among the stars which moved out of his way. The moon was a shepherd leading his flock of stars. The clouds were the breath of God puffing life into little fishes. And all of these, heavens, stars, winds, and fishes were created so that the land would be verdant and flower; like an illustrated picture book from which a boy could learn lessons less dreary than the Latin and Greek which good Father Anastasius fondly believed were a similitude of classical European studies.

The river and the land were as one. From his sheer sensuous enjoyment of the one, he could learn the true appreciation for the other. If the river was the great aorta of the circulatory system, then the land was the body itself, the body of Russia. The grasses that covered the body of the land were like the living things that covered the body of Russia - its people. Gropingly, the young Ivan had conceived of the thought that his God intended all creation to adorn his people; and emulating God he gradually transferred his objectless love of the land to a more limited love for the people on the land.

There were plenty of people to engage his attention on his father's land. A few were tenant farmers reduced to great poverty by the burden of taxes and rentals to which they were subject. For the most part, the people were serfs who had remained on the estate from one generation to another. They lived in clay huts along the commons far to the rear of the great house. They seldom spoke to the members of the aristocratic families, but like puppets pulled by invisible strings, they bowed and bent and shuffled in silence. It was the latter whom the boy Ivan wished most to love, "because they need me most," he told the chiding old priest. "I want them to talk to me, Father Anastasius," he cried out, one day. "Are they afraid I shall beat them with my whip the way father does? I want only to ask them about the things I do not understand. I want them to like me!"

And they had come to like the strange boy, to smile at him when he rode among them on his horse, or sat himself beside them while they worked. He would chatter to them freely, but they would continue with their work as stolidly as did the beasts who understood nothing one said. The asses, the big bellied cows, the restless bulls, the fowls that strutted hither and yon, seemed less inarticulate than the men and women who hoed, dug, lifted, and carried as unweariedly, or at any rate as unprotestingly, as the animals.

The colonel, reminiscing as he often did during this period preceding the divulging of his plans to his wife, experienced a pang of regret at the thought of cutting himself off from these people of his father's land. Leaving Russia would be tantamount to deserting these voiceless serfs who had no one to represent them, who were almost on a level with the black slaves of Captain McClellan's country except for the fact that these serfs were not creatures from another world, almost another geological time. They were Russians. They ought to be free citizens!" As men they were equal to any officer in the army!

"If only they would cry out! If they would resent their status! If they would turn to ask for help! But no! They are acquiescent! It is not their fault, but how hopeless is the prospect of helping them who seek no help save from their God! They tremble if lightning bolts across the sky and they tremble even more if the Cossacks ride through the village."

More than ever he chaffed under the weight of the silence he attributed to the serfs. More and more he saw himself hampered in his inner development as long as he had to endure serfdom or the knowledge of its perpetuity. Repeatedly he turned from it to the thought of America and took to studying atlases with a view to familiarizing himself with the topography and geography of America. In a matter of weeks, he could have drawn up an acceptable geographical map of the United States, one that would have done justice to a student of the subject. He could visualize the tremendous mountains, the irregular long coastline so excellent for defensive purposes, the great river basins, and the plentiful inland lakes which studded the map like jewels on an empress' bosom.

He knew his native land with the same attention to detail and he found in the study of its contours and features the same sort of pleasure a mathematician finds in the devices whereby he apprises himself of mystical and metaphysical possibilities that logic and axioms suggest. He spent endless hours comparing the lakes and rivers of Russia with those of the beckoning land he dreamed of. "Ah, lakes and seas are the same, barring differences in degree. Rivers empty into lakes and seas all the world over. All rivers are burdened with the waste products of life and death. Their Mississippi river empties into the Gulf of Mexico; our sea of Azov widens into the Black Sea. A handful of dirt here in not unlike a handful of dirt in America! I shall do it! I must tell Nadine!"

That very evening, he took time to broach the subject with his wife. Above everything in life, Turchaninoff wished the happiness of this slim blond girl, his young bride, Nadine. He had given serious thought to her part in his venture. He envisaged with no light heart the arduous journey, the sudden change in their lives, the removal from people and sights she was fond of; for should she hesitate, he knew he must suppress his wishes and give heed to hers.

"Nadya!" he began diffidently, "Is the thought of home very sweet to you?" And when she looked at him with shining blue eyes in which a subtle humor played, he leaped hurriedly into a confusion of details and reminiscences which delayed the disclosure until her direct question brought him to a sudden simplicity and starkness. "I am sick of the dark feudalism of Russia! I wish to go to America! Will you come with me?"

Instantly she was beside him. Their army tent was not dim enough to hide the radiance of her golden hair or her startlingly blue eyes which, with their film of tears at this moment, sparkled indeed like brilliant sapphires. "Wherever you go, I shall want to go, also," she said.

They laughed together and whispered into the late night. Darkness descended mercifully in cool vapors over the parched and feverish men lying in wait for one another next to the hot cannons whose deadly breath was held until a hazy day opened their mouths once more.

"We shall collect us memories as eventful as all of ours here," he guaranteed her. "The things that are beautiful to us here will be duplicated in America. Only we shall not have the ugliness of ignorance and backwardness to mar it. There can be no nameless waifs like ours in a land so young and vigorous as America!" He had thought of the dwarfed deaf-mute with whom he had grown up on his father's land. This deaf-mute had been his favorite companion at an age when it was necessary for him to have more than the river to address. He had held endless soliloquies with this grinning but uncomprehending audience. He recalled one now and related it to Nadine. How he had, on that occasion, dramatically scooped up with his hand, some of the moldy earth from the roots of the oak; how he had held it under the poor dwarf's quivering nose and declaimed upon its virtues. "See this dirt! It has no feelings! It can't cry or sing or laugh the way people can, or sweat and gape and make foolish faces the way you can. It can't whistle the way I do; it is in short, only a lump of nothing. But see you, dwarf, it is a wonderful lump of nothing, for out of it comes everything. It produces everything, even dwarves like you. And what is its reward? That it may not utter a word, that it may not move away, that it may not speak in its own behalf; for it does not know how to speak!" That was what he had said in childish arrogance to his father's dwarf

"I believe, I wish more than anything, Nadine," he cried happily, "to go out into that land across the ocean, to a world which is young and to meet its citizens, clasp their hands and teach them the speech whose vocabulary our old travails in Europe have fashioned, without their need to acquire it by the foolish method of trial and error. I have something for America and America has something for me."

She was a good and dutiful wife. She was ready to follow wherever he led. But she was practical where he was impractical and now she set her mind on other than yearnings and desires; a way in which to affect their departure as soon as the war was over.

Having decided to take the irrevocable step, they began to think of all the old ties which must be broken during the years which would follow. They often talked far into the night, but the talk was good, furthering their resolves while it afforded them a means through which to speak their unspoken farewells.

"They are good, these silent people in Russia," she said one night. "They are as you say, like tall wheat, bending and swaying in a field."

"Yes and from over the seas they will hear us better than they can here. When the echoing of our voices reach to them it will be like a wind before which they bend and listen."

"And what then, Vanya? What then?"

"I do not know. Perhaps they will awake and realize they are not vegetables. Perhaps they will hear tales of America and begin to feel the oppressive weight of silence and bondage. They are men and women. Why should they not feel as men and women ought to feel? They laugh and cry and kiss each other under their crushed silence. Some day they will throw off this silence of theirs. By example, shall the new teach the old and force them to learn."

They spoke of St. Petersburg where they had met on the day Turchaninoff had received his appointment, his new rank, and his first compliment from Crown Prince Alexander. All the famous old buildings, the pride of the ancient city built by the renowned Czar Peter, they saw again in their mind's eye. "We shall never see St. Petersburg again," Nadine said wistfully.

"There will be greater cities to see," said he, "Cities which, when we walk on the streets, will not make us shiver because of the murdered dead who died unpitied in the marshes underneath. The Czar built a modern city upon the whitened bones of his victims! There is little beauty to regret in that."

She sighed in resignation. St. Petersburg was the city where love came to her. St. Petersburg was her first home as a wife. Upon its famous old bridge over the Neva, she had walked in the misty fog until a crepuscular gloom enveloped the city during those wonderful moments between night and day, before the flickering gas lights were lit in the distance. These things she would miss, these and the friends who dotted the great land, some living in Moscow, others in Poland, still others here in the Southland. She would miss the boat trips with gay officers and lovely ladies. She sighed again, but she was a good dutiful wife.

"In St. Petersburg, we students read, Nadine. We prepared for soldiering, but we read. Between the leaves of our schoolbooks we read Pushkin's poetry and the seditious pamphlets of Alexander Herzen. Most of us forgot what we read, but I have a closer knowledge of nature than many of my colleagues. I did not forget."

"You read me love poems in the fog, remember?"

"And bought you hot chestnuts on the Nevsky-Prospect! Yes, I remember. But because I remember, there is all the more reason why I wish to go into a new, a younger life."

"We shall go when we can," she promised. "After all, Vanya," and her voice was delightfully gay, "we can find other bridges, or if in America they have no bridges, you can build them bridges and we can still read poetry in salt mist. They have oceans, have they not in America?"

"They have everything we have saving only wars. They have ships and seas and land and lakes. They have lights and railroads and richness of life."

CHAPTER III

Weeks and months rolled by after the visit from the American Military Commission, with Colonel Turchaninoff and his wife planning secretly to leave Russia at the first opportunity. Meanwhile, the war was going badly for Russia. Sevastopol was doomed and the men, mainly peasants from the Northern provinces who had marched hundreds of miles into the Crimea, perished like flies. The humid climate was more deleterious to the common soldier, who had to camp in the ever damp earth, than to the cannon or bayonets of the British. Among his men, Colonel Turchaninoff had thoughts for nothing but their welfare. Day and night he rode among the sick and wounded, his wife at his side and tended them with his own hands. He spent himself to save them and the knowledge that his efforts were futile, caused him to grimace with unavailing anger.

The profligate amount of death angered him though Turchaninoff himself was strong and led a charmed existence against the dreaded swamp fevers and miasmas to which the others succumbed so quickly. He also resented the attitude of the ruling classes toward the prosecution of the war. In Kerch and other seaports, reports of wild gaieties and shouting revelries came to him, while his men lay dying or dead. In point of fact, the commanding general rarely made so much as a token appearance in Turchaninoff's sector; apparently content to trust him explicitly.

Above these and countless other irritations came the news of the old Czar's passing and the accession to the throne of the young Crown Prince, a man Turchaninoff disliked for his pronounced arrogance and ruthlessness. As a commissioned officer he had served under the same Prince. "But I need not bow to him as my Czar," he cried to Nadine.

Yet for all his protest, it appeared at first as though Colonel Turchaninoff must comply with custom and make ready to pay homage to the new Czar, Alexander II upon his formal coronation. Expecting orders to this effect, he received instead a hurried command to leave the Crimea on a mission to Poland where it was feared the Austrians might venture to push through the fortifications and press on to Russian soil. On the Austrian frontier, Turchaninoff strengthened the fortifications and defenses and had to endure the rigors of a frigid winter after the sufferings of a miserable summer in the Crimea. It was enough to try his patience, but even that was not so provocative of his final wrath. As the war came to an end, he received a sudden recall to Moscow where he was ordered to take his footsore men and force them to stand in review parade to celebrate the coronation of the Czar. "I have fought their war; I have suffered their fevers and endured their swamps and bunglings! But I will not take my sick men, first roasted and then frozen and condemn them to march to Moscow!"

A late winter snowstorm was raging outside their field tent. The world was a whirling desert of glittering snow. The dispatch rider who had brought the colonel's orders from field headquarters was shivering outside. Colonel Turchaninoff flung the written communication away and roared for the sentry to conduct the rider within. He poured the frightened young man a stiff drink of his own brandy, then gruffly ordered him to find shelter and rest; there would be an answer later, he said.

Nadine had picked up the order and read it carefully. A smile appeared on her face as she handed it again to her husband. "Read it once more, Vanya," she suggested. "You do not see the fine praises your general bestows upon you?"

"I see them well enough. But what do I care about praises? Take my men on a march through this blizzard to Moscow! Half my lads will be dead before I get them partway. I should be sick at heart if I found joy in being praised in the same breath I am asked to murder these boys!"

"But you have in this praise, the opportunity you have waited for. See!" She eagerly explained herself by pointing out that in view of the general's commendation for services already rendered, it would not be a matter for suspicion should the colonel send back a report of sudden illness and fatigue and a request for a leave of absence in order to recuperate before proceeding to Moscow, a long and arduous trip at this time of year. "The general cannot refuse you, Vanya! It is plausible. It is very human to become sick."

"What then?"

"We start, say, for the Marienbad, but actually go elsewhere, reach the border, fly through Germany and into England."

For long minutes, Turchaninoff eyed his wife solemnly. To tell a deliberate falsehood was not acceptable to him. For her to suggest he tell a falsehood was perplexing to him. Only the encouraging and frank solicitation decided for him to do as she suggested. Quickly, he penned an answer and signed his name with a flourish. She, taking the letter up, scanned it briefly. "It is the last time you sign yourself colonel of the Imperial Staff," she said. "It is a serious, a drastic step to take if we send this letter off without your firm resolve to carry through to the end either what you plan or what you have written."

"Send it off. We shall presumably go to Marienbad."

When, several days later, his request for rest was granted, the colonel and Nadine made hasty preparations to depart. First of all, Turchaninoff wrote a long letter to his brother, exhorting him to free his serfs, inherited from their late father. Then he sent letters to his bank in St. Petersburg with orders to forward to London his current cash and finally he secreted Nadine's jewels carefully in the lining of his violin case. The violin was the one thing without which he would not leave Russia. The violin was an old masterpiece of craftsmanship reputed to be priceless. He would never let it out of his sight until they reached London.

Part of the rough journey over the icy ruts and frozen rivers, they made by sleigh. For days they travelled half buried under blankets belonging to a Polish farmer whose wagon and horse they hired for two pearl earrings. In Germany they took a train to the coast and at last, weeks later, they arrived in London.

Turchaninoff had no need to explain to Nadine why London was the place from which they would sail for America. For several years, even before their marriage, she had heard him speak of one Alexander

Herzen, a name, said he, to conjure with. This Alexander Herzen was the most eminent of living émigrés from Czarist Russia and was the fountainhead of such inflammatory literature as managed to elude the police within Russia. The sum and substance of all Herzen's writings was the abolition of serfdom. To accomplish this, he cried for every means and any ends. His writings were widely read in spite of police surveillance and one of his greatest admirers was Colonel Turchaninoff. The best known of his pamphlets issued regularly was a sheet called the "Bell". Provided with a copy of this, Turchaninoff prepared to locate the publisher and meet him face to face. "From what he dares to say, from the sincerity and truthfulness and selflessness of his writing, I feel in him a kindred soul," he explained to Nadine. "I could not think to leave Europe without speaking to this great man."

Forthwith, almost as soon as they had taken lodgings at a small waterfront inn, they began to search for the office of Alexander Herzen. They hired a horse cab and made a tour of the district where all the publishing houses were lined up in a row like so many withered old gentlemen with dusty spectacles on their noses. They had no success.

On successive days they made the rounds once more and finally despaired entirely. On the last day of their search for the elusive publisher, having driven about in the rickety hack all morning, being chilled with the clinging fogginess to which the waterfront smoke added no alleviation, they alighted on a dirt street darkly illuminated by fog lights. Here in a small cafe they sought some refreshment and discovered to their ineffable joy that the barkeeper was a Russian exile, an old man who claimed to have been one of the rash nobles who attempted the abortive revolution in 1825. He was instantly able to give them Herzen's address, after carefully ascertaining the colonel's business and being assured that they were indeed self-made exiles themselves.

Herzen's office was not far from where they then found themselves and consisted simply of the basement front parlor of an old fashionable house. To this house they made their way on foot and soon stood before a small iron railing, almost unnoticeable in the gloom, directing one down a short flight of steps to the unlettered door on which hung a heavy knocker, the worse for wear and weather. With a bound the colonel was at the door and wielding the knocker vigorously.

Footsteps were heard within the apartment and the door opened wide enough to emit a thin stream of light. No further did the door give, as a firm foot kept it in place against the colonel's impatience. A slow voice demanded the knocker's business. With a touch of hauteur the colonel stated that he had no business but to visit with Alexander Herzen. The door, opened only partially, and the time that ensued between the question and his answer, dampened the colonel's ardors. A man of quick impulses, he could not tolerate a deliberation which could rise out of nothing but an unwillingness to trust a stranger; it was so, that he construed the delay. It was enough, he reasoned, that a friend knocked upon your door. The enemy stealthily clambers through the window; only the friend knocks, or the authorities on official business. "I am a free man come to consult with another free man who like me has heart and tongue that he offers to humanity, for the service of humanity. Whosoever comes to Alexander Herzen as a friend comes as I do. Were I he, I should fling wide the door and greet all who share my ideals." So he thought and scowled at the door. The scowl still lingered when at length a brighter lamp was turned up in the interior of the room and the door flung back upon its hinges.

A tall stooped man dressed in gray, surveyed them incuriously. He showed nothing of any emotion on his face whatever. Moreover, it was a face from which nothing could be learned, either of himself or his thoughts. Yet, it bespoke an unfathomable loftiness which, while not attracting, did not repel, only withheld, a fact the colonel sensed rather than reasoned out and which at once coiled the impetuous warmth with which he had ventured to call. Carefully the gray man removed his silver rimmed spectacles and with an ink stained kerchief began to polish the lenses. When he had quite done so, he calmly replaced the glasses upon his long nose, motioned the Russian couple to follow him inside the room and took a seat immediately at a small table where nothing but a stack of leaflets was visible.

"Yes?" he spoke the single word and fixed his eyes upon his callers, as though seeing them for the first moment. "I presume you seek Alexander Herzen?" He waited without eagerness for an answer.

"Are you Alexander Herzen?" Turchaninoff demanded unbelievingly.

"Yes. And you, may I ask?"

"We are Colonel and Madame Turchaninoff," the colonel stiffly gave reply.

"So! And what does a colonel wish of me?"

"Oh, Mr. Herzen, you must think us impolite indeed." Nadine gave him a sweet smile. "We are Russians. We are taking passage for America. We have read "The Bell" and wished just once to meet its distinguished editor and publisher. If we interrupt you, we are sorry."

"I should not have thought it a presumption for an honest man to seek out another one, even a busy and important one," the colonel stated. Herzen paid no attention to him, turning his near sighted eyes upon Nadine who flushed under their intense scrutiny.

"Russian, eh?" was all he said and sank into a deep thoughtful silence.

"Does that make a difference?" Do you not address yourself to everyone?"

"So you are Russian, are you?" Herzen spoke slowly. "Well, I speak to Russians, those who are bound to Russia. To those who are free I have but one word to say; how does your freedom assist the unfree to gain theirs?"

A deep flush stained Turchaninoff's cheeks, an unmanly blush of anger and outraged self-esteem. The man's cool self sufficiency, his cold appraisal of the visitors, his harsh words, no matter how close their truth lay to the colonel's own heart, now estranged him from his former idol. The closed narrow vent of his mind was not the clarion call his printed messages rang with. How could a great mind, for the writings of this man described him as such, be such a petty functionary as this gray pedant showed himself? All desire to converse with him drained away. Unconsciously, Turchaninoff's attitude became that of the Russian officer and with such an officer's arrogant pride, he stood and gave his arm to his wife. "Mr. Herzen, at your service!" said he coldly and formally.

Herzen had a curious disdainful smile on his pale lips. Nadine was flushed with embarrassment. "Please sit down again, Ivan," she begged. "I am certain Mr. Herzen will grant us a short interview when he knows how anxious you have been to see him. He is an exile, you know and must take great precautions. Now that he sees we are sympathizers, not spies, perhaps we will understand one another."

"Yes, please remain, Colonel Turchaninoff," Herzen said more cordially. "I grow impatient too quickly. There is so much to do and so little time in which to do it. Every moment counts." In this way, though he tried to be conciliatory, he managed to make Turchaninoff even more uneasy and resentful.

"I have observed, sir," said he that when there is the greatest urgency there is always time for an honest man. It is little men, those scrambling toward the top of the heap, who have no time to grant to anyone. The big men know that time is endless."

Herzen now bent his eyes away from his visitors. He seemed in fact to have departed in spirit altogether. The colonel made a move toward the door, but was halted when Herzen suddenly spoke. "Your place is to fight serfdom if you love your country!"

"My fight," said the colonel, "even yours, which I have for years admired, will be of little good in destroying what is the backbone of Russia's economy. You should know that to fight serfdom is to fight God in Russia!"

"The time is closer at hand than you dream, colonel," Herzen said with a quick smile which transfigured his somber face with passing warmth. "You are an impetuous man, colonel; let an older man have his say! But I shall welcome your assistance here with me, if you choose to remain in England."

"I have a dream about America," was Turchaninoff's quiet answer. He was quickly mollified and now was in no hurry to leave.

"But if you hate slavery, remember in America there is a black slavery as vicious as our white slavery in Russia."

Turchaninoff smiled expansively. "It is different there. It must be different there, not so deeply ingrained in the fiber of the land. In America, slavery is regional, confined to small areas of the South. I ascertained that from an American Captain. It is not likely to spread, for being a sickness it must be routed by the health and youth of that young republic. I believe that. I believe that slavery will vanish out of America because it is inconsistent with the idea of America."

"But colonel," Herzen laughed wryly, "slavery in America dates back prior to the country's national entity. Before the first puritans from England drifted to American shores, the first slaves were already digging American soil. That is history. I believe my fight to free the Russian serf is less futile than the probability of your vision."

"No fight against ignorance and inequality is futile," Turchaninoff said. He grew cold and haughty again. He had hoped to gain a measure of approval, though he should have scorned merely polite approbation. He wished for some intangible bond to spring up between his mind and Herzen's; that such a phenomenon had not occurred convinced him that their minds worked at cross-purposes. If Herzen felt a similar repulsion from the colonel's mind, he indicated it only by a half smile and lifted eyebrows. They faced each other, the older man and the young one and shook hands without purpose.

"You do noble work," the colonel said politely.

"May you find what you seek in America," said Herzen.

"I cannot fail. I know my objective," answered Turchaninoff.

And they parted thus mutually untouched. The solid door closed behind the Russian couple. The dreary chilliness of the heavy fog caused them to shiver and hasten their steps toward the friendly Russian barkeeper at the neighborhood inn. "You see how it is, Nadya," Turchaninoff exclaimed impatiently. "A great man with a great idea. But where is the warming humanity in him? He has not time for that! The head does business by itself and leaves the heart to do the same. The little man in the cafe acts the nobler part."

She said nothing.

CHAPTER IV

During the many small tasks which fell to Turchaninoff, incidental to the actual boarding of the ship which was to take them to America, he could not rid himself of the natural irritation begot of the thwarted rapport with Alexander Herzen. What the great Russian publicist was for the abolition of serfdom was almost sufficient to override his angered pride and injured amour-propre which had come forward to mar the pleasure of the longed for meeting. There might perhaps have been even a small degree of boyish anticipation thwarted. He had desired to share his proposed endeavor with the one mind who he fancied was able to congratulate him with true comprehension, without veiled malice or overweening flattery.

Thus, while collecting their money, he had entertained a fleeting impulse to make his way once again to the basement flat and there to grasp, in the complete expression of his brotherly feelings, the hand of the man who had written words that beat in his breast. This man he had wanted to consult that he might have from him, sympathetic understanding. To this man he felt able to explain what seemed inexplicable to others; that it was because he loathed serfdom in Russia that he could disentangle himself from it and face willingly the prospect of residence in a world where another sort of slavery existed. Herzen's should have been the mind to conceive of the true nature of this choice; he should have envisaged the far reaching aims lying beyond the immediate problems of a slave economy in a new land; he ought readily to have agreed that slavery and youth were antipathetic.

Once he was aboard the ship, out on the open sea, his disappointment subsided. The fretfulness which had marked his features and which had revealed to his wife some element of his feelings, gave way to lighter moods, to flashes of gaiety delighting all the passengers who came to enjoy the Russian couple. This was not unnatural in view of the fact that Nadine possessed a rare beauty and a graciousness of mien, which soon won for her, nods and smiles and the countless courtesies which can improve a sea voyage. In addition, Turchaninoff himself, on the third day out, appeared with his magnificent violin, which he fondly explained was an heirloom, a priceless Stradivarius already at that time more than a hundred years in his family's possession. Being a musician of some skill, his contribution to the life of the ship was welcome; nor was he abashed to regale the company as often as requested. He was fond of native Russian airs which he rendered with vivacity and joyousness, remarkable when one noted the stately lines on his face and overlooked the solemnity in the brilliant blue eyes.

One passenger on that voyage appeared indifferent to the colonel's efforts to relieve the tedium of endless days on the ocean. This was a solitary young gentleman of distinguished bearing and fastidious dress, but of a pale and almost sickly hue and a savage sullen droop to his mouth whenever the evening concert began. It was apparent to Nadine, who had noticed him during their first few days aboard, that he made only ill disguised efforts to tolerate the musical sessions in which he took no part. Every evening he withdrew from the guests and made his way on deck to the loneliest quarter of the ship, where he would lean far over the rail in an attitude of dejection. Several times Nadine had followed him out of the salon, but he had never noticed her. There was, about the young man, a quality which appealed to her, though she could not have stated exactly what it was; not to her curiosity, certainly, was this appeal, for she was not one to be stirred by idle questions concerning things or persons forming no integral part of her life. There was no air of helplessness about him; on the contrary an aura of reserve and arrogance proclaimed the man's own estimate of himself. Despite this, however, some intuitive knowledge led her to the belief that the man wanted companions. An underlying warmth of feeling propelled her toward him as though a desire to offer friendship. This desire Nadine had in common with her husband, if not so vociferously and freely as was permitted a man to display. How well she always understood the colonel's lament that it was a pity indeed when two kindred spirits encountered one another, for empty conventional standards and forms to choke the spontaneity before it had an opportunity to generate the least human warmth.

She sighed lightly as these thoughts flashed through her mind one night, the fourth night at sea. The atmospheric pressure was heavy; she could feel the penetrating bite of the March wind as it blew her light hair across her face. Intolerable heat in the salon, combined with the poignant Gypsy melodies the colonel's violin was delivering this night, had finally induced her to steal out of the laughing crowd clustering about Turchaninoff. On deck it was cold. She shivered in the moonlight, more from a feeling of being aimless and weighted than from the clear coldness of a wintry heaven full of stars. Here she did not have the high resolves to which she gave constant attention in her cabin, wherein her husband never tired of the plans his imagination executed.

The sky hung low over the black unruly waters. Small bursts of icy wind puffed up and out in the same instant. She leaned against the ship's rail, unconsciously imitating the unknown young man who had interested her. The gleams of lighted portholes from below deck cast wavy ripples of gold over the sea and upon these her eyes fastened, feasting on the directionless profusion of the lights.

A dark form took a place beside her and an elbow brushed close to hers. "Pardon me, Madame," a low voice with modulated mockery interrupted her reverie, "but it were far wiser to look up, you know, than down; anyway, so they always tell me."

Without verification, she knew the speaker to be the same young man who had caught her fancy and likewise she knew she need make no reply. With barely inclined head she acknowledged that she had heard his words, when he continued. "Look, there up above. Notice the velvety texture of the heavy-laden clouds. They would be called angry clouds by our romancers, but I call them honest clouds; they grow full, they empty out; no fuss, no melodrama; that's left to the dreamers!" His voice ended in a faint sneer.

In short order the two had become acquainted. No smiles or fine words passed between them, rather a peculiar communion, not with one another, but with some quality of impersonal passion that clung to the night. "We Russians!" his voice was moody, "we are all fleeing into the future; yet out there," he pointed into the dark sky, "it sweeps over us always, something we cannot escape; tomorrow is a vastly distended cleric dominating the heavens in his heavy monastical robes." He leaned on his elbows. "Do you see it, Madame Turchaninoff? Only this night his diamond encrusted crucifix is discreetly covered."

To this Nadine had answered that he was full of furious fancies and his retort had been that this occasion was the last. "When I arrive in America," he stated, "I leave my fancies on this ship, they will travel back and forth with other people, but they will never find me again. I have determined to see no love in the ravage of a rose's heart when a bee descends upon it. Think me mad. All of us are mad; only I know it!"

At this juncture in their low conversation, the colonel, having tired of playing and having noted the absence of his wife, had come in search of her and seeing her, white and beautiful in her black shawl splayed by her pale gold hair glistening in the moonlight, stepped forward to take her arm. "This gentleman, the Baron Trofimov," Nadine eagerly made introductions, "goes also to America!"

"Trofimov?" the colonel repeated the name. "Then you are Russian! Yet, I fancied you two were speaking French."

"This lady is one to whom one instinctively speaks French," Baron Trofimov replied with a bow. He answered the colonel in Russian but immediately lapsed into the French tongue as some whim took possession of him and he added: "Pay no attention to my title. It is not real. I find myself impelled to a curious truthfulness with my compatriots to whom I do not mind admitting the usefulness of it."

This last brought an understanding smile to Turchaninoff's face, for his mind grasped the full significance of the younger man's unasked for declaration; here was an honest man who had forthwith seen in a fellow traveler, no wish for deception and had responded as one man should to another of quality. Frankly, he extended his large firm hand and the two men for an instant appeared to avow a common understanding, almost an unspoken sympathy.

"I do not mind owning to you," Turchaninoff said unaffectedly, "that it rather comforts me to know another Russian is aboard and reaching over the seas to a new life."

To this the other made no direct reply. Instead, he smiled with a strange amusement in his eyes at Nadine who quickly retired in her husband's shadow and savored his enjoyment as much as she might the effects of her own efforts in engaging a new friend's attention. His glance meanwhile clearly said to her that the suggestion of homesickness detectable in the colonel's remark was nothing short of sentimental and therefore ludicrous. "Apparently, colonel," he observed, "you are one of the exponents of the ridiculous theory that once a Russian, always a Russian!; that sooner or later, all Russians succumb to a nostalgia for their old home!; that some portions of longing to return will crop out in all of us!"

"No one ever frees himself of dear memories; of people and places and associations; of the sources for our very beings; of the earth whence we rose," said Turchaninoff. He was beginning to sense in the other man objectionable traits of contradiction which annoyed him as they impinged upon his mind. Ordinarily he was not the man to make a summary judgment upon another man without much thought, much weighing of pros and cons. Nor was it characteristic of him to cling to an opinion once he had formed it, if further experience warranted a change. In Trofimov's case, however, he unconsciously formed a prejudice and never thereafter quite attempted to understand a mind he felt rather than knew to be antagonistic to his own. He had little patience with qualities of personality which he considered to be at variance with common sense. "Did the man take him for a fool to offer such jejune comments on a subject anyone with a grain of reason would at once admit to have as a basis in fact and have done with it?" So went his silent thoughts following this first encounter with Trofimov. "Where was the superiority in decrying one's past life. The past was necessary to prepare for the future. To remember what was finished and done with as far as a man's future was concerned was a far cry from a morbid attachment to the unattainable. "Bah!" He said later that night to his wife, "I am not impressed by the antics of your new acquaintance. He is an unstable character; no credit either to Russia or to us." That last he uttered with a new tone of proprietorship concerning the land lying as yet in the fogs and the mists of the unknown.

His words had the effect of inclining Nadine favorably toward the young man. She remembered his curious words in the way one sometimes recalls the faint melodies of a symphony, not so much to recapitulate an air, as to recapture an emotion which the air evoked. "What do you suppose he meant by saying his title was not real?" she asked suddenly, quite unaware that Turchaninoff had digressed to another subject.

"I should have thought at first," he cheerfully turned his mind to hers, "that he intended to present himself in an honorable light to us; that he appraised us justly for people who had rather know him honestly. However, it is apparent he had other intentions. One can scarcely estimate the extent of such a man's intents."

"It is rather quaint for him to adopt a title which cannot have much weight or meaning in a democratic land like America," she laughed lightly, though her unspoken thoughts lingered long upon Dimitri Trofimov.

The young gentleman had remained on deck long after the departure of the Turchaninoffs. The coming of a night storm at sea intrigued him, in a sense resolved him of nameless obligations which he scorned to consider. He was replete this night with the satisfaction of a vast emptiness. He knew no one and no one knew him. He had nothing and was morally free by his own august consent to acquire whatever he chose. His was the choosing! Let the elements struggle; let the heavens dramatize the battle of the everlasting ages. He had cut himself free of all ties; love, home, kith and kin, in short everything binding upon him as a European. And as a future American? He asked himself that, as the long expected raindrops began to pelt him, as the sea spray was dashed upward into his face, as he still stood on the deck of the ship. He wondered what it would be for him to make himself an American. What was to be his calling, beside Baron Trofimov? In which of the cities should he sojourn? Everyone wanted something and the Americans wanted the most. This was a philosophy of human behavior deeply ingrained in his mind; that always, when the subterfuges and evasions and false delicacies were stripped away, the raw contours of the simple bargain became manifest.

Standing at the ship's rail all through the brief but furious March storm, Trofimov frankly summed himself up in the nice manner he had used on former occasions, in order to apprise himself of values either to be bought or sold. From city to city in all the countries of Europe and Asia Minor, he had wended his restless way these past dozen years. He had been clerk and merchant, emissary and interpreter, scholar and scoundrel, dissident and devotee as the fancy took him, or as chance presented itself according to his needs which were at all times extensive so far as money was concerned. And always he had been troubled by an exiguous purse, the remedy for which lay in a necessary ruthlessness or in good fortune.

Certain bitter lessons he had learned since his eighteenth birthday: namely, that honesty was only a useful word; vanity a useful ingredient providing one carefully allowed it to one's victims; that love was a foolishness which begot senseless burdens and that the good life would be defeated by scruples and self doubt or an aggravating conscience.

Obviously, what such a man as Trofimov proclaimed himself to be was not likely to win the admiration or lasting respect of Turchaninoff. The cynicism of the one violated the ardor and vision of the other. The difference between the two men lay in this: that Trofimov was incredulous whereas Turchaninoff from the first believed every word any new acquaintance yielded of himself. Warm liking could not well be established between such men after their first meeting and was not more possible in the unavoidable contacts made during the remainder of the long voyage when conversation was inevitable. Questions as to reasons for emigration from Russia started the two men off on their series of fruitless discussions which Trofimov would fain have avoided save that by doing so he must, of necessity, have kept himself apart from the colonel's wife. To be near her was a growing pleasure he would not forego and therefore, with some annoyance, he lent himself to Turchaninoff's exuberances and enthusiasms. For the most part these consisted of long eulogies of the land. It seemed to Trofimov that the colonel was rather fanatical in his love for mere land.

"Really, sir," he interrupted several times to say, "I see no great difference in one kind of land rather than another, if it is the physical fact of the land which elicits these commendations from you."

He was excessively bored with a mind that reveled in concepts which to him appeared somewhat disjointed. No love for his native soil lent him sufficient apperception to share Turchaninoff's binding attachment to the ancient Russian earth; he was incapable of delighting in the information that a rich earth contained an acidulous vitality prone to increase both fertility and productivity. He saw no subtlety in a mind, infected, in his opinion, by an overweening confidence, treating in an offhanded manner the most widely divergent subjects - from involuntary servitude to military science, from wars to the sustaining of backward unprogressive power to a philosophy of grandeur based upon vast quantities as compact masses of dirt out of which he imagined he might, with as much ease as a magician with a wand, call forth new delights of life itself.

"That is because you do not understand the poetry of the land; how its size, scope, its tremendous challenge add up to great adventure, providing the whole is sunk in the fastness of freedom based upon progress and enlightenment. Those things we are slow to obtain in Imperialist Russia. Those things we may hope to achieve in a young land where there is a will to be free," exclaimed Turchaninoff.

"You appear to have the zeal of a missionary," was Trofimov's only response to this.

"Perhaps I am that," Turchaninoff returned coldly. "Perhaps a new world wants missionaries with zeal." Then, forgetting that he considered Trofimov unsympathetic, he added, "I see in much land, much room, much opportunity, and much abundance. Space, air to breathe freely, enough work for every man, for each to have his share to till; enough to raise cattle, to fatten the land, to turn darkness and despair into light and good. There will be gold where there is mud and the gold will not destroy a young nation that has no greedy hierarchy. In such a land of space and progress, men like I can come and lend our skills to new endeavors."

There was both conviction and triumph in his voice as he finished and he gazed intently at the other man as though to challenge denial from those thin, smiling lips.

By the time the boat arrived in New York harbor, neither man was especially cordial toward the other without a previous determination not to be otherwise. Nadine, in the weeks aboard the ship, had confined herself to a book which she invariably opened when the two men engaged themselves in conversation. Periodically her eyes would fasten upon Trofimov, but when his own chanced to return her calm study, a sudden smile disguised her innermost thoughts and made her eyes illegible to him. She maintained a grave friendliness toward him and this had the odd faculty of calming him, often causing him to make foolish resolves to remain close to her, even if thereby he invited a continuance of Turchaninoff's acquaintance. At the last, however, a cautious self-protection from Nadine deterred him in any expression of such a wish and he became as casual as she. He generously admitted that the lady drew him more than was wise; that she was not the most beautiful woman after all; that it were wiser for a man to be curt than to be hurt; that at thirty only romantic fools let moonlit nights before a storm become confused in their memories with a woman's pale hair and a pair of unfathomable eyes that seemed drenched in dew. Yes, her eyes were like wood violets, but Trofimov preferred the more sophisticated flower, he insisted to himself.

"We shall see you again," Turchaninoff promised, in a burst of spontaneous friendliness, as they left the ship together.

"Perhaps so." Trofimov bowed. His tone clearly said otherwise. His dark mocking eyes looked after the Russian couple with something like regret shadowing their depths. "He goes to pursue his dreams; I go to find wealth; we can never meet, for he will at best certainly be only famous, not wealthy! But she has eyes like wood violets. They go well with dreams," he mused.

CHAPTER V

Arrival in the New World proceeded for Turchaninoff with the same regularity as had all the events since his first meeting with McClellan in the Crimea. New faces, new language sounds, new features of landscape; all of these came to him with some sort of pre-experience for which he could scarcely account. Accustomed to the concrete simplicity of mathematical thinking, he found it enough to start all speculations on one set of axioms: land was land; you could pick up a handful and taste it like food, know whether it held promise or sorrow; people were people whose basic needs were your own, if once you learned to converse with them; and all people were conversable in the same way that all problems were solvable once you accepted first principles.

After a few days in the shabby hotel to which they had been directed by a coachman, an opportunity presented itself for the purchase of a farm site in Long Island, about thirty-five miles from Brooklyn.

"Two things we must do at once," he said to Nadine. "First we must familiarize ourselves with the language of the people, the common language, not our literary and stage English. Then we must buy land away from the congested city. We begin in a small way, with a few acres of American soil. It will teach us to know these American people better than a hundred years of residence in a great city like New York."

"You propose to become a farmer?" she asked, smiling at the idea in spite of herself and the seriousness of her husband's trend of thought.

His idea was to establish themselves on a farm until he felt orientated to a degree enabling him to find suitable employment. "I must first taste of this life before I contact Captain McClellan." That was the tenor of his mind at this time and it was comprehensible to his wife, who, better than anyone else, understood the independent nature of the man. It was a matter of personal pride to him that he be able to prove his rugged ability to stand on his own feet before turning for advice to another. That he knew little of the work entailed in farming unknown land did not disturb him. That he had hardly any knowledge of the climatic conditions which a winter in Long Island would disclose to him was of little moment now, when New York was green and resplendent in its early spring garb. The sparks were alive with youth and newness. The heart of the city was full of busy people, no less bright than the banks of flowers on the square where the hitching posts stood clean with new paint.

"It is all wonderful and hopeful," he averred over and over again. "You can almost feel the city grow, but like all cities this one is already growing out of bounds and before your eyes the healthy new grows old and spotted with the signs of an hidden sickness."

He was dissatisfied with the aspect of New York in that one respect, for he believed firmly that to be happy, people must spread out on the land, not crowd into cities. Cities ought to stretch far and wide, he believed, so that even in close proximity with other men, a man would remain closer to nature and to goodness, the two concepts being ultimately one in his mind.

Thus he hastened to arrange the deal for the farm in Long Island, never once doubting that his wife shared his own feelings, never noticing how longingly she lingered before the new emporiums the city was boasting, before the flower stalls and book shops. And while the spring advanced full and strong in the city, they drove in a hired carriage to the new farm home set amidst a grove of trees and wild shrubbery where the phoebe birds chirped.

The farmhouse was ancient and in great dilapidation. Many windows lacked panes and only one iron cooking stove was available for use. The furnishings were obviously of the poorest sort and indicated long disuse.

The surrounding land was utterly useless for immediate cultivation. They saw that much work must be done before they could look to their garden for some measure of sustenance. Weeds and woodland creatures had ravaged what must have been at one time a sizeable trucking farm. The dark forests looming on every side seemed almost to have made a calculated encroachment upon the meadows of the property. The connecting road could only be reached from one side of their road and this road led to the neighboring farmhouses. These were so widely separated that for all practical purposes it seemed to Nadine that they might be isolated in some remote village in Siberia, save for the lack of ice and snow. Came the first winter, even this distinction disappeared in her troubled fancies.

Several weeks had rolled by before Nadine had her first polite visitor, the wife of a German farmer some five miles distant. The scrutinizing glances of the good woman, the frank disbelief in her eyes as she saw the careless arrangement of the farmhouse and the lack of the barest essentials of farm life, did not escape Nadine. As always, when meeting hostile criticism, she drew into her quiet patrician reserve and met her neighbor's unvoiced criticism which she interpreted at once to be haughtiness and queerness. When the neighbor took her leave, Nadine watched her sturdy figure marching stolidly over the brambles, grass, unbroken ground and neglected road which the colonel had not yet cleared of debris.

When told of their first neighborly visit, Turchaninoff smiled broadly, well-pleased both with Nadine's accurate description of the woman and with his own right thinking on the subject of neighbors.

"You see, I told you these people will recognize our sincerity if we start on the land," he pointed out with approval. "You must be like them, Nadya and soon return their calls. I am sure I shall shortly meet all the farmers. They will welcome the suggestions I have already outlined with respect to the soil and general topographical factors I have observed in my walks. Reconnoiter; one has to reconnoiter first."

But no further signs of communication were forthcoming. Nadine had attempted to make her return call, but had lost her way through the woods. On another occasion, both she and the colonel had walked to their next neighbor's lands, only to discover from a tall lad swinging on a fence that, "Pa allows no callers on the Sabbath."

They might have made some sort of entrance into the communal life of the region had they ventured to attend the church services held some distance away and preached by a lay minister. But this did not occur to Turchaninoff who, though not a practicing observer, nonetheless would never have condoned the idea of religious avowal of a faith not his own. He acknowledged that it was quite right for every man to seek to commune with God in his accustomed way. Still, in the final analysis, the outward manifestation of belief was not vitally important to the development of character. He would honestly have asseverated, upon questioning, that the place of organized religion was beyond doubt in any society. This he would accept without impairing his equally strong opinion that all religion lay in an explanatory parenthesis beside science and knowledge.

"Religion does for us until knowledge pushes back the darkness of not knowing," he used to point out. "First there is faith that we are intended to know," he would earnestly continue during the chill and silent nights in the country, "and then there is knowledge to confirm faith and make it beautiful and enriching."

Sitting huddled in several shawls and periodically poking alive the wood embers in the kitchen stove, Nadine would hear him out to the end without interruption. Occasionally she turned over bits of bark and twigs which she was drying for use. Now and then she rose and lighted an oil lamp. Sometimes she annoyed him excessively when without warning, she changed the subject and remarked mildly that only so much of their precious small fund of dollars remained, or that the supply of bacon and sugar which they had brought from the city on their last trip was running low.

In time they acquired a large sow, a goat and a few chicks which occupied Nadine all the rest of the year. They had discovered the art of trading with their neighbors, but never the art of becoming neighborly. The farmers were mostly of distant Dutch and German extraction, scarcely anyone being a first generation foreigner. Yet despite their origin, they showed no intentions of adopting among them the Russian couple.

It was, indeed, a day of joy when Nadine cheerfully brought the colonel the extraordinary news that their heavy sow had begotten a litter of nine porkers. The grunting of the sow and the whining of her young were for the couple the sweetest and most promising music they had heard since they had attended the ball at the Petershof Palace.

A week later Nadine noticed that one of the sucklings was becoming noticeably thinner. This was the tiniest one of the lot. The others always managed to squeeze him out from his legitimate place by the side of the mother sow, the place which in all justice was the tiny porker's inalienable right and privilege.

Nadine looked sorrowfully at the tiny feet and belly of the suckling and decided to feed him goat's milk. She walked over to the mother sow and the litter and lifted the starving suckling, which was still struggling for a place by the side of the sow and walked away a few steps. The suckling whined and squealed and aroused the motherly instincts of the large sow. Furiously the sow jumped to her feet, dispersing the rest of the litter and rushed upon the intruder.

Nadine looked frantically for cover, but there was none save the stacks of drying hay. Towards these she ran and reaching them, she fled first around one and then the other. "Vanya, Vanya!" she cried, but the more she called, the fiercer became the sow. Nadine dropped the little porker in the path of the raging mother, but this belated restitution did not appease the rampaging animal. Around the stack they ran, the sow in close pursuit of Nadine when the colonel came rushing out from the field brandishing a large stick in his hands. Almost completely exhausted by now, Nadine gratefully heard her husband shout: "Run here. Run toward me!" This she promptly did, still pursued by the sow. In a moment his swift steps lessened the distance between them and his stick now fell heavily upon the sow's hide, quickly subduing its rage. The sow reared back and showed confused surprise, then lowering its snout, it ambled away back to its litter.

Spring and summer went by and a grim fall and winter followed. The neighbors looked askance upon Turchaninoff's bluff heartiness since there seemed little purpose in his confidence. They saw the stumps of fences and the broken beams of the shed. Their women noted the delicately embroidered curtains, the product of Nadine's fancy needlework, the overly ornate gowns so unfitting a good woman, the frills and lace collars and graceful crinolines and not the sturdy homespun any sensible woman should have owned. Often a pert lad might be seen studying with amusement the solitary goat which Turchaninoff awkwardly attempted to milk in the shed. Stories of weird goings-on circulated among the farmer folk; that the Russians were spies; that they lived at night and slept all day; that they drank tea and worshiped before a huge metal idol of gold, though they owned no kettle as the first observer had reported.

Not only the kettles and pots and pans of the usual farm household were wanting, but also the commonest objects to make winter life in the country endurable. No one ventured to inform Nadine of the needs to be provided; all waited for the lady and gentleman to come-a-begging. Nadine was well aware of this though her husband scoffed at the idea.

"They are poor, even poorer than we were, for we have had much and have the ability to gain much. You do not realize how kind people are underneath. You have to understand people. I like their being reserved. That shows honest pride. It means that they give us the chance to find ourselves. Then they will see what we are."

Convinced that he was correct in his estimation of his neighbors, he was not at all daunted when the few children he encountered, stared at him with that frank and blank curiosity which reflected their parents' sentiments.

Once, he laughingly repaired a child's rough wagon caught in a rut near his property and then let his laughter boom out into the frosty air as the little boy scampered off in unfeigned fright. He had the happy imagination where children were concerned to see him as he imagined they saw him. This day, arrayed in an old army jacket and a Cossack fur cap, a new and gleaming axe over his shoulder - he had been in the woods marking trees to fell - he appeared as a fierce vision, what with his beard spiked ferociously with ice and snow.

Yet, for all his attempts to cut trees, repair the shed, help in the tasks about the house, the winter months reduced them finally to the point of sacrificing the chicks not yet fully grown. One by one they had to eat them. Neither the killing of them nor the preparation of them helped them to enjoy their life. And when at last it came the turn of the old sow, they sat in mute despair and looked at one another helplessly.

"It is not that I have grown fond of the pig," Turchaninoff defended his reluctance to take the axe to it.

And when his wife reminded him that the five shoats they now possessed were starving and had better be disposed of, he suddenly came to a rapid decision that he must sell all the pigs. He would not admit even to his wife that, strong a man as he was, soldier or engineer, the thought of a pig's frantic squealing under his knife was unendurable. In conversations he was prone to advance the opinion that all animals were intended by the laws of life to furnish fodder for mankind. That weak squeamishness where animals was concerned, could well result in a confusion of mind; for it were far better to eat animals, to consider them thus destined, than to destroy intelligence and soul, which properties distinguished man in particular.

"Let us kill animals when we must, but we must never kill man," he opined, yet for all that, he failed to grasp his wife's silent commentary in her answering smile of amusement. He had faced death at men's hands and had taken life with precision, this hater of war, this husband of her bosom who had great merit as a warrior. The professional soldier turned citizen amused her especially when he could not bear to kill a pig which consumed more of their food then they did.

The problem of selling their meager supply of animals went unsolved. In the first place they owned neither wagon nor horse. Secondly, neither one knew how to approach their neighbors with a sale of shoats in mind. And finally, when they decided to take the pigs into New York, they met with open derision and refusal on the part of the hack driver who came once a week into this area of the Island.

"Even if you was to pay passage for them danged critters, I'd not permit a pig to ride in my coach where decent folks sit," he exclaimed and afterwards told the story with relish and much to the delight of the country folk. "Them queer furriners wanting to take a pig to town in a coach!"

Thus even before the first warming winds began to sing in the trees, before the thick buds burst on the boughs, it became urgent for them to leave the farm. To accomplish this, Turchaninoff made several trips to agents in New York and finally, for much less than the original price paid, he sold his land.

"This has not been the proper time," he exclaimed. "I shall return to the land again, but then I shall know more."

CHAPTER VI

After their return to the city which was again evidencing the tingling vibrancy of life which Nadine loved, the spring sunshine, the emerging crowds that seemed as glad to shunt off the winter's lethargy as she was herself, it became necessary for Turchaninoff to bethink himself of George McClellan once more. For almost three years since his first meeting with the American, he had held his card as a talisman to be used on exactly such an occasion as now presented itself. Though McClellan was indeed the only person whose name he knew in the United States, the only man whose address he was cognizant of, still it was difficult for him to approach him. He knew nothing of McClellan's feelings; whether he might remember the Russian colonel; whether he was as yet occupied in a military capacity. Now suddenly, Turchaninoff wanted keenly, the protective garb of his former rank and title. It was one thing to meet a captain of a young and not overly important country when you were on the Imperial Staff, when you were the one conferring privilege. It was another matter when you were unknown, without resources and an alien requiring patronage. Quite naturally he struggled with many doubts and qualms before he resolved to write McClellan a letter.

At the time of the writing of that first letter to Captain McClellan, that young gentleman was but recently disengaged from the Army and had taken a responsible position with the Illinois Central Railroad as vice president. An important change had come over him since his carefree days in the Crimea. At that time he had not yet won his wife and therefore he had been known to be gay and brilliantly charming. In this wise,

Turchaninoff and Nadine recalled him. Marriage was quickly to mature McClellan, though it would not eradicate the essentially commendable traits first noticed by the colonel. He was to grow more thoughtful and aware of the responsibility that both his new estate and his new career perforce were to impose upon him, but as yet he was not materially altered from the man who had admired Colonel Turchaninoff. Therefore when the colonel's letter reached him, he received it with evident pleasure and an allowable self-satisfaction that his lightly spoken words in a foreign land had apparently produced this unexpected result. His first reaction was undeniably auspicious on that account. He was a man inclined to cherish the validity of his own first judgments and less inclined to amend them even when circumstances justified such correction. He paid scant attention to the outward circumstances of which Turchaninoff briefly told him and chose, rather, in a spontaneous gesture of friendliness to write the Russian colonel as though there yet clung to him the aura of prestige and authority which had greatly recommended him formerly.

Carefully and in his own hand, he penned a polite letter in return, making such suggestions as he fancied might serve the colonel to bridge the obvious differences which he must encounter in a new country. He made courteous reference to Turchaninoff's indisputable ability; he was confident that in short order he must find a welcome place in the business or industrial life of the country. He was sorry that he could not be optimistic in this respect concerning the prospect of a military commission, the Army being in size and importance quite without the status armies held in other lands. He concluded with a suggestion that Turchaninoff interview a certain gentleman whose address he enclosed. This was a man of many parts, one Alexander Bache who descended from a distinguished line of American patriots and who now held an important post in the Coastal Survey.

It was undoubtedly a friendly letter and McClellan himself was well pleased with the result. His was the type of mind which was easily prevailed upon to make plans. He had a quickness of perception for opportunity which was remarkable. It fell easily to his mind to allocate the right things to the right people, the right people to the right places. In the case of Turchaninoff, he felt justifiably magnanimous, considering the slight acquaintance upon which the colonel presumed.

Having dispatched his friendly and helpful letter, he promptly forgot Turchaninoff. Perhaps he thought never to hear more from him. It might almost be thought that the changed station of the colonel had, absolved him from any further concern, that he justly deemed himself relieved of further commitments. But if these thoughts were creditable at all, they had their base only in McClellan's unconscious snobbery, in a natural haughtiness and pride of class, not in any true obliquity of character.

In any case, until his letter of advice reached them, the colonel and his lady remained in New York where their days were as usefully spent as people with little money can spend days, having time above everything else to part with freely. And if one were to have followed them about at this time, one might have concluded that not a worry in the world harassed either of them. Nadine was rejoiced to feel again the subtle flavor of security which large towns and cities accorded her. She, unlike her husband, had from earliest infancy been accustomed to the life of cities, though it was a fact that in her young girlhood she had made many sojourns in camps during campaigns. Her father, a widowed general of note, was enabled by rank and wealth to indulge her in such privileges.

The colonel too, appeared to be relieved of a sense of failure which it would not have behooved him to articulate on the farm. He recognized that leaving was tantamount to an admission of failure, yet this in itself did not perturb him as much as an open avowal of defeat might have. He reasoned that he had elected to leave and having established as much, he was free to permit himself whatever amusements New York could bestow upon them. They walked in the spacious parks and attended a music hall. They took long walks as far as the outskirts of the city, sometimes even further than the forties which constituted the suburbs.

"I feel somehow as if we two were specters, not real people at all," Nadine had once exclaimed. "We walk and talk but always only with one another." She sighed deeply. "It is as if no one sees us, no one is aware that we are among the living."

In a measure, her husband also felt a noisy silence all about them. He sensed that it was not enough to be a spectator. Within him, rose an old longing to approach one of the ladies or gentlemen promenading on old Broadway, reach out his hand confidently to him, as though assured that it would be taken, that friendly eyes would know his inner man.

They were directly in front of a book shop. On the sidewalk in front of the shop were ranged two long tables creaking with the stacks of books they supported. The windows of the shop were interestingly dusty with what seemed almost a scholarly dust, therefore permissible, even desirable. The interior of the shop stretched far into black shadows, for no ray of the bright sunlight outside seemed capable of penetrating past the towering array of volumes crowded near the entrance itself.

"Let us stop here in this book shop," he said. "Books are real people; they are the important parts of people; they reveal everything about a man."

They had no idea what to seek in the shop, though each of them, without communicating his loneliness, began at once to scan the shelves lining the walls of the shop. Carefully Turchaninoff drew first one volume and then several off their shelves. Something gratifying clung to his fingers with the ancient dust of the books. There were French novels and German philosophies, histories and poetry. Together they gave him a sense of purpose in searching over the shelves; he would perhaps find a copy of Pushkin's poems. Always it dispelled an uneasiness and vague mistrust of himself to find an objective in whatever he undertook to effect. It was not enough for him to find himself acting aimlessly in any capacity whatever; he had to define for himself an incentive, a purpose and goal toward which he inclined throughout the accomplishment of his smallest office. So now in searching for a volume of Pushkin's work, he was enabled to throw off the momentary gloom of their virtual isolation in New York. His search for his best loved native poet created the illusion of familiarity no events of their life in the States had so far evinced. The fact that there lay no doubt in his mind but that he would encounter his old favorite among the strangers sitting mutely on the shelves, lent further substance to the gentle evasion which his mind allowed to him.

Nadine, on the other hand, was frankly less interested in the thousands of books than in the figure of a young man she took to be the indifferent clerk, absorbed in a book of his own choosing, only casually aware of the two customers who had not yet turned to him for service. Unlike Turchaninoff, she considered each person an entity quite disparate from all other entities. Where her husband reduced everything to generalities, she found it simpler and more natural to begin with an acceptance of unique differences. Her husband fought differences and sought ever to unite likenesses, but she took likenesses for granted, finding only the differences intriguing. It was the oblique, the grotesque, even the distorted factor of the unusual in an object which irradiated it with subtle meanings for her.

Unobtrusively she neared the reading clerk, who, upon lifting his eyes from the book in his lap, returned her silent observation with a warming, inviting glance. Quickly he rose to his feet and met Nadine where the counter swung toward the back of the shop. He laid his book away without marking his place and began to address her with an odd obsequiousness which varied greatly with the alert intelligence shining in his eyes. She could not determine whether they were light eyes or dark and furthermore, after a moment's inspection, decided that it mattered not a whit, for the sparkle and life in them made the onlooker forget superficial attributes instantly. In like manner it escaped her attention that the man was strangely uncouth in his attire, that his hair was disarrayed, his beard untrimmed and his shirt carelessly open at the throat.

"May I be of assistance, Madame," he spoke quietly. As she was about to answer, the colonel neared and answered for her.

In careful English he asked for a copy of Pushkin and watched the obliging clerk return behind the counter where he busied himself at a less accessible case of books. Once or twice he turned about and flashed a friendly smile at Nadine, who answered with one of her own.

"I am sorry not to be able to oblige you," he said regretfully at last. "The bookseller is absent at present and I am but waiting on trade until he returns. Perhaps if you call again he will be better able to help you than I."

His voice was rather rueful, as though it were a matter of personal distress that it lay beyond his powers to serve them. Coming again to the store side of the counter, he unexpectedly addressed the colonel, whose entire face thereupon lighted up with pleasure, even before he had uttered one sentence.

"You will forgive me my curiosity, but I could not help but note in spite of your excellent English, that you are strangers. French perhaps?"

Everything about the man was kindness and to Nadine his kindness seemed indeed no careless accident, but a direct response to an inner knowledge he possessed. Some men have educated heads, she reflected, but this one has an educated heart.

In a matter of minutes, her husband was deep in conversation with their unknown acquaintance. They discussed the famous Russian poet for a few sentences and then with fervor followed this trend of thought until poetry in general and a meaning of a man's song to other men became their chief topic.

"It interests me that the first book you wish to buy in a new land should be a book of poetry," the young man said, his eyes all alight with a pleasure whose provenance neither of the other two could suspect.

"First comes a friend," Turchaninoff answered simply enough, "but failing that, it is a man's privilege to find a substitute for friendship. In the songs a man sings, one can find the comfort of friendship; so I believe."

To these words and others for the few minutes that their interview endured, the temporary book clerk listened, nodding his head now and then, leading Turchaninoff on skillfully with only a word or a look until it seemed to Nadine, observing it all, that no secret in her husband's mind could remain so for long. At length, however, the actual bookseller returned and put an end to the discussion.

"Thanks, Walt," the bookdealer said in a hurried tone of voice which carried with it the implication that he and time were at great odds, that he always had to catch time by the forelock. His brisk glance at once took in the two people upon whom he immediately cast his professional smiles and invitations. With a bare nod he saw his friend Walt take leave of the shop, book in hand. Hastily he explained that he had remained away but a short while and that if they had been discommoded in any way...

"Sometimes my friend speaks out plain and frank," he apologized in advance. "He means well, though and I like to have him come in here; lends an air to the place. He's something of a poet and you'd be surprised how some people you would never expect, enjoy talking to a real poet who does not act anything but a regular fellow when it suits him. Name's Whitman."

Here he reached under his counter and came up with a small green volume which Turchaninoff received from him. "Leaves of Grass" was written on the cover. In touching the pages which fluttered through his fingers, it was as though he were clasping the hand of a friend. Without further ado, without even mentioning Pushkin, Turchaninoff bought a copy of Whitman's poems.

As they left the book shop, much of the same quietness fell upon him as before their entry there, with one difference, to be sure; then he had felt a sad loneliness, against which in a strange land it seemed impossible to protest. Now he felt loneliness composed of comprehensible factors which time and opportunity must remedy. That had been the promise in the glance and approach of the poet.

"It is as though that young man had given us something to look forward to," he spoke happily to Nadine as he tucked her fingers under his arm. And indeed, with the book for companionship, once they returned to their rooms, this was true enough. The great city now seemed to accept these new citizens. They were welcome because a single unknown man had been kind.

CHAPTER VII

Until George McClellan's letter reached him, Turchaninoff held himself forcibly aloof from the anxiety which his wife less successfully controlled. He was confident that the Captain must recall to mind the details of their former acquaintance, must be immediately appreciative of the fact that so much time had elapsed while they were in the United States without their need to have recourse to him. Self-reliance like that would have revealed much of the man's fortitude to him and consequently induced him to ascribe to McClellan a like reception of such intelligence. That his wife felt this to be supposititious thinking was of no matter, for he persisted in his belief that basically all men were composed of similar stuff and that all must perforce respond by an inner consciousness to a sense of right which would leave no doubt of their sympathy and compassion. He therefore drew much comfort from his own assurance and remained confident that the next post should deliver them the letter of a friend. Repeatedly he pointed out the slowness of trains, the distance separating them from Chicago, the need for patience during the period of expectancy and waiting and all because he felt the importance of that awaited fate; the sign, the avowal, the certification of their actuality and worth.

During the days of expectancy the colonel chose to remain almost exclusively in their rooms. He took to polishing the fine inlaid woods of his violin until the instrument obtained the luster of a mirror and gleamed warm encouragement to its owner's heart. Nadine, less certain of McClellan's good intentions, maintained a discreet silence, preferring to read rather than pursue fruitless discussions. Whenever she did speak, it was to ask information or to repeat some lines from the volume of poems they had purchased.

"The title 'Leaves of Grass' puzzles me," she said once in tones of helpless submission, pleasing to Ivan who constituted her mentor and intellectual guide.

Immediately her husband crossed the room and took the book from her with a jealous disdain of whatever aspersion her feminine obtuseness might imply.

"It's because you don't listen and hear the man behind the words. It is because you are critical without first liking the man in the poet. But I understand him, this Whitman. He draws lessons of life from nature. To me he speaks like a brother. I know what it is to lie in the tall grass in a far field where a river flows. At first you feel like a huge heavy mass weighing cruelly upon small, helpless little things; you seem big and ruthless, overpowering; the inarticulate world is only greenery blowing over your mouth; you have no thought of the miracle of one blade of grass. Then suddenly you feel humble; your size diminishes; your eyes open up so that you can see the finest thread, the tiniest creature for which a blade of grass is as a tree is to you."

"The title of those poems means all that to you?" Nadine was incredulous, though these infrequent insights into her husband were not utterly unknown to her. She could not explain the mingled respect and repulsion these insights gave rise to. She believed his intensity excluded her from his inner life, though his penchant for ecstatic enthusiasm rendered him praiseworthy in her sight. At rare times it was vouchsafed her to perceive the images and figures which peopled his inner world and these rendered her thoughtful to the extreme, even when they infused into her a degree of confidence which outer circumstances refused to grant her. As in the present case, she seemed capable of grasping the intangible truths which were the lessons of his text; with a contagious illumination she recognized his solemn credos, saw as lucid that which was ordinarily obscure and vague to her more practical mind. With a curious lifting of her spirits she could enter into his passionate fancies, receive with affection his own concepts of nature and man's relation to it; see in a sudden comprehension his identification of men flowering on the earth with grasses springing unprejudiced out of every species of soil. This flashing perspicuity would not remain with her as an essential ingredient of her composition, but while under its influence her emotions lent themselves to his conviction that each life was a facet of a boundless masterwork, a detail, whether flawed or a stroke of genius in a grandiose work of art.

At long last McClellan's letter arrived and was succeeded by a further exchange of friendly letters in which tacit promises were made to secure proper connections, with Alexander Bache, preferably, but with others should Bache prove unavailable. McClellan suggested Mr. Bache as the best first contact for Turchaninoff because he was the one man able to appraise the significance of the Russian's outstanding accomplishments as engineer to the Czar. Behind this selection of Mr. Bache there may have been an intended compliment to Turchaninoff, to his former title and rank, which considerations stood high in McClellan's esteems. He took a pardonable pride in his own family ties and connections; in the honors and distinctions that had accrued to his house; in his excellent record at West Point and afterwards in the Army. Though McClellan had now entered upon another line of endeavor - railroading - and received a salary ample to his needs, enough to invite marriage, he still clung to the traditions of his class and would have been perplexed at the colonel's social defalcations had he known the complete story. As it was, however, it was natural for him to introduce two excellent men, engineers, exponents of true aristocracy as he conceived of that station.

As has been said, it flattered McClellan to be instrumental in conjoining suitable types. In his new estate as vice-president of the Illinois Central Railroad, it was a simple matter for him to become Turchaninoff's patron. He knew he was complimenting Bache in referring the Russian colonel to his attention, paying the older man a tribute in memory of his former connection with him in Washington where they had met while on similar business; both had had dealings with the Secretary of War; both were men of narrow vision and traditional patriotism and had seen eye-to-eye on matters of national defense; had talked as equals might on this all-important subject.

Bache had attained the most dignity and honor in McClellan's esteem by being the great grandson of Benjamin Franklin, a fact upon which he based Bache's claim to an aristocracy he openly admired. He was connected at this time with a noted engineering school in Philadelphia and it was this school which McClellan had in mind as the proving ground for the colonel, preparatory to his future occupation. Here he sent Turchaninoff who readily acceded, aware that his first American schooling was a good beginning. With letters of recommendation and with correspondence to pave the way, Turchaninoff at length removed to Philadelphia and to Bache's sponsorship.

In spite of the failure to affect the start of a career in Philadelphia, Turchaninoff ever after remained grateful to McClellan for his efforts on his behalf. In later years when the military and political fame of General McClellan was on the wane, when a country looked with aversion upon his declining grandeur, Turchaninoff inclined to remember a gentleman's tact and generosity toward him, found himself exculpating McClellan from serious charges of dilatory duty and creating for him an exoneration based principally on his own feelings that McClellan operated under laws higher than strict logic; and this he deduced from the remembered sympathy that he had ascribed to McClellan in the past.

In any case, Bache stood prepared to welcome the colonel and Nadine. A fussy and somewhat querulous gentleman, older than Turchaninoff by several years, he nevertheless made an effort to befriend him after an initial inspection, much as an Airedale might sniff at a new dog in the kennel. Apparently satisfied with his preliminary survey of Turchaninoff, he soon abandoned his original superior tone and assured Turchaninoff that he had an excellent opinion of Russians whom he preferred to the British, for the obvious reason that Russians were not land hungry.

"We are a gullible people," he informed Turchaninoff almost immediately. "We won't believe in the perfidy you Europeans take for granted."

Bache had an habitual air of worry which he plainly showed to derive from something more than his extensive responsibility as superintendent of the Coastal Survey. This post had more linguistic prestige than factual; a fact which he deplored bitterly.

But he was a sincere man possessed of an honest fear for his country and this impressed Turchaninoff favorably; a man with a mission was no laughing matter to him, for he understood the pain such a one must endure, due to the purblind obtuseness of politicians. He thought Bache wrong in fearing some foreign invasion at a future date, for what was less probable then this where covetousness of strong and grasping powers was checked by a land's blessed purity? But Turchaninoff won the other man's heart by admitting the dire possibilities of foreign invasion and by manifesting at once a hatred for this anticipated hostility which did not seem odd to Bache who nodded his approval.

"You will make a fine citizen," he said kindly; then bethinking himself he added, "You are now a better citizen then some whose blood is the tested blood of patriots!"

At this time Bache was pleading with Washington to vote him money for more detailed research and study connected with a system of adequate coastal defense. The entire coastline of the eastern seaboard offered opportunity for enemy treachery, as it was then bereft of necessary forts and guns. If his main fear related to the strategic dangers threatening his own fair city, this could be excused. He was rabid on the subject, quick to flare into anger when he met with opposition he attributed to sheer indifference and ignorance.

"They see only what lies directly under their noses," he raged to Turchaninoff. "We need men like you in the Service and you deserve to be well paid! But do those selfish old men stuffing their gullets with the fat of the land understand that? They expect patriotism to flourish on high standing verbiage! Meanwhile, if I want something done for their good, I am to pay for it myself! Mine is not a service to my country in their opinion but a smug sinecure for which I should be properly grateful!"

This forebode no good for Turchaninoff whose pride suffered, while Bache continued to lash the government for refusing to make appropriations which would have enabled him to put Turchaninoff on his staff. As it was, because he truly admired the Russian's indisputable abilities and because he was truly animated by sincere patriotic fervor, he made him as liberal an allowance as he could reasonably do, in order to benefit by the extensive knowledge the other possessed.

Bache had frequent consultations with Turchaninoff in which they discussed everything from mathematics to poetry, from guns to bridges, from poetry to philosophy. Turchaninoff attended lectures at the Engineering Department of the Philadelphia University, saying to Nadine that this was necessary until he could accustom himself to the American way of doing sums, as he put it whimsically. Always he assured Nadine that it was merely a matter of time before he established himself with an adequate income. He pointed out to her how Bache, an important man, already trusted his judgment and wished to attach him to his personal staff. Bache had only to persuade Congress that the coastal survey appropriation is a vital necessity; and that was a mere trifle.

"Do you imagine it will be difficult for such an exemplary American to procure whatever proves necessary for the good of the country?"

However, the developments did not justify his optimism. While working in Bache's office in Washington, Turchaninoff had many occasions to visit the Senate chamber and there noted with much surprise that every Senator from the Southern States was violently opposed to giving the coastal survey anything approximating an adequate appropriation. A burly Senator from Florida was persistently vehement in denouncing the Coastal Survey and said repeatedly that any appropriation for the Coastal Survey was an appalling expenditure of funds. The result of such opposition from high places was that the revised appropriation was not only defeated, but in fact, the existing appropriation was materially reduced and Bache was compelled to curtail his current small staff, which included Colonel Turchaninoff. A few years later when the Southern States seceded, Turchaninoff was enabled to see why the Southern Senators had objected to the increased Coastal survey. The future secessionists in the South were even then preparing ground for the dissolution of the Union and it was to their advantage to keep Washington as ignorant as possible concerning the topography of Southern harbors.

Happily McClellan, with whom the colonel kept up a correspondence, at this juncture offered to arrange for a position which the Russian might fill in the near future. This gesture from the American went far to confirm Turchaninoff's increasing devotion to this land which he now determined to adopt in every way that a man can adopt a land - in spirit, in effort, in dignity and in loyalty.

Until his departure from Philadelphia could be arranged, he occupied himself for the most part in Bache's rooms, where he not only discovered, with unending pleasure, ancient newspapers and magazines, many of whose publishing houses were now defunct, but also yellowed journals which belonged to the historical archives of the city, save that Bache retained them with a dragon-like obstinacy. He allowed Turchaninoff freely to peruse these old publications and also many old documents and letters; often he sat with his new friend and explained the origin of values and customs among early Americans. In this, he took great pride as he did in all things pertaining to the glorious record of the Founding Fathers. Everything he did and proposed with respect to the security of Philadelphia derived from an apprehension for the security of the entire country. Strategic coordination of men to work in time of crisis; gun crews and supply lines of ammunition and food; foundations for gun emplacements all along the splendid coast line as yet but slightly bruised by batteries; positions for underground storage facilities in case of a long siege - these were the basis for all else upon which he discoursed. When the Russian mildly wondered at his unusual concern with military matters and remarked upon the peacefulness and plenty with which the land emanated, Bache had ready and impassioned replies.

"We in this city especially, are a race of sharp, astute men: shipwrights, builders, men toiling in the earth and on the sea; our instincts are sharp too. The sons and grandsons of men of the sea hold dear the land they clutch from the sea robbers. We marched in civic pride when this country was born. My ancestors participated in the first grand military procession on the fourth of July in the year 1788. Believe me, we in this city are in the position to feel the pulse of the nation; and we fear for the nation's future."

He was sincere in his conviction that the foes of the land lay without, not within. The evils within frightened him in no wise. Over these, including the agitated political struggles, territorial accession, slave trade, the Fugitive Slave Law and the Taney Decision, he shrugged his shoulders philosophically. These matters he did not surmise to be of the bellicose and inflammable quality to create the death and destruction of war. Turchaninoff, heeding his words and well-considered sentiments carefully, felt inclined to agree with him. European as he was, it came to his mind as more likely that, with growth and wealth, the United States would become the coveted prize to be fought over by England or Spain, rather than the battleground for her own sons and daughters in an internecine slaughter.

Agreeing as he might with the distant possibilities Bache fearfully envisaged, Turchaninoff nevertheless enjoyed himself immensely in the discoveries he was making among the historical antiquities. Each evening he recounted to his wife the excitements he experienced in his literary rambles over the pages of America's young past.

"Somehow it makes me feel that all things I long for are possible; there is but a brief survey to make of the past years and having made that, I shall be caught up with my contemporaries; I shall be an American like them!"

And he firmly believed this; so firmly indeed that all thought for Nadine and her feelings appeared wanting. To her fell the lot of worrying about the few dollars remaining to them. She quietly accepted a loan from Bache and she incessantly planned small economies whereby they might accumulate enough money to leave Philadelphia when new opportunities should open to them. Already they knew the name of the western town where McClellan had thought it advisable for them to remove. She could not be overly blamed if her husband's interest in Philadelphia's history assumed less significance to her than to him.

He who loved the future must scan the past, he claimed. She, chaffing under petty irritations which colored her every thought, began to harbor natural resentments; she angered over the plight they found themselves in; she wished this new land held newer opportunities for women who seemed improved upon the European women. Often her thoughts were filled with plans which in Russia or France or even England she might have carried out with some modicum of success; run a small school or even make attempts to enter the new profession of nursing in which skill she was no novice. These things were less than possible here. Her eyes sparkled dangerously as she listened to her husband relating with animation his discoveries. Had he noticed these resurgent signs of dissent in her, he might have paused to inquire their origin. But he accepted the feminine half of the world with the equanimity with which he accepted a sunrise. He longed for a world of active brotherhood and took for granted the silent sisterhood of women. His wife, with no clearly defined intellection on the subject, accepted this also and when her dissatisfaction rose to articulation, she was at a loss for definition. After all, she was a woman of her age and not of that heroic mold which ventures upon untrodden paths. With him at her side, it would seem normal to dare the unknown. Without him she sank into the helplessness which was little affected by his rousing enthusiasm. In this new world, she found her position greatly inferior to what it had been in Russia. Here, the established social milieu in which she had moved with honor and approbation was wanting. Here she could be a partisan only to what Ivan was a partisan to. Here she must subside more than her birth and station had demanded of her in Russia. Sadly she felt herself traitor to the impulsion which extended her husband's selfless ambitions. She made haste to push all recognition of this treachery from her mind, to smile the more brightly at Ivan's progress in historical research, and to pretend sympathy for his efforts which in no manner or form held merit for her. "He really mistakes thought for action," she thought repeatedly and no sooner had she alleged this than she began to doubt herself, to fall back on him. Perhaps, she concluded, in the long run thought was action and action thought.

Finally this rather involved meditation reduced her to fatigue and she would abandon it for something concrete to do with her hands. She sewed and tatted lace and sat complacently in her role as auditor to Turchaninoff.

"What makes these researches of mine important," he was fond of declaiming to her, "is that they reveal to me that this city contains a cross section of all the country. Do you realize, Nadya, that Philadelphia, even more than New York, is the veritable hub of the country's life? Why, in knowing Philadelphia, a newcomer knows the people everywhere; one finds it difficult to acquire any sectionalism. If only I might infuse in you my own fervor about this amazing democracy, this constitutional democracy which thrills a man's soul, I tell you!"

To her it was one and the same whether this city they hoped soon to leave held historic mementoes or not. With resignation she heard her husband laud the city's participation in the War for Independence. Nor would she brave his wrath by voicing her own private thoughts that such matters were less vital to her than the closer issues involving happiness and personal success. She had seconded his desire to leave Russia in the belief that his greater personal happiness depended on it; therefore, she could not see his present suspended state without sorrow and a sense of shame, which was as active in her as in him. Never before had her pride and self-esteem been so sorely tried as in these months; never since their flight from security and certainty. It began to appear to her that they had rushed headlong into the tenuous stuff of a dream, which, with its prolongation, was gradually assuming the aspect of a nightmare.

With her cupboard bare of essentials, leave alone niceties, to which they had in better times been handsomely accustomed, it was not simple for her to glow as Ivan did when he expostulated upon the unaffected honesty of the great city's origin; that its pioneer stock consisted of house builders and shipbuilders, sailmakers and shipjoiners, ropemakers and cabinetmakers, instrument makers, gilders, coopers and cane makers; that these were the people he loved; to them he would turn for confirmation in his creed of progress and brotherhood.

His best gifts obviously did not lie in the field of social analysis. He approached the idea of action too resolutely to find contentment in mere diagnosis, in mere logic which often leads to satisfaction with and of itself. He was void of calm satisfactions. In the absorbed studies he pursued among Bache's papers, he perceived no indication of social patterns by which to follow out new lines of cogitation. He saw only variations of the pervasive dream Herzen in London advocated and which he, in every act of his adult life, espoused. When he found evidence of early social unrest among the Americans, which he did find in old periodicals and records of a generation or two ago, the tone of strong individualism made him jubilant. One magazine, "The Young American", especially delighted him, for in it he found an article listing the rights and claims those earlier Americans had wanted added to the written codes of the land. The first of these demands consisted of man's unalienable rights to the soil, the homesteads, to a just distribution of the fruits of his labor. Other claims sued for drastic action against excessive ownership of land which might tend toward land monopolies and still others against debtors' laws including imprisonment for debt. Rights for women and a marked departure from the constraining puritanical laws with regard to the mails on the Sabbath finished the list and the last proposal delighted Turchaninoff as much as the more serious ones.

In this way, they waited until McClellan had effected an opening for Turchaninoff at Mattoon, Illinois, then a mere hamlet in the vast land grant of the Illinois Central Railroad; a slight bud on the young branch of the spreading industrial tree. There was a great need at the time for construction engineers and architects. These were required to erect sufficient dwellings for the increasing population of adventuring men who, having been led to seek in their westward push that wealth and security that the more settled areas of the country denied them, were crowding the railroad junctions until they inflated them into towns.

Eventually, they boarded a west-bound train and proceeded to their new destination.

"I feel young and strong," Turchaninoff exclaimed. "I want to roll up my sleeves, roll down my collar and breathe deeply; for I go to take a part in the making of a new world. Actually every man takes his share, but how wonderful to be cognizant of it, to be unafraid of it!"

CHAPTER VIII

Another traveler was speeding at some fifteen miles per hour in the same direction as the Turchaninoff's. This was the young shipmate, Dimitri Trofimov, they had met nearly two years earlier. Chicago was his destination and it is to be doubted that, had he known his compatriots were in the next coach, he might have been overly surprised. His was the belief that a fate directed each life, provided the individual went halfway to meet it, but that anything was likely and significant by its chance. Never go the entire way for anything; never reach too high, nor yet too low; never give too much, for that prevents the other fellow from having room to give at all: cardinal points for him. Above all, never be thrown out of countenance; that robs a man of poise and stance and affords undue advantage to the other man whom you assume to be either an adversary until proven otherwise, or a means to an end.

How he had fared these many months since his advent into the United States must remain a matter for conjecture. That he had managed, without noticeable resources, to survive at all, could not be doubted from the fashionable attire he sported. He was a young man of many and varied gifts. Therefore, the problem of eking out an existence was less worrisome to him than it was for another man in a like position. He was seldom above creating for his purposes either talents or references which opened avenues of opportunity denied many a more worthy gentleman. He had wandered in and out of New York, Boston, and Philadelphia on one business mission after another. And when it suited him, he advanced upon the newspapers where he succeeded in impressing editors, if not by his writing skill, then by the names he pronounced haughtily and with familiarity and his own noble surname which he discreetly implied was a name to reckon with in Moscow or St. Petersburg. One month he might pose as a retired millionaire; another as an exiled rebel against the Czar; still another as a collector of secret military information to be used against the French.

However he managed, manage he did, flitting from one city to another, from one fashionable, foolish dowager to another, all of whom he entertained vastly and according to the lady's pretensions, either with titles of nobility, or his intimacy with the noted wits and charmers of two continents.

This westward move he was embarked upon was the result of a chance conversation in which, though not officially participating, he nevertheless had pricked up his ears, always ready to receive such suggestions and hints as might readily be turned to good usage. He was not one to underestimate the favors which fate sprinkled about indiscriminately. As regards the fortunes of the world, he was humble enough; considering humbleness the proper virtue for men with their fortunes yet to be made; with the proviso that humbleness be directed toward the mollification of those basking in success; in any other situation it was the height of folly.

In a gentleman's club where he was frequently introduced by members led to sponsor his pretensions, he had discovered the potential strength of the West. The matter under discussion had been the expansion of the railroads and the lands granted to them by an indulgent government. Chicago was mentioned as a city fast becoming the Mecca of the new industries springing up in the West. New wealth and new talent were beginning to mark out widening trends. Trofimov was not slow to surmise that opportune moments in history often announce themselves in just such a casual manner as this. Throughout the tedious days of journeying to his new field of conquest, he found sufficient amusement for himself in his own thoughts and but rarely took his place on the observation platform of the train. Had he so followed the fashion of the travelers, he might have chanced to encounter Turchaninoff who was never content to spend his hours within the stuffy wooden coach and chose rather to feast his eyes upon the wonders of a shifting landscape.

For hours on end, the colonel deserted his beautiful lady for the beauty of a greening countryside to which, as the train sped, he attributed virtues and promises sweeter than the dreams of success that Trofimov was envisaging.

It was inevitable, however, that so many days en route should bring about a meeting between these strangely met people. Nadine was the first to recognize the figure of their former acquaintance when they stopped in the station yard at Cleveland. Many of the travelers had left their seats to seek refreshment and relaxation for the short interval in which the puffing iron engine was refueling. With an ill-restrained gladness she called attention to herself, though blushing the while she did, for it was not her custom to bemoan herself ordinarily by this form of behavior. In a matter of minutes Trofimov was at her side, bowing over her hand, admiring with one arched glance the elegance of her bonnet and the freshness of a skin as pearly and tender as a young maiden's. In a few more moments the two were laughing and chatting easily; he with the consciousness that two years had not diminished the lady's charm's for him; she without much curiosity but with an instant happiness in his presence and eagerness which lifted her spirits and animated her entire being, so that her eyes grew darker and brighter and her face faintly roseate and girlish.

"You say you are not to settle in Chicago?" Trofimov was somewhat surprised and had not quite caught the name of the small hamlet which she had hurriedly confided to him. "What then will the colonel hope to accomplish in the hinterland, not that this town of Chicago can be much superior to any hinterland?" he said deprecating Turchaninoff's selection of site.

Nadine shrugged her shoulder ever so slightly, though she was aware that at other times she should have grown immediately provoked at this scarcely veiled derogation of her husband. She had suffered the unvoiced censure of their unrelenting Long Island neighbors with more chagrin than perhaps the situation warranted; but always she had felt herself prepared in any case to support her husband, much as she might disapprove of many of his "impractical" evaluations. Her loyalty to him had never been questioned; her alliance with him was an immutable fact in her thinking. In this respect she was again the natural product of her age and she should have been the first to recoil in horror at open rupture. Marriage was not an institution one entered or left; it was an ineluctable truth which depended upon no demonstrable instances. Looking into the baron's spellbinding eyes she felt no wifely anger.

This anomaly, perhaps, was significant to her as she stood in the station yard, the sunlight of a bright day beating down upon her and her companion. Later she was to reflect upon this exception and store it away as women often do, for future study and beguilement. Now she smiled and enjoyed the mild banter to which Trofimov treated her, the studied courtesy by which he was enabled to persuade any woman that she was an especial delicacy only momentarily tendered him for his reverent worship. Nor was she sorry to rejoin her husband and leave Trofimov's care.

Her mind was innocent of guile. She had no suspicion that her interest in the young Russian nobleman, or pseudo-nobleman, stemmed from other than accountable motives. Frankly, had she consulted her innermost thoughts, she would have conceded at once that the colonel was by far the worthier man, that for all his visionary disquisitions, he stood pre-eminently in her mind as an admirable man. Always he had without profession or explanation, allowed her a liberty and freedom few women of her acquaintance could boast. He had turned to her ear, if not to her mind, with a frequency she could not fail to translate truly as unfeigned love and respect. Troubled as she might be by what she termed his vagaries, and much as she might secretly despair of his success in the knight-errantry he upheld, she was not the one to falsify her husband's claim to merit and moral grandeur. At this time, however, it never occurred to her to make comparisons between the two men. She merely enjoyed the novelty of scintillating and witty conversations; the peculiar polish Trofimov gave to language; the opportunity to relegate the actual problems facing them to the future rewards which Mattoon, their destination, held forth.

In Chicago the three parted with idly spoken promises of renewed contact. Trofimov disappeared into the peopled wilderness of the great town, while Nadine and Ivan figuratively girded their loins as they proceeded to Mattoon.

This small town, like many others in the West of those days, was in the throes of a building boom. A feverish activity marked every phase of life among its bustling inhabitants. There was a smile of welcome on every face in town for every other face and this friendliness above all else, appeased Turchaninoff at the very start; he having had his fill for the time being of unpeopled grandeur in the virginal woods of Long Island. This happiness rose from the knowledge that he and all who were willing to build the temples of the lord, so to speak, were hailed and acclaimed. It suffused his days and even his nights; for he threw himself into the work of planning and surveying with such heartiness that little room was left for the steady furbishing of his hungry mind with reading and studying.

In Mattoon, nothing was established, everything was to be done. Therefore all doers were vital creators. These were his thoughts and Turchaninoff projected them into the earnest, if heavy, faces of the rough toilers he consorted with. A smile of common variety was treated by him as an invitation to fraternal affection. The casual inquiry became the reaching hand of a friend. The mild jocularity of an Irishman, chewing his wad of tobacco, attained an international significance that the tobacco chewer would have denied with vigor and resentment.

Officially his appointment in Mattoon was in the capacity of architect. This profession entailed something other than the drafting of plans and blueprints. It encompassed surveying, employment of workers, construction in its most elementary form, and not infrequently, actual labor with an intent to demonstrate the work. On his arrival, Turchaninoff found that in spite of the urgency in the community, there existed but little more than a hundred buildings worthy of the name. The need was great for all sorts of ability in laying the groundwork for the life of the town. That such a life was springing into full bloom, with the ruthless determination of healthy virility, was manifest by the interest every worker in Mattoon took in the political doings of the day. In the back country, even in the purlieus of New York where the Turchaninoffs had ventured to make brief entries, nothing of this personal interest in the political life of the nation had been apparent to the newcomers. Nadine, a lover of cities, was less surprised at this vitality of mental life in Mattoon than her husband, for she had the perspicuity to perceive, if not too clearly, that removal from the individualism of the land accounted for the greater contiguity of people with one another and afforded them incentive for their concerns with national affairs.

"A new broom sweeps vigorously," she laughed. "A new town is a true cross-section of a country."

Here it was that the colonel met with the first zealots of the newly organized Republican Party which was making which was making itself ready to take part in the senatorial race of the State. Nothing could have been more to his liking than the eagerness with which the proselytizers sought him out upon every occasion; the way in which burly men lent themselves to his expiations on general ethics and morals; the interest their faces openly showed when he explained his flight from Russia; the welcome his strength and personal power was given. All of these more than justified to the colonel the fervor of his far-reaching visions. Gladly he appended his name to the rolls of Republicans and took a silent oath ever to support the party's democratic precepts. Not that he did this lightly, let it be understood. On the contrary he studied its text and objectives seriously and discussed its role in the nation's life with a sharp acumen. The Republican Party, then but two years old, he identified as the true voice of the people. He learned to identify the Democrats with the vested interests of the prevailing slave economy which he looked upon as a decrepit, hanger-on fossil in a new age. It did not overly disturb him that this should be so, for he expected no violent changes whereby these remnants of obsolete castes might be eliminated. He was absolutely sanguine that of itself, the vast agrarian plantation rule in the southern states must inevitably yield to the progressive onslaught of the peoples' claims in a forward-looking area such as Illinois.

As he integrated himself into the life of Mattoon, he grew more and more partisan to the local peculiarities which marked the party line in this section of the country and was prone to overlook the larger significance which the emergence of this party indicated. As if his former opposition to inequities were a cloak worn loosely over his shoulders, he now dropped it carelessly and appeared to forget the property lines of division he had noted, even so recently as the Crimean War. The fact that the outspoken clamor of a portionless people, heretofore more silent than not, gave good indication that a fundamental economic change was occurring. The further fact that new techniques, without being thoroughly understood, were casting their shadows, endowing all men of the age with new hopes of material grandeur; that as might be expected, these hopes were evoking the subtle and entrenched foes of change. He saw none of this.

In a curious fashion, he nourished an illusion about the United States, that it stood like a blessed Isle, like a pearl in the fluids of an irritated oyster, a veritable symbol of man's triumph over chaos. In 1858, he conceived of no raging floodtides which might sweep over the placid prairies or the gentle knolls so divinely sodded with the green wealth of the land. When he began to attend political meetings, he expected anything but the furious storm of passion and feelings which small matters like the territorial acquisitions aroused. Perhaps he expected discussions of generalities, which, in the main, were the essence of his own thought; but soon he became experienced on behalf of his nascent patriotism.

At first he saw no import in the vast Southwest territory which, like a worm at the root of a plant, lay at the bottom of the political frenzy of the day. So far, his American experience had not exposed him to the current history of the past decade, the most telling decade in an altogether changing and evolving century. Ten years of Russian history were as a mere puff of wind; how likely was he to impute to ten years of this country's history, a more compelling place? The men who worked with him, who laughed and scolded and swore and gloried in their limited achievements, seemed unaware of the hammer-like blows which the past ten years had dealt them. They saw, if at all, only extremely dim outlines of the conflict beginning to take shape out of the mists of misunderstanding, a sort of evil genie mounting to the heavens out of the close confines of a bottle foolishly uncorked.

But they did see one thing and he saw it too. Namely that they must protest against the spread of slavery in the new territories accruing to the United States. Not that the existing institution excited their indignation, though, to be sure, there were some who cried for the complete abolition of the hated system of bondage; their concern was the furthering of an evil whose economic necessity they could not view sympathetically. These early members of the young political party were not embroiled in the entangling complications of cotton, tobacco, and the foreign markets hungry for American raw materials. They had vast uncultivated land to populate; they had the abundance and fertility of generous and variegated food stuffs to sustain them in a rugged independence; they were understandably passionate in their endemic prejudices and principles, believing truly to be representative of all that the Founding Fathers had intended when the Articles of Federation were drawn up.

Living and thinking with these people in Mattoon, then already a town singular in its difference from the towns of the East, it was not surprising that Turchaninoff's political philosophy became deeply colored by them. The people were of many nationalities, from half a dozen European countries, still close enough to foreign traditions to be a source of encouragement to the colonel who noted only the resolution and courage they showed in departing from them. His heart warmed toward these older citizens and he strengthened his resolve to be as like them as possible.

Aside from joining the Republican Party, he took yet another step toward Americanization. This was the changing of his name, which step he celebrated by a convivial ceremony with his neighbors. He first came to the idea when one of his workmen, also a vehement politician, despaired of pronouncing the name Turchaninoff.

"In this country we don't attach much importance to a name," the workman stated, "but since every man has to have one, let's have names we can say. Now take me. I had one of those long names, all right in Hungary. Now I am Joe Papp. Everyone calls me Pappy. I'm happy."

"You think it better that I change my name?" Turchaninoff asked. He was rather perplexed, for this aspect of his Americanization seemed trivial and somewhat removed from any that merited attention. "You think my name too long?"

"Sure," Joe answered, undeterred by the deep frown he rightly read to indicate the colonel's fastidious protest, the old pride which lies deep in the fibers of a man's being. "I know it is a fact that a name hard to say keeps people from talking to you. Now take a name like John. That's easy to say." Joe smiled and nodded his head paternally. He was a strong and forthright man with iron gray hair and an enormous beard of which he was inordinately proud, refusing to trim it though the men who worked with him took every opportunity to deride him for its patriarchal proportions. He had a kind heart and an unfeigned sympathy for the newcomer into these parts. He was not exceptionally communicative even had he been endowed with more ability to express himself than he was. He had resided long enough in various cities, however, to be aware that certain small matters, likely to be overlooked by an ardent man like the Russian, would, if neglected, be the cause of much aggravation, the more annoying because the Russian might never suspect the cause. In Turchaninoff, he recognized a warmth and ingenuous honesty he knew to be vulnerable to the many pinpricks his distinctly foreign name would provide.

"Yes," Turchaninoff acceded slowly, "John is a fine name." He furrowed his brow in deep thought. "Also Basil is a good name, not too much different from Vasilevich, eh?" Then with a face that seemed to reflect his mood, he accepted the other's suggestion and acknowledged the truth of the words spoken by a friend. In an effort to abide by the decree intended in the words, he clapped his great hands together so as to emphasize the fact accomplished:

"Turchin! That will be the way I shall call myself! Now, Joe, what do you say to such a transformation?"

This decided, the colonel thereafter wrote and referred to himself as John Basil Turchin. In the willingness to hear advice, once he was convinced that it emanated from the heart as well as the head of a good man, he unwittingly discovered and employed one of the endearing traits which attracted people to him. In Mattoon he was a great favorite for a time, both with the foreign and native elements. Had he been content to accept people as he found them, he might have retained the goodly number of adherents which he had then obtained. This was not his way, however, to think merely in terms of the pleasant and most enjoyable. He was of the opinion that a man's friend meant exactly that: a friend was one to whom one must speak the thoughts dearest to the mind. The paltry doings of the day and the superficialities in which women delighted were not the fit subject for a friend to discourse upon. A friend had moral obligations, if he were a true friend. And should he perceive the error of his friend's way, it was his duty to himself and to all he held dear, to declare the failing aloud and to stand by during the emendation of the fault.

True to this doctrine, he found that, despite all his comradely affirmations, for all that he could look every man squarely in the eye, he soon alienated the very men whose friendship he wished most to retain. Especially the foreign born, whom he made hostile with his constant exhortations on the score of loyalty to the new land of their adoption. In addition, having once joined the Republican Party, he seemed unwearied in his quest for more members. Almost every evening he made his way to one family or another to plead the cause of the Party. His neighbors, many made uncomfortable under his lashing arguments and willingness to lay bare their intentions and ambitions, began to look upon him as a man rather to be avoided than admired. His flashing eye and his charming smile, after a few arguments with him, no longer invited confidences. But it was his wife who received the outer manifestations of the coolness. The ladies no longer stopped before her gate. She was not invited to play the piano at weddings. And the good wives acquired that skillful quirk of the eyebrows which disapproving matrons know how to use so well in administering rebuke or abjuration, the nature of which they leave to the culprit to discover.

Nadine discovered this easily and withdraw, as was her wont, into the haughty silence she imposed upon herself. By nature not made to endure silence or reproaches, desirous of warmth and gentle gaiety, expecting as her right the respect and admiration so easily won heretofore, she abandoned all efforts to fraternize with her neighbors. She added to this, with no reasonableness, an indifference to the turbulent problems Turchin's friends pondered, whether it be on the front lawn of their house, the barber shop on the corner or in the offices where the construction gangs met each morning.

It was not that she, in effect, was blind to the situation her husband outlined as thoroughly as he could to her. Her mind was excellently schooled, not only as befitted a noble lady of Russia, but as would have done ample justice to any Bluestocking of the day. Her accomplishments were many; musical skill, linguistic excellence, nursing experience, knowledge of military matters and a high degree of mathematical ability, the last of which was a constant source of husbandly pride to Turchin. She joined him in a deep and abiding love of letters and had read, with him, the noted works of the masters in four languages.

She was alive to the compelling enthusiasms with which her husband militated against current evils, of which he seldom particularized. But she was in her own right, sufficiently a critic to appraise them properly, the while that she recognized that in his mind they were of a quality to encompass only huge stratagems, without functioning equally well in the execution of the necessary and subsequent details.

She had arrived in the country with the intention of following her husband in every matter he should elect to interest him. Her main interest, nonetheless, was their personal life. She had no feeling of great loyalty to this new land, for she had no belief in the validity of transplanting. Turchin was thirty-six and she close on thirty. To have been uprooted so late in life was strenuous indeed. Therefore, to her mind, their first aim must reasonably be to exert every effort toward fashioning a new security. Her problem was, however, to convey this intelligence to Turchin in such a way as to keep intact the even flow of their lives; to do that which she had to do in order to ensure his happiness by a complaisance in itself dangerous to her success.

Happily Turchin was too busy to take heed of these undercurrents, either of the town's aloofness or of the gradual resentment to himself and to his sententious utterances which he delivered in extremely good faith. Joyously, he went to his meetings and sat with a curious civic pride for all he saw in the animated men in the crude halls. He met with white-haired congressmen and portly solicitors in frock coats. He listened with interest both to Lincoln and Douglas on a platform, and afterwards was inspired to compose a graphic cartoon for Mattoon, whereby he hoped to display his own evaluation of the man Lincoln, whom he saw as towering not only literally but figuratively over the vigorous and suave orator Douglas; he hoped to imply with his clever pencil that the true giant was Lincoln, toward whom he conceived a boundless admiration notwithstanding the lawyer's unpleasant falsetto voice which hardly did justice to the power and conviction of his words.

"He simply stands there as though indifferent to any blows that may fall on him," he said as he recounted his first meeting with Lincoln to Nadine. "He has a weak voice and some people jeer at him as if that mattered in the least! The moment I saw him I knew that way deep inside that man, there was stuff of greatness; the terrible pity for all of them who cannot see their common tragedy, their common hope!"

"You take these matters too seriously," she replied without looking up from her work basket. "You attend altogether too many of these public debates as though you were not aware that we are, after all, bred in old ways, which have been put to both the test and the sword. Will you not believe that this new land advances along the same sort of path? Are you truly blinded by the clamoring voices which speak endlessly about votes? Don't all the voters come to the sword for arbitration? Have they not already had wars in this land? Leave these native quarrels to those who thrive on them."

To these pleas Turchin lent a deaf ear, hearing rather the voices of Lincoln and Douglas, and of Joe and the rest of the Mattoon citizenry.

His response was in no way unexpected. "In Europe the people are hemmed in by thousand-year old bigotries. No tongue can appeal to the lacerated credulities of a suspicious populace. Old people are even more cruel than savages, for their cruelty is dark, like a rayless heaven and greedy for the last flicker of light. European ways are like old people compared to the youth of this land! It is in that youth that I glory and place my trust! Here we will outlaw wars by no decrees! We will outlaw them by destroying the grounds upon which they breed! We can elect the kind of world we want to live in! Look at this Republican Party. It grew spontaneously in response to the demand for a better world! It steps forth to strike where fearful men hesitate. I like that!"

He made reference to the role devolving upon the Republican Party, to lead the more spirited elements in government, to take a firmer stand upon the troublesome issue of slavery's extension in the new Border States. The staid and old Democratic Party was inclined toward a policy of leniency on this and other matters which might be viewed hostile by the sensitive new States. He tried to explain to his wife the purport of this leniency and succeeded in delineating the shape of troubles to come without apprehending them himself. It was she who first caught a glimpse of the great division of sentiments which was cracking the solid unity of the country, like a vast fissure cleaving the base of a mountain.

"As I understand it," she remarked, "the Southern States want the right to take their slaves wherever Americans may go; the slaves are chattel goods, yes?"

"Slaves are human beings, Nadya!" Turchin thundered in reproof.

"And these Border States are divided in their belief that slavery should be extended wherever it chooses to go?"

"It is inevitable that slavers will attempt to pollute every suitable area with their filthy practice!"

"Yet the government in Washington does not dare to ban slavery?"

"Not yet! Not yet!" Turchin was irritated with the attitude of Nadine. Somehow the trend of her questions displeased him and doubly so because he discerned in them a subtle criticism he did not then choose to consider. Instead he enjoyed a spurious sense of superiority over his wife's reasoning by telling himself that she, like many others, failed to see the drift of this constitutional battle involving the new territories, the appeasement of the Border States, and the multitude of other State affairs of which she was scarcely expected to be aware. Most of all it aggravated him, even if he did not choose to discuss it, that he himself plainly saw why a man like Lincoln, obviously a hater of any slavery imposed by some men on other and less fortunate men, chose rather to skirt the problem of slavery as such and exert himself in behalf of more abstract issues. He, himself, realized only too well that millions of dollars of invested capital lay beneath the squalor of the nine million Blacks. Capital could never be idle capital; it had to increase itself or be destroyed. This knowledge made him unhappy. He avoided the subject with his wife thereafter and continued his education in suffrage and politics without recourse to her matter of fact mind.

Little more than a year had passed since their coming to Mattoon and during this time they had exchanged only brief notes with their patron and friend McClellan. Then, with no forewarning, Turchin received an offer from him to accept a post with the Illinois Central Railroad in Chicago. The reason for this invitation, McClellan did not feel called upon to explain, though he subsequently elucidated his selection of the man he remembered to be adequately equipped for the job of surveying and other engineering offices.

If the nature of the times affected the colonel, how much more so a man of McClellan's marked qualities, both as a former army man and as a rising industrialist? He certainly used with success his ability to gauge other man's talents and no doubt bethought him of his Russian acquaintance in a moment of no insistent urgency. Whatever it was, send for him he did and moreover actually found himself rather pleased when Turchin accepted. Certainly, McClellan realized, changes were occurring, though it is to be doubted that he perceived exactly what their nature might be. His own star was in the ascendancy; he felt expansive, not troubled by the bickering in Congress. Railroading was a prospering business; engineers were important. He was ready to welcome Turchin personally.

CHAPTER IX

The problem of Dimitri Trofimov getting settled in Chicago involved more than the matter of selecting a suitable establishment for young bachelors or an appropriate occupation for a man who designed to make a splash in the best circles of the city. It rested upon the successful discovery of the circle in whose beneficent influence he might, in the shortest order, gain the ends he sought. The first he did easily by locating that section of the city which had the air of seclusion he knew denoted the moneyed class. The second he settled by offering himself in his most velvety tones to the editor of a large newspaper. That he was accepted goes without saying. There was, in the young man's handsome appearance and obliging attention, which he offered in a manner that resembled a presentation of a gift, that which pleased rather than offended his hearers and bespoke his abilities more than a proof of probity or experience. It must be said, however, that in the matters of journalistic reporting and editorial commentary, Trofimov was not lacking in either qualification. He, like the Turchins, had a ready facility in several languages and he attested to his quickness and insight by a precise and accurate directness easily comprehensible. He carried about him on his person, several letters from newspapermen in London and Paris; these made a considerable impression upon his prospective editor-in-chief. Accompanying his modest approach and subdued eagerness, which he knew to be acceptable to executives in almost any branch of work, he allowed a certain playfulness to warm his interviewers, who invariably responded favorably to his smiling dark eyes and the charm of his person which was elegant without being simpering and fashionable without being ostentatious or vulgar. Altogether, with his low voice and his princely bearing, the kindliness he willed into his every expression, he found no difficulty in obtaining immediate employment and in making his first contacts with the most important lady connected with the newspaper.

This lady was a young widow. She had inherited from her husband both many thousands of dollars and a portion of the newspaper. It was her wont to appear regularly in the editorial offices and to supervise such material as pertained to the supervision of the virtues and vices of the day. She was quite an attractive woman, Trofimov found, except for her habitual air of absorption in the evils of the world, which he delighted in defending whenever opportunity afforded him the chance. She spoke willingly to the fine looking young foreigner, seemed taken with his apparent noble lineage and laughingly complied with his request to be introduced to her group of friends.

In her intimate circle of acquaintances he found little favor. Her friends consisted for the most part of young men and women who had elected the more severe and less appreciative tasks of enlightening the world on such important doctrines as universal suffrage, abolition of slavery and Utopian societies, the nature of which they heatedly differed in defining to the Russian nobleman.

"You have amazingly curious friends for so brilliant and fashionable a lady," he complimented her. His laughing dark eyes took in every detail of her costume and person and seemed to declare his boundless admiration for both.

"They have intelligence," she replied somewhat coldly. "It is in my power to consort with more influential persons than these," she added in a softened tone, "yet I prefer to sponsor groups of such people," indicating the knots of young men who were occupying her drawing room with familiarity. "They make an effort to study something more serious in life than the qualities of a pair of roans."

This last comment interested Trofimov exceedingly. He congratulated himself upon his good fortune in chancing thus to make her acquaintance and redoubled his efforts to attach her to himself, but to no avail. There was a bright cheerfulness about her despite her open addiction to intellectual pursuits, which often belied the serious vein underlying her activities. Without condescending to unvarnished truth-telling, she managed to prevent Dimitri Trofimov from making any headway in his persistent suit. Instead, apprising herself of all such statistics as were available for her to judge the man's intentions in all their possible light, she frankly informed him that he must look elsewhere for the sort of achievement that was his desire and which she could not guarantee.

This was his first failure but Henrietta Morrison was, fortunately, in no way able to bruise his self esteem. They became friends in a manner of speaking and later when she presented him to her cousin Susan Brewster, he quite forgave her own indifference to his charms.

It was Susan who comprised all the expected foibles of young womanhood as he had learned to know them and to play upon them. She was a much more beautiful girl than her cousin and not burdened with the other's seriousness or habitual aura of gloom. There lay beneath her garrulous chatter a certain shrewd sharpness not yet too noticeable in either speech or manner. She was over-conscious of her appearance, of the patent superiority her costly attire permitted her to display as her due. She had a restless, roving eye that was quick to gleam with jealous resentment over trifles, but particularly over a lack of respect for the attributes of station and class which she held dear. Immediately on observing the young Russian and seeing with what unusual courtesy he hovered about Henrietta, she aspired to divert his attention to herself, little dreaming that the baron knew instantly that his actions would so affect her.

It was not long thereafter that Baron Trofimov became an intimate in the home of the Brewsters. So easily was this accomplished, so lacking in the normal restraints he expected of young ladies who presumed to dominate their social world, that a secret contempt made him hesitate to disclose all his arts in that house. His reticence, however, had the desired effect of increasing his value to the young woman of willfulness and affection, making her positive where before she had been supercilious. She was an only child of newly wealthy parents, who had long given up directing her in a day and age when so many things were rapidly changing, when the air itself resounded with the clamor of things yet unsaid. They were content if she was happy and it must be said that secretly her father, especially, took rather a pride in his fine child and encouraged her in her worst faults of snobbishness and selfishness.

Mr. Brewster was far from an insipid man. He had risen from obscurity and poverty to a position of wealth and eminence in the business circles of Chicago. He had made no secret of his origin, of his youthful struggles, of his rise, taking instead somewhat undue credit for the success he had attained. Success was the keynote of all his computation. What was not successful was not good. Being in a position to arrange success more or less as he chose, he enjoyed the emergence of these same tendencies in his offspring, even inflated them with the privilege of an absolute sovereign. In all her pettiness and vain posturings, he saw an expression of his own power and privilege. He demanded only that she oblige his vanity by making at least a pretense of seeking his approval. The young lady had learned early in life to yield that to him and consequently they were extremely good friends and understood one another with unusual indulgence. When Susan bluntly stated to her father that she wished to become the baroness Trofimov, that the title amused her, that she thought it a feather in her cap to achieve this in her second season in society, to obtain such rank that it would make many a young lady like Ellen Marcy, that most aristocratic young lady who was to marry George Briton McClellan, certainly envious and perhaps eager to renew their casual acquaintance,... he laughed and agreed that she might marry her baron. He allowed this in a tone which described his inner thoughts to his daughter; that he could well afford to buy her any toy she sought; that she might do much better in other waters where bigger fish swam; that all the usual fears for the tender welfare of a loved child were unnecessary with this Miss of his. And in a manner, he rather admired the element of ruthlessness her pretty soft face contained. No namby-pamby mincing and bowing and scraping for her. In her own way she could conquer in her times as he fancied himself to have done in his.

It rested now with Susan to prevail upon her baron to ask for her hand. She was confident, with a toss of her dark head, that this was a simple matter. With boldness and even a sort of malicious pride she confessed her intentions to her cousin, Henrietta. Despite Henrietta's objectionable concerns with the abuses of the drink habit and the sins of slave owners, she had free access to the Brewster house, where, if ties of blood were not the prime inducement to family cordiality, her substantial fortune was. Henrietta's sarcastic congratulations were too well couched in polite terminology to carry much weight with Susan. Once she had decided upon something her mind gave no heed to objections or objectors; moreover, she was not fond of the older woman and that was enough to constitute a basis for disregard of anything she said. In her own mind the affair was settled; the matter of Dimitri Trofimov was settled.

It was at this stage of the baron's affairs that the Turchins arrived in Chicago. Neither the one nor the other had given much credence to their old polite wish to meet again. If perchance Nadine favored the baron with a thought now and then, she kept the fact concealed from her husband. She would have preferred keeping the same fact concealed from her own honest mind, were that possible and thereby deceiving herself that her passing fancy for Trofimov presented some danger threatening her stable situation. Never in her many colorful peregrinations had she known such an impact of a personality which she recognized as hostile to her own way of life. Always, the gallant flatteries she received at the hands of ambitious underlings or presumptuous youths had been a matter of mirth which she had gaily offered to share with her husband. It distressed her no little bit to find herself referring with guilty starts to her excitement and pleasure in the remembrance of the baron.

Nadine and the colonel, now established in Chicago, were becoming somewhat familiar with the byways of the city. They occupied a most charming little house on Division Street near a pretty park, when they chanced to meet Trofimov who was promenading along the great boulevard with two charming young women at his side. The ladies were Susan Brewster and her cousin, the widow Mrs. Morrison. The two groups met, stopped, exchanged bows and then blended into one group. The men were animated with the novelty of their encounter and clasped hands in friendly fashion. The ladies were less vivacious, Nadine remaining completely silent as did Mrs. Morrison after a few polite remarks. Susan, however, with a perverse forwardness, for which nothing seemed to account, turned her full batteries upon Nadine.

"I have heard the baron refer to you and your husband frequently," she deigned to say with just a shade of condescension, surprising to Nadine, who bowed her acknowledgement. "It is indeed a small world. One manages to meet everyone sooner or later."

To this Nadine found no ready reply and left it to Mrs. Morrison to continue a desultory conversation mostly with Susan, who, in the meantime, made constant calls on Trofimov's attention. Soon the two small parties separated, but not before Trofimov had requested and obtained from the openhearted colonel the address of his home.

Afterward, the colonel said to Nadine cheerfully, "I feel that America is improving our friends," well pleased to have met with the baron. "I am ready to admit that heretofore I have found myself irritated by his cynical smugness and that I have had small patience with a man who rejoices in his preference to live in a vacuum instead of a world of living beings."

Nadine, quiet and troubled, had nothing to offer to this and Turchin continued.

"I hope he wakes up in this more vigorous atmosphere and that he begins to enjoy the poetry of positive thinking, learns that it is empty business to be a shadow rather than substance. Only then will he be conscious of his proper place in life, when he feels with people and feels with his heart open to people, feels the beat of a nation's pulse. As it is, he feels, I am afraid, only for himself."

Believing sincerely that Trofimov was more mistaken than misanthropic, Turchin was happy to receive him when shortly thereafter the young man made his first call upon them. The manner in which Trofimov entered the small drawing room and his slightly arched eyebrows, revealed nothing to Turchin, but Nadine seemed to sense the inner conflicts which the baron would have disdained to reveal. For his part, the baron chose to believe that his tumbled emotions were due to an accurate measure of the fruitlessness this visit presaged. By this he meant that he willingly went forward to waste time that he might better employ to secure Miss Brewster and that he was conscious of an involuntary attraction toward Nadine which was based on other than the sound principles which guided him steadily toward his selected star.

It angered him that his mind was unable to dispel the dreamy enchantment he associated with her; the way her pale gold hair seemed brightened by its own tame fire in the light of the moon; the way her filmy black gown had simultaneously clung about her slender frame and seemed to enfold her in its diaphanous draperies; the way the wet spray had hung in sparkling globules on her satiny cheek. Therefore he took a seat in her sitting room appositely furnished for his disquietness, with its unpretentious furniture and unrelieved simplicity and he kept on his fine-skinned gloves rather longer than friendship commanded. With his cane he dug small holes in her carpet while the colonel became ready to converse with a friend.

"Does it not trouble you Colonel, to find yourself reduced to this petty dwelling, these obviously inadequate accoutrements for the son of a nobleman and his lady."

"You mean, baron?" Turchin did not follow the meaning in Trofimov's discontented eyes, nor did he see the odd accusation which lingered in them even after the baron had turned them deliberately from the fringed lamp under which Nadine sewed complacently.

"I mean that I fail to understand how you saw fit to come to this country at all! How you find it tolerable to begin of necessity all over again!"

"You are, perhaps, commiserating with us?" Turchin's voice was low with menace. His wife looked over toward them and with her quick glance conveyed a pleading message to the baron. He felt a grudging admiration for her and he began to smooth the soft felt of the tall hat on his lap. He felt that withal, he bore Turchin no ill-will, that in fact he was willing to share with him some part of his own conviction concerning adjustment in this new land. Pressed to state an attitude, he would have maintained a sturdy defense of his goodwill, would have insisted that the thing that most irritated him was the setting for failure which he read all too easily in Turchin's approach to matters. He promised himself at that instant to study carefully his relationship with his compatriot, though in doing that very thing, he professed to himself a determination to cling to something else which, though his sentiments urged it, his cool brain derided - his inexplicable attachment for a woman who willingly accepted her own husband. Yet, he would have been the first to confess that this was a sort of irrationality. As his long slender fingers rubbed his hat brim, he turned the act of irrational behavior over in his mind, amazed that with the awareness of it, he did not immediately reject it. Perhaps every man has one exception to his well-laid plans; he was curiously satisfied that this should be sufficient justification for him.

"You employ rigorous terms for the slightest circumstance," he languidly answered Turchin who was, in truth, standing now with undisguised antagonism written on every feature of his face.

"Gentlemen", Nadine laughed lightly, somewhat embarrassed, "With all topics of the day to discuss, must you anger one another over trifles? We are here. Let us think about that only."

Like two truculent children, the baron and Turchin settled themselves to a civilized discourse and the hour of visiting moved smoothly on a stream of impersonal topics. Momentary flickers of pique could not help but intrude, yet both men made polite, if obvious, efforts to remain calm.

"You say that you have met Mr. George McClellan? That you spoke to him? On what occasion, pray?" Turchin was interested immensely, feeling that if such an interview between his patron and the baron had occurred, it would not be particularly to the latter's credit. He felt that the airs and posings of the baron would not acquit him as easily with McClellan as they seemingly did with other notables.

"In his offices," Trofimov informed him. "I had rather a fine talk with him. He has the cultivated tastes of a gentleman."

"He is indeed a gentleman."

"He did not own to knowing you, colonel," Trofimov continued with a touch of malice.

"He is a busy man."

"He has curious visitors, has he not?" Nadine interposed with a faint smile to offset the implications he might read in her words.

Nothing daunted, Trofimov, with a long look in her direction, expatiated upon the various individuals he had seen entering and leaving the offices of the vice-president of the Central Illinois Railroad. "My interest with Mr. McClellan concerned politics," he volunteered. "You see, unlike yourself, dear colonel, I have observed that politics are a great weapon."

This ambiguous remark was not lost upon Turchin, who evinced his scorn. "If you must know, I am a Republican. The wrong people take it upon themselves to construe politics," he retorted. "What interest do you have in political affairs which would be consistent with an American's honor?"

"Such high sounding names and words," Trofimov laughed. "I suppose you were not aware that so fine a patrician gentleman as your good patron McClellan interested himself in partisan politics?"

"If Captain McClellan is partisan, well, then what he is partisan to is right!"

Trofimov enjoyed the trap he had sprung upon the colonel and now lost no time in informing him that McClellan was a staunch Democrat, that he was strongly partial to the orator Douglas, had, in fact, supported his candidacy generously during the senatorial race the year before.

"You see, my dear colonel, you inter yourself in a small village and through it, as though it were the small end of a telescope, you hope to see great things; I am openly opportunistic, you may say and yet I actually contemplate the ways of my neighbors more accurately than you. You mentioned you were a Republican and leave it to me to find out your most admired friend is a political adversary."

"That is a libelous accusation to make upon a man like McClellan!"

"It is none the less quite true. Ask him yourself. Ask him, too, my foolish friend, who paid for the cannon booming on Douglas' campaign train? Ask him what lengths he went to, to ensure Douglas' victory over his opponent." He paused, well satisfied with the look of dawning credulity he saw on Turchin's face. "And incidentally, the ways of these Americans are even stranger. The very day I spoke with your paragon, no other than the defeated candidate, a Mr. Abraham Lincoln - I believe he is some obscure lawyer, or, if not obscure, then officiously forwarded by the scalawags who support him, upstart lawyers like himself, no doubt - came to seek a moment with McClellan. It surprised me to learn that for all their political opposition, the two men had business with one another. Let that be a lesson to you, my friend, an object lesson as to how men act in this land; that they are not different from other men in other places."

"You actually saw Mr. Lincoln at close range, this fine orator, Mr.

Lincoln?" Turchin forgot the purport of Trofimov's long address and chose to hear only that he had been close to the man he revered with almost an acolyte's devotion.

"The colonel admires this Mr. Lincoln excessively," Nadine spoke up softly. "And so much do I respect his judgments, that I doubt not that Mr. Lincoln is indeed an admirable man. It is said he is honorable and sincere." She had no wish to encourage Trofimov in felling Turchin's idols. She knew rightly that her words would be support for her husband, that without realizing their intent, she would rally his spirits against the baron's purpose with them.

"I have no objection to admiration," Trofimov responded. "So-called great ones always tend to cling to one another in a society of mutual admiration. I do object to blind worship. Why not see men for what they actually are?"

"Would that suffice for your purpose, baron?" Nadine had risen and come behind her husband's chair. It gratified her to see the faint color of discomfiture spread over the darkly handsome face of the baron.

"You mean Mr. McClellan and Mr. Lincoln as examples?" Turchin had folded his wife's white fingers into his broad palm.

"Certainly," Trofimov replied instantly. "This Lincoln about whom even Henrietta Morrison rhapsodizes, was not above asking the Illinois Central for a five thousand dollar fee when it suited his interests. Five thousand! He sets himself up rather highly, eh?" Trofimov felt uncomfortable and angry though his outer manner of casualness remained with him to a large extent, or so he fancied. "I dare say, my wise humanitarian, that you had no idea your Mr. Lincoln worked for the Illinois Central?" Then, seeing the open surprise, he continued, "Or that for all his expressions of Republican views he quite as readily defends the Railroad against the honest man and as I have heard, defended the slave owner against the poor persecuted run-away slave." He paused sneeringly and glared at the contented picture of domestic harmony that Turchin and Nadine exemplified. "What does it matter what two politicians speak? Mr. Lincoln and Mr. McClellan, although separated by every sort of distinction, have in common the reality of life. They preach the philosophy of success first of all and they can be verbal foes without losing their real alliance."

"Your words are infamous, Sir," Turchin's voice rose in anger and he disengaged himself from his wife's hand roughly. "You have a wicked mote in your eye, a black mote that sets its dark spot on everything you see. You hear a noble name and you besmear it with mud so that you can recognize it for one in your vocabulary! But that does not dim its radiance! That only convinces honest men the more, that you, baron, are neither a citizen nor a baron!"

Trofimov rose with a spring from his seat, as he could well be counted on to do under the stinging lash of Turchin's open anger.

"I see there is nothing for it but to let you plunge into the stupid vapidity where you belong," he lashed out coldly, his very words containing the chill of his summary decision. He stood in the middle of the room, two spots of faint color on his high cheekbones, his eyes seeming to sparkle with topaz fires, with one more moment's hesitation. A slow smile hovered at the corners of his mouth and showed the control that he had quickly recovered over himself. At that moment he felt rightly wronged, though willing to confess to an unwarranted temper. He believed himself to have spoken on a friend's behalf. He believed the colonel suspicious and jealous and not merely loyal to a lawyer for the Illinois Central Railroad. He truly held with the belief that Turchin was deceived in McClellan's friendship and unworthy of his own. Under the circumstances, he felt condescending to say the least, warmed as his self-esteem was these days by Miss Brewster's languishing ardors and Mrs. Morrison's agreeable recognition.

Were it not for Nadine's quick interposition, Dimitri Trofimov might then and there have departed the house, never more to re-enter it. It was she who hastily came between them, skillfully turned the conversation and charmingly laid her hand upon the young man's shoulder while the free one was held out to her husband.

"Ivan is reputed to be a Cossack," she repeated this old joke to Trofimov. "You, a countryman of ours, ought to know how quick and foolish is the wrath of the Cossack and she accompanied this with a merry laugh in which Turchin, already contrite for his outburst, joined her. He was not really of the Cossacks, though the relationship had often been imputed to him in the past, as though it were an admonitory finger pointing out his noted shortness of temper and acerbity of tongue.

"Perhaps you mean well, Baron Trofimov," he half apologized. "You are my countryman, now twice over," he said gallantly, "and you must wish us well. To you, I am at fault for not pushing advantages. Well, maybe so. But each man must answer the call he hears, yes?" He came close to the other and frankly held out his hand in amity. The baron took it silently, but not enthusiastically. "We will not discuss Mr. Lincoln, nor will we discuss Mr. McClellan. We will be friends and be interested in the adventures this fine and good land offers to each of us, yes?"

"Of course we shall all be friends," Nadine answered for the baron. She brought Ivan's old priceless violin which she laid wordlessly in his arms. "It is time to forget politics," said she saucily. "Play for us, Vanya." Then, turning to the baron, she led him sweetly to a seat near her own. "You have only to hear him play to learn to love him," were her final words, but her eyes lent a curious stress to her words and dispersed the baron's disgruntled mood.

CHAPTER X

The things Trofimov had referred to in his remarks lingered long in Turchin's mind and grew even more discomfiting with every brief contact McClellan granted him. Following the visit of the baron, he sought out the busy young vice-president with an assurance his great faith in the man commanded him to sustain.

Since the day he had taken up his duties as surveyor and engineer for the line, he had not presumed often upon the earlier acquaintance he claimed with McClellan. He sensed that the other man would prefer to leave the past relationship to his own discretion and this was quite understandable to the Russian. He told himself that he must act like a gentleman who was self-assured enough to accept the necessary relationship between the executive and the employee. It was not his part to be lowly or unnaturally humble, to be sure, but it behooved him to respect the distance changed circumstances imposed upon them and to allow for McClellan to make such advances as would reveal his wishes. For all that, it gratified his honest pride that the vice-president was neither too busy nor too lofty to spare him occasional moments for friendly discourse, often on other matters than those pertaining to the business of the railroad. At such times both men were unrestrained in their mutual respect, preserving a curious balance between them which offended neither. As though it were tacitly understood between them, no reference was made to their social lives apart from the work they shared.

On the morning that he decided to question McClellan with respect to many matters he considered important, Turchin entered the younger man's office with grave seriousness. Instead of greeting the former Captain as he usually did, he stood somewhat stiffly before him until, almost involuntarily, McClellan rose from his desk and extended his hand to him.

"Something on your mind, Sir?" he questioned with a friendly tone. He motioned him to a chair and reseated himself comfortably. He thought, as he watched his surveyor lay aside a roll of charts he had brought with him, how fit the man appeared, how distinguished, how representative of good bones and good breeding. He congratulated himself for estimating the man accurately and felt generally well disposed toward him.

The Russian took rather a longer time to answer than pleased the younger man who immediately assumed a severer expression, whereby he checked his indulgence, and composed himself to cope with reason instead of sentiment. He leaned forward in his chair as Turchin began to speak, to tell him his ideas of the character of true loyalty and respect; how a man must feel identified with the nature of his employer's outlook; how it was incumbent upon an honorable man to know with certainty that his superiors, in a common work, stood not to contend with him, his basic loyalties.

"It would be a shameful deed for a new citizen, especially," he announced earnestly, "were he to devote his best efforts in the service of men not as loyal to the country as he was asked to be upon the first assumption of his new status as an American."

"It has reached you already!" McClellan observed, getting up and moving toward the window whence he looked out over the thronged boulevard below. "I presume you are referring to all the clamorings with which the journals are filled! Those infernal gossip sheets! Rabble rousers are what they are! Presumptuous proxies for a public which daily grows more careless of the splendid heritage my father's fathers bequeathed them." He seemed to be speaking to himself, and paid scant attention to Turchin whom he invited in no way to make reply to his thoughts.

"There was a time when the men who had the right to be leaders rose and led the country to health and prosperity. No one seemed to be afflicted with a sudden love for humanity which today sounds hollow, indeed. Why should there be such a disturbance over the question of slaves!" He turned swiftly upon his engineer. "It is not as though those black savages were suffering vilely. But they are ignorant wretches, and serve to front for the vain ambitions of pretentious upstarts!" Then, recollecting himself, he came back to his desk and took his seat formally. "Forgive me, colonel, what is it you seek me for? I am sorry to trouble you with my irritabilities. You wished...?"

"To know something of these things you mention - slavery, and what it is, and what it means when men like Mr. Lincoln rise to speak against it; what it then means when a man can defend a slave owner against a slave?"

McClellan eyed the other man with interest.

"So you have heard about Mr. Lincoln! Perhaps he will make the whole railroad famous for his occasional services to us!" He was sarcastic to the extreme, indeed betraying displeasure with Mr. Lincoln which he strove usually to conceal. Not that his displeasure with the Sangamon Lawyer, as he privately named him, was entirely of a personal nature. It was only that he saw exemplified in Mr. Lincoln, trends and tendencies which he could not approve of. It may have piqued him also, that Mr. Lincoln had virtually held up the company for an enormous fee and that the line had had to pay it to avoid suit or scandal. Another factor he could not stomach with equanimity was the growing political importance of Lincoln which certain Republican spokesmen were fostering. Black Republicans, he called them.

"Colonel, you must not pay too much attention to the unjustified political bickering you read about. Do your own job and we shall all be satisfied, and you will be the sort of citizen you long to be." He rose from his seat once more and stood next to the perplexed Turchin. "Believe me, Sir, when I say that it requires much farsightedness to understand the nature of the legal stormings we hear these days about Constitutional Rights, Territorial Rights, and Slavery. From the beginning of our country's national life, slavery has been an accepted institution whose inception we might deplore but without wishing in the name of premature philanthropy to create confusion and disorder. Hot-headedness and the noisy fire-eaters in Congress, notwithstanding, these unruly periods in our national development will pass over."

"You do not like the Republican Party?" was all Turchin could say. "You are indeed a Democrat?" He seemed so palpably unwilling to believe this that McClellan burst into laughter.

"Colonel, you will learn that we operate on a bi-party system. You, I am afraid, have been misled to attach yourself to the wrong one. But be that as it may, in time you will discern the sheep from the goats. You will recognize lawyers' quibbling and know it for what it is, anything but a disinterested patriotism! All I may say now is that it is a sad day for the country when lawyers become the spokesmen for a people, while the men who really represent the nature of the country and are best fitted to arbitrate its concerns, must either haggle like fish vendors in order to gain a hearing, or retire in favor of those who stoop to any level in dealing with office holders and office seekers."

With this the interview was ended and Turchin politely dismissed himself. The effects of this conversation with McClellan, however, remained long with him, often making him pensive and thoughtful during his tenure of office as surveyor. Periodically he recalled word for word both McClellan's speech and the baron's insinuations and he was saddened and depressed by both. At one moment he vowed to discontinue his relationship with both men, only to meet with Nadine's curious insistence for delay and tactfulness toward both. She prevailed upon him in time to separate his duties as engineer from his position on slavery and slavery's extension. Likewise she persuaded him to circumscribe his obligations as a gentleman and compatriot of Dimitri Trofimov's from his condemnation of the latter's morals and intellect, both of which the colonel unhesitatingly labeled as specious.

In the one case it was a simple matter, requiring only a form of concentration in his work, whose plannings derived not from the vice-president solely, to develop a manner of cool impersonality; he had only to remain distant from the central office which was easy to maneuver. On the other hand, it was not quite so simple a matter to disengage himself from Trofimov, who began frequently to call upon them and always with such a marked politeness and courtesy that to take umbrage over his nicely couched satires was to lay oneself open to a just criticism for an overweening sensibility. Turchin had too long been accustomed to permit Nadine a voice in the matters of their home to begin now an autocratic rule against which so proud a woman as she would chafe unforgivingly. Plain it was, that Nadine distinguished the baron with her respect and admiration and though obviously there was no real harm in this mark of her esteem, it nevertheless occasioned many uneasy moments. Gradually, almost in spite of himself, Turchin fell under the spell of the baron's indubitable charm and allowed that young man's artifices to allay his suspicions, even to educe from him some measure of admiration for the astuteness of mind not wanting in the baron.

Either by a stroke of genius or by a cleverness for which Turchin would not have given him credit, Trofimov further endeared himself by accompanying Turchin to various political meetings. That he had many interests to advance by this practice may be assumed to be true. He wished to ingratiate himself to Turchin for Nadine's sake; this was a fact he no longer denied to himself if ever he had been so inclined to do. Also he found that attending lectures offered a relief from the insistent sweetness of Susan, whose patience was long indeed where her baron's noble reticence was the subject; for in no other way would she view the strange silence he maintained whenever inviting opportunities arose in which to make his avowals. Lastly, led by some masculine pride or by some quirk in his nature which though not cruel was yet vain, he used his pretended interest in the debates he attended with the colonel to induce Henrietta Morrison's interest and goodwill; flattering her in the meanwhile that he sought her good offices as advisor in matters difficult for a foreigner to encompass. She, however, concluded that the impecunious nobleman was enlisting her aid in forwarding the match with Miss Brewster. The idea pleased her in a feminine way, for, with proper values, she deemed him worthy of a young woman who, in her own manner, was as ruthless as he was in his. This, at least, was the rationalization she used for joining him and Turchin at meetings, where only her wealth and social position exempted her from hostile criticism. Ladies were not interested themselves in politics and she read the surprise at her daring in the colonel's face when she encountered him in public meeting halls.

Yet it was not really surprise she had read on that face; it was admiration. Not admiration for her face or figure, nor for her courage in defying convention by attending a political rally, but an admiration for the interest her cool set features clearly bespoke as they composed themselves to listen intelligently.

She, in her turn, when the handsome Russian colonel was no longer a stranger to her, perceived something in the sincerity of his address, the manner of his greeting, the honesty of his blue eyes. These attributes were so marked in their contrast to Trofimov's and drew her toward him, exciting her interest as no cleverness of the baron's had been able to do.

"I dare say, Colonel Turchin, that you find it surprising for a woman to interest herself in these problems of slavery?" She smiled gravely upon him until he returned her smile with his own.

"No, Madame," he returned, "I find it gratifying. Why should not women be interested in matters which ultimately affect them at a great cost?"

"What an ominous undertone your words contain," she exclaimed. "Surely you find nothing of such portentous nature in the debaters! They hate slavery and militate against it. Were I a man, I would do so myself!"

"The colonel is enough of a military man to detect the aura of warfare even in the utterances of academic humanitarians," Trofimov obligingly explained.

"That is correct," answered Turchin. "Hot words foment unrestrained passions. Fulminations demand action and that in turn demands resistance. Otherwise, why have the debate?"

"We Americans like discussion", said Mrs. Morrison. "We perhaps like to do our fighting on a platform." Mrs. Morrison was enchanted with Turchin, and openly indicated her partiality by ignoring Trofimov completely, even casually taking Turchin's arm as they made their way to her carriage.

"Perhaps, Colonel Turchin," she invited simply, "you will honor me by calling. It will be a great privilege for me to receive you."

To which invitation he made a smiling assent, mentioning that he and his wife should be happy to further an acquaintanceship which had begun so auspiciously. Having said as much as that, his mind returned to its absorption with the subject of the debate they had heard and he forgot all about Mrs. Morrison, paying scant heed to the dark looks Trofimov tendered him.

"So you like Mrs. Morrison," Trofimov later demanded wryly.

His mocking glance might have told him that the very question was ironic, that in the baron's opinion, Turchin was incapable of liking or appreciating any woman, including his own wife.

"Like Mrs. Morrison?" Turchin seemed surprised at the question. "Of course I like her. She has intelligence. She feels for those poor victims of an unlawful practice. She talks well and is a true gentlewoman."

"She's an abolitionist," Trofimov informed him sullenly. "She can afford to be almost anything she likes with impunity. If I had her money and influence, I might dare also."

Trofimov's characterization of Mrs. Morrison as an abolitionist, interested Turchin at once and he plied the baron with endless questions concerning her, meanwhile determined to make her further acquaintance for that reason alone.

"Not that I hold with women in such matters," Turchin said, "but her wealth and her widowhood lend her some protection from gossip. The problem of slavery and its eradication, I should think, is too wide a topic for women's sympathies alone to cope with. You heard tonight how slavery is at bottom but one of the factors in the dickering going on."

"Oh, Mrs. Morrison will soon inform you differently," Trofimov yawned. "She will endeavor to prove to you that slavery is the major concern of Christians. She'll tell you about one of her friends who wrote a book about the American slave. You are welcome to her," he added peevishly, as though making a large gesture toward his friend. "She wearies me."

Trofimov was not pleased with the turn the evening had taken. He would have wished to be rid of his companion, but refrained from making this apparent lest he lose the opportunity of accompanying him home. In him, there was this night, a need to see Nadine, to renew his own self-importance, which he always managed to do when in her presence, when able to bask in her unfeigned pleasure, her unstudied efforts to entertain him. With her, in short, he relaxed. Her smiling ways impressed themselves comfortably and comfortingly upon him, like a mold which assisted the outer form to adopt more engaging outlines. She was the European woman he knew. Here was no strained, pampered doll with snapping eyes or domineering mannerism. Here was tenderness as innocent as the flower she reminded him of. Here was appreciation for what he deemed himself to be, without inquiry into reason or motive. Here was a grace of mind and bearing pervasive enough to sustain the colonel in all his ardent pursuits. Trofimov turned to make some paltry remark to Turchin, with a sincere envy in his breast. At that moment he might have been willing to love Nadine more than himself.

Later in the evening, while Nadine was drinking tea with them, Turchin stated to Trofimov, "I forgot to mention to you a happy chance which befell me today. I had the honor of speaking with our chief debater this forenoon. Trofimov, did you notice his hat tonight?"

"Yes. A very tall hat and obviously not custom made."

"Indeed, I was witness to its recent purchase," Turchin laughed. "I had occasion to buy a hat myself and therefore stepped into a haberdashery near our offices. Inside the shop was only one other customer, and although I have never spoken personally to Mr. Lincoln, I recognized him at once."

To this Trofimov made the remark that the man was certainly distinguished by all he lacked rather than all he possessed and this succeeded in rousing Turchin's ire, which, until now, had been kept securely buried in the varied pleasures of the day.

"Would that you or I had half his heart," he snapped fiercely, the pleasure of his story departing.

"Go on, Ivan, what happened when you saw Mr. Lincoln in the haberdasher's shop?" Nadine was anxious for him to retain his pleasant, friendly attitude toward Trofimov. Her eyes, meanwhile, turned with soft reproach upon the baron, who subsided meekly under their impact.

"What is the sense in telling Trofimov anything? He scoffs at good and bad alike, which might be commendable if he were not so... so..." But in the end he was coaxed and cajoled until he continued his tale.

"He was about to buy a hat," continuing his tale, "and he stood there in the shop as humble as a simple clerk. The haberdasher looked from him to me and seemed about to turn to me, only I reminded him that Mr. Lincoln was entitled to service before me. He looked from me to him and from him to me," Turchin made a comical gesture which elicited a faint smile from Trofimov.

Mr. Lincoln was startled that I should know his name. He grew confused and embarrassed like a school boy and appeared ill at ease as if I were reprimanding him for some fault. "You know who I am?" he asked me and I was glad to tell him that I had gone to hear all the talks he made and that because of him I was proud to be a Republican even if my patron and friend was a Democrat.

Then he asked me who my patron was and I told him it was McClellan. And he smiled a quiet smile while he picked out a new hat and took out a small leather purse which was very slim, I can tell you. All the while he seemed conscious that he made a less imposing figure to the shopkeeper than, perhaps, I did. His modesty was a lesson to me." Turchin dwelt long on this point until Trofimov openly yawned.

"He was pleased it seemed to me, when he learned that I was a surveyor. He told me he was a sort of a surveyor too and said he hoped I got more than buckskins out of McClellan. 'Maybe I am a better surveyor than lawyer, sir. I fear Mr. McClellan would concur in that he told me plainly enough he thought me not so worthy a man at law as Daniel Webster.' Those were his words." Turchin finished his story and then seeing the blank indifference on Nadine's face as well as on his friend's, he glowered with an uneasy knowledge that neither the one nor the other saw the piquancy of the encounter in the same light as he. The air itself seemed to reflect their boredom with his narrative.

"Everything has to be humorous and obvious for some people to appreciate it," he mumbled as he turned on his heel and strode into his own room. To his mind, whosoever failed to regard Mr. Lincoln, failed to respect him.

In his room he sulked, child fashion while the murmur of Nadine's voice continued for some time and there he reflected that since coming to this country and their meeting with Trofimov, the intimacy and confidence which had always belonged to him and his wife were ebbing. He felt an irresistible sudden dislike of his friend and a desire to seize him. Several times he might have risen and re-entered the other chamber in order to expel the baron, save that each time he restrained this impulse; for he was too honest to deny that much of his anger was inspired by an irritation begot of the unfeeling lack of response that he attributed to Trofimov. Quickly he exonerated his wife. Once she understood the basis for his resentment, she would conclude with him that because of men like Trofimov, men like Mr. Lincoln were condemned to remain unheralded and unsung. As thanks for their insight and their efforts to awaken a lagging social and political perception, such men received the unrestrained jeers and vulgar calumny of the obtuse.

In his role as active citizen, Turchin felt called upon to evince an interest in the matters which orators fanned into violent blazes. The truth which sought to establish right was an ichor reserved for the drink of compassionate men. And would a man not drink thereof, Turchin would angrily call such a man unworthy and withdraw from his quarter, the tolerance he put forth everywhere else.

In the awkward appearance of Mr. Lincoln, his weak voice with its poorly controlled rise and fall and in Mr. Lincoln's rising position in the Republican Party, Turchin saw omens he would fain have discussed with Trofimov. Instead, sitting alone while the other two were heard to laugh, he bethought him of Mrs. Morrison; not her face, not her silken flounces and long silken gloves; but her rapt attention to the speaker, Mr. Lincoln, and her observable comprehension of the subject. Perhaps for the first time in his life, he gave another woman than Nadine more than a passing thought. He resolved to become better acquainted with Mrs. Morrison and acting promptly on this thought, just then fixed in his mind, he strode into the sitting room and waited to announce his intention.

"Mrs. Morrison would not find it a small matter for me to have met Mr. Lincoln personally," he stated, once the lady had been mentioned again.

"Mrs. Morrison is a follower after fashion," Trofimov deprecated with an amused glance in Nadine's direction. Nadine became interested and demanded to know more of Mrs. Morrison.

It was not the usual thing for Trofimov to discuss one lady with another. He had no just reason to bear Henrietta Morrison a grudge, despite the fact that he was daily more certain of her cool appraisal of himself. What he said now rose from the depths of his ego rather than any spite; he could not forgive the lady's disregard of himself in favor of Turchin, though in fairness to him, Turchin might not have known this.

"She fancies herself a Bluestocking," he was led to say by an angry and disdainful glance from Turchin. "Her late husband left her a sizeable interest in a newspaper, which immediately endowed her with acumen and a privilege of diagnosis you can read any weekday in the paper." His tone was condescending with emphasis on every adjective supposedly descriptive of the young woman's talents. "It is the fashion to support indigent lawyers this season," he continued, "and she is no doubt influenced in her choice of Mr. Lincoln by her determined affinity with the common man, which subject offers rich widows a broad field for good works." He walked to the ormolu topped table and opened the humidor. Selecting a plump cigar, he lit it slowly and walked twice across the room before resuming his topic. "This, Mr. Lincoln is famous by way. It is said of him, so great is his forensic ability, that his name has but to be mentioned in connection with a case to ensure a reasonable belief of its success. Now, who can blame Mrs. Morrison for choosing the object of success for her favorite?" He rocked gently on his heels, as though immensely pleased with his own rhetoric.

When the baron at last took his leave, he left, if nothing else, at least a much firmer determination on the part of Turchin to seek out the lady whose character the baron has assayed neatly to delineate. And so, not many days later, the colonel and his wife sent in their card and were duly received by their hostess. This first call was followed by a regular and frequent exchange of visits which pleased Madame Turchin, who enjoyed in Mrs. Morrison's beautifully arranged drawing room the first freedom from strangeness she had known in the United States. The quiet good taste of the lady, the simple yet elegant decor of the room, the fragrance of flowers and polished woods soothed her into an answering charm.

In time it happened naturally that Turchin began to meet Mrs. Morrison in town and not infrequently she invited him into the small newspaper office reserved for her use. There both of them enjoyed long, discursive conversations ranging from the simple to the most complex problems of the day. There Turchin learned something of McClellan's part in the Douglas senatorial campaign.

"Mr. Lincoln, even though he occasionally does legal work for the railroad, is allowed only an annual pass to ride the cars free of expense. This privilege and munificence," Mrs. Morrison explained with some asperity, "did not extend to the campaign. On that occasion the Illinois Central showed open partiality for Mr. Douglas, allocating him a private coach, with a platform on which thirty-eight signal guns were mounted. Mr. Douglas travelled up and down the states in that car, free of charge.

Turchin was visibly moved by this expose and he asked how Mr. Lincoln had retaliated against this bias his employer showed towards his rival.

"Mr. Lincoln's managers asked for thirty-eight women to represent thirty-eight states, and I am happy to inform you," she blushed becomingly, "that I volunteered my own services for the occasion. We stood festively decorated on the platform of Mr. Lincoln's coach."

When he smiled at this she rebuked him gently and chided him for belittling the use of feminine persuasion to counteract partiality and discourtesy.

"Madam Morrison," he gallantly responded, "I sincerely believe women the repositories of true beauty and thus related to truth. Why not parry partiality with beauty?" He laughed heartily and gripped her arms affectionately.

So it was they talked. She, warmed by his laughter, told him many things, even the small arts and usages of the day which he received with pleasure and gratitude, the quality of which he was always anxious to communicate to his wife.

"It is not impropriety," Turchin said defensively at one such report of his activities, "for me to be closeted with Mrs. Morrison. She is not like other women." He floundered and flushed somewhat while his wife smiled indulgently upon him, assuring him that even if Mrs. Morrison were an enchantress, notwithstanding, she admired her as much as he. "She thinks like a man and somehow it is becoming in her. Besides, she always has her male secretary near her!" When Nadine laughed merrily at this juncture, he reddened and stalked off in high dudgeon, which, like all his brief bursts of anger, quickly evaporated.

Not without much amusement, did she relate this to Trofimov and even ventured to recount her husband's extreme reticence and obliging delicacy to Mrs. Morrison herself.

"I do believe the colonel has a delightful prudery," she confided with gaiety. Her eyes indeed were sparkling with friendly raillery. In their depths, Henrietta Morrison thoughtfully read an unconscious approval of his prudery and assigned its origin to a wifely over-confidence she was not yet ready to deem justifiable. Mrs. Morrison's quick intelligence had not failed to note the touch of exuberance in the voice of the Russian woman and she rightly ascribed its inspiration to the baron, who had accompanied Nadine.

She made rapid deductions from the sight before her, and though outwardly she did not swerve from her gracious friendliness, she nonetheless grew imperceptibly reserved in her behavior until Colonel Turchin arrived. With the colonel's presence, she brightened visibly, thus enabling the baron to study her with the same peculiar intensity with which he had been scrutinizing Nadine.

The baron was satisfied with what he believed to have discovered of the widow's emotions. Getting up from the settle where he had been attending to her, he walked toward the magnificent mantle, which was marked by a portrait of her late husband. This he observed with respectful silence until all the eyes in the room were drawn upon it and him.

"I presume this stately gentleman to be your late husband," he said after a time with a glance over his shoulder toward Mrs. Morrison. Receiving an affirmative nod from her, in which she made no effort to impart sorrow or regret, he praised the noticeable strength and nobility of the face and features.

Turchin, drawn to the portrait, stood before it thoughtfully. "One may not judge a man by his outward features," he ventured at last.

"No." Mrs. Morrison said noncommittally, but her mind censured the stern face in the frame. He had been a successful man, a good man, as the world judged. He had openly derided the weaknesses of man and boasted that he knew and encouraged them. And that as long as stupidity was entrenched in the minds and hearts of his fellows, it pleased him to shape it to his ends. The important thing was to observe the outer form while understanding the inner nature of the times. These had been the tenets by which Mr. Morrison had lived and prospered. Of these matters, delicacy prevented her from giving a hint; nor could she inform her guests that all her days now were spent in a quiet attempt to atone for her husband's policy. Not that she fancied herself high-minded; but she was of that strange composition which made a sense of righteousness and fairness of itself her highest goal. As a wife, she had been bound by the strictures laid upon all wives, especially those of wealthy and prominent men. As a widow, she was free to express her sympathies in the manner she saw fit and this she did in a thousand small ways and so successfully that she had not impaired the name she bore, nor had she impaired the character she had long received for both integrity and charm.

"No," she repeated, looking directly at Trofimov, "it is not the act of wisdom to judge by outer appurtenances, whether of face, figure, or, for that matter, anything else."

"That, Mrs. Morrison, is what I constantly enjoin upon the colonel when he would praise or blame men or institutions on the basis of their appearance to his mind." Nadine spoke with unusual warmth and conviction and the two women's eyes met and held for an instant, as though the meaning implied in the wife's words contained more import than the friend was willing to acknowledge.

"The colonel is prone to feel that because he resides here with much of his European habits, he is therefore equipped with a sounder perspective in all matters than the citizenry who are too close to national events to judge them properly," said Trofimov, well pleased with his observation, which, he saw, was taken variously by his three listeners. "He will not believe that at the bottom, despite all his enthusiasm for causes, he remains essentially European, Russian if you will; that what concerns him most is the role Russia must play in the life of this country, though I'll wager you the colonel would deny this promptly."

"I take the liberty of doing so for him," Mrs. Morrison interrupted.

Later, the conversation turned to Mr. Brewster and his influence in the city. Trofimov, for his part, lauded the qualities of the man and his contributions to the welfare of the community, citing the many plaques and citations affixed to Mr. Brewster's office walls. Mrs. Morrison, on the other hand, with a sense of outrage, impugned Mr. Brewster's motives as self serving and self aggrandizing. "Nothing that man did, did he do for others, but only if he could see a profit for himself," she asservated. "And what is wrong with that," retorted Trofimov, "as long as it also benefits the community." Turchin, embarrassed by the turn of events, felt the need to intercede. "Maybe," he suggested, "it would be better in such matters to have the benefit of actual proof before arriving at a determination." Unfortunately, this bromide did not serve to allay either party and the evening soon reached it's somewhat less than satisfying completion.

CHAPTER XI

To Nadine, the conclusion of what had promised to be an eventful evening became something garish and repulsive. She suffered herself to be led to Mrs. Morrison's carriage in silence. But throughout the short journey home, her mind was in a whirl; how had it all happened in such an unfortunate manner? How had Ivan so far lost his sense of the appropriate as to dispute with his host? How would it all effect their future social life, of which there seemed little hope to buoy her up?

The colonel, however, was beset by none of these worries. In his mind glowed a righteousness that nothing could diminish. Where there had previously been a heartfelt wish to know Brewster and the superior qualities he felt must operate to make a man quite such a figure in the city as Brewster was, there now also existed a sort of sadness that so fine a man might after all, be confused by false gods, purblind to the interests of his country and a declared enemy to progress and enlightenment; a man who hung his deeds on his walls, not that these might inspire him, but that in effect he might hang others in effigy. Of this he spoke not a word to the two silent ladies.

In the weeks that followed, he could readily forget his discomfiture amidst the agitations which were, as early as December, already hovering, like evil spirits, over the land. Chicago itself, like Turchin, became more and more openly the advocate of federal authority, which had for its end the preservation of the country and the subjugation of resurgent elements originating in the Southern States. It pleased the colonel to identify himself in every respect with the character he ascribed to the city, which was for the most part, outside its own regional influences, like a stranger when it clashed with the well established Eastern communities.

Chicago stood as an outpost of the westernmost reaches of commerce and industry at this time. It was certainly the most vital center in the great Northwest and the depot for the straggling farm outposts leading into the unknown wealth of the West. Into that Wild West and its dangerous frontiers came the men and guns of the army. These made their way through the city, and brought with them tales of the Indian menace, to guard against which, the city had organized its own regulars, and now possessed several well trained regiments which met regularly for drill and boasted an adequate supply of stores and equipment to maintain a citizens' peacetime army.

In addition to its own preparedness with reference to the problems close to its interests, the city was alert to the affairs of the country as a whole. Its newspapers were making historic strides in journalism, often rivaling the older newspapers, and challenging their established prestige. They were all strongly partisan one way or another, though bound, except for one or two, in an over-all sympathy and fierce loyalty to the Cause of the Union.

It was Mrs. Morrison's opinion, freely confided to Turchin, that the secession of South Carolina was merely the defiance of a sulky child, that it signified nothing but a meaningless grimace and empty gesture toward the in-coming president. "We shall have to coax South Carolina back to good behavior," she said of the affair, utterly oblivious of the fact that a movement was going on in the South, known to many in Congress, to organize a government of rebel states. Few there were who were aware of the haste with which this conspiratorial body was organizing a government. Still fewer were forewarned of the clever blow therewith intended; to the end that Mr. Lincoln should be all the more confounded when the time for his inauguration was at hand.

Differing strongly with him, in views on these matters, was a new friend that Turchin had acquired at the offices of the Illinois Central, in the person of Nathaniel Banks who had arrived late in the year to take up his duties as vice-president of the railroad. Mr. Banks had been previously interested in the Russian engineer, and once he was established in Chicago, took every opportunity of inviting him to his office where they indulged in a variety of talks almost more intriguing to Turchin than those he shared with Mrs. Morrison. Banks was a superior mind, carrying about him an air of factual intelligence which appealed more to Turchin's mind than the impassioned and often intuitive predictions of Mrs. Morrison. The current situation, preceding Fort Sumter plainly worried Banks and he was not loath to admit as much to Turchin, with whom indeed he seemed to find a meeting ground for almost every phase of his multifarious affiliations. He worried mainly over the hostility which the air itself contained these last days of the year of 1860.

The secession of the recalcitrant and bitterly infuriated South Carolina was of itself not so dire a portent as the swift imitation it induced in six other states, making a total of seven, who formed the secession bloc, at whose head reared the former cabinet member, Jefferson Davis. Mr. Banks was not one to undervalue Davis, as was the case, at first, with many less far-sighted men than he. He confided to Turchin that he had not so sanguine an opinion about the easy redress these rebellious states would accept. Nothing short of submission to their claims would satisfy those among them who were crying loudly for their just deserts and were quoting in legal thunderings, the Constitutional citations to corroborate them.

"They'll get their just deserts, I am afraid," he spoke solemnly to Turchin early in the spring when news had reached them that a de-facto government was now fully prepared to establish its right to existence in the South. "It won't be what some of our braggadocio friends imagine," he added thoughtfully. "I do not envy Mr. Lincoln, who has the job old Buchanan left in the making."

Banks was an able man and knew as well as Turchin that, when a group of men intent upon seizing power, create a cabinet, elect officers, organize a political organ like a constitution, commandeer the wealth of their territories, and quickly begin to draft men to form an army, something more imminent than a political debate will be the result.

"Is not all that fanfare just so much bombastic fist waving? Do you imagine that those rebellious states can hope to win against a great organized country? They think they can tear into the vitals of this country by threatening?"

Turchin, soldier as he was, was unable to conceive of the boldness which would make millions of men in the Southland dare to launch an attack against opponents who were obviously superior in every important detail. In the North were the major industries necessary to implement a war. The commerce and lines of communication were there. The iron foundries and the mills were in the North, leaving the vast Southland solely a granary which though indubitably important in waging war, was yet secondary to the modern techniques of warfare.

"If they go to war," Banks informed him, "they will have one superior advantage over us, despite our greater wealth and means: They have the best officers of the land; a third of our highly placed officers are Southerners."

"I do not anticipate open war," Turchin observed. "It would be national suicide; it would be brother against brother and that is a fruitless war no matter which side wins. The right is on our side. Mr. Lincoln will guide us through this and I am certain such a man will prevent so horrible a scandal as a war between brothers."

In this way the two men, whenever they chanced to spend a few minutes together, exchanged friendly opinions, each one always leaving the other more favorably disposed. At length it began to seem that Turchin had finally achieved his proper stride in his work for Banks to appreciate his accomplishments and he hoped that this would augment his aspirations for advancement. Nadine was quite pleased with the favorable turn of events. She was even beginning to make her way about the city in a familiar manner. She was warm hearted in her dealings with shopkeepers and tradespeople and unfeignedly delighted with the little children and their nurses, whom she encountered in the park. This excited a reciprocal congeniality in which she bloomed radiantly. Returning from these happy little jaunts, her spirit bubbled with such contagiousness that Turchin, looking upon her, also felt cheerful.

Thus, in March, 1861, the inauguration of Lincoln gradually transpired with perhaps a shade less pomp and formality than was the wont at such important national events. Nathaniel Banks went to Washington for the ceremony and Turchin scanned the Chicago papers for every word of criticism or encomium he could find. Comments varied concerning Lincoln's ability to deal with the delicate problems of the country, which every day were becoming more precarious. Some voices brashly accused the new Cabinet of employing a mean non-committal strategy in order to force the Southern claimants to show their hands in an unfavorable light. Others applauded Mr. Lincoln for the same reason, believing that a compromising though firm stand, would drive the hot rebel heads to open hostilities and concomitantly win increased support for the Union.

Then the incident at Fort Sumter happened. South Carolina, upon secession, warned that all Federal property within its boundaries would be considered belonging to a foreign power intolerable to the State. The Star of the West, a supply ship sent to refurbish the low food resources of Fort Sumter, had earlier been fired upon and prevented from delivering its supplies. The out-going Buchanan, when the repulse of the relief ship occurred, made no official effort to subdue the rebellious State, and consequently Lincoln's polite attempt to send food, and only food, to the men in the Fort, left the belligerent observers of the South indecisive and nervous in proportion to Lincoln's growing determination.

The incident of the hard pressed men at Fort Sumter was well calculated to stir the indignation of the entire North, and the outcome of the affair was looked to with apprehension and excitement. These emotions were not lost upon Turchin, or Banks and they discussed the situation exhaustingly. Banks, whose admiration and friendship for Turchin grew every day, heartily declared to his companion, "We must furnish our men with food; that goes without saying."

"You think it possible they will fire upon the Fort?" Turchin queried.

"I think it very likely; something must break soon. For a while now, South Carolina has wanted to gain possession of the forts along her coast. The forts were basically built along the country's potentially weak points in case of a foreign attack. The coves and bays are ideal spots for hostile powers to occupy and anchor their fleet. Having seceded from the Union, it is not surprising South Carolina demands these forts. As a matter of fact," he smiled seriously and continued, "the Federal Government had originally, and with due formality, purchased the land sites for the forts from the states in which they are located. There was even a legislative act whereby these sites were ceded to the sovereignty of the Federal Government. Now, however, South Carolina wishes that these forts and sites revert back to her." He shrugged his shoulders without further comment.

"So you believe they will use force if they cannot repurchase these forts? Well, then," Turchin added in a more optimistic tone, "Major Anderson must defend the Fort in case of attack. It is not possible that the rebels can demolish a United States Fort. No, that is impossible."

The whole affair weighed heavily upon Turchin. He wished to share his perturbations with someone, but aside from Nathaniel Banks, only Nadine was receptive to his worries and even she thought little of them. Mrs. Morrison had departed the city for some weeks, and Trofimov had accompanied the Brewsters to Columbus, Ohio, where they were visiting friends.

However, much as Nathaniel Banks admired his engineer, there were certain reticences he clung to, for it was his policy to keep his thoughts predominantly to himself. Moreover, Banks sensed that the colonel was able to grasp the national character of the emerging struggle despite his ardent espousal of Americanism. McClellan then resident of Cincinnati, might have been a better confidant for Banks, had not his ambitions moved him to a certain obtuseness, rendering him insensitive to the problem as Lincoln viewed it: the threat to the Union.

Then, on a fateful April day in 1861, all speculation concerning the role of Fort Sumter dissolved with its bombardment by a howling and gleeful handful of South Carolinians. A seventy-seven year old Southern gentleman was said to have pulled the lanyard from which rocketed the first shell into the not yet finished fort. Only a handful of soldiers, commanded by Major Anderson, were at hand to defend the fort.

The whole world was stunned. Everyone waited for an explanation and ominously anticipated retribution. Many things in these early months of Lincoln's administration, remained obscure to Turchin, and he anxiously sought out Banks for enlightenment. The amiable Banks iterated the whole affair of the Secession, including the firing upon the Star of the West, and the purport of the admonitory words of Lincoln, uttered upon his inauguration. "Mr. Lincoln', I believe, stated his opinion and his policy clearly in his inaugural address," pointed out Banks on the day following the first astonishing news reports that

Major Anderson had capitulated to Beauregard, the general who was commander on the spot during the tense days preceding the incident. Beauregard was already then known to be a brilliant young soldier and had been commissioned by the newly organized Government of the Confederacy, to treat with the Fort Sumter defenders.

"I have read that address many times," Turchin nodded his head.

"Then you must recall that the President makes it a matter of solemn duty to himself and to God to keep and defend the possessions and properties of the United States." He rose from his leather arm chair and took to pacing the room where they were meeting, in such a troubled manner that Turchin hesitated to say more, though hoping Banks would of his own accord relate further.

"I have an admiration for Mr. Lincoln, for his sincerity which I believe transcends the claims of his party leaders. More than that, I sense in him a native shrewdness which should not be underrated. The President knows that this open challenge to him consists of daring defiance and arrogance, which no one thinks will mean war; a horrible challenge thrown to him as though to defy him to take such action as is his right and duty." He took another turn about the room, clutched his hands fiercely together behind his back, and brooded over the whole business for a few minutes.

"Do you see the dilemma Mr. Lincoln is faced with?" he asked rhetorically, for he did not believe Colonel Turchin was advanced sufficiently in American politics to see the nature of the strategy he believed dominant in the President's actions at this time. "He leaves it to the South to interpret his address however it chooses, and to react to it in such a manner as to leave no doubt in the people's minds regarding the aggressive nature of this incident now perpetrated." He was referring to the Fort Sumter calamity which was shaking Chicago to its marrow. "All the while Mr. Lincoln is aware of the necessity to win the support of our new Border States which lie so strategically between us and the rebellious states, in case of open conflict of arms. Their sympathies, and therefore loyalties, must be naturally divided, and their intelligent comprehension of this crisis must be ensured."

"I think I begin to see what you mean," Turchin assented, though not too sure he truly understood.

"Good! Then you may understand why it was that Mr. Lincoln gave orders right from the start of this rebellion - and I have it on good authority - that the forts in the Charleston harbor were to avoid any and every collision with the Southern patriots, except only upon open attack. And that Major Anderson was bound to hold the fort as long as possible, and which we have learned today he has done ably with his less than a hundred men and his few guns. These must have been almost worthless, what with the lack of ammunition he openly confessed."

Again Turchin nodded his head. He had a quick picture of the scene at Fort Sumter, where the men had little food. He knew what it might mean to lack movable guns; to have what few guns there were, mainly unused, lacking in carriages or recoil mechanisms; to have the hatred and contempt of such shore merchants on whom an isolated fort must rely for the necessities of life.

He took that picture home with him and lived with it in a mood of mingled compassion and indignation. When days later it was learned that the courageous Major Anderson had been hailed in New York as a hero, he felt somewhat relieved, unwilling entirely to see in the capitulation of the fort, some ulterior advantages which Banks had tried to demonstrate. "Don't you see, man, that Lincoln has made the South open the fight! It is a moral victory for us, and after all, the shelling of the fort, though a dastardly wound to our national pride, still cost us no life."

When Baron Trofimov heard this version of the incident, he deprecated, "That's a fine battle. You can see how the temper of a lot of shoemakers is easily inflamed to its senseless hero worship! They cheer this Major Anderson who does nothing! Their fort is demolished and you think it is a victory!" He threw up his hands, and made a mock gesture of resignation.

"But it was an unequal fight!" Turchin protestingly roared out. "Only nine officers and seventy-four men, they say, to defend a fort against seven thousand enemies. What do you expect, miracles? The guns were defective, lacking screws, scales and tangents, if you can understand in the least what that means!" He was angry and discourteous as he said this last and included his wife in the dark glance he threw at Trofimov.

"But the flag was lowered after less than a day and a half of fighting, remember that, and your fellow zealots call it a victory! That is all I am asking you to notice!"

"It took their thousands of men and good guns two days to lower our flag," Turchin roared even more loudly.

"Our flag! Just listen to our patriot," Trofimov prodded him further with a strange recklessness. He addressed himself to Nadine who judiciously kept herself aloof from the argument which was touched with fierce emotions.

"He is not satisfied to be a Russian gentleman; he has to become more American than the Americans!"

"I was a Russian gentleman, and that is more than can be said for some pretenders," Turchin snapped back. "Now I choose to be an American. But at least God has so far endowed me with some reason and some moral courage that I may choose! In any case, my friend, to be a gentleman depends on no national boundaries. Only a snob, with extremely subtle foundation, would presume otherwise."

Trofimov, usually more careful of his words, was now nursing a wounded pride. He had consented to journey to Ohio with the Brewsters where many charming events and occurrences had lent him stature and value. The houses he had visited, the charming women who had clustered about him as much as a rigid decorum permitted them, the wealthy gentlemen he had become acquainted with, all endeared the small city of their sojourning to him; until the news of Fort Sumter reached them. Immediately, Mr. Brewster had become engaged in many activities from which he excluded Trofimov, curtly informing him that his best efforts lay in Chicago; that here in Columbus his prestige and title amounted to a row of beans. "Your best activity, baron," he had said with unmistakable sarcasm, "is to attach my girl before she changes her mind, that is, before the fad for Russian barons disappears."

Furthermore, intending to follow the advice of the other, he had accepted the wry advice insolently tendered, for him to accompany the ladies to Cincinnati, where Susan hoped to seek out her erstwhile friend, as she loved to call Mrs. McClellan, whose acquaintance with her went only so far as to permit Susan to bow to her. They met some seasons ago in Washington where perhaps half a dozen sentences had been exchanged. Upon these few casual words, Susan, not to know Mrs. McClellan was fashionable, depended to add tone to her interview.

"You will find, dear baron," her mother had cooed into Trofimov's ear, "in this city where my daughter's distinguished friends reside - he is president of a railroad, and at his age, too - something of the spirit of a culture we lack in Chicago, I am afraid."

They had left their cards at Mrs. McClellan's door, and that was the end of the matter. Mrs. McClellan had ignored their existence and thenceforth incurred Susan's lasting dislike and malice. Her ill-humor upon that occasion had marred the usual sweetness of her temper with respect to Trofimov, and although he was almost ready to gratify her desires, to give her a title and the envy of her friends, she seemed truculent and withdrawn. This was so indifferent that her behavior threw Trofimov upon the mercies of the confidential Mrs. Brewster. At once she informed him how much more she always enjoyed travelling, which was much better than arriving, for once arrived at a destination there was nothing more to expect, since people were very careful to avoid displeasing her, and so enraging Mr. Brewster, who was a very powerful man with powerful friends like Senator Vallandigham. Her discourse ended with their journey.

Discontent with himself now activated the baron in his carelessly chosen words, and would have precipitated a quarrel for which there might have been few appeasements, had not Nadine interposed herself now, and in time been able to divert Trofimov and Ivan from their dispute. Hers was such an art to please, that only hard-hearted individuals might resist her gentle importunities to friendliness and gentleness. On this occasion she brought forth her precious samovar and treated Trofimov to an account of their trials in Long Island, not a few of which stemmed from their possession of it. This had engendered deep suspicion among the severely pious neighbors, who had considered it an idol. "We were the infidels, the perverted Canaanite, suppliant before the golden calf," she laughed and glanced toward her husband who also began to smile as he recalled those days which now seemed to him remote indeed.

As it was, the evening ended safely, though not happily. Each person in that small drawing room in Division St. was ultimately grateful for this outcome; Turchin for the fact that an element of friendliness remained to permit Trofimov's future visits; Nadine that neither man had exceeded the limits they tacitly permitted each other and thereby enabled her to savor of the happiness they accorded her in their disparate ways; Trofimov that some touch of "home," as he put it, was left for him to cling to in the delicate and tortuous path he had elected to follow to success. He had for some time now, admitted the salubrious effects these compatriots exerted upon him. He wished to retain the right to frequent their undistinguished home where, better than anywhere else, he could restore the inner confidence upon which he sustained himself against the stings incurred with Mr. Brewster and the gentry he consorted with.

In taking issue with Turchin, he did not so much wish to imply an utter ignorance of national affairs, as to find a harmless vent for his ill humor. Had he chosen, he might have lent, to the sort of talks Turchin longed to have with him, many facts formerly unknown to him, but which were now made available through Mr. Brewster, whose fingers reached far into the political doings, not only of Chicago, but Washington as well. However, he was pledged to a secrecy which, with a peculiar honorableness, he resolutely preserved.

From sources not accessible to Turchin, Trofimov had heard how, on the receipt of the news of Fort Sumter, the President's cabinet had convened in great haste. He had some idea of the men composing this august body, chosen to support a man with not much other following in high places. Brewster, rubbing his hands with irritated jerks, as he often did when under stress or excitement, had fully described these important men and the role they were called upon to play, with Lincoln as their chief. Brewster had declared, in no uncertain terms, that every man, with the possible exception of old Salmon Chase, the Secretary of the Treasury and Montgomery Blair, the Post Master general, were actively concerned to bring about an amicable settlement of the whole agitated problem; that all wanted to avoid armed conflict. "Why old Winfield Scott," he thumped his fist on his great mahogany desk, "the ablest man they have, chief of staff in what some are pleased to conceive of as an army - army indeed! - said plain out, weeks ago, that a force of 21,000 men would be needed to hold Fort Sumter! And what have we to look to in order to retake that fort? There is not even a decent provision,

Vallandigham told me, for legislative action, even if they tried to take back the fort, which would be war! We certainly do not want war! That would upset our whole economy!"

Trofimov, listening intently, had remarked in answer to this: "Wars have always been profitable, if you know how to get the profits. That is reasonable enough, else why would there be wars? War is only business gone amok, I say, like an open and unsmiling announcement to ruin him who is weakest." He hated war because it was ugly and stupid and not clever. What was not clever, what had to be stated in bald terms, leaving no room for imagination, alienated the baron, forever attached to the evanescent, the fleeting, the intangibly lovely. Even the ugly factors of existence he strove to clothe in operations that bore the stamp of charm whenever he could so manage it. He recognized how contradictory his tendencies were in this respect to his stated plans. He explained his dislike of Mr. Brewster adequately on the basis of those same tendencies or sentimentalities. He knew also why he was reluctant to close the affair with Brewster's daughter, namely because he sensed a certain vulgarity in her display of what she termed quality; being himself a pretender to his title, he scorned with redoubled fervor all parvenus; being a seeker after easy gold, he despised the sharp dealer so much the more fiercely.

Some days later, following his visit to the Turchins, he listened to Brewster's sneering account of what had transpired in Lincoln's cabinet meetings. After having made a comment or two, he subsided into the slightly mocking audience Brewster desired. "Do you know what they resorted to now?" Brewster raged while thumping his hand with righteous wrath on his desk. "They uncovered some old dusty Militia Act of 1792, last invoked in the "Whiskey Rebellion which you would not know about. And with that miserable instrument for authority, this Mr. Lincoln proposed to draft his first war proclamation. And I hear he has ordered, if you please, that treasonable combinations disperse! Who is he to know treason? Are combinations of sincere citizens, who take issue with the government, to be called treasonable? Ha! We were fools, indeed, to abide by that dictum. The dictum of a second-rate lawyer raised beyond his abilities! I say! And now he demands 75,000 volunteers for a 90 day enlistment! The man is a fool. I'd be surprised if any sane man pays attention to that, leave alone takes arms against other Americans at his mad request."

But Brewster erred, not only in judging Mr. Lincoln, but in judging the effect upon the peoples of the North. Almost to a man, among the workers all over the northern states, the people rallied behind the President's decree, and the necessary volunteers were quickly raised. Among the first to offer his services was Colonel Turchin, though the examining officers in the recruiting station thought it wiser to refuse his enlistment until his abilities were properly estimated, or in other words, until he could be commissioned to a post that would enable the forming army to utilize him at his best level.

"We need officers even more than soldiers," Banks had said laughingly when he learned of the colonel's amazing determination to enlist as a private soldier. "We need especially men like you, Colonel Turchin, to help us organize and train an army. This is no short order affair, I think. We have a long pull ahead of us, but I think a victorious one, God willing!"

CHAPTER XII

Those were feverishly anxious days which followed upon the President's war proclamation, and they affected the lives of everyone. First to leave the circle of Turchin's acquaintance was Nathaniel Banks himself, who received his commission in May, and soon thereafter departed for the post assigned to him. Before leaving his friends in Chicago he performed one last friendly office for Turchin; he being one of the most insistent that the colonel refrain from enlistment but wait instead for an appointment in the capacity for which he was fitted. He wrote McClellan, asking that old colleague to bestir himself with the Governor in Turchin's behalf. McClellan was but a short time wed at this date. He had, as became a former officer, at once obtained a high command in the Ohio Volunteers. Like many sincere men of that time, despite his personal antipathy to Mr. Lincoln's policy, he had dedicated himself to his country in its time of need. Another such man was Stephen A. Douglas, Lincoln's great rival of former times. It was this same fiery "Little Giant," as the papers were fond of terming him, who stood beside the President at his inauguration. Douglas felt it not beneath him to hold Mr. Lincoln's hat and to offer publicly his wholehearted support, signifying that when a national crisis faced Americans, party distinctions disappeared to make way for unanimity of action.

By the time Banks had left, Turchin had gained some measure of understanding as to the deplorable state of unpreparedness with which Mr. Lincoln was to cope in these early weeks of the war. Not only was there a very real military situation to confront, but there was an army to create, almost from the bottom up. At first this realization was shocking to a man accustomed to conceive of a nation's military arm as an essential ingredient in the construction of the country. Despicable as futile wars of aggression seemed to him, he took for granted the normal precautionary means employed to withstand hostile aggression. However, he expected a peacetime army of more than the 1,500 regulars whose sole experience consisted of routine duty on the Indian frontier.

It was this last fact which made him check his ardent feelings when the first call to arms came and when he saw the hordes of young men begin to respond in every section of Chicago. Trainloads of gay, young lads rode out of Chicago daily, and the sight made him restless and impatient. All these lads without competent leadership faced grave dangers from a better trained and better led enemy. This fact enabled him to endure patiently the time he must waste until Governor Yates, of Illinois, confirmed his appointment. Always he was sustained by the honest pride and faith he had in the aid he could offer, not only to Governor Yates, but more directly to Mr. Lincoln. The President had grown in such stature that it would have been worth a mouthful of teeth to Trofimov if he were to malign the man in the White House.

More than being simply and grandly a citizen of America, Turchin felt himself peculiarly a citizen of Chicago. The response which this town gave to the President endeared every stick and stone of it to the colonel. Turchin now made it a practice to wend his way to the receiving station where he could observe the touching scenes between the young lads and the families, who sent their sons and sweethearts and husbands to do the will of God. He watched these boys earnestly. As each wooden coach pulled out of the station yard, he vowed that each lad was to be his own special charge, his own son; that each parent's tears were to be a reminder to him of the grave responsibility he waited to assume.

Mrs. Morrison had driven by in her carriage and catching sight of her friend, had ordered her coachman to stop. She got out and smiled gaily as half a dozen young fellows greeted her with rousing cheers and cast admiring glances upon the fresh prettiness she embodied in her green linen gown with its festoons of gay ribbons and clusters of flowers. She had not seen her friend for nearly a month now. Making her way with graceful steps in his direction, she was free to look upon him without attracting particular notice. Despite the happy disturbance her appearance had created in the small circle close to her carriage, Turchin's notice was not attracted. With her womanly intuitiveness she guessed the trend of his feelings and thoughts as he stood alone and watched Chicago's offering to the Cause of The Union. With an increased heartbeat she noted that his lady was nowhere in sight and that he was indeed alone. This surprised her immensely and convinced her he was a spectator, not yet a participant. Judging him from what she knew of his feelings, his former rank and title in the Russian Army, she had supposed him by now to be in uniform, to be acting as a colonel. It was the practice during early recruiting, to assign to former officers the same rank they held in previous service. Apropos of nothing, the mere sight of him brought a happy pride in her and a delicate flush of pleasure to her cheeks. Shyly she discovered herself to him by touching his sleeves with light fingers. "Colonel Turchin! What a happy surprise finding you here", she said.

"You are back!" were his first words, unconsciously betraying the happiness her presence gave him and the loneliness her protracted absence had caused. He grasped her hand and crushed it between his palms. "There is so much I have to say to you; so many things I wish to discuss with you. You always understand me better than almost anyone else!"

"Yes, I have been away much longer than I thought to be," she answered smilingly. She gazed into his frank blue eyes and saw in them nothing but the unaffected friendship he vouchsafed her. A small sigh escaped her as she collected herself. "I have come to see off a young friend of mine whom you might enjoy knowing," she looked about her hurriedly. "I have often thought you two might be most congenial acquaintances and hoped soon to make you known to one another."

To this Turchin made some proper remarks, though his eyes were once more occupied with scanning the groups of men and boys out of whose undisciplined ranks he already envisaged regiments and brigades, camp workers and drilled units. These would be something more effectual an opposition to an enemy than so many sacks of meal into which an enemy might fire shell and canister.

"He is another of your mettle, colonel," Mrs. Morrison explained, though she noticed and forgave his absorption in problems which she knew lay beyond her province. "He comes to my workingmen's cultural group and is, like you, an ardent new citizen."

"Do you think, Mrs. Morrison that I acted wisely in waiting as I now am doing, for a Commission? I had as lief enlisted as a regular than stand about and wait for things to happen."

She was about to make a reply when her fingers tightened on his arm. "There he is," she said and gently pushed him forward toward a small cluster of men and women surrounding the young man to whom she had made reference. He was a tall, rather heavily built young person with rugged features of such outstanding clarity and pleasing construction that he attracted notice instantly, though it were hard to say what single feature about him elicited such attention. An unstudied heartiness of manner or the effect of light coloring conjoined with deeply glowing dark eyes might account for it; as well as the commanding size of his strong frame and softness of manner. This was instantly observable from the small courtesies he bestowed among the female relatives gathered tearfully about him. He was waiting to join the many recruits the city of Chicago had mustered for Mr. Lincoln. Nowhere else except perhaps in the city of Boston was such civic cooperation shown the President as in this city where, in little more than six weeks, thousands of men were provided and equipped out of a population of 160,000.

Observing this young man and the hundreds of others milling around the station, was a young parson who, though unobserved by the colonel and Mrs. Morrison, was drawn to direct his kindly, interested glance frequently upon them. He was a minister from Rockford, Illinois, who had just succeeded in enlisting as chaplain and was now waiting to entrain with the regiment he had joined. Seeing the direction in which Henrietta was guiding Turchin, he followed with curiosity and was immediately arrested by the appearance of Geza Mihalotzy, the man awaiting Mrs. Morrison. Mihalotzy saw her nearing with Turchin, and his personal welcome gave way to a polite smile in which was no effusive gaiety and no inordinate heartiness. Casually, he occupied himself with the numerous cousins and aunts tearfully bidding him farewell, as though they, not he, were destined for the dark adventures of war and death.

"Captain Mihalotzy," Henrietta intruded herself gently amidst his family, the while her eyes begged forgiveness and immunity of them all, who, recognizing her innate quality, made instant way for her to reach Mihalotzy, to whom she presented her friend Turchin. "You see, I have come to pay my respects to a gallant gentleman, and I have brought with me a good friend."

Mihalotzy without a word extended his hand to Turchin whose own was as ready and prompt. The two men clasped hands warmly, looked into each other's faces and smiled almost simultaneously.

"I am proud of our young captain," Mrs. Morrison said kindly in order to overcome the first strangeness she sensed these men might feel in one another's presence. "He is the sort of man to make every woman in America proud of our men! He is like you, colonel, a firm believer in a better future. He has your kind of faith in mankind, have you not, captain?" She deliberately used his military title with the intention to compliment him, to approve his efforts, which she knew to have begun in the service of his new country even before the President's call for volunteers.

Mihalotzy was a foreigner by birth. Like Turchin, while still a young man, he had chosen to abandon the insurmountable obstacles he found in his native land, Austria-Hungary, in order to establish a brighter happiness and freedom in America. Not unlike the Russian, he believed, with boundless faith, in the height and breadth of the possibilities this new land offered. He was of good plain birth. No morbidness claimed him. It was the world, in its mere existence, that furnished him with sufficiency of motive to extol its merits. He had no intellectual passionateness, no disease of pride or ego, and yet no overweening satisfaction, either. His eyes held a humor which never did less than comfort the most self-absorbed stranger once his eyes were caught. Afterwards the fortunate passerby might stop to wonder what magic inspired the lightness and elation left on his palate.

No folly of mankind grew disproportionately repulsive to him. If he made no extravagant claims to defend man's natural fallibility, he however yielded himself to its perpetuation with such an unvoiced sympathy, which in the most intolerant, there was always a lack of suspicion and animadversion. He appealed to women without thrusting them into moods or attitude where they could reproach him. He was beloved of the older and more fearful folk, to whom he gave freely the sincere credit he maintained they deserved for first venturing across the ocean in hopes of betterment. He often became their protagonist when they shamefacedly confided their inability to adjust to new ways.

These things Turchin, naturally, could not divine at first glance, but the compelling and inviting gladness of the man made them evident from the start. "You were a Captain in the Hungarian army, perhaps?" he asked after a few minutes of pleasant conversation.

"It is not for any former military distinctions that Mrs. Morrison honors my rank," Mihalotzy laughed, nodding with affection toward Henrietta, who had graciously stepped to one side and pretended a deep interest in the various scenes about her. "It is because I am trusted now to enter the service. I am not sure I quite deserve my elevation."

"He is overly modest as becomes a true man," Henrietta boldly praised him. "Why colonel, he was perhaps signally important in organizing the Lincoln Riflemen, at whose head he will serve us now, if he was not entirely responsible for its being. He must learn to take credit where it is our honor to bestow it. Goodness knows, many men claim it on less merit." She was making an allusion to her cousin Brewster, who had largely and apparently handsomely, contributed to this very regiment when first Mr. Lincoln had granted permission for its institution. She knew her cousin Brewster well and was perhaps condemning his propensity to demand applause where an obvious act of righteousness was appropriate. She held other opinions, and many doubts, about her cousin Brewster, but was too much a gentlewoman to betray these to anyone. Being in a position to know many unrelated facts and being, moreover, an intelligent woman, safely past the dangerous periods of first, girlish sentimentalities, she was able to correlate many actions which all pointed in her mind to the machinations of her wily cousin. Not the least of these was his long standing friendship with Clement Vallandigham. To him, she ascribed authorship of much of the hostile journalism which was growing ever more undisguised and audacious; winning toward itself some very able leaders in the life of the city, as well as the state as a whole. She had lately heard rumors of the organization of a new secret society, especially suspect for its anti-Union doctrines. Trofimov had dropped several hints unguardedly, as late as the day before. It was a simple matter for her to see the concatenation: Trofimov, Brewster and finally Vallandigham, the latter being the fountainhead.

"The time is coming, I believe," Turchin spoke seriously, "when we new Americans shall prove whether we deserve what a good and honest people confer upon us." He uttered these words humbly and in grim earnestness, without reference to the colonelcy he expected any day.

"That is exactly what I tell these foolish women," Mihalotzy replied in quick, smiling agreement. He turned toward the anxious faces of two older women, who stood respectfully at a distance, while this meeting took place. No one in this family gathering understood a word of English. Their eyes carried an ancient haunted memory of comings and goings, the wounds of war, the wounds of life, before and after wars. "These are my people, Colonel Turchin. I must comfort them and reassure them. They are so proud of me, you see, that even if they fear for me, they believe I may positively will it to live or die," he laughed merrily over this last. "They can really all do exactly what I have done, that is, all of them who are not too old, but because I have done it first, learned to talk the American language, to read American books, they believe me superior to themselves. They are very wonderful, my people. Excuse me colonel and Mrs. Morrison. I must bid them take heart and have true faith, not in me, but in something higher than all of us." He bowed somewhat awkwardly to Henrietta and again held out his hand to Turchin. This time Turchin took it with such emotionalism and brotherly feeling, that the young minister, who had witnessed this little conclave of relatives and friends, took special note of the group. He would have been pleased to know at that time, that both these expressive men were henceforth to become well known to him, that he was to see confirmed by them the many convictions of his sturdy creed and gospel of liberty.

The parson was the future chaplain of the 19th Illinois Volunteers, the very regiment Colonel Turchin would soon command. His name was Augustus H. Conant, and he served with undeviating devotion during the entire enlistment of the Illinois regulars, until 1864.

The griefs that few anticipated that day in the station yard of Chicago, he was to carry like a heavy cross on his own shoulders.

Younger and stronger ones grew weary and hopeless and sick with the longings which all, engaged in the bitter struggle, whether in Blue or in Grey, were to know to the fullest. This onus of human grief he was no stranger to, having already at this date exposed himself to the heaviest censure a man of God can evoke, for his battle against it. Early on he had the temerity to speak up, to stand up in the support of such principles of human liberty as had not yet been adopted by the pillars of his church or the solid citizen, comfortable in the settled doctrines, which were in no serious way handicapped by the existence of a slave population thousands of miles away.

Once he had come to the conclusion, that to preach to men the Word of God, must entail a will to uphold that Word for everyone, free or unfree, black or white, rich or poor, nothing could stop him from tampering with the whole slave problem, regardless of the price. At that first instance of his integrity and courage, he had been but newly ordained. When he announced fearlessly, that as a man of God, it was mandatory for him to hold up the issue of slavery in the face of God's sunlight, many of his best friends severely castigated him. They considered such remarks as foolish self-indulgence and a consequent disregard of the tender feelings in worthy supporters of the church, who did not enjoy the airing of a debatable subject from the pulpit consecrated to divine worship.

The expected results from this youthful ardency soon necessitated the young minister's removal from the church and the community. He came to Chicago where he published his provocative sermons in pamphlet form and added to his first convictions the further emphasis of open avowal to the cause of the abolition of slavery.

Came news of the first guns of Fort Sumter, Conant prepared himself for the war he knew to be inevitable. By this time, after many years of effort and experience, he disdained the "Peace Democrats" who could either support, or allow a nation to support, so vile and evil an institution as human bondage. The shells that tore into Fort Sumter were a clarion call to this passionate man of God, who wrote, if not as well, then at least as courageously as the fierce, one year dead, John Brown, captured at Harper's Ferry after leading an insurrection on behalf of a defenseless people.

In his last sermon, before enlisting as chaplain, he quoted Jesus as expressly commanding him "who hath no sword, to sell his garment and buy one." For the closing anthem that last day as officiating pastor, he selected the National Anthem which he sang with such deep fervor and grief that his audience wept to a man. He further enjoined his congregation not to weep, but to act in such a way, that they could identify themselves with every one of the Union boys who would thenceforth be of their spiritual congregation; the boys he had referred to were these very lads now entraining.

The signal to embark had been given and the many clusters of friends and relatives broke up. Mrs. Morrison and Turchin followed the young men, who fell clumsily into single and double files as they made their way to the coaches waiting to receive them. Caps were thrown into the air. Shouts of cheering rose and drowned out the piteous cries of mothers and wives. When Mihalotzy entered the coach, an old woman flung her arms into the air and shrieked aloud. Henrietta instinctively moved closer to her and put her arm about the wildly weeping woman. Turchin stood stiffly nearby, a worried frown etched on his forehead. He was already taking stock of the inadequacies he saw clearly attaching to the task of creating an army out of these raw young recruits, not one of whom was departing with so much as a uniform. The only sign among the future soldiers that would indicate their new roles was a rolled blanket given each man which they carried strapped about themselves at the shoulder. The disposition of the men smacked too much of an outing and not of a serious mission. It was not pleasing to Turchin who, in the matter of army details, was demanding and who stood fully resolved to remedy much of this deplorable unfitness as soon as he had taken his place among the men. He never doubted but that this was inevitable in the near future.

When the last coach had rattled out of sight, headed for Cairo, where the first training was to be supplied, Turchin remembered Henrietta who had quietly moved to her carriage, where she stood waiting for him, though unbidden to do so. Often she questioned the sudden streams of compassionate understanding with which she felt herself imbued when in this man's presence. And the explanations her steady mind and heart returned her, cautioned a carefulness which, considering that she was at all times decorous and deliberate, sometimes manifested itself as an aloofness which, fortunately, Turchin did not perceive. As she caught his remembering glance, she nodded her head beckoningly and made a move to enter her gig.

With a few rapid strides, he reached her side. "Forgive me, charming lady, for neglecting you. I become absorbed in the problems which I see are only now growing visible. I am impatient to join this State's regiments. I can hardly tell you how impatient, for they need every man who knows even the most elementary facts." He looked at her appealingly, wanting her approbation of his concern, and she accordingly nodded.

"I look upon them, these mere children in the way of war, and I can't help thinking how far from their experience is this thing, war," he pursued quietly. "I am glad Madam Turchin is not here to witness these leave-takings. They would upset her, though she is a valiant woman. She spent much of her girlhood in military camps," he added, a note of pride creeping into his voice. "She is such a brave creature, for all she is delicate and helpless in appearance." He laughed as he lapsed into a momentary reminiscence. "And what a nurse she would make for those good lads going to meet they know not what! She is quite learned in that art. Once she tried to gain permission to locate and meet Florence Nightingale, that noble English lady who came to the Crimea."

"She was a nurse," Henrietta said quietly. "Yes, I read about her. We will need brave women now, I fear, as much as England needed her." She stood with the shadow of sadness on her pale face. The station took on the appearance of a lonely deserted place, pervaded by an air of impatience and callousness, which the mere continuance of routine functions, following the former bustle, lent to it. Slowly she climbed into her carriage, which she proposed to drive herself, having dismissed her man. She perfunctorily offered Turchin a lift home, which he as politely refused, on the grounds that he had not yet finished his work in the office; that his presence was due to the fact that he was unable to desist from this participation of the first day's entrainment; that he had several errands to accomplish for Nadine. In short, with a bow and a friendly smile, he saluted her and allowed her to drive away. Nor did he see, some few paces further on Dearborn Street, how Henrietta's gig stopped and how a tall slim gentleman climbed in beside her with something of a triumphant air. The baron, for it was he, seeing her and paying her a pleasant salute, was not loath to enter her carriage, though it somewhat mortified him to be seen sitting idly beside a lady who refused to discharge the reins to him. "Her cursed independence," he thought and hoped he inspired something other than her cool humor when he nonchalantly gave her the address on Division Street as his destination. For this Henrietta responded with an enigmatic smile and a brusque nod. What her thoughts might have been as she conveyed to Turchin's house this man she suspected to have more than a casual interest in Turchin's wife, she carefully refrained from airing. That she might have had, perhaps, a secret longing for Turchin beside her rather than the baron, she also concealed carefully from Trofimov, who remained in complete ignorance of her recent encounter with the colonel.

"How well, Madame Morrison, are you acquainted with Senator Vallandigham?" he inquired after a long silence had ensued.

"Well enough not to like the gentleman," she returned with more directness than she usually employed when the slightest denigration was intended.

"I think him a man of unusual perspicacity and power," said he.

"Some scoundrels have the virtue of believing, at least in their own sincerity. I should not hazard as much for Senator Vallandigham."

"The more credit then, to such a man, for succeeding in winning many supporters. There are thousands of persons who would follow him blindly."

"So he says', she answered wryly. "It is peculiar that you yourself, astute and observant, fail to note a most common device utilized not only by him, but by many others we have to suffer. No matter what they say, so long as it serves their ends, they have only to say it often enough to convince first one and then another; or if they do not convince, then they succeed even better in that they demolish the security which reposed in their listener's mind ere they instilled hate and suspicion."

The baron laughed unpleasantly. He disliked women with a turn for words, unless those words were designed to transmit what he believed the proper purpose; emotions and feelings relative to himself or to men in general. The way Mrs. Morrison delivered her opinions, without much hesitancy; the way her eyes shone with a fighting challenge; the line her otherwise lovely mouth made of itself, as though to demonstrate will and forcefulness; all united to antagonize him. He knew but few ways to relate to such a woman, either to pique her vanity or rouse her envy and jealousy. These methods were of no avail to him, with a lady on whom his presence had no effect, and so he finally lapsed into as non-communicative a mood as hers, and she was in no hurry to disturb it.

CHAPTER XIII

The days dragged on without realizing for Turchin the speedy appointment he was so confident of receiving. He continued to hold his position with the railroad, although the work had grown distasteful to him, as it would to anyone, he reasoned, who felt himself wasted in this sort of occupation when a higher duty called him elsewhere. It was not that he failed to esteem the railroads for the important role they were playing during the preparation and prosecution of the war. It was that he saw a more urgent and more immediate necessity to organize an army, where nothing fit to be called by that name now existed. It required more than hot words and balled fists to effect a military situation. Mr. Lincoln would need more than so many dead men, no matter how valorously they died, to accomplish his purpose, Union, which at this stage, Turchin accepted without question. He was willing in his thinking, to keep the subject of slavery in abeyance, as though he had a sure knowledge that, with the struggle openly waged in the field and in Congress, with the land united against the exponents of a slave economy, with a decisive victory obtained on the battlefields, much more than formal terms of peace must emerge. More specifically, the end of a loathsome toleration of slavery which could not endure once the nation won a people's war for Union and freedom.

McClellan was already in uniform; Banks was also properly serving Mr. Lincoln. Why were those in the state house, so slow to allocate him? "When war comes, then the warrior is more important that the statesman," he argued with Nadine, who insisted he remain calm and patient. Anything else she may have felt in her heart these days she wisely kept to herself, for she had come to the conclusion that whatever her husband decided to do would be her way, also. The fleeting pleasures she had known in the fall were now entirely dissipated. The winter, with Turchin's absorption in the election and Secession, had left her lonely indeed, with only Mrs. Morrison's infrequent visits to warm and cheer her. The spring and the war further isolated her. Not intentionally, had Mrs. Morrison lessened the intimacy which Nadine had hoped would increase. That young woman, like Turchin, had been swept out of her accustomed social duties by the problems she took more seriously than many women of her kind. She continued to call fairly often, but seemed unable to extend her hospitality in return, as had at first seemed probable. She worked tirelessly at the Tribune, with whose editors she was particularly friendly and with whom she often spoke in whispers of the conspiracy she intimated seemed a-brewing in the circle of her cousin, Brewster's acquaintances. "We may not presume to name as traitors such men as saw fit to oppose the President," she said once, "for some of those same men, now that a national crisis is on hand, openly take their stand beside Mr. Lincoln; like Mr. Douglas, for example."

Joseph Medill, a man with a kindly mouth, sat in deep folds of worry and anxiety and patted her on the shoulder. Henrietta was a special favorite of his and he welcomed her contributions in his paper, the Chicago Daily Tribune, though for the most part, he discouraged women's participation in journalistic pursuits. Medill was a strong anti-slavery man and often braved his publisher's wrath on questions of policy with regard to the war and political partisanship. Throughout the Senatorial campaign of '58 he had been strongly in favor of Mr. Lincoln and during the presidential election was one of his most ardent protagonists, which part he continued to play in the succeeding years. Particularly he was pleased with Mrs. Morrison at this time because he admired her independence in openly disagreeing with her powerful cousin, Brewster, whom she affronted by her passionate democracy which was galling to that tycoon. Brewster, who for his own mysterious reasons still permitted her association with his household and even sourly engaged her himself in controversies, the nature of which he left her to guess. She tried little to fathom his intent and cared less for his dubious indulgence.

Brewster had, soon after the election, joined the Republican ranks, as he had promised Vallandigham to do and this he disclosed, in Henrietta's presence, to his good friend William Storey, who was editor of the Chicago Times, a paper openly hostile to Mr. Lincoln and the Republicans. Mr. Storey had listened with a broad grin on his face, a grin which added no sweetness to the hard-bitten lines sitting oddly upon a face crowned with fatherly gray hairs. "Perhaps, Brewster, you had better be careful," he joked heavily. "Mrs. Morrison works for my competitor. Medill is scarcely fond of me and I dare say, even somewhat afraid of me!"

"Mr. Medill is afraid of no one," she retorted sharply. "If he has any fears at all, they are the fears any true patriot feels; that not our enemies, but our friends, reside within the wooden horse!"

Mr. Storey and Mr. Brewster exchanged knowing, patronizing glances and then blandly commended the young woman for her knowledge of the Classics and for her astuteness in quoting oppositely when it suited her, regardless of the soundness of the facts she hurled about, wounding as she would.

Listening to Mr. Storey discount thusly, she bit her lip in vexation and resolved to hold her tongue in better check.

"Mr. Brewster tells me Medill has the advantage over me in having secured the services of the accomplished Baron Trofimov," Storey suddenly changed the subject. "Why did you not send him to me, Brewster?"

"I shall be delighted to inform the baron that you have been so good as to make him an offer," said Henrietta before taking her leave. She was followed into the hall by the hearty laughter of the two men.

From this house she had gone to the Turchin's where luckily she found the colonel just returned. "No news yet?" she inquired pleasantly, while pulling off her gloves.

"He is too impatient," said Nadine. He goes every day to the station yard and judges hastily from what he sees there, which is exactly what one would expect to see when a country first begins to mobilize for an unexpected outbreak of war: confusion and a lack of that martial discipline the colonel deems absolutely essential. He frets about it all day and all night," she sighed and smiled faintly at Mrs. Morrison.

"It is something to worry about when I see our boys sent off daily, to camps which are not camps, for training which is no training." Turchin made no effort in this humor, to play the host and indicated clearly that the inexplicable delay, as far as he could reason it out, was irritating to him. "I need not tell you Mrs. Morrison, how loyal I am to Mr. Lincoln, nor how I feel about this terrible Armageddon now come upon us. But just the same, what is a soldier to think when he realizes that it is civil direction for the prosecution of this war against rebellion and not military planning our untrained troops have to depend on?" He began to walk to and fro in the small sitting room where they were warming themselves against a late spring chill at the low fire in the mantle. After a few minutes, during which Nadine assembled her tea things and samovar, Mrs. Morrison took her favorite seat near the bay window, Turchin once more attacked the topic closest to his heart. "Now, though I respect Mr. Lincoln's judgment highly - and I hear he was a soldier for a while in the Indian Wars - I find myself unable to understand why he and others in Congress seem more anxious to send troops, raw troops, at that, into our neighboring loyal States instead of training our men and guns on our enemies. Mrs. Morrison, do you see much sense in sending troops among our friends?"

"You run the risk of falling into the trap Mr. Storey and Mr. Brewster spread out temptingly for all who are easily discouraged," Mrs. Morrison said less gently than was her wont in speaking with her friend. Having just come from the presence of her cousin, her mind was still somewhat angered and on the defensive. "Loyalty means, my dear colonel, at least for a simple woman like me," she was led to smile, realizing the sharpness of her tone, "the determination to accept the wisdom of a leader, until it becomes feasible to publicize his reason for his actions. We select a given leader only because we attribute to him more aptitude in holding together the intricate threads of our political lives than we are able to muster for ourselves individually. What, Colonel Turchin, do you suppose would happen to this entire region, where our resistance to the rebels is most important, should our Border States join the secessionists?" She smiled appealingly now and immediately he felt a glow of admiration for her; not realizing that he truly appreciated the last yieldingly feminine admission implied by her question; that she ultimately relied on him to supply troublesome answers.

"Yes. I see that now! Of course! How right is Mr. Lincoln! I know from their proximity to the slave region that the Border States verge on loyalty to both the slavery interests and ours. Naturally there are bound to be disloyal contingents within those States themselves which must be resisted." He fell into deep thought for a few minutes while the two women exchanged amused glances resulting in mutual smiles. "I should have seen this before!" he exclaimed happily, his brow clearing amazingly, leaving the fair face alight with a peacefulness it displayed whenever he succeeded to a final clarified conviction. "Yes, sending troops first of all to Cairo, Illinois has definite meaning now. Good military meaning!" he concluded with approval. "From now on I shall have the sort of faith in Mr. Lincoln that you mentioned, Mrs. Morrison."

From then on he viewed the initial movements at Cairo with a consummate interest, seeing the strategical importance of gaining at once this vital point of juncture for road and river traffic which was to play so indispensable a part in the western campaigns. The Mississippi and the Ohio Rivers conjoined at that point and constituted a vital position for the movement of Northern shipping and supplies, as well as for Southern commerce. The South would logically be supposed to attempt the securing of this river juncture at the very outset of hostilities.

More than ever Turchin longed to join the men at Cairo, to share with them the problems in facing the emerging fighting force of the rebels. He hoped especially to be assigned to the Infantry, for he had an aversion to cavalry duty which at first might appear odd indeed, he being admittedly a skilled horsemen and the new Northern army requiring a cavalry almost more than any other branch of service. In those early days of army organization, the cavalry performed in the field much of the duties of reconnaissance which later days and customs allocated to Secret Intelligence. The cavalry also served as the advance scouting parties so necessary to reconnoiter the terrain and the general topography which was not adequately mapped or charted. Often during maneuvers a whole army moved by instinct and guess work rather than by detailed planning, which was found wanting in those early months of the war.

Despite this, the extent to which Turchin guessed at, he preferred active duty with the infantry; for to him this arm of the service represented the field in which he felt able to exercise his highest skill. Besides that, he truly preferred to work with the concrete human being he was called upon to mold and direct, than the paper work of an officer in other capacities. There was a peculiar dislike, resident in him for many years, of leading horses into battle. Animals had always held a high place in his regard, mainly because they were inarticulate to a large extent and were consequently dependent upon human will to control their destinies. He had learned of the meager preparations made for the boys at Cairo in the matter of quartering and provisioning and he was filled with impatient anger because of it. How much more so would the plight of horses have affected him, had he known then how, during the war, animals were often forced to endure even greater hardships then the men. If food were lacking, they at least could find some solace and consolation in a common cause and the companionship rising out of mutual sentience by the light of a camp fire crackling in a mist of smoke from wood and tobacco.

At Cairo, the newspapers reported, after the first contingents of soldiers had arrived, that there were only a few vacant cattle sheds in which to house the men. No provisions for the life of a camp were made in the desperate haste with which recruiting officers dispatched those men to their stations. It was no unusual event to see advertisements, in the newspapers, for such common items of daily use as cooking utensils and basic bed clothing, asked for individually by the men.

Appeals of this sort wrung his heart and caused him to bestir himself without stint in order to secure supplies, or promises of such, from everyone whom he encountered, not forgetting even unlikely prospects like Brewster into whose office he strode one day and boldly solicited aid for the boys at Cairo. This temerity and officiousness surprised Mr. Brewster who, under no circumstances, would have demeaned himself, as he afterward said, before those who had plainly shown him coolness socially. He allowed to the Russian, a measure of pride, nevertheless and was compelled to recognize another motive for his appearance in his office rather than a mere method to push himself forward on one pretext or another. Watching Turchin's eyes he could almost believe him unselfishness, but not quite. Not easily prevailed upon himself, he was unable to believe in anyone's selflessness, especially when it appeared to transcend self-esteem. His own eyes gleaned with satisfaction and contempt.

It is to be doubted whether for any cause, other than to help the soldiers, the colonel would have consented to visit Roger Brewster's premises. Yet, his coming to this rich man was understandably simple. He himself was a man of limited means. He gave more than Nadine felt they could afford to do. Nor did he scruple to make it sternly clear that he was willing to give until he literally hurt, until he ached all over. "What is giving at a time like this, but the best investment a sane man can make?" For which passionate intellection he received only her reproachful sighs, however well she might think to understand his emotions. She was willing to give lavishly; she would give of herself, her time, her work, her money; but she was not willing to give until she herself approached the line separating the giver from the receiver. "Things should be done circumspectly," she frequently murmured. "There are Americans better able to give of their substance than we, who have barely enough to keep us from being pauperized. After all, it is their country, surely, Ivan, as much as it is yours." He missed the touch of irony her words held and caught instead the hopeful implication of them. It was this sudden new source of help for the soldiers which induced him to seek out wealthy citizens on behalf of those he hoped soon to have under his command.

Outwardly, Brewster received him courteously, even invited him to take a seat. He listened carefully and politely while Turchin explained his mission. After listening attentively, he shook his head and informed him that in his opinion it was a mean reflection on the military capacity of the White House, that private citizens should be subject to abuse in their own homes, being made to seem picayune by appeals to their charity. When private citizens were badgered for saucepans, it was time the government considered its means to wage war before striking its pompous and meaningless poses. "As a matter of fact, however," he added as he saw the darkening anger on the other's face, "I feel that I have already done a fair share in that way. I and many others that I know of generously supported the State Militia and were not loath to equip what we considered a reasonable number of riflemen. I must own to you, colonel, that I can not countenance this war brought upon us by unscrupulous power politicians, who would have us believe that to slaughter our dear children is the end of true patriotism! This is nothing but utter madness! Believe me, for we are miserably inferior to those gallant and able Southerners." He paused and turned a serious face to Turchin, whose face showed incredulity and astonishment.

"You are not an American, Sir," he continued and you have no feelings about this sort of war, comparable to ours, who know those people whom some are pleased to call our enemies. I am as good an American as any. My people blazed the trails over which your company is laying its iron rails. Your Mr. Lincoln himself is originally a Southerner, as are my ancestors. Is it not reasonable to suppose that, if millions of our brethren claim a right, are willing to die to defend that right, we ought to listen to them, at least as open-mindedly as we listen to a lawyer who proposes to interpret the will of God himself! Would God wish us to exterminate our own countrymen?"

The other made no reply to this disquisition, but rose, without a bow or other sign of courtesy and stalked out of the sumptuous room. His mind was seething with rage and outrage, yet he was undaunted in his efforts, never believing for a moment but that Brewster stood alone in his flagrant disloyalty. Resolutely he approached other men of prominence and money, but with few variations received almost entirely the same response, if not worded so boldly, nonetheless purporting to be righteously aloof. If a mad government performs mad deeds, the sane elements of a community need not condone the procedure. It was an American's privilege to speak his mind and operate as his conscience decreed. This is what in substance he learned from most of the men he interviewed.

From Mr. Storey, oddly enough, he received a promise of monetary assistance and that gentleman gave his promise with a mockery which made his liberality gall to Turchin. "I have been most opposed to Mr. Lincoln," Storey stated blandly, "and this lamentable condition at Cairo only proves my contention that an incompetent sits where we need a man of vision, tolerance, and balance. But I shall contribute something, not for Mr. Lincoln, but for this State which is very dear to me. You see, Colonel Turchin, we Americans are not like you Europeans. We feel that true patriotism begins at home, literally, right at home. We love our State first, then our country. We were originally so organized as sovereign States." He was expansive and not quite so offensive in manner as his friend Brewster from whom he had, of course, already received some hints as to this Russian colonel. "Now take that excellent General Lee from Virginia. Do you happen to know that Mr. Lincoln would have been grateful to heaven if such a commander had consented to take the position which I know on good authority, was offered him? Do you think General Lee was insensitive of the honor a promotion of this stamp would have brought with it? But no! He chose the way of a true soldier and true American. As his State went, so went he, not that he loses much thereby. I am fully confident that General Lee will stand to gain both honor and glory by the time this matter is settled, once and for all." His words said not half so much as his tone implied and from him Turchin went with heavy heart and many natural misgivings for Mr. Lincoln's sake; Mr. Lincoln who was less popular to Mr. Storey than a rebel general!

Among the employees of the railroad and among the workers of the newspapers, from small shopkeepers and saloonkeepers whom he next applied to, he managed to accrue a bountiful supply of goods and moneys which Mrs. Morrison, who herself had given a large portion monies, helped him dispatch anonymously to the boys at Cairo. Even Trofimov, though he accompanied his promise of assistance with many stinging observations not dissimilar to Mr. Brewster's, was led to match Mr. Storey, if not for the same reason, at least for the same amount. "This overweening paternalism is a mere gesture impressing no one," he said to Nadine when the colonel had rushed off to attend to some further business. "Is this the manner in which a people hopes to equip an army? Are private citizens to be molested and embarrassed continuously while this regional strife lasts?"

"He is like a man possessed over it," she answered resignedly. Then, catching Trofimov's leaping glance, she hastened to add, "But it is his life; he is never happy thinking only of himself. The situation, with which he sees a land he loves confronted, becomes a personal matter to him." She glanced with uneasiness at Trofimov and the uneasiness was not on Turchin's account. It was on her own, because she vibrated to the baron's vitality, which was like the advent of a spring day. She had never seen him so handsome and vivacious. Even the scornful phrases, which her remarks evoked from him, seemed charming, coming from his smiling mouth; for with Nadine, no matter what topic they discussed, he never departed from the old world graciousness which was indeed genuine for her.

"Almost I wish his commission were here and he gone!" burst from him suddenly and he took a determined step toward her. She evaded him by sitting down quickly in the nearest chair where he followed her and before which he planted himself, looking down at her with as tender an authority as her indulgence permitted. "You will not of course, go with him, will you?" His voice betrayed both his desire and his uncertainty. He recalled how she had on former occasions participated in Turchin's campaigns.

For a long time she made no reply to this. She had given much thought to this same question even since Nathaniel Banks had written the governor on Turchin's behalf. The fact that she had pioneered the question at all troubled her. Before, there had never been a doubt as to her choice in matters of this sort. She had been his willing companion in the Crimean campaign and had just as willingly shared his rough life in wintery Poland the year before they had immigrated to the United States. But now the scenes her mind depicted in advance, represented a mass of confusions and unfamiliarities with which she was fearful to cope. At any rate this was her first explanation which she discarded when her honesty revealed the truer motive for her slow willingness to follow her husband when his call to duty should come. Her conscience upbraided her, forced her to speak at least part of the truth, namely, that she was reluctant to leave Chicago where the baron's company alone compensated her for the alien world in which she could not, as wholeheartedly as her husband, abandon herself and what she had been. Further than this she could not probe; that she had conceived a deep attachment for the baron, so deep that it threatened to break for her a habit she had followed since her marriage; that it appeared to her almost more cruel to see nothing of him than to part with Ivan. In women with as high a moral turn as hers, with as sensitive a response to the highest ideals one could arrange to preserve, to have knowingly entertained these feelings would have been tantamount to an admission of treachery and abasement.

At last she looked directly into Trofimov's questioning dark eyes and answered his question firmly. "Wherever Ivan wishes me to go, there shall it be my desire to go. I do not feel about these matters as he does and were it seemly for a wife to criticize her husband, I should feel free to criticize Ivan. But it is not and I do not, save only where I have the hope to mitigate some of his enthusiasms. Even when it is difficult for me, for always he has me confounded, when I must confess that it is justice and right that impel him; then I, too, must applaud at least the intention with which he stands up against evils he will not call by other names than evil."

"Oh, his intentions are solemnly grand, I agree," Trofimov sulked. He turned away angrily and took a sullen stand at the window from which he could look out upon her small garden which was beginning to bloom with the delicate new flowers she loved. He threw back the shutters and drew a deep breath of the spring-laden air and fancied it was the accent of violets he breathed, though in truth, it was nothing but the steady, gentle intoxication he experienced in her beloved presence. Where she was, was always spring for his wayward heart and like a distant voice caught on the mild winds, he seemed to hear such facts declared. If he felt a brief satisfaction with this, he confessed it in no way, keeping his back turned upon her in such a young stubbornness, that she, watching him longingly, smiled. As if it were secretly given her to comprehend his unspoken thoughts and feelings, she divined his emotion.

"The trouble with men like Colonel Turchin," he turned and confronted her steady glance, "is that they are so infernally perfect. Such perfection is insipid as well as false! Even the rarest beauty is appealing only when some touch of imperfection exists in it to describe it by contrasts!"

"Oh, Ivan has his flaws," she stated positively. "There is no more contrite sound than his when he is conscious of error."

"When?", Trofimov laughed harshly. "He takes my patience when I try to make him see sense. Nadine, to what heights might his abilities carry him if he would but listen to reason! But no, he must play the hero, the avenging angel, Prometheus bringing immortal fire to clay! Brewster could do much for such a man if he were not so damned righteous! It is every man's duty to make the most of himself, not worry about the next fellow's chances!"

"I cannot agree entirely with you, Dimitri," she sighed softly. "A little of each of you, I think, makes a better whole than all of either of you. Though," she laughed a clear merry laughter, which tingled through him pleasantly, making him think in sudden contrast, of the nervous shudder Susan's voice induced," If one has to have simply one set of qualities, I believe I should prefer Ivan's!"

"You lie atrociously, Nadine!" he retorted disbelievingly, taking two strides toward her.

They were at this point interrupted by the return of Turchin, who now came in with a transfigured face. He had received good news at the recruiting office and was heartened by the early prospect of joining his men. He thought of the boys in the 19th Regiment as his, for he was reasonably assured that of this regiment he might receive the colonelcy promised him. What additionally pleased him and made him a joyous companion this day was the astonishing intelligence concerning the present colonel of the regiment designated for his command. Colonel J.R. Scott was a young man in his early twenties and already much beloved of the men who had enlisted with him in May. Colonel Scott, upon hearing of the contemplated assignment of Turchin, offered at once to resign his command in order to facilitate the appointment of Turchin. He had heard, through various reports, that the Russian's considerable experience in warfare, must make him a valuable acquisition to the regiment and therefore, in sincere patriotism, exercised every zeal to secure him, even offering to take second command in the regiment if this would entice the colonel to accept immediately.

Nothing could have rewarded Turchin more than this appreciation from an unknown and unseen man. He could speak of nothing else for days and weeks thereafter.

The summer was fast coming upon them, a hot, muggy summer, which promised little pleasure for any of them. They all lived in the tenseness of expectancy, aggravated by the idleness Turchin endured during the few weeks before his duties actually began. He had already given up his position at the Railroad which, though deploring their loss of him, praised him for his loyalty to the country and proudly added his name to the long list of employees already serving the colors. It was quite natural that the most advanced technological organization of the day should be called upon to furnish a disproportionate number of its employees, these being largely men with engineering skill, so sadly wanting these days when there were rails to lay, bridges to build and repair and roads to cut through wilderness and rough terrain, to mention only a few of the tasks.

One day in June, the whole city was shocked with the electrifying news that its idol, Stephen Douglas, he whom the people fondly called the Little Giant, he whom the city honored greatly in spite of the fact that he had opposed Lincoln, was dead of typhoid fever. He had been among the first to outline by his meritorious and exemplary behavior, the pattern of true patriotism, when he rose above party disputes to support the Union. The news of his death affected friend and foe alike, but especially it attained a deep significance for those already disheartened by the inauspicious beginnings of the war which was as yet accomplishing more signal triumphs in the newspapers and lecture halls than on any battlefields, a fact made much of by the political orators and writers in Brewster's secret "Knights of the Golden Circle". In the passing of so likeable a politician, they made hustle to see a portent of things to come, a diminution of the Union's chances to subdue the South. And these calculated pessimisms had the desired effect. When the funeral procession marched with the dead statesman's bier, a saddened city followed disconsolately even though men like the Tribune's Joseph Medill, had hurriedly published as many encouraging facts of the war's progress as could be obtained. The Tribune described the victorious encounters the Cairo men had had with enemy craft, the amounts of small arms and stores seized from rebel boats plying the Mississippi, a river boat rammed and taken prisoner. But this was a feeble substitute for the beneficent voice of Douglas whose loss the army mourned as did the citizens. Several regiments were ordered to return from Cairo in order to escort the bier and to symbolize a nation's grief and respect for the loss of a noble son.

Nadine, Turchin and Mrs. Morrison attended the funeral ceremonies in order to observe the honors bestowed upon the distinguished senator and leader. They followed the slow procession through the city decorated fittingly to commemorate a good and great man. The troops stationed themselves south of the University where a camp, later to be called Camp Douglas, was created. Here the three friends stood and paid deep reverence to an honorable American. No one felt inclined to words. The evening dusk, the soldiers relaxing after their long hours of marching, the doleful aura of the city, reduced them each to his private sadness. As the crowds began to thin and disperse, they suddenly heard the clatter of horses nearby and discovered that the Brewster family had just arrived. Mrs. Morrison smiled wryly and remarked to Madame Turchin that her cousins always managed to sit in at the last round, "just to be counted; a quaint custom some of us natives have."

With them was Trofimov who was in Susan's good graces this day, a fact Nadine noticed with one brief glance.

"I say, it is unfortunately the wrong men who die too soon," Brewster remarked by way of greeting when the two parties bowed.

"I agree with Mr. Brewster," Turchin spoke loudly and distinctly. "The wrong men die too soon!"

CHAPTER XIV

At long last the assignment to duty arrived and both Nadine and the colonel made ready to join his men. Their books, the violin and the samovar, without which she would not stir, were all packed and ready. The gowns which she had brought with her five years previously, were all neatly stowed away in wooden chests which were to remain in the house, which they had purchased with a mortgage loan and which they were assured, would be taken care of by Trofimov who offered this service with a touch of embarrassment, never quite knowing in what manner Turchin might receive an offer of assistance. To his surprise Turchin was grateful and took his hand with such unfeigned friendliness that a small disgust immediately rose in Trofimov, who somehow could never forgive the generosity of spirit which moved his friend. With a curious directness he allowed that the colonel had cause indeed to name him other than friend. Some remnant of old fashioned honor reminded him that by coveting his friend's wife, he was forfeiting any claim to affection, especially Turchin's, who was too ingenuous to conceive of base feelings in the bosom of a man who entered his house as a friend. Sometimes the baron wished that Colonel Turchin would surmise what desires lay in him and forbid him the house. Discovery would be a solution, would settle affairs, be something definite, and put an end to the romance which seemed without inception or conclusion.

There were times when the baron strove to remain absent from Nadine's presence. Often, when driven toward Division St., he would utter a muffled imprecation, order the cab driver to turn about and deposit him before some saloon where infamous women with execrable manners served to detain him until he was certain it was too late to make his contemplated call.

When it was plain that Nadine was to accompany her husband, the baron was both relieved and disaffected. He suddenly found the entire city an unlovely place to be; found no spot where he could enjoy what always seemed palpably simple, when at the back of his mind, he was cognizant of Nadine's presence not too far way. In his newspaper work he took such slight interest these days that his dismissal came with no surprise. As a matter of fact, Brewster had decided that his efforts were more useful as agent of the Secret Society which was flourishing splendidly since the outbreak of the war, than in the newspaper work. Brewster's hold varied in its strength upon Trofimov, who would as well have expended himself and his talents on behalf of the one or the other party to any dispute, so long as he personally stood to gain. Not so much safety of his person, as safety of his security, bothered him. In reality, he was not a pusillanimous man and had more than once in his career crossed swords with a haughty challenger who had regretted the day. His prowess with a pistol was noteworthy and he might have boasted as steady an eye and finger as Turchin; yet without as much truthfulness could he have withstood the rigors which a disciplined life might have demanded of him.

There were days when Trofimov felt for his colleague much the sort of contempt Turchin had shown for Brewster on first collision with him. These days came mostly when he felt himself more drawn to Nadine than to the blooming, bursting Susan, whose vacillating moods were trying to her suitor and continued endurable only because her fortune cast a wide shadow. At length, driven by a discontent which resulted from Nadine's decision to follow her husband, he brought himself to make a formal request for Susan's hand. This proposal had been so long expected, that no one showed surprise, least of all Susan, who still fancied a title of nobility as rather smart and distinctive. It fretted her only that her friends now found military titles more intriguing; that Ellen Marcy should be the wife of a general; that even the pale and bloodless Russian lady, as she referred to Nadine, should be the wife of a colonel, that no one seemed envious of her contemplated elevation to the dubious rank of baroness.

Following the happy consummation of this match, Trofimov was to engage in certain business transactions which, Brewster said plainly, would give him sufficient income to keep Susan satisfied until she should come into his money.

"I can't see what is so important in papa's Secret Society to warrant your constant attention," Trofimov's new fiancée said one evening, as they were returning from a farewell visit to the Turchins. The occasion afforded Susan scope to indulge her malice and unrestrained humor respecting the drab and poor dwelling on Division Street. "A place not fit for a servant," she said, "and just what could be expected to produce Union officers. I think it would look very well indeed if you went into the army. You'd look more distinguished than mama's Muscovite. An army ought to have only handsome men in it."

"Which army would you prefer me to join, my sweet?" he asked with heavy sarcasm.

"Oh," she replied, missing the barb in his question, "I suppose it doesn't really matter, though I should imagine since Ellen's husband is a Federal, you might be with General Lee, only then you'd be likely to run poor General McClellan right back into Ohio." She laughed brittlely and cast a long sidewise glance at her baron. "I do think you might spare his life, though Mrs. McClellan certainly offended us in Cincinnati."

"Well, settle yourself, my dear," was his sardonic advice, "for I take orders from your papa and he has other uses for me. He's never figured out how my presence in the army can benefit him, but I might suggest he try."

The fact that he made little effort to conceal his irritation with her father added to his charms; the lovely Susan having enough of her sire in her bones to enable her to enjoy the added flavor of the suppressed struggle which her baron made against her father. She did not of course really believe that true dislike lay between them; for she had never witnessed emotions other than dominance and submission, the former of which her father customarily displayed toward everyone. Herself headstrong, accustomed to her success in outwitting her father, in allaying his suspicions, in wheedling out of him her every wish, she relished the element of struggle and combat with him and looked upon contention as a natural concomitant to association with her father. How often she had stealthily on tip toes listened at the library door while her father castigated in cold fury one or another unfortunate, closeted there with him.

She thought of her father and his mysterious associates this day as she and Trofimov drove away from the Turchins. She also wondered why Mrs. Morrison had absented herself, being content to send merely a note in which she regretted her necessary occupation elsewhere. How sorely Turchin had seemed to miss her! How fondly he spoke of her! How vulgar of him to announce that she would be the first recipient of his letters! And though she chattered of other things, she was quite glad to see the last of Nadine.

At Camp Long, Turchin and his lady joined the men of the 19th Illinois Volunteers, the greater part of which had been sent from Cairo on the occasion of Senator Douglas' death a few weeks earlier. There were, of course, several companies other than Chicagoans in Turchin's regiment, but he viewed them collectively as a sort of extension, not only of the city, but of the new self he had become in that city. This feeling of paternal pride illumined his countenance when for the first time he came face to face with the companies, which were called out in review before their new leader. Several officers at first were predisposed to resent Turchin, due to a misplaced loyalty to what they called their "own sort" and viewed with hostility, the incursion of the Russian, as though he came not to aid them, but like the legendary tartar, to despoil them. Were it not for the frank approval and willing co-operation of their former colonel, young Scott, who was on hand to welcome Turchin and present him to the rest of the regiment's officers, reverberations of the officers' hostility might have become perceptible to the emotional Russian. As it was, he saw only what he desired.

"Men," the stalwart and beloved young Colonel Scott addressed the assembled companies, "we are fortunate in having this eminent soldier consent to teach us and lead us. I, for one, feel it an honor as well as my highest duty to obey him in every respect, to oblige him in every way suitable to the dignity of an American and a gentleman. Colonel Turchin has served the Czar of Russia with unassailable distinction; how much more he may serve us, a free people, depends upon us all."

After this eulogy, there was nothing for it but to accept the serious faced new commander who, standing tall and stiff before them, gave no inkling of the turbulent feelings with which his chest was choking. His eyes, looking over the thousand faces before him, saw not individual features; he saw the conglomeration of all that he elected to believe was the stuff of a new world, rich and poor, young and old, high families and low - all gathered together and united by a bond of unity which was more potent than the threat of a scourging whip or the fear of the rack or the wheel of torture. Free boys, young boys, with all their lives to live unhampered, as far as the wide expanse of the land permitted, voluntarily joined themselves together by a creed and a belief which were the embodiment of the deepest and holiest reverence; knowing without erudition or expostulation, that freedom and a way of life, wrested out of the darkness of ancient hatreds, were worth fighting for, even if the fight was against one's brother; knowing that a brother was not a blood relative alone, but only a brother if he stood with them, not against them, stood to preserve their freedom, the while he trusted them to preserve his.

Colonel Scott had taken second rank to Turchin, but judging by the glow on his face, an observer might have imagined he had just received a new promotion. He stood beside his superior and presented the entire staff to him, not excluding the Reverend Conant, who had been present when Mrs. Morrison had come to bid her protégé, Mihalotzy, farewell in the Dearborn Station. The minister as he shook hands with Turchin, at once recalled his person, though he did not betray his former glimpse of him, mainly because he remembered the darkly lovely lady on his arm then and was too tactful to make references of identification in the presence of the colonel's present lady, who gave him her hand with grace and sweetness which left nothing to be desired. The young officers were as much taken with Nadine as was Scott with his chief, to whom he hastened to expound upon the innate virtues of these men who would in time be a fine fighting unit. "We have not all raw recruits," he boasted boyishly. "The Chicago Zuaves, of whom you may have heard, colonel, form part of this unit."

"We shall have the best drilled and best trained and healthiest men in the army," Turchin promised instantly and with a brisk order, he demanded that every man in the entire regiment file past him. With each man, whose name he repeated with a smile, he eagerly shook hands and managed to convey almost to each of them that the handclasp was a covenant of friendship, "Each of you is an important person," his handgrip seemed to imply. "Each man here is my friend!" A line of Whitman's poem flashed through his mind as he stood beside Colonel Scott and received his official welcome: "Passing Stranger! You do not know how longingly I look upon you!" Yes, each man before him was one he looked upon longingly, not patronizingly but longingly; wanting to know him, wanting to shield him with his greater knowledge, wanting to join him in the expression of unbending loyalty to Mr. Lincoln and the United States of America.

If the informality of his first greeting elicited varying shades of regard from his men, the impromptu address he delivered later in the day won him, at least among the rank and file, spontaneous respect and trust, which, in many cases, endured throughout his affiliation with this regiment and even longer. The review was over and the men stood awkwardly in the hot sun of the day. Nadine and the minister were chatting under a tree which stood on a small hillock. Here Turchin joined her and ordered the men to fall out. "You are at ease, men," he began in an ordinary tone of voice, "But before you go to spend the rest of the day as you please, let me say this to you: It is my honor and duty before God and my fellow citizens to instruct you and lead you safely, wherever the exigencies of this war may dictate. It will be my highest reward if, through the time we are bound in our common duty to this magnificent land of ours, you men will deem me worthy of your confidence and trust, your faith that I shall be unremitting in my services to all of you without consideration of rank. I believe all honest men equal and equal to the restrictions which order and discipline impose on everyone. You are all able and loyal men, else why would you be here? Mine is the duty, before God, to add my might to your much; to make you valuable instruments in the saving, not only of your lives, but of your country; and the saving of the one is the true saving of the other. Let us not underestimate ourselves. War makes men ruthless, driven out of themselves; let us therefore be ruthless in the right!"

Several junior officers frowned upon this manner of address to the men in the ranks. Such a freedom of speech, such imputed fraternization, boded no good for the formation of an army where already the rules were slack enough, where the material being molded into a fighting force was an independent country stock of boys, who would as lief walk home as not should they feel themselves affronted or curbed in the natural liberties they stood ready to defend. The President's war proclamation had asked for ninety-day volunteers, which left the officers little more to work with than the basic good will of the soldiers, on which they had to rely during this period and with which they hoped to gain a quick service. But few had the sanguine hope that the rebellion would be under control when the enlistment period was over. There was no way in which to coerce men to remain longer than their volunteered period of service, since no conscription law existed. And it was not until the following year that such a measure was introduced into Congress.

Turchin discussed this problem of voluntary military service with young Scott, who pointed out this was a uniquely American trait in conscription. "What, do you mean that with war declared, nothing is being done to ensure our victory?" He was incredulous. "We no sooner beat the hay out of their hair than we lose the soldiers and acquire a new crop of untrained boys?"

When Scott laughed and shrugged his shoulders, he grew serious and lapsed into troubled thought. At last he brightened up and asseverated strongly that in his regiment, no American would think to lay down his arms without having used them first in the defense of his country. "We will so train our men that they shall scorn returning home while a single rebel still lives to fire upon us! We shall so appeal to the loyalty and manhood of every soldier under our command, that no hardships will frighten him back to the family fireplace until every man in America is free to return to his own."

Perhaps somewhat highhandedly, but certainly with a will and a purpose, Turchin began to shape his regiment into the fighting force it afterward became; one of the best in the entire army. For one solid month he drilled his boys until they nearly dropped in their tracks and often cursed him saltily for his pains and theirs. When they were not marching and drilling, they were digging and cleaning and scrubbing and shining until they grew disgruntled, finding in these homely chores but little of the glamour they had envisaged when the first flush of wrath and patriotic indignation had called them, whether from the fields and plains of the country or from the shops and offices of the city. Many indeed were pallid and ill postured, which fact such papers as the Times made much of in contrasting the unpretentious Union soldiers with the vaunted hardihood of the Southern soldiery, reputed to be both better equipped and better endowed by nature for the conflict, which as yet raged more fiercely in words than in deeds. "You may not see the immediate need for the rigorous training," he told several officers who objected that his publicized methods were preventing enlistments in the regiment and were likely to drive home the lads who wanted to fight and who were not happy cleaning sanitary wells and cisterns. "Yet these same grumblers will thank us some day for preparing them to put up a good fight, not to yield their lives cheaply. A victory is significant when the cost to life and limb are at the minimum!"

In time the regulars grew fond of their colonel, who was not above joining them in some of their meanest chores and who often treated them to a series of stories which, when repeated from company to company, gained him the reputation, not only for a spirited will, but for a great sense of humor. Added to this was his quaint combination of tigerish accuracy and uncompromising demand for exact detail, the noncompliance with which was enough to transform his smiling countenance into a mask of fierceness warranted to frighten the hardiest man. But if these mannerisms estranged his men one day, the next they readily forgave him, when with a fine spontaneity, he brought forth his violin and played for them, at their request, even the new melodies he had learned in Chicago.

In these musical hours, the chaplain heartily joined Turchin and often, they enjoyably discussed music, for the Reverend Conant had a rare appreciation not only for the medium of music for its own sake, but for its part in the subjugation of the less amenable qualities comprising the human being. The minister was fiery in theory, but gentle and latitudinarian in practice, being willing, nay anxious, on occasion, to give the fallible mortal a second and third chance to redeem himself. In music, as he said to Colonel Turchin, men had ready at hand the finest means devised, to speak the intentions of God. He was all the more ready to fall in with the Russian's plan to organize a vocal group in the regiment which would lead the men in singing. "When men lift their voices together, be it only to praise a pretty face", he spoke pleasantly and respectfully, "it is in effect like prayer. I have often observed how prayer seems of itself to justify and explain itself, when commonly supplicated in the humble unison of a congregation."

Turchin, growing ever fonder of the preacher, who at first had not appeared singular to him, unwittingly retaining a slight reserve with the clergy, on no surer or more reasonable grounds than that a professional sanctity prejudiced him, now beamed broadly. They had been playing chess in Turchin's tent where Nadine sat in her usual calm peacefulness and attended them quietly. "I know that feeling exactly, Sir," he answered. "I am not strictly a religious man, follow no prescribed doctrine, that is, but I have sat in the light, which pours through stained glass windows with almost a proof revealed in the holy effulgence and found myself believing, perhaps not in the ritualistic words, but in the noble spirit of that which lies beyond the light itself.

In this wise, a month of preparatory training and drilling passed. Turchin, no less than his officers or men, grew impatient under the lengthy delay preceding final allocation to duty. Camp Long was not designed for extended sojourns and man and beast grew restless as the hot summer sun of the daytime and the choking mugginess of the night, closed in upon them all. "The concept of war which obtained was," the colonel often remarked to his wife, "an unreal mirage, composed of their childish valor and inexperience. They are free men and sons of free men and this war is one of their choosing, lest they lose all choice. In a democracy it is so arranged, that a man feels convinced that he acts when he follows out the orders of those leaders he knows to have been elected. I am ready to do likewise, yet if orders come I shall have to state my opinion that my men are far from ready for active duty." He, more than distant authorities, had knowledge of the immediate realities of his regiment and the high toll which an inaccurate gauge of them might exact. Often during an evening, when the cheerful camp noises filled the air, creating the only stir in the motionless atmosphere, he walked slowly to the horse stalls and patted the beautifully curried animals who, like his young bucks in gold braid, reared their necks and longed for release. When at last, orders came to strike camp, he submitted, though grudgingly and made his men ready for their first field experience. This he expected to execute at Quincy, once they arrived there. At Quincy, Missouri he spread out his companies strategically for the performance of the routine duties consistent with the task assigned him, which was to guard the towns along this sector of the Mississippi River. He was to stand ready to relieve the 21st Illinois, stationed at Palmyra and Hannibal in Missouri. This regiment, then as obscure as Turchin's 19th, was commanded by an equally obscure colonel, Ulysses Grant. The two colonels met perforce and exchanged civilities. Grant wasted no time on ceremonious gestures and taking his cue from him, Turchin also confined himself to brief necessities. But each man in a moment had esteemed the other, for only one criterion weighed much with either: loyalty to the Cause they supported; the tremendous responsibility resting upon them, though they marched the remote westerly boundaries of the war theater, where no momentous battles were expected in 1861. The whole country, as well as the military high command, such as it was in those early days of the war, looked to Virginia and Maryland for whatever bloody struggles were to ensue. Here in Missouri the task for both Turchin and Grant, as well as the many other officers delegated to this area, was to guard the communication lines over the river, protect loyal citizens, prevent demolition of bridges and give the enemy tradesmen using the river as much trouble as possible.

Turchin's erstwhile friend, George McClellan, was now rising in favor with Mr. Lincoln and his Cabinet. To him had fallen the honor of heading the army which was expected to withstand that of General Lee, then massing troops over the border in Virginia. Turchin, completely reconciled to McClellan, for it was patent proof of the man's abiding loyalty and good faith. He had come forward as the sturdiest pillar for Mr. Lincoln's support and had longed for the opportunity to serve under him in the East. No spark of envy touched him that the younger man, a man who had been but a Captain, when first they met, should have now arisen to the post of the most pre-eminent defender of the Union. Perhaps the only personal emotion in him at this time, the only one which might have an element of pride in it, was the one growing out of the vindication which his first attachment to McClellan now received. It pleased him to have judged the young Captain correctly, to have believed that a good soldier presupposed a good human being.

What he did not reckon with, what became a stumbling block between him and many other officers in the army of Tennessee, was a code of behavior and tradition to which McClellan, as well as most of his contemporaries from West Point, were addicted and pledged by their training and instincts. This was so peculiarly American, so wrung from the mingled heritages deposited in the heirs of the Colonists, that it could not possibly have been apprehended by so logical a mind as the colonel's. Therein was a deep-seated regard for property for its own sake, for decency and personal value of the individual, any individual, which the officers wished operative, despite the war. "They want me to be gentle," Turchin Nadine in their tent one night. "They do not like my grim realism. But what is war but realism, which allows for no further compromise, which had done with fine surfaces and soft evasions?"

He was making special reference to the growing antagonism his brigade commander, General Hurlbut, was evincing toward him; for his doings, his familiarities, his unorthodox drills and activities had found their way, with piquant additions, to the brigadier general. Hurlbut was indubitably a fine regulation officer with a serious intention to do his duty as he had learned to do it. If he tended to domineering methods, he could easily be pardoned; for in those trying first months of the war, almost every commander was burdened with the necessity to undertake responsibilities which should have devolved upon a general staff. It was hardly the time for army innovations, Hurlbut charged. Moreover, he went so far as to threaten Turchin with a summary court-martial, should he defy regulations henceforth. He had become impatient and tired of the 19th's colonel's vehement clamoring for more and better camp equipment than was furnished to others. He had grown irritable at the colonel's incessant demand for better uniforms for the men, for more and better food, in fact even for better cooking.

Harassed as he felt himself to be, General Hurlbut in exasperation referred Turchin's inordinate demands and the reported disrespect he was reputed to have shown toward the property of the local gentry, to his superior, General John Pope, who arrived to inspect matters for himself. His arrival in camp caused Turchin no regrets or fears, but induced, instead, a passion of resentment against the blindness and uncomprehending stubbornness to which he ascribed such difficulties as he had been meeting with.

"Property!" he fumed to Nadine, "Is that all they think about? What do they think these men of mine are doing? Playing games? So a few of my reckless young ones take a few chickens from these fine patriots, who have not the grace of God in them, else they would bring those chickens to us and bring them ready-cooked. As it is, they reduce us to borrowing them. My lads merely borrowed a taste of fowl to keep their courage up and their homesickness down! Am I to spoil their every jollity by punishing them? Will not every man of them reflect on our hypocrisy, that we come to wage war on a rebel government, the while we esteem their property as sacred?"

His wife listened to him pensively. She, going about among the men in the camp, smiling and chatting with the artlessness which endeared her to everyone, was discomposed by none of these sentiments. More quickly than Turchin, she had apprised herself of the curious nature of these Americans. Nothing she discovered about their manners shocked her, for she expected all peoples to show differences and deviations. She did not labor under the delusion that the common experience necessarily brought common sympathies. She was more willing than her husband to allow for the operation of opposites; she had none of his passion for reconciliations. Turchin would reconcile what, by its own pristine qualities defied reconciliation; yet he would not reconcile himself to natural limitations; compromise was a hateful sin to him.

She finally interrupted the angry silence he had preserved after his outburst and opined that he himself, upon more mature reflection, must realize his error, which lay primarily in his excess of sympathies. "Not to do enough, dear colonel," she said, "as we all know is lamentable. To do too much can easily be construed to have other motives than yours, as a basis. As a soldier under Alexander you would hardly have exceeded the duties assigned you."

"My duty is to guide my men, to fight my enemy, to destroy him in the field!"

"Your chiefs have the same idea, or believe they have," she countered, feeling that it was important that Turchin see the nicety in the point she was about to make. "They are prepared to fight soldiers in the field; the farm at home, the chickens on that farm, the weeds themselves are not apparently opposed to them in the field. These Americans are not fighting the Southern people; they are fighting the rebel government."

"My boys do not feel that!"

"No," she agreed with a sigh. "Yet, because you are remiss in teaching them this distinction, you are summoned like a fledgling lieutenant to account for yourself to General Pope."

He was plainly grieved at her unexpected defense of such men as he privately and sometimes not so privately named disloyal. He saw only justification for his leniency toward his men when they stole food in the neighboring farmyards. He cared not a whit for the form and tradition of the officers, who fed not on stale bread and hard junk, as he put it, salt pork fat back and the meanest foods besides; those fine gentlefolk who upbraided him did not shiver at night under thin and insufficient blankets; they did not suffer themselves to be paraded about with ancient guns, rusty bayonets and cooking utensils not fit for jackals to dine from.

"I think what you have done is praiseworthy," she hastened to say, seeing his dismay. "But is it not unseemly for you, dear, to write vehement letters which Mrs. Morrison prints, decrying those conducting this campaign? Think of the dignity of your position! What has a colonel to do with demands for oilcloth and linens? Think how such doings reflect upon all?"

"That's it!" he retorted angrily. "He is concerned with appearances! The sufferings of men hungry and cold, forced to exist, not as men fighting to save our country, but as the meanest felons condemned to die, that is as nothing beside appearances! Are we supposed to impress ourselves? A battle for human liberties faces us and I am asked to worry about how I shall appear because I am not ashamed to act like a man and ask in the name of those who have less voice than I!"

In this frame of mind he was preparing himself to face General Pope, save that Nadine prevailed upon Colonel Scott to convince him otherwise, to temper his indignation, to persuade him to a more suitable demeanor and cooperation. Finally it was happily arranged, to everyone's satisfaction, that two or three men accused of chicken theft should own up to their crimes. These men appeared with Turchin and took upon themselves, the entire blame. If an unusual levity shone in their eyes the while they stood humble and contrite before the stern Pope, he at any rate missed the levity of their manner. The entire situation was cleared up.

Turchin did not cease to correspond with Mrs. Morrison, who had his permission to publish whatever portions of his letters that she deemed worthwhile. His letters after General Pope's visit, contained less complaint than formerly and more hopefulness that his regiment would soon be incorporated into the Army of the Potomac, where he was anxious to serve with McClellan. He had good reason to hope that such a change was imminent for him and the 19th Illinois and was constantly thinking of this expected change. One day his wife showed him a newspaper article written in response to his published advertisements for money and other help.

"I show you this," she said, "that you may see how futile your campaign is to alter things for those who see no fault in what grieves you." She held out the newspaper and he read that a certain lady from Chicago ventured to inquire of the editor "Why should Colonel Turchin's regiment be furnished with oilcloth or rubber blankets in preference to any other." The lady further asked, "Is not the pay of the soldier sufficient for them to make purchases of such necessary articles? And would they not take better care of them if they made the purchase with the ample pay allowed by the government?" ($13.00 per month)

Ripping the news sheet in two, he flung the pieces from him violently. This, if anything more could have done it, angered him to the point of distraction.

Nothing daunted, though in her heart she rather pitied him, Nadine picked the offending sheet up and matched the torn ends. "You may as well finish it," she said and when he shook his head, she decided to do so herself. "The lady concludes," she said laughingly and read, "In behalf of those who desire to have their sympathies and benevolent feelings directed into the right channel, will not some persons who are well-informed give us their views."

"Benevolent feelings! Sympathies! My God, Nadya, what sort of mother or wife could that be? Facts she wants! Give me a pen! Get me some paper! I myself shall tell her some facts! What does she think war is? Whom but her are we protecting, here in this marshy hinterland?"

"All people, you see, do not feel so strongly as you do," said Nadine.

"Let them think as they will when no emergency threatens us all. Let them think in two, in ten, in ten million ways, when we have given them the peace and the freedom to think at all. Until then, we who are soldiers are the chosen instruments with which justice is to be written. If we are weakened and crippled from behind, what sort of instruments of justice will she or they have?"

To this tirade his wife merely answered that he had little patience with the human race, a fact which cast oblique reflections on the nature of his love for it. And he refuted this by claiming, that only with such purposefulness as his, did a man prove his love for anything; that acquiescence and weak tolerance resulted at last in precisely the sort of intolerance for which a national bloodletting was the last cure.

They came to no agreement.

CHAPTER XV

Late in the month of August, Mr. Brewster summoned his prospective son-in-law with a peremptoriness he permitted himself as a sign, no doubt, of his willingness to accommodate Trofimov in his family circle. By this time he had dropped all artifices with the young Russian, going so far as to suggest coldly that the title he sported was probably false and if not that, then useless to all intents and purposes. "You have a gift of languages, which happens to suit us now. You have a winning face, which you are clever enough to use to your best interests. I admit I like the utter crassness which marks you, my dear baron."

With this kindly introduction he gave the baron to understand that he had already arranged with his good friend, Mr. Storey, of the Times, to make available a position for him. "Mr. Storey is a man of real farsightedness," he informed him. "The Tribune has a news-gathering faction following our local boys in the field. We feel you, being a friend of the colonel of the 19th Illinois, are the best prospect for what we wish done."

Trofimov listened unmoved. He was standing before Brewster, who no longer bothered to make so much as a motion of rising. "And what is that, Mr. Brewster?" he asked with a faint smile. "Am I to slay the gallant old fool, my friend?"

"I should not put it past you if I had not a fairly certain conviction that my girl's dowry is more tempting to you than the blond lady on whom your heart - that is if you have one, which would be downright stupid and maudlin - is fixed." This last remark he guessed shrewdly as he looked knowingly into the younger man's attractive face.

"No," he continued with a short laugh, "nothing so drastic is asked of you, however. You are to report to Storey who will give you details." He paused. "And money," he added significantly. "You have an idea, I believe, of what we expect of you in addition to the prattle you will be sending to satisfy inquisitive curious readers. You know what we wish promulgated. You know how to insinuate yourself into the good graces of all whom you meet."

"My argument will be that this dastardly war must be ended quickly." Trofimov followed Brewster completely. He was still smiling, though his mouth had grown narrower and his eyes more sparkling.

"Exactly", Brewster complimented him for his astuteness and dismissed him so that he could return to the pleasantries of his wife and daughter.

Some days thereafter, Baron Trofimov, equipped for reportorial duties in a campaign, arrived in Kentucky where the 19th was finishing its last field maneuvers preparatory to the removal to the east which Colonel Turchin daily anticipated and the order for which actually came in September.

When Trofimov showed himself to the colonel and Nadine, he was a welcome sight, especially to Turchin, who plied him with questions about the city, about the degree of success in enlistments, the reasons he saw for their declining and not increasing and Mrs. Morrison, whose letters, he said, had grown inexplicably short and irregular. Nadine, on the other hand, held herself aloof from him throughout the evening, though her soft blushes and stealthy glances at him, assured him that he was still high in her favor. That special knowledge rendered him sparkling and witty, a gay companion, which added to his natural vivacity in this woman's presence, a will to please, not all of which was according to Brewster's orders, nor yet Mr. Storey's.

"I thought you were a hater of wars," Turchin suddenly remembered, when the baron's proposed endeavors were laid before him in their prepared light. He eyed his friend skeptically. "What made you ask for such work? Do you fully intend to follow us until we beat the rebels?"

"Or until they beat you, colonel, which will not be so long, I fancy, despite your friend McClellan's grand army. I hear the uniforms his men wear are better than the wearers; that there is so much gold braid and brass buttons gleaming in his regiments, that Washington has to depend on the glare from all this brilliance to blind the enemy whenever they decide to push into the Capitol!"

Nadine, despite herself, laughed, but quickly looked away again as her husband jumped to his feet and stood menacingly over Trofimov. "Will you never have done with your stupid sarcasm? Does it make you so much taller to malign a good man? Do you think your careless words will macerate a nation's foes and not the men you sneer at? Those boys with their new uniforms may be dead on their bellies or backs, in ditches or rifle pits, while you find it sport to mock them in their innocent moments!"

"We are getting ready to join the Army of the Potomac," Nadine hastened to speak while Turchin caught his breath. "It will not be proper for you, Dimitri, to derogate General McClellan's army, if you are to come with us."

"Who says he is to come with us?"

"Irrefutable authorities, colonel!" Trofimov replied coolly. "In fact, such authorities that your generals will think twice before disputing my presence."

Turchin was truculently silent, convinced albeit unwillingly. Nadine took this up quietly. "It will be an advantage to have a newsman with us. So much that is false is being reported, that..."

Trofimov had risen and was moving about the double tent which was the only home the Turchin's had here. He felt cramped and small; a state of mind which did not add to the slight guilt Nadine's words had given rise to. As though to dispel this guilty touch of conscience, derived of his curious attachment to her, which warred with the loyalty he had pledged to his conferees, he did not doubt that he would use all his efforts to create as much confusion and doubt and misgivings among the men as was possible. Still he clutched about in his mind for a topic which should remove him from the defensive position her blind gullibility placed him in. "Is it false, Nadine, the news which is being bruited about Chicago, that the colonel has hired a professor of music to attend the musical wants of his regiment?" Then, turning to Turchin, who had his back to them, he inquired with mock innocence: "Tell me, colonel, when you were on the Imperial Staff, was it customary to fight in ballet form?

"Please, Dimitri, do not badger him. We had much rather hear what news of the outer world you must have brought with you. How are Miss Brewster and Mrs. Morrison?"

But Trofimov had a better piece of news than gossip. He could not resist displaying his greater information to his friend, whose superior and righteous airs annoyed him more than usual today. Looking upon the fine military bearing of the colonel he felt a double desire possess him; to pierce and wound the man's self-esteem, thereby to punish him because he was a constant reminder of their differences; to grip him by the hand, as one would grip a stanchion for protection against something dark and foreboding, but unseen. He was conscious of one definite fact; that as long as Colonel Turchin stood well and alive before him, he Dimitri Trofimov need not come from behind the bland mask he wore, need never make that final decision, the very nature of which terrified him out of countenance; the decision about Nadine, to be sure.

"Colonel," he began, "You imagine because I do not go into a passion over other people's business that I am in the dark about national affairs. What would you say if I told you that I know for a fact something you do not? He rocked on his heels in his favorite pose and invited the other to remark upon this intelligence. Turchin, of course, became at once interested. "You see, it pays to know influential people and to be agreeable to them. For instance, I have learned that the Czar has interested himself in the paltry doings of this country!"

"Is that bad?" Turchin snapped sarcastically, already prepared to oppose whatever Trofimov said.

"You ought to know how far to trust the good will of the power-hungry politicians in Europe and Russia! Would you take seriously the sudden friendliness the Czar manifests toward this country and toward Mr. Lincoln? Is it compatible with the system which prevails in Russia? Ha! They with their slaves, commiserating with Mr. Lincoln, battling a slave-holding South!"

At this juncture in the conversation Turchin's assistant, Colonel Scott arrived and was introduced to Trofimov for whom the young Scott immediately felt a great friendliness and took his hand with a youthful spontaneity surprising to the baron, who was always wary and careful, never ready to accept people at their face value. Soon Scott was drawn into the subject that his coming had interrupted and he at once opposed the baron's position on Russia's friendliness. "I have indeed seen the newspaper accounts of the Russian minister's presentation of the Czar's letter to the President. The editors say the letter breathes a spirit of unrestrained sympathy. I understand that the Czar is almost ready to free all his own serfs. Do you suppose that is correct, Colonel Turchin?" He deferred to the older man's opinion with such a charming and unassuming air, that Trofimov looked sharply at him, suspecting duplicity in such admiration thusly expressed for Turchin.

"I don't know about Russia nowadays," Turchin, somewhat mollified by Colonel Scott's warm friendship, answered. "It is possible the serf will someday be free. However," and he turned brusquely to Trofimov, "concerning Russia's friendly attitude to this country, you had better consult an elementary history book, where you will read expressly that, as long ago as Catherine's time, Russia supported the claims of this country; in 1775, in fact. There has always been a bond of kinship and spirit between these two lands - the love of the land! Russians like Americans love their land, love the freedom and health of the land! Yes, I believe Czar Alexander sincere in his offer of continued friendship and I am sure Mr. Lincoln believes it too. Russia is the one great power that has never deviated in her partiality to the United States."

"What is odd to me," Colonel Scott puzzled aloud, "is the strange indifference England seems to show toward our fight here. This fight will turn into a fight for freedom, don't you agree, colonel? And if what is rumored is but half true, England is more favorably inclined toward the rebels than to us."

To which the other two made appropriate comments indicative of their character; Trofimov, utilizing an opportunity to discharge his obligations to Brewster, averred positively that British intervention on the side of Davis, should it come about, would be a good thing, in that it might hasten the close of a shameful war; Turchin, asserting with equal positiveness quite the contrary, shouted that the people in England and France would rise in a body and declare themselves against such actions from their rulers.

Trofimov in this instance carried the last word as he pronounced: "Believe me, gentlemen, if foreign intervention could be enlisted by

Jefferson Davis, there would be no doubt as to the war's outcome and in the end, millions of needlessly sacrificed dollars and men, too, would be spared. It is just a matter of one's point of view. I'd rather be a living man with any name or degree than a dead hero." His private thoughts were that a foreign intervention would be better for the Southerners than several divisions of men in the field, but this last he discreetly kept to himself. It mattered little to him who won the war.

Though Turchin worried constantly over European embroilment, particularly England's and France's, he found himself surprisingly grateful to his former country, for its weighty role in the assured friendship. He knew, when translated into concrete terms, that this was in effect a warning to England and France and that their intervention in America would bring about Russia's intervention on Mr. Lincoln's side. But pressing concerns forced him to dismiss these more distant problems in the face of the immediacies with which he had to treat. His was the task of transferring the whole of his regiment to Washington and it was no simple matter, the journey being long and difficult of itself, despite the fact that he foresaw no rebel opposition in transit. The railroads were much taxed by the war needs in those days and the rail lines were in a deplorable condition, which demanded ceaseless supervision and repair. Iron rails and quickly over-heated iron engines, pulling wooden coaches, created hazards well known to a man of Turchin's knowledge and experience.

Still, once set upon it, he was impatient to start on the journey. So far had he restrained his critical propensities under Nadine's constant exhortations, that he was quite ready to submit himself to the dictates of his superiors. Speaking often with Trofimov, who was a favorite with the men and was welcomed wherever he showed himself, he actually became happy over the baron's determination to continue with them to Washington. In an impulsive moment, he forgave him the many stings and aspersions suffered at his hands, just as he would have been ready to forgive almost any personal affront, were the offender in this respect joined with him in the lofty cause of defending and loving America. In no other guise did it occur to him to interpret Trofimov's presence with them. To follow a campaign involved one in dangers perhaps even greater than those due the lot of the soldier prepared to defend himself. Trofimov, disdaining weapons, seemed doubly brave to Turchin.

At last the time to entrain arrived. It was a beautiful day which was designated for their departure from this westerly area. Turchin rode to the station on his restless gray horse, followed by his men in fine order and excellent spirits. The lads marched along the road with an abandon and cheerfulness which was contagious and soon Turchin was humming under his breath.

Trofimov and Nadine followed behind the regiment in an open carriage hired from a farmer who trudged by the side of the road with his two sons, who periodically skipped into the loose lines of the men. The farmer was going to the station in order to retrieve his buggy. Nothing in the entire scene, not even the singing columns of men, appeared war-like. Everything had the fulsome and plentiful aspect of satisfaction. Great trees with their red and gold trim, lazy cattle munching stubble, a delicious apathy in the air and a fantastically blue sky knit the baron and Nadine, sitting side by side, into the intangible web of romance which neither the one nor the other wished to destroy by so much as a word. Once, with reckless daring, he put his arm about her shoulders, but almost instantly removed it without comment.

The whole regiment began the trip. All night they rode over the plains and the next day made a change of cars at a village named Sandoval, from which place they hoped to proceed to Cincinnati. The trains they boarded here were two; the first being occupied at once by five of Turchin's companies and his regimental staff, including himself, his wife, and the baron Trofimov. The second section of the train was devoted to the remaining five companies comprising the regiment and the regimental equipment attached to it. When they began to move, the entire company was in the highest spirits, matched only by the bustle and excitement of the villagers who had been drawn near the train; for thus far so many soldiers in a body were the closest appreciation they had of the fact of the war, barring a few border skirmishes which barely merited official report.

The colorful autumnal landscape, with its changing aspects of sky hues and meadow flowers, wild brush and serpentine rivulets threading cornfields and pasturelands; the homely farm houses modestly receding from the roads, screened from view by enormous stacks of hay neatly molded in rounded hillocks; suggested a sadness and drooping loveliness to Nadine. She saw in the fullness of the harvest time the reminder of winter and death, cold rigid sleep holding no hopes of change or condition, only finality without emendation. Sitting in her coach seat beside Trofimov, she indulged herself in this painless melancholy whose essence seemed to reach him also, so that the curl of the lips relaxed, inducing a sweetness of expression to the mouth. They did not speak much and seemed to be recalled to their surroundings only when the colonel, who spent the greater part of his time marching from one length of the train to the other, took a few moments now and then to join them in their contemplative study of the scenery which seemed to fly past them.

At last they came to a bridge crossing, where Turchin left them in order to take his post on the platform of the train. It was a creaky old wooden bridge which had barely sustained the weight of the train in the crossing. As Turchin gave it a backward glance, it seemed to him to be extremely frail; the piles which supported it in the stream showed large seams and fissures, marking the ravages of weather, strain and time. Anxiously he thought of the second section of the troop train, which was following behind them. During the first hours of their departure from the junction at Sandoval he had been able either to see it behind them, or to hear it in the distance. Now he could do neither. Uneasiness held him fast to the platform which he determined not to leave until he was reassured about his men, until he knew them to have crossed the bridge.

The night was fast descending upon him, but he was for once indifferent to the opalescence of the heavens, the gauzy outlines of the moon, the sudden freshness of winds laden with wine fruit scents and scrub pine. Nervously he bit the end off a cigar and lighted it against the wind. He puffed slowly the while he listened for the sound of the train which ought to be following them. All the sound his ear caught was the rattle of his own train, the periodic screech of its wheels on the iron tracks, the groan of the sagging coaches, and the strident scream of the train whistle. Where was that train? Why did he not hear the rush of its engine? How far away from the bridge were they? He tried to recall the name of the town just beyond the bridge crossing, but failed to remember. Throwing his cigar overboard, he stamped his feet heavily and re-entered the coach where Trofimov and Nadine were still musing over the purplish twilight which was enfolding the country-side.

"My other boys must have been delayed somewhere along the route," he said unceremoniously to his wife. "They must have crossed that bridge we came over, some time ago."

"Worried, are you? Do you think the whole rebel army is come north to waylay you, Colonel Turchin?" Trofimov could not resist this opportunity to persiflage.

"I am deeply concerned with the condition of our roads and bridges," Turchin continued to Nadine, not deigning to make any rejoinder to his tormentor. "When a people gear itself for war, it was folly indeed to neglect to strengthen roads and bridges and all manner of cars and vehicles, whose good or bad condition could help or hinder a campaign. Our communications depend largely upon roads, rivers, and bridges."

"Always doing the thinking for the entire military staff; always fighting this war all by yourself!" retorted Trofimov.

"He is right," Nadine interposed swiftly, putting her fingers on Ivan's arm, "Surely these things are as vital as he says. It is honorable for an officer to think always of such devices whereby the lives of his men gain so much more protection." She was profoundly annoyed with her friend for his continual belligerence toward her husband. To such a degree did she value his friendship that she dared to rebuke him for blindly jeopardizing it by his tactics. However, no sooner had she spoken thus, then, she offered him her hand and her smile in so winning a fashion, that his momentary anger with her relented.

Before he had formed the next thought, the engineer suddenly set the raucous bell a-ringing and the huge iron engine came to a grinding jerking halt. Two riders were seen pulling their horses alongside the steaming engine. Men and horses were perspiring, giving evidence of extreme haste and excitation. "Colonel Turchin! We seek Colonel Turchin!" they shouted together. Turchin sprang instantly to his feet as other of his soldiers followed suit. They made a headlong dash to the exit and almost fell upon horses and riders alike. In a moment the colonel's worst apprehensions were verified; something had indeed happened to his boys. And what had happened was the worst of all possible catastrophes, a train wreck.

For an awful moment Turchin stood dumbfounded and stricken. He scarcely heard the garbled account which the riders related. He could not believe so dreadful a thing actually had taken place, until the couriers recounted the screaming and shouting of those trapped beneath the frightful wreckage of the second troop train. "There are many dead," the witnesses said, "and God alone knows how many are lying half dead, crushed in the mud of the river; for the train crashed through the rotten timbers of the bridge near Vincennes." It was the same bridge, which had raised fears in Turchin's mind earlier and though he did not know it then, six cars had smashed to their doom in the river flowing under the bridge.

"Let's not stand here, Turchin," Trofimov said sharply in Russian. "Let's do something!" He was carried beyond his usual bland indifference, perhaps wrought upon by the grief he saw on Turchin's face and the white pallor on Nadine's.

Turchin, overcome by a terrible grief, a woefulness for which there could be nothing of words, but only a feeling of horror, nodded his head and left it to Colonel Scott's initiative and resources to send the engineer speeding his train back along the route they had so recently traversed.

The sight that met their horrified eyes when they came back to Vincennes was long to remember. Hundreds of local folks had convened at the scene of the disaster and presented a fantastic spectacle to the arrivals. Darkness was falling in heavy folds, as though to blanket from sight the scene of swift and terrible death. But no merciful blackness could drown out the screams of the mangled victims clinging desperately to the heavy wooden planks of the smashed coaches.

"Lights!" Turchin roared out. "Where are lights?" And almost as suddenly as he spoke, oil lanterns blazed up and torches were held aloft. "Now!" he yelled, "An axe, somebody!" and stripping his coat from himself, he sprang into the river's eddies where he began to wade in the direction of the cries for help. Immediately he was seen to brave the current, other men followed in his lead and among them was Trofimov who, no less promptly than Turchin and with as little regard for his fine coat, plunged into the river behind the colonel.

Then began a night's work, which was indeed like a garish nightmare. Men hacked wildly with axes at the imbedded splintered sides of the wooden coaches and risked life and limb in superhuman efforts to extricate maimed soldiers almost drowned under the debris. Relays of other men carried the wounded to shore where Nadine, with the help of several local women, gave whatever aid she could. Some screamed and others fainted when limp arms and legs yielded to the touch. Trofimov held dying boys in his arms during the last convulsive shudders of their passing. Turchin worked like a madman, seemingly endowed with a fabulous strength enabling him to lift prodigious weights and even, it appeared, hold back the volume of the river.

When the last man was laid out on the sand, when the dead were separated from the living, Turchin took his place beside his wife in her tireless administration to the grievously wounded. Both he and the baron unhesitatingly tore their shirts into bandages, while Nadine without shame, removed her petticoats and helped bind the bleeding. By the time a rescue train reached them in the morning, the banks of the river were grim with their burdens. In his own arms Turchin conveyed to the train the lads most seriously injured and with the tenderness of a mother he laid each on the piles of blankets arranged for the purpose.

He was less concerned with the lifting of the crushed coaches from the river bed, which took the remainder of the night, than with the damages wrought upon his regiment by the destruction of its two companies in the disaster. Between grief for the dead and rage over the conditions responsible for the wreck, he was both a spent and an angry man. The axe he had swung all night with a vigor which would have splintered stone, leave alone wood, was still beside him.

Trofimov, his dark hair damp and disheveled, slowly and carefully put on his bedraggled coat. "Well, my dear colonel," this seems to be the end of your trip east." He tried to insert in his tone the same light impertinence which was usually able to anger his friend, only this time the other nodded in disconsolate agreement. More than that; Turchin dropped his head in his hands and openly wept.

"So that brings you to your proper size, does it?" Trofimov snapped, because the sight of Turchin weeping was too moving. He was aware that not the frustration of Turchin's plan, but the sacrifice of his boys had bowed him down. The night had taken a heavy toll of him also, to a greater extent that he was willing to confide. A hundred bits and scraps of information which he had gathered in Storey's and Brewster's offices warranted the development of a deep uncomfortable suspicion that the bridge disaster was no accident. For an instant a fiery wrath burned in him against Brewster who was informed of Turchin's movements and who must have known that he, Trofimov was travelling with the regiment. This anger subsided quickly. There would be no motive in Brewster's callous consent to this or to his personal destruction had Trofimov really been cognizant of any plans to tamper with the bridge. He did know, however, that it was part of the campaign of resistance to the White House, to wreak as much damage as possible to all trestles and bridges; that it was not beyond the limits of possibility that some overzealous Copperhead should have been directly responsible for this bridge's collapse.

His tired eyes fell upon Nadine who had sunk exhausted upon several blankets left lying on the bank. Her hair was wildly disordered and had fallen about her shoulders in girlish fashion, emphasizing the fragile face smudged and fatigue-laden. Seeing her worn and helpless, Trofimov had to strike out against someone in order to find for himself release from the awkward sense of culpability he could not rid himself of. "Now you can see why sane men decry the bloodshed and agony which a war, none of you is prepared to fight, brings to everyone. Men are destroyed even before a shot is fired! Perchance this night's cold bath, my friend, will temper your hot ardors! You will, perhaps, see that sensible men know what they talk about when they cry down this needless sacrifice! No money, no soldiers, no decent equipment; only rotten bridges, rotten railroads, rotten coaches! That's your true picture!"

"Enough!" roared Turchin, roused to vent his anger and grief upon him who showed the least understanding or compassion for those who had suffered this night. "If you cannot weep, if no heart beats in you with one touch of love for your fellow creatures, then respect the claims of death itself! You cannot love life! Love then the still death you offer instead of the warmth of life my boys will never more ask of you or anyone!"

Some time later the remnants of the 19th Illinois boarded a train sent for them and were taken to Cincinnati, the largest city in that region with sufficient facilities to accommodate the sick and wounded. The entire city was roused to a demonstration of cooperation and sympathy which at other times would have gratified the colonel, but who now had no thoughts save for his men, his regiment and its future allocation in the war. Not until nearly a week had passed in Cincinnati did his proper indignation over the train wreck begin to assert itself above his personal grief and pity. This indignation, nothing more than outraged justice, received a sort of corroboration by the courtesy and kindness which the citizens of Cincinnati showed the entire regiment. That strangers should be moved to pity by the plight of unfortunate people convinced him that all Americans were generous and compassionate, that at least, all who were informed of the true state of affairs. If tragedies like this one came about, they owed their being to the negligence of authorities, not properly controlled by the will of the good people. He repeated this conviction until the baron was exasperated.

"What divine goodness you ascribe to anyone who pleases your fancy!" he sneered. "The good people! Those who come trooping in with jellies instead of sense. It would never occur to you that these sudden ladies of mercy actually look forward to the chance you afford them so opportunely to prove their saintliness. What an occasion for them to come bobbing with their feather bonnets and silken flounces before these helpless men, unable to resist them at last!"

The colonel forgave this badinage, for after resting and becoming calmer, he was not prone to forget how his scoffing friend had, for all his talk, swung his axe as fiercely as he, torn his fine white shirt as readily as he, succored the dying as tenderly as the Reverend Conant himself, who that night had been as heroic as the bravest man in battle. He smiled now and almost agreed that the sight of the good ladies bringing their pretty baskets of jellies and soups, with their best embroidered napkins, might deserve his accusations. He was led to say something kind to Trofimov. "After what you have been through with us, Baron Trofimov, I begin to suspect you are really one with us, an American."

"Is that supposed to be a compliment?" Trofimov demanded. He repulsed any further attempts on the colonel's part to thank him for his part during that night of the disaster. "Pay your compliments to the Hebrew that the chaplain seems to be taken with."

He was making reference to the distinguished Jewish clergyman whose acquaintance Turchin had made the day before. This was a Rabbi by the name of Billienthal who had offered his assistance to the Reverend Conant when the regiment first arrived in the city. The two clergymen had found one another extremely congenial and Turchin, who was fond of looking upon the Jews as a people singularly suited to explain the laws of God, was delighted by the friendship. "The laws of God," he once said to the chaplain, "I well believe to be revealed to the Jews; the love of God to all who are able to abide by the law without falling, like lame geese, upon the empty symbols of the law."

Now he was happy to speak with Trofimov, regarding the Rabbi Billienthal. "He is a European by birth, as you and I are. He's a fine man, honest and sincere, but a human being above everything else. Jew or not, in Russia such a man would be a better Russian than you. In America, he is a better American than you."

"I have never claimed to be an American and anyone is a better Russian than I," was the baron's cold rejoinder.

"The truth is you are a nothing!" Turchin angrily declared. "You are an empty imitation of a nothing with the manners of a lap poodle! You select a silken pillow and sit foolishly on it, even if the pillow perches on a pile of dung. From that vantage point you see only faint outlines of things and people and you decline to see anything else because to see more involves apperception by the heart. Dr. Billienthal is not afraid to feel and believe in something. He dares to be what he is. He makes men admire him for what he is, without the need to twist their sense first."

"I've had enough of your subtilizing," Trofimov said curtly. "Let us hope your magnanimous and upright principles keep you from being court-martialed for this disaster!" Having delivered this thrust, he stalked out of the room and left Turchin to glare after him balefully.

CHAPTER XVI

How long they had to remain in Cincinnati neither Nadine nor Turchin could guess, but in the time they spent there they were warmly and hospitably entertained, being invited into the best homes in the city, where Trofimov, on the pretext of news hunting, joined them. There was no real excuse for his loitering in this pleasant city whose atmosphere and cultural aura, though pleasing to him, was essentially profitless at this time. Brewster had already recalled him to Chicago in no uncertain terms; and still, with a spirit of careful defiance, he lingered.

For the most part he spent his time in the spacious hotel rooms where the Turchins resided as the guests of the mayor. With the tragedy of the train wreck so close to all three of them and with each hurling censure and blame for the disaster upon other causes than the true one, they drew into an intimacy different from any in the past.

Trofimov could not rid himself of the growing dislike he felt for the role he had heretofore willingly undertaken. The stark scene near Vincennes haunted his imagination: the smoking torches yellowing the blackness of the night river fog; the limp bodies he had carried to the bank of the stream; the blood smears on his arms; Nadine lying worn and exhausted on the head of wet blankets; Turchin with dashed hopes, with his head in his arms like a child, with a man's tears rolling over his checks. No, he would not forget all that soon and consequently, in response to a nagging guilt which he could not utterly discard, he showed a chastened and more conscientious attention to Turchin, going so far as to send truthful dispatches concerning the condition of the army to the Times.

Turchin, on the other hand, contrary to his usual kindly attitude and despite Trofimov's unstinting assistance at the disaster, seemed to grow resentful of the other's constant presence and pettishly coincided his removal gradually from him with the awaited signal from Headquarters for the Regiment's reassignment. His looks and frowns, which did not escape his wife, were frequently cast upon Trofimov.

She meantime, was troubled by disquieting thoughts and feelings. First, when the initial horror and suspense of the accident had worn off somewhat, she had concerned herself only with her despairing husband whom she could not abandon in those moments of deepest need. She realized that the entire regiment was now broken and disorganized and that Turchin himself would strain every nerve to see it reformed; that he was too honorable to relinquish it even if he were offered a different one to command. Knowing his loyalty and pertinaciousness, she could understand his attachment to these men whose broken ranks were like broken bones of his body to him. More than a hundred dead, many more to die later, equipment lost, officers wounded. These were no light matters to him whose one care was to bring about a consciousness in the public's mind, a public-spirited consciousness that he felt would be evinced beneficently by the prevention of any further such needless tragedies as the bridge disaster. Day and night he labored over a letter that he was composing for the newspapers, dealing with the entire affair as he saw it. Day and night he drew diagrams of the fatal bridge and discussed with all who would hear him, its span, its age, its tensile strength; whether it were possible to have avoided the tragedy by proper supervision and unmitigated inspection.

Against her will, Nadine wearied of this topic and was duly grateful when Dr. Billienthal, the Reverend Conant, or various other sympathetic dignitaries of Cincinnati occupied him away from their suite and left her to the stimulating companionship of Trofimov. Toward him a new element made itself visible. Where she had been the self-proclaimed friend and protagonist, conferring patronage, she now became self-conscious and uncertain in his presence. For one moment during the night of the train wreck he had held her in his arms, had lifted her aching body over the edge of the river-bank; and in stealthy shame this moment persistently recurred in her every dream until she opened her eyes and faced the fact that she harbored for Dimitri much more than a simple friendship, that what she felt ought to be repulsive and was certainly dishonorable. All this made her fearful of herself, yet that fear instigated an unfamiliar boldness which her former guileless attachment would have forbidden.

This conflict in her mind and heart grew more desperate daily. It left her room for little else. In her pendulous wavering between distrustful desire and torturing self-doubt, she sorely wanted a trusted confidante, one in whose ear she might safely whisper her secret passion. But there was no one, nor could she look to some kindly member of her own sex for this comfort. She thought of Mrs. Morrison, but shook away the thought at once. That lady would have opened astonished, indignant eyes on Turchin's behalf; for her partiality to the colonel was obvious to Nadine, who was not unlike most wives that were complacent in the love of their spouses, ever watchful and thoughtful when admiration grew marked and suspect in other women. She was convinced she should never find any sort of rapport with the clever widow and equally certain that the vain Susan was undesirable even if available.

She was thrashing these problems out in her mind one day when the baron himself arrived with the challenging statement that he thought it fit to return to Chicago and to Miss Brewster whose fair society, he said, was no longer resistible. To this Nadine made a demure reply, suggesting that his return was reasonable and profitable; that a young man with clear vision had little to realize in commiserating with a distraught friend embroiled in troubles he could not remedy.

"You wish me to go back and marry Susan?" He had come close to her where she was sitting and sewing. He did not doubt the beautiful Nadine's answer. Her heart was an open book to him.

"I wish for you what you wish yourself," she answered him noncommittally and looked away from his face on which was mirrored more truthfulness than she had ever read upon it. Yet, what was there for his truthfulness to confirm? She watched him pick up a pad and pencil. Suddenly, he threw them down and took several turns about the room. Finally posting himself directly in front of her, he said, "Shall I tell you what I wish, Nadine?" He challenged her with a smile on his craven mouth.

"No! No!" she said in a flutter and rose as though in sudden flight from her seat, brushing him as she fled to the other side of the room. "I truly mean what I say, that it would be a good thing for you to return to Chicago." Her words made a flimsy barrier between them.

"That is another story," he retorted as he took the seat she had vacated. "I spoke of wishes, not fact."

She came back and stood, as he had stood, in front of him. He did not rise, only looked at her with his dark eyes sparkling with meanings. Nadine could swiftly translate. One long minute they probed each other's heart, then his eyes darkened, grew sadly stern, like waters calming in order to reflect a passing cloud. "Wishes can be facts sometimes," she whispered persuasively. Then, driven by an impulse she could not restrain, she bent forward, cupped his face in her palms and kissed his mouth softly. Her hands were cool as the petals of freshly gathered flowers. He tried to capture them in his as he reached for her form which instantly repelled him, but remained close in a stiff and frightened stance. Her widened eyes stared at him in purple confusion.

"You do care something for me!" he cried out. He had jumped up and now stood with his hands gripping her shoulders, hard fingers pressing into her flesh with cruel unconsciousness.

"No!" she attempted to evade what she had sought. "You are our friend. I love you as a friend!"

"Do you think me capable of marrying Susan?" he demanded, not releasing her.

"Yes! Yes! I believe you are capable! I believe you must!" She was frightened and not quite clear as to what she said or meant. But whatever else she might have blurted out in this moment of intense emotion, she was spared from revealing, for at that moment Turchin, bringing the minister and the Rabbi with him, entered the outer room. He came into the drawing room to find Nadine seated and Trofimov studying the view from the window. "I have finished the letter to the papers. Their Excellencies, the Reverend Conant and the Dr. Billienthal have been so good as to help me phrase it more accurately. I wish everyone clearly to understand what I feel."

The two clergymen made their greetings and paid note with small attentions to Nadine, who lighted up radiantly under the praise and compliments both men lavished upon her. Handsomely, Turchin included Trofimov in the invitation to hear, in its entirety, the speech he had just written. He was proud of it, proud of his sincerity, proud of the stand he felt he could honestly make in presenting it. He had just returned from the field of tents where his remaining companies were temporarily camping and there he had been greeted with such hearty cheers and good will from the men that his face glowed and clearly betrayed his deep gratitude. Among the men, he had encountered the good Conant who seldom left the camp and the cultivated Rabbi who came often with his gifts and encouragement to cheer the boys in their forced inactivity.

"Don't you think, my dear Rabbi," Trofimov addressed himself to Billienthal, "that by sending an explanatory letter to the papers, Colonel Turchin implies thereby some sort of culpability, which is extremely foolish?" He cocked an eyebrow and waited for the Rabbi to make answer. Dr. Billienthal, with a deeply serious expression, meditated on the other's words. A slight smile warmed his eyes and then his whole face, where as a rule nothing but a deeply ingrained courtesy manifested itself. He was a handsome man in his forties, possessing a graceful carriage and a sensitive face. He appeared to be a man of letters rather than a man of God, for in his speech he betrayed more of the academic habits of mind than the exorbitant turns of the pulpit orator. Originally an Austrian, he had completely overcome any tendency to linguistic reminders that English was not his native tongue. Before he could reply to the baron, Conant answered in his stead.

"You can hardly know, Baron Trofimov, whether the colonel's letter will imply culpability or not. You surely cannot know what is in it and if it pleases Colonel Turchin, perhaps he will read it now for us all to hear."

This Turchin at once consented to do and the men disposed themselves about the room in readiness to listen. He began: "In the name of my poor soldiers, ingloriously perished on account of that miserable structure; in the name of my other soldiers crippled for the rest of their lives; in the name of humanity and the sacredness of our Cause, I ask the intelligent public of these United States to take in their hands the management of these railroads and insist upon the appointment of Boards of Supervisors to inspect the railroads and to stop the butchery of citizen soldiers, who have sacrificed their dearest personal and special interests and have flown to the ranks for the defense of their country.

I am an old soldier, but never in my life have I felt as wretched as when I saw by moonlight my dear comrades mangled and disfigured, stretched motionless on that pile of rubbish, below agglomerated cars and heard the groans of agony from the wounded. The railroad must be answerable - the families of the killed and wounded must be amply indemnified by the managers, or the friends of humanity will give up their hope to find justice in our free country."

He stopped and looked at Trofimov who casually leaned against the mantle. A sarcastic smile hovered about his mouth and gave to his face a saturnine aspect which of itself spelled disapproval and Turchin knew it. "Well?" he dared the baron. "What is wrong with the letter?"

"You had better ask these saintly gentlemen. They know more about God than I do and they better than I can advise a man who plays God!"

Turchin gasped with unrepressed rage. Conant frowned unhappily and the Rabbi smiled again, very slightly. Conant said, "The baron probably means that your tone, Colonel Turchin, is not calculated to appeal to the railroad people; that perhaps you are hasty to fix the blame for that disaster upon them. Is that what you mean, Baron Trofimov?"

"I mean that he is too officious; that he speaks his piece with an authority he does not possess. I am his friend so how can I stand and see him make a fool of himself in the sight of all respectable people! He tells the public what it must receive in redress for the accident to its citizen soldiery! Bah! He further tells the whole world what reparations the railroads must make to the victims for their negligence! How can he be so sure they are responsible?"

"Perhaps the colonel appeals to others than the merely respectable," Dr. Billienthal answered, still kindly, still showing traces of a quiet mirth in his eyes.

"He's right in appealing to the people," said Conant defending the contents of the letter. "Where, but in them is justice resident? In the benevolence of the people, a good and God-fearing people, we can look for justice."

"And to touch the springs of that benevolence, Reverend Conant, we must appeal to that in them which is attuned to reverence and a love of humanity." Dr. Billienthal spoke these last words almost under his breath, yet everyone in the room heard him and Nadine cast a swift, startled glance upon him and then fleetingly upon Baron Trofimov. "If there is aught to criticize in your letter to the public," he turned to Turchin and spoke gently, "it is that you are a little too fierce in your insistence upon justice and might therefore induce some people to misconstrue pure justice as wanting in the temperance of mercy."

But Turchin, roused to a fighting wrath, announced he would not eliminate a single word and indeed he sent it to Mrs. Morrison exactly as he had written it and had the satisfaction afterwards of seeing it published. When, on his return to Chicago, where it was decided he and the regiment were to nurse their wounds and refill the gaps made by the large toll of death the disaster had levied upon them, he noted with additional satisfaction that many accounts, submitted for the information of the people, gave heed to his recommendations.

For the remainder of the fall and early winter Turchin's crippled regiment was assigned light duty in Elizabethtown, Kentucky where a few skirmishes of no great importance occurred occasionally and lent some reality to the fact of war. For the most part, however, the duty was galling to a soldier like Colonel Turchin, who was geared for action. Finding himself inactive or semi-active was an ineluctable personal defeat, for it denoted no intention on the part of the High Command to delegate him or the 19th Illinois to McClellan's army in Virginia. One fact cheered him at this time and that was the acquisition of a printing press which his boys took over when the terrified owners, rebel sympathizers, fled the town. A Regimental sheet was started and carried on with great success. It was called the Zouave Gazette and offered the colonel what he most needed at this time, an avenue for self-expression. He wrote many interesting articles pertaining strictly to camp life and drill functions. Carefully he avoided the insertion of his opinion on matters dealing with affairs not pertinent to the Regiment; Trofimov's sarcasm on his former writings still rankled and stung.

Yet, he could not refrain from excoriating slavery and soon it was well known in army quarters that he was an uncompromising hater of slavery, that he felt he was fighting to see slavery vanquished. This procured him numerous critics, making him the target for all manner of barbs, even in the matter of his drills and tactics. As to his fellow officers, they considered his comments on slavery as unwelcome as were his sentiments on political or social themes.

His waiting and wondering had grown nearly unbearable during which time he had completed a military manual upon which he had worked incessantly since the train disaster. One day, late in December, Trofimov, who had meanwhile returned to Chicago and was busy in the work of recruiting, not for the Union Army, but for the Knights of the Golden Circle, came on a visit to the camp. He had unpublished information that the 19th Illinois was to be sent to Camp Quincy Adams. He said cheerfully that this was the purpose of the visit, though his brilliant eyes spoke of another to Nadine. They told her that, alluring as was the wealth and riches which his activates were drawing him, she was almost as tempting; that when the winds blew icy blasts off Lake Michigan, his memory of her transformed them so that they grew perfumed and balmy; when frost bit into his face, when sleet, like knives, slashed the quickened flesh, they seemed mere tools of a mighty artificer, who created wrought beauty out of ugliness and death. But that was all they told her; nothing of decisions which a woman might expect from such confessing eyes.

Turchin was angered to hear about camp movements from him. He knew nothing to this effect. "You come here to tell me this? Am I to receive military intelligence from you? Or are you attempting, in your subtle way, to inform me that the military, too, is controlled by your Mr. Brewster?"

"Even when I am unselfish," Trofimov laughed, "he suspects my good will. This is the season for good will, Colonel, remember?"

"For him there has to be a season for good will," Turchin snapped.

"There is a season for everything and you might learn, my old compatriot, that unseasonable things, like unseasonable facts, are unwelcome and vulgar. I hear you are to have a commander who is meticulous about seasonable things." He was referring to the new head of Turchin's section, a General Don Carlos Buell.

"Next we shall be taking orders as well as advice from you," Turchin sneered at Trofimov in an effort to disguise the reluctance with which he accepted what in his heart he knew to be the final truth: he was not to go eastward, not to take part in the real battles which he calculated to be fought in the East. Camp Quincy Adams was definitely in the western theater of operations. Angrily he stalked out of the tent, into the clinging dampness of the night. His feet sloshed through numberless ruts filled with slime and mud deposited by endless rains and storms. The winter was bitter cold and Kentucky was a mud hole designed to make men miserable. The wintry days were gloomy and chilly, bleak for man and beast forced to endure them. This was the first winter under canvas for the men of the 19th and the discomforts attendant upon it discouraged everyone, bringing nagging illnesses to many, depriving most of incentive and worst of all, encouraging desertion, against which the colonel and young Scott strove ceaselessly.

Sloshing about, forgetful of Trofimov, who was left to enjoy Nadine's society, Turchin was an unhappy man. His own troubles were manifold and his future not very bright, if Trofimov was right, which fact curiously enough, he did not doubt. Yet what irked him silently was the lack of progress of McClellan's army in which he desired to serve. Reports had reached him that McClellan, the handsome white-haired boy on whom a nation depended for vindication, was still sitting immobile in Washington, while a rebel army laughed and jeered. It was being rumored that Mr. Lincoln was fast losing patience with him and was naggingly seeking the reason for his reluctance to advance against Lee.

Other news also came which was even more painful to the ardent colonel. With consternation he had read of the battle of Bull Run. It grieved and enraged him, too, that Union men should have turned on their heels and taken flight at the first taste of bullets. Why Mr. Lincoln should insist upon troops in this sector of Virginia was another of the irritating questions he tussled with. It seemed only good sense that all men should be deployed in the East in order to deal Lee a telling blow at his very vitals. Why did not McClellan do something? What was he waiting for? Was he afraid to fight? Why was that colonel of the 21st Illinois not more able and persevering; like Colonel Ulysses Grant. Turchin remembered him well and had read with pride of the account of his recent masterful capture of forts Donelson and Henry in Missouri.

This sort of unrest and bitterness of spirit Turchin had to endure until February when it became fairly certain that the regiment would remove to Kentucky. With this knowledge, not only Turchin, but also the disheartened men began to revive in spirit and confidence, being further inspired by the appearance of the distinguished General Buell himself. He made an impressive appearance which recommended him to all the men, especially to Turchin who thought his upright and strict military bearing augured a promise of action in the field. The men wanted both movement and baptism in battle; otherwise their weary months of training would appear to many no more than a scene in a comic opera. The fact that Buell, himself, the Department Head, rode several times to inspect the columns and showed himself sensitive to the needs of the army increased Turchin's respect. Certainly, Buell's cold but thorough appreciation of new drills and tactics may have had something to do with Turchin's favor. Turchin, in a most humane manner, warmed to anyone who showed real appreciation for his aims and efforts. Buell's commendations and faint praise were all the more welcome to the colonel because the general was admittedly a man of the most esteemed West Point traditions; and a tribute coming from such a source lent a measure of authority to the manual of drills he had unceremoniously introduced. This proved to him that the traditional was not unalterable and sustained him in the brief confidence he was enjoying. What he could not conceive of was Buell's willingness to accept that which he wished, the technical value of his colonel, without a liking or admiration for the ear or the mind of the man devising the innovations. To the Russian, it was an intolerable idea that a good soldier could be anything save a good man, a kind and sympathetic man, with an eye to the common good.

Quite otherwise, in his appreciation for Turchin, was the Division Commander, General O. M. Mitchel, an excellent engineer and a man not devoid of the necessary human qualities which augmented his soldierly attributes. Not talkative or demonstrative, this man was ever aware of the pulsing good will emanating from Turchin and he saw the good which concomitantly accrued to the regiment. Better coordination, better hygienic arrangements, more thorough preparation and knowledge, were evidence enough. He himself rode into camp to inform his subordinate officers that the time had come to strike camp and prepare for the march on Bowling Green where a large force of rebel troops was expected, supposedly bent upon Grant's destruction at the lately captured forts in Missouri. Turchin's men were given the mission of preventing enemy reinforcements from reaching Forts Donelson and Henry, a task not likely to overjoy Colonel Turchin who patriotically resented the implication that his men and his whole section were nuisance value for the defense rather than a strongly aggressive striking force.

A year of belligerency, he reflected, was almost ended without anything significant gained or determined. He rode slowly over the ruts and breaks in the icy roads and his men trudged before him in silence and wonderment. A bleak February morning was no inducement for that merry singing which Turchin had made a part of camp life. The one wry consolation he had was that their road led southward, that the frozen gushes in an unrelenting earth, marked by the icy scalpels of winter, would soon be behind them if all went normally, if they could continue southward into the bosom of the rebels' territory. He pulled his horse to the side of the road and waited for Nadine to join him. Suddenly through the greying of the cloud-laden sky, a spear of gold was thrust and husband and wife watched it together as it broadened into a band along the rim of the heavens. "See how that light gilds the icy rocks," she remarked, "and how the valley is alive with mercurial lights!" Her words were deliberately cheerful as though with them she hoped to obliterate the reality of frozen mud and penetrating cold against which her horse whinnied and shivered while they paused.

"It will not be a sunless day," he answered and patted her horse. "The men will see clearly the ravages of the passing rebel army and it will hearten them, I am certain. Look, there across the road, do you see those caverns cut into the earth? Deliberate vandalism! See those fallen trees strewn in our path? Deliberate! They expected us to move this away! It is their manner of hindering men whom nothing but death shall halt and even then we will march against them!"

Later on he gave orders that no man was to drink from any of the water holes they passed; for near the holes and in them, too, were carrion and refuse placed by a wily enemy, along with sick and half dead mules, whose staring empty eyes turned Turchin's stomach. "They will use their dead to impede us, if their living fail to do so," he said to Colonel Scott who had joined them. "We must establish some sort of medical unit as we proceed. We must see that our soldiers have relief and first aid on the spot if they shed their blood for our common good, I t's the least we can do." And turning to his wife he said, "It is lucky thing for us all that you are with us."

"In the end, Madame Turchin, our strongest men will be in your safe keeping!" Colonel Scott complimented with a gallant bow from his saddle. "Because we are all aware of your ability, General Mitchel permitted your presence while other army wives have been denied the right to accompany their husbands."

In this manner they made their march until they reached the outskirts of Bowling Green, reckoned to be a stronghold of secessionist strength. A river separated the contingents of rebels from the troops of Mitchel's army, which had spread out fan-like along the banks of the river whence they could see and be seen by the hooting rebels. From the frantic activity, the fires, the smoke and the confusion raging among the enemy, Turchin divined that for some reason, the city was being abandoned to the approaching Federal troops. He could plainly see the field batteries trained upon his men who stood indecisive on the river bank where they seemed helpless to interrupt the steady retreat from the burning town save with derisive curses and empty threats. No bridge was available for crossing and the rebels shouted their derision with impunity accompanied by random shells aimlessly fired to cover their retreat. In an instant Turchin leaped off his horse, the state of affairs obvious to his trained eye; that which the rebels could not take with them, they destroyed. The citizenry helped the enemy by assisting in the demolition of stores, which would have been of incalculable value to the Union army if only they could have gotten to them soon enough.

The river which presented the obstacle to their pursuit was the Barron, at this time of the year already swollen by a rush of icy spring waters just freed from the frozen grip of winter. Quite naturally, men and horses hesitated to ford this river; not so Turchin, who was ready to dare anything except acquiescence and he began at once fearlessly to explore among the reeds and brush of the river bank until, some distance away, he spied an abandoned old mill beside which, rocking slowly in its bed of slush, snow and debris, stood a flat-bottomed antiquated ferry. In this his ingenuity saw a means to cross into the city and immediately he ordered the rigging of rafts and whatever other floatable objects could be quickly devised. At the same time he ordered batteries to be placed in full view of the enemy, who had overlooked the worm-eaten ferry boat. This battery was to fire desultorily, lest the enemy be led to suspect an undue silence and attempt to frustrate the colonel's plan from being put into operation.

By nightfall, the slow ferrying of men and material was executed a half mile below the enemy position. Then followed a surprise rush which cost Turchin's regiment little trouble and enabled his men with expedition, to take the town and seize the precious stores the rebels were forced to abandon.

The city quickly subdued, was sullen but submissive, making no effort to pretend a welcome for the Union men who now were strategically placed to endanger the southern rear of General Johnson's men. Citizens surrendered what stocks and stores Johnson's men had left behind. In a week the regiment could safely hold the town with only a nominal force while the main body of troops proceeded forward to Nashville. Here too, Turchin met with a quick and as he thought, sensible surrender. "I like good sense. They cannot hope to win against us and I hate to see my boys killed unnecessarily. I hate even to have to consider their misguided southern people as murderers." Such was his attitude when the mayor of the Tennessee capitol surrendered the town without a shot in its defense.

If the colonel of the 19th Illinois had a further satisfaction in Nashville, it was in the fact that at least he had come into the real cotton south, or so he believed. If this was not strictly accurate, he was led to this conclusion by the sight of vast numbers of colored folk who, with their household rags, a few pots and pans, dilapidated sticks of furniture and bedding, lined the roads on either side and lifted choked voices in mournful songs and tearful jubilation. "They think we are their liberators," he said movingly to Nadine as they rode like conquering heroes through the dense lanes of these dark peoples. "They think we are marching on Glory Road," she answered wistfully, not knowing precisely whether she pitied the hopeful faces, which stared up appealingly at her, or her husband's stern faith, the more.

"Sir, you will have to order them back home; they are bent on following us," Colonel Scott rode up to tell Turchin.

"The young men ought to be enlisted into the army!" was the angry answer. Then, realizing Scott was looking anxiously for his reply, he said, "At least these ignorant and downtrodden folk have one faith some of our better people lack; they know in their hearts that our flag will not defend their masters, even against them who are not yet free men. Tell them to go home," he conceded, "but tell them to believe that, once we secure the safety of the Union, we will altogether destroy their bondage." Suddenly he remembered that he had heard from Trofimov the confirmation that Russia had freed her serfs. He stayed Scott and said, "If a thousand years of shackles could be removed by a decree of the Czar, how much more logical is it that, when we have defeated the traitors to humanity, we shall build us a totally free America!"

CHAPTER XVII

Turchin's men were pushing from Nashville to Murfreesboro, thirty miles away, with a retreating rebel force scattering at their approach, unwilling to come to a pitched fight against superior numbers. At the same time, Henrietta Morrison, in addition to men like Joseph Medill and owner and publisher of the Tribune, Cyrus McCormick, carried out a campaign to root out the growing scourge of Copperheadism. At that time, the followers of Vallandigham were particularly potent and persuasive in Ohio and Southern Illinois and their appeal was spreading to New York as well. Unfortunately, the foreign papers and agencies were often deluded by Copperheads, and consequently, they sowed the discontent and disloyalty which was beginning to be felt in Washington.

Vallandigham's men cleverly and covertly disseminated their malicious and flagitious lies, while Senator Vallandigham himself continued high in repute. Intelligent persons failed at first to suspect him as the leader of the secret war against the government. Henrietta ascribed her dislike of him to no more than a purely personal aversion. Certainly she could have not been prevailed upon to dine with him at her relative's home, which was growing more distasteful to her because of Trofimov's continual presence in it. But she did not, at this stage, take Vallandigham for anything more lacertilian than her cousin Brewster, and accused him of short-sightedness rather than anything more reprehensible.

As it was, she found herself one evening amidst her kin, with something of pleasure in the anticipation of news she hoped to elicit from the baron. The news she sought, though she wished not to betray her special interest, was of Turchin. She had gradually diminished her steady correspondence both with him and Nadine, giving as her excuse nothing but vague causes which did not deceive the wife and were soon forgotten by the husband who was now completely engrossed by the details of his campaign. Henrietta knew, however, that the baron kept up a regular contact with his Russian friends and from him she hoped to extract such as she could from a recital of Turchin's progress and prospects.

A splendid feast was laid out for Mr. Brewster's guests this night, and nothing was lacking to make this dinner party sumptuous and elegant, congruous with the distinguished gentlemen and ladies invited to partake of it. When the trivialities of the day had been exhaustively dealt with, inevitably some gentleman mentioned the Chicago boys in the field. "They do say," he declared laughingly, "that the army marching into Tennessee has to build its way as it goes. The clever men of Johnson's army know how to confound our lawyer-generals!"

"Very clever of them," Trofimov said coldly, and catching Mrs. Morrison's eye, he informed the company: "Colonel Turchin had to build 1,200 feet of railway in ten days."

"I believe that a remarkable feat," she spoke up. "I heard from as reliable a source as the baron that much credit goes to Colonel Turchin for his fine leadership at Huntsville, where the 19th Illinois is now stationed. I understand that he devised a brilliant plan which surpassed any arrangements the generals had for taking Huntsville!" She looked about her, where Brewster's guests sat with sundry expressions of boredom on their faces, and she felt herself impelled to defy them all by continuing. "Doesn't this sort of news affect any of you? Is there not one father or mother in this room with a son or an anxious daughter involved in the affairs of the war? For my part, I wish our men, now striving to break the Confederacy's line of communications with the East, success!"

"How well informed you are," Mrs. Brewster said slowly. "My guests will pardon you when they know you are a Bluestocking, a lady writer for Mrs. McCormick, I am sure."

"I require no pardon, cousin," she retorted with a deep blush. "I find it strange indeed that American gentlemen and ladies can be so indifferent to the fate of their country. Gentlemen, if I may be excused?" She departed with no backward glance despite the sudden hush which fell about the table. Even Susan was speechless, though her eyes were shiny and malicious as they followed Mrs. Morrison from the room.

Henrietta was quite agitated as she drove off in her carriage. She had good cause to feel bewildered and upset, for never before had she seen how callous were these people in whose company she spent her social and leisure time, little as it was. More than that, she had sat through dinner with the dreadful news of the initial setback at Shiloh, a fact she kept concealed lest it embolden Brewster, a satisfaction she wished to deny him.

One other person present that day, the baron, knew of Shiloh, of Grant's plight, and of the many military affairs relative to Turchin's division, which facts Mrs. Morrison might have welcomed. He might have added to her small knowledge of Turchin's success at Huntsville, of which he had only that afternoon apprised himself. But so much pleasure he would not willingly accord the haughty widow. He could easily have told her how, with startling maneuvers, Turchin's men had stealthily attacked the enemy town; how they had captured 170 prisoners and 15 locomotives, whose rolling stock the army needed desperately. And in addition to the locomotives, 150 passenger coaches and freight cars were captured.

Instead, after her abrupt and discourteous exit, Trofimov regaled the guests with witty tales of the havoc and confusion his scouts had reported from all sections of the state. "Every man who ever sat behind a plow is now fitted to direct the war," he began.

"I'd say every woman, too, only Henrietta has too much money to be accused of plowing," Susan commented brightly.

"I heard," said Trofimov, "that recently the engineers had a private war in a certain roundhouse, to decide whether Davis or Lincoln was to get the engines!" But the audience was unresponsive.

"Like stupid children," he reflected, "who are gay and brilliant while they play and cheat and are not shown up, but who sulk and fret as soon as the slightest difference occurs."

"I hear, also, that my old friend, Colonel Turchin, has gained a lot of booty at Huntsville."

"We'll see about that," Brewster acidly interrupted. "What does he think this is, a peasant war?", whereupon the company laughed. Mrs. Brewster then began to delight her guests with tales of the Turchins. "Her gowns! Heavens, what curious things! And she had us believing they came from Paris and London. Though she was a countess, I believe. Still, those gowns! Positively immoral."

And the mention of Nadine, with her snowy shoulders in her soft lovely gowns, with the lace in clusters of frills about her arms, softened Trofimov, actuating his withdrawal from the general tongue-lashing Turchin was receiving at Mr. Brewster's hand.

Fortunately, Turchin was beyond the reach of either Mr. Brewster's vindictiveness or Mrs. Morrison's affection. To the one, he should have answered with pride and scorn, and to the other with his usual uncomprehending casualness, for he neither little guessed nor would have believed, what tender sentiments that beauteous lady nourished in her bosom for him. For a brief span of time he, in Alabama now, was elated with the success he had known thus far in his southern march. There had been several stiff skirmishes of which he rightly boasted that no man need be ashamed, they not having once been bested. His brilliant plan for taking Huntsville had received encomiums not only from General Mitchel but from General Buell himself. And Colonel Scott was of the happy opinion that the Russian would merit a citation for his achievement; that in fact, a promotion might not be too much to expect. Colonel Scott was utterly devoted to his superior.

Only one slight cloud appeared on Turchin's auspicious horizon during this short week of success. He had found a current journal in which the Tsar's letter which lauded Lincoln for his peace efforts was characterized as "sniveling and false." The same article applauded and quoted Britain's Lord Palmerston's letter deriding the sincerity of Russia. "Only traitors could denigrate a powerful country's good will," Turchin growled to his wife. They had pitched camp in Athens, a small town some miles from Huntsville where the colonel had detailed a small force of men to maintain order in the surrendered city. "It is easy to see whether it be England or Russia, who stands most to lose if America emerges strong and even more able to make the British shopkeepers whistle for their pennies. I tell you Nadya, what England is afraid of is Russia's fleet. Whatever we Russians are, we are loyal friends," he laughed heartily. "Some think that even I am a Cossack! Isn't that a good joke? We are such a small country that every one of us is a Cossack! But they'll appreciate the Cossack when he whips the rebel to his feet!"

And then an incident occurred in Athens, Alabama which, though seemingly only a normal expectancy during war and occupation, suddenly reared itself into a terrible specter, and brought down upon Colonel Turchin one of the most drastic misfortunes of his life.

Some soldiers misbehaved and some outraged southern gentlemen brought furious charges to General Mitchel. Eager tongues carried exaggerated rumors to General Buell, and the storm broke over Colonel Turchin's head just when the warmth of his Huntsville success was sweetest to him, when the first glories of a southern spring began to awaken his tenderest emotions.

So ubiquitous is the evil breath of scabrous malice, that Mrs. Morrison and Trofimov in Chicago heard of the incident in Athens almost as soon as Turchin himself, who received the first inkling of trouble when his aide, Colonel Scott, rode in one day and abruptly, imparted the intelligence. "Buell is on a rampage," he said unceremoniously. "Mitchel is coming here to see you. It is bad, Colonel Turchin!"

"What is bad?" asked Turchin and Nadine simultaneously. This time she could not guess whether her husband had asserted himself in an overweening manner or proffered supererogatory services. And when they subsequently heard Turchin's men accused of all manner of misdemeanors, both united in positive denials.

In Chicago, the affair of Athens embellished by men such as Vallandigham, attained serious proportions, complicated because neither Scott nor Turchin were there to tell the story honestly. Only Mrs. Morrison, who read the startling facts as reported, staunchly denied Turchin's alleged part in it. She, furthermore, denied the veracity of the case generally, though indeed she had to confess that if a commander had to be responsible for his men's actions, then he, poor Turchin, might well be the scapegoat for almost any folly his enemies wished to ascribe to him. "Men like Colonel Turchin always make enemies! They who are most worthy of respect and love, they are the very ones chosen to vent spite upon!" she said.

Luckily for the nerves and tempers of the Brewster house, Mrs. Morrison was not present when the Athens affair came under discussion there. So angry and incensed was Mrs. Morrison that it is not likely she would have left her cousin's home with restrained humors, particularly had she endured the slights made of her friend by Senator Vallandigham.

"Russia!" Vallandigham began the topic. "First we have all this to-do about a barbarous country playing polite politics with that incompetent Lincoln, who has not the sense to see through their game! Only a country bumpkin would treat with the Russians. But that is not enough; we in this great Northwest entrust thousands of our innocent lads to another Russian! And what happens! Just what you'd expect when wild people with the blood of Tartars sweep down upon civilized citizens! Turchin allows every indecent license!" He turned to Mrs. Brewster who looked the picture of mortified innocence. "This, dear lady, is no language for your ears. Robbery of women's virtue, and by his permission, if not express, then by his command! Gentlemen's property ruthlessly destroyed, probably by his orders. It is a wonder he has not had all men shot while the women..."

"Oh! Heavens! What a terrible monster!" cried Mrs. Brewster.

"These things are fact, Senator?" Trofimov asked sarcastically. He had quietly attended Mr. Vallandigham's outburst, and now was openly moved to defend his friend. "After all, every man in Colonel Turchin's regiment is not Russian, and all Russians," he smiled cruelly, are not Tartars!"

"No offense meant to you, baron," Vallandigham instantly smiled. "You are a gentleman and that makes a difference. You have the good sense to judge properly."

"Come now," Trofimov said boldly. "You mean I have the good sense to agree with you; a different matter entirely." He followed this with laughter in which Vallandigham joined reluctantly, while Brewster found his future son-in-law witty and clever. At that moment he probably liked him more than at any other time in his life. Men are of such curious compositions, that they sometimes find joy in the condign punishment their fellow sinners incur. No less treasonable than his friend and unable to mete out retorts to him because he in effect was his leader, it pleased him immensely that a rascal like Trofimov should have the temerity to flaunt his impertinence in the face of the Senator from Ohio.

"Russia has no right to concern herself with us," Vallandigham resumed his subject, somewhat irritated by the laughter which still lurked in Brewster's face. "England, if she deigns to view our confusions and shameful internecine struggles, is at least blood cousin to us. She has a right."

"Would she have the same right, Senator, if Lord Palmerston instead of Prince Cortchikoff had offered friendship to the President?" said Trofimov.

To this Vallandigham, with his face beginning to flush wrathfully paid no heed. "Perhaps it is a good thing this incident at Athens happened. It will serve to illustrate the point sincere patriots are vainly trying to make: that the whole war is an insanity, a bloody dream of a demagogue; that our men are not only not fit for wars but are led by even less fit officers! The first time our poor boys saw the muzzles of the Southern guns at Manassas they turned tail, and suddenly lost all interest in what was no business of theirs to begin with.

"I hear however, Senator," Trofimov replied without raising his voice, "That recently those same poor boys and their unfit leader, Ulysses Grant, I believe, gave the Southerners quite a taste of blood at Shiloh."

"Do you call slaughter, war?"

"Yes, and other things too," was the unfriendly reply. "I for one don't believe a word of this scandal you choose to view as significant. Whatever Colonel Turchin is, he is a gentleman, Senator Vallandigham. He would not countenance things that some, called by that name, easily would. He outgentlemans the gentleman!"

"He is an insult and injury to us all! Vallandigham blustered, losing his self-control. "It is exactly such gratuitous nobility as he is reputed to boast, that gives our foolish and gullible populace its insane belief that they shall beat to their knees the sterling stuff our South is made of. Quality, true quality is stacked against them. The kindest thing we could do would be to facilitate a quick compromise. That's the way to prove true patriotism, not by empty words! I call it a cheap patriotism which sacrifices the flower of our youth for a cause which, no matter how you view it, is both unconstitutional and tyrannical."

Turchin heard such sentiments often after Scott initially reported the incident. Amazed and incredulous, he immediately set about investigating the situation. "It was wonderful if the things we accomplish at the risk of our lives were as faithfully and expediently reported as the small deviations are! What happiness can our detractors find in publicly maligning us?"

But what was an outrageous incident in the Chicago Times was scarcely an untoward disturbance on the spot. The town had been occupied, and a provost marshal delegated to attend to both discipline and order which was necessary in a town admittedly hostile toward its occupying army. Turchin's orders had been obeyed, obeyed so well in fact that when a band of Confederates had assaulted some Union soldiers, natural reprisals had ensued, as was to be expected, especially as the citizens were known to have aided and abetted the attackers, to have shielded them in their houses.

But of this uncomplicated war occurrence, what stories were recounted! Rape of women; looting of private homes; pillaging of town property; revenge and barbarianism, were but mild details. "I shall not reply to such nonsense," Turchin declared irately to his wife. "Mitchel may come and investigate. He shall find my boys as decent and mannerly as any in America! Vile traducers notwithstanding I am willing to defy them all, to back my boys to the hilt!"

The one thing which worried him with respect to the tales told, was that preceding the time of the small unsuccessful uprising of Southerners in the town, he himself had ridden to a neighboring town. To guard the scene, he had left an excellent company of Ohio regulars, among who was his friend, Mihalotzy. He had sought out at once for full particulars and lamented the evil chance which had drawn him out of Athens. Being an exacting honest man, this absence at a critical moment troubled him, and helped create room for doubts until he should establish the truth. This he set about doing at once and secured the co-operation of Scott, Mihalotzy and Mitchel. They found indeed that the townsfolk were bitterly hostile, making the most of their rights as citizens the while thumbing their noses at the Government itself. Mitchel ascertained that upon being attacked, the Ohio boys had been shown neither mercy nor courtesy, and moreover, that vicious warfare against federal troops was deemed proper, far more proper than the use of confiscated supplies to feed these Ohio boys who had subdued them. For the rest, there were nothing but idle rumors and unfounded denunciations based upon nothing, save harmless familiarities young men will take with servant wenches.

That there had been several burnings of public buildings did not worry the colonel, for his orders had been explicit in this respect. General Mitchel, presumably with General Buell's knowledge, had commanded that wherever the army met delaying action, wherever the people were active in their support of the rebel army, punishment was to be meted out, and a few buildings burned as a warning.

Turning these matters over, apprehensive and yet singularly free of apprehensions, he awaited the coming of his superior officer, General Mitchel, who rode over late in the day. He was accompanied by several junior officers and one lieutenant attached to Buell's staff. The men saluted and attacked the problem at once. "Buell is in a rage," General Mitchel said to Turchin in an aside, whereupon the colonel showed surprise and consternation. "Whoever made it a point to inform him, certainly had colored the facts violently. He is ready to come down here personally to clean up the messy business."

"What is there to clean up? Is it not by his express orders that resisting towns are to be seized and punished where punishment is due?"

Mitchel nodded wordlessly. He seemed more intent upon his gloves than the face of the excitable Turchin. As his fingers stroked the long fringes on his cuff, he said: "It's the same old story, Colonel Turchin. It is the basic contradiction we face in the prosecution of this war. General Buell, like his model, General McClellan, is a stickler for keeping up the dignity of their West Point ethics, in spite of the nature of this war which we all know is predicated on no civilized ethics to begin with." He sounded tired, and his face showed worry lines deeply etched in it. "But what would you do, colonel, when our top-ranking leaders by and large are dedicated to a genteel policy of leniency toward the Secessionists. We are to impute nothing of warlike sensibilities as we oppose them civilly or militarily!" He turned his back upon him and the several officers who attended the meeting, and began to walk restlessly about the colonel's tent. "It will come to this, gentlemen," he exclaimed sharply, "that if the Army of Tennessee wins a victory, we shall all stand to get court-martial!"

"I fail to understand all the excitement," Turchin persisted stubbornly. "I left a few men here to hold the town; they were attacked without warning by returning rebel soldiers. They were macerated by these, except for such few as escaped and fled the town, and whom we met on the road as we came to assist Stanley. We retook the town, and perhaps our boys did not feel kindly toward people whose hands were still red with their comrades' blood. We found a few snipers secreted in buildings, from which vantage point they bravely shot our boys in the back. So we set a few buildings afire. Perhaps a few women screamed."

"That is exactly what will infuriate General Buell," Mitchel stated. "The ladies of the South flatter him, and he thinks their kith and kin as full of niceties as their womenfolk, when they hold rifles against us. We are asked to wage war against the men folk while he dawdles with the ladies, and then we must punish our boys who believe we mean it when we say fight!"

"General Buell will find that nothing untoward can be said of my men," Turchin promised. "Who says my lads are barbarous, committed crimes or indecencies, lies in his teeth!"

"And what is this about your harboring run-a-way Negroes?"

"Only one, sir. A human being could do no less than we, Madam and I, in giving succor to a lad who looked to us as the liberators of the land. To have sent him back to his master would have meant to set upon him the unleashed, retaliatory vengeance of these people. To the town, that colored boy is a renegade and a traitor. Do you realize that wherever a colored boy has been found to have given information to our army, we find him strung up on a tree afterwards?"

Mitchel did not press this point, and continued to worry over the affair more than he was willing to disclose to Turchin. A few hours later, he was ready to act. He proposed that with Turchin's and Scott's help, sufficient evidence was to be accumulated from the townspeople themselves in order to prove to General Buell the utter baselessness of the tales he had heard. He summoned the mayor of Athens, and ordered depositions to be taken of all those who preferred charges against his occupying regiments. Every person was called upon singly to make his statement under oath, and then the accusers were called to hear and scrutinize each soldier, to indict him who had been guilty of pillage or rape as averred.

Not a man was identified, not a man indicted. As far as Mitchel was concerned his men were totally absolved, and he had documents to prove the complete fabrication of the stories rampant in the papers. But this was not satisfactory to General Buell, who, all the evidence notwithstanding, appeared to have developed an implacable hostility toward Turchin. He received the depositions which Mitchel forwarded without comment, waved aside the attestations of citizens in Athens who exonerated the whole regiment and refuted entirely the story of the supposed outrages. He was plainly not to be appeased by solid facts. He gave all to understand that he was dissatisfied and ready to make an example of the incident. Until he came to a decision, the corps was forced to a standstill in its southern march.

Outwardly, Turchin endured the necessary period of waiting for General Buell's judgment patiently, but inwardly the delay and anxiety were wreaking havoc with him and with his wife, too, for whom these unfortunate reverses in their fortunes began to connote an evil fate and to give off an unpleasant odor of dead hopes and ambitions. Often, under the Alabama stars, she would stand unguarded; her little hand clasped about the dagger she wore at her waist and permit herself the luxury of tears. The past five years seemed to glide by in relentless review in the sky and she experienced a sense of loss for their passing; for out of the five years had come nothing to her but Baron Trofimov and he, like her dreams, was a passing figure in the sky. She dared not bring his image close to her conscious mind and therefore turned to her husband's present difficulties with dogged purposefulness, as though by concerning herself with them, little help as she could be, she guarded herself from the claims the baron's elusive smile made upon her.

"Poor Vanya!" she thought as she stood alone and contemplated the velvety heavens. We come through a hundred villages and hamlets and everywhere he feels like the shining knight errant bringing the truth, only to find rudely, as he pauses to rest, that he has been mistaken for a ruffian, a vile persecutor and heretic!" And at that moment the tears which fell from her eyes were truly for her husband; not one for Trofimov, who was to marry Susan Brewster and who selfishly tendered Nadine his undemanding love, more searing than dislike, more wounding and upsetting than hostility which could be construed as springing at least from a spontaneous emotion.

"He tries so valiantly, so gamely," she said to herself of Turchin. "I wish I could ensure his success!" We are two hundred miles into the heart of the Confederacy; the fortunes of war are not with us, yet he complains not at all; we are threatening the second line of the enemies' defenses and depriving them of the river lands, yet he is discontented, wants ever to go faster and do more!" She did not utter the thought which nagged her, that for all his pains and his enthusiasms, his rewards were slight and if any accrued at all, he had to fight valiantly for them.

For long minutes she stood outside their tent and watched the movements of clouds in the night sky. She had only now returned from her nightly inspection tour of the hospital tents where lay the boys wounded at Huntsville and Athens. Since Turchin's men had quelled the uprising in Athens, scarcely a single shot had been heard in the region and her comings and goings at all hours were comparatively safe. Tonight she had been humbly escorted by the colored lad who had joined them in Huntsville and she saw him making long shadows near the mule shed. A smile flitted across her face and a deep thankfulness for this humble sentinel, filled her. A sudden impulse seized her and she stepped towards the mule shed. Two of the beasts brayed loudly and the black boy's face glowed with delight as Nadine approached him. She above all others he adored mutely and now waited to hear her purpose in seeking him. "I want to see that wound on your arm," she said and waited until he rolled back his sleeve. "I see you do not wear the uniform the colonel furnished you," she reproached him pleasantly.

The boy made no answer at first. A wide smile curved his mouth. "Why do you not?" she asked putting his arm down when she had finished her inspection of the flesh wound.

"Da Cunnel have plenty trouble 'tout gittin folks riled bouten me," he answered simply and was thereupon nonplussed as his shiny "Cunnel's Lady" as he called her, turned abruptly away from him in tears.

Returning to her tent, she found her husband fallen asleep in his chair. The day had been nerve-wracking and trying to his strained patience. No word had as yet come from Buell and the entire camp felt like a whiplash because of the restlessness their colonel labored under.

Finally fatigue had claimed him and his head now lay lax on his arms over the desk. The kerosene lamp had burned out; only such starlight as her entrance had enabled to shine in, lit him up. His weary mind had shut out all sounds and sights. Nor did he stir when she gently unfastened his neckband and eased his head with a small cushion.

The next morning, when a bright, clear daylight pervaded the camp, when the rows of tents reaching toward the river were brightened under an assertive sunlight, Turchin woke and stretched his cramped limbs. Nadine, already clothed and fresh in the neat plain garments she adopted for use in camp, was steeping tea for him. The aroma was strong and invigorating as he sniffed it. Bill, the runaway slave boy, made his appearance with a platter full of corn cakes, the sight of which heartened Turchin who quickly made his morning toilet and was once again rosily prepared to defend high faith and good appetite. He called the lad into his tent for the execution of small chores while he and Nadine breakfasted.

Between mouthfuls of corncakes he pursued a pleasant, edifying conversation with the young Negro, who by this time fairly worshipped both Turchin and Nadine. "You may shine the buttons on my uniform, son," Turchin laughed, "but only in order that you shall prepare yourself to shine your own. Soon you will be able to wear your uniform proudly. You are only to have faith."

Before Bill could make his untutored reply, Colonel Scott rode up in clattering haste. He had come all the way from Huntsville with the dispatch General Buell had sent there, instead of to Athens, where Turchin expected it. From the dismay on his face, Nadine inferred the contents of the document he waved aloft even as he leapt from his horse and strode into the tent without further ado. "It has come, Colonel Turchin," he said thickly with grief in his voice and eyes.

"What has come?"

"Buell's answer to Mitchel's report."

"Why to you, Sir?" Turchin rose and frowned angrily upon his young friend who, understanding the emotions with which he must be struggling, took no umbrage at his tone or implied superiority of rank.

Without another word, Scott handed the dispatch to his superior and stepped back as Turchin perused its contents. No one in the tent looked upon the face of the colonel and even Bill, after a frightened minute, stole quietly out of the tent.

Nadine had guessed the contents of the documents which had clearly saddened and decomposed Scott. To her surprise, Turchin, upon finishing his reading, laid the paper carefully on his desk and looked about him with calm eyes. "Like a deer just shot, not yet aware of pain, just startled at the occurrence," she thought. "Like a man struck from behind," Scott thought.

"Well!" Turchin uttered the one word with flat finality. "I suppose they all know by now, Mitchel, Mihalotzy and the rest?"

"Mitchel knows."

"Knows that Buell is about to institute court-martial proceedings against me?"

"Knows, and is about to hand in his own resignation. He says he will go to Washington if Buell continues his persecution!"

"You, my boy, must not resign," Turchin hastily cautioned, reading the other's intent in his tone. "Buell wishes to suspend me, well and good! Let him! I have nothing to fear; I shall not hand him my resignation, which is what he probably expects me to do. I shall stand trial and I shall challenge them to discharge Colonel Turchin dishonorably. So far, Justice won't be defiled!"

Some days after this, Turchin and Nadine packed their belongings and set out for Chicago where it was decided they should wait until Buell's plans matured; either a recall or a court-martial. Their departure was quiet at Turchin's request and only intimate acquaintances like Conant and Mihalotzy, who had come to Athens from Huntsville to express their regrets, accompanied them to the station. Colonel Scott was inconsolable, while the young colored boy openly wept. When Nadine gave him her dagger and ordered him to carry it always, he threw himself upon the ground in a frenzy of grief. He was but sixteen years old and his gods were few, which accounted for his desperation at their sudden removal.

CHAPTER XVIII

Henrietta Morrison had an admirer whose tender feelings for her she never suspected. This was Geza Mihalotzy, whom she had not seen since that memorable day when he had entrained with the 19th Illinois. Mihalotzy was attached to the 24th Illinois and had formed a part of the forces which had occupied Athens. At the time Turchin was suspended and subjected to General Buell's displeasure, he too was in the shadow of that offended general who was definitely bent on making an example of recalcitrant officers, as he dubbed them and who had incurred his displeasure by their actions or words. In due course of time his military housecleaning, as he looked upon his stringent castigations and swift court-martials, reached down to the ranks of the captains and thus a week after Turchin had departed for Chicago, Mihalotzy followed suit, he being charged with complicity in the disorders at Athens.

It was not in the nature of Captain Mihalotzy to harbor against Buell the antagonism men like Turchin developed. He was always ready to accept criticism and even chastisement, with an open mind. It had not touched the well-springs of his being to find himself under a cloud, for clouds did not exist long in the light and joyousness of his bland personality. More tolerant than Turchin, he viewed the people of the South simply as people; that they were enemies he attributed to their weaknesses rather than their evil intentions. Moreover, military life had not for him the innate fulfillment of united intelligence it had for Turchin for whom such a life was, all unbeknownst to himself, the glass through which he made his studies and took measure of all actions and behaviors attendant upon them.

It was hard for Mihalotzy to grow wroth with anyone and upon returning to Chicago and seeking out Mrs. Morrison he failed to mention his own imminent discharge in his anxiety over Turchin's. If the sight of that fair lady's troubled countenance, instantly shadowed with concern for Turchin, caused him to feel a pang or two, it did not evoke resentment against the colonel, for Mihalotzy expected no requital for the deep affection this American lady had awakened in him.

Not often in his life had women stirred the grand passion in his bosom; not readily could he presume to make her whom he knew to be far beyond his reach, aware of his desires. It was sufficient for him to have free access to her, to be permitted to correspond with her, to have her abiding interest in himself and his efforts to master the details of complicated social life in Chicago.

Therefore, with unfeigned good-will, he accepted with alacrity her suggestion that they two seek out Turchin immediately. Henrietta said, "It is not seemly that good friends shall stand on ceremony, wait for a friend in trouble to call upon them! We must rise above petty social form; make the first amends to him for the cruel prejudice pitted against him. It is nothing short of that, Captain, which impales the honor and integrity of men like Colonel Turchin!"

Quickly, she summoned her coachman and in a matter of minutes, she and her companion were on the way to Division Street. So moved was she at the sight of the house and the thought of the man she fancied brooding within, that her eyes prickled uncomfortably and she heartily wished she had not a witness to observe her agitation. Upon alighting from her carriage she attained a measure of composure and the quiet dignity without which she would have felt herself as compromised in Nadine's sight as though she had committed some unbecoming indecorum.

They were received with surprise and some dismay by Colonel Turchin, who, himself had answered the door. No simple matter was this for him to find himself the object of pity, which emotion he thought to detect in the faces of both Mrs. Morrison and Mihalotzy. "Well, colonel," Mihalotzy began. "You see, your friends find you out in your most remote hiding place." He held out his hand with warmth and eagerness to him he knew was sorely wounded by the past events.

"It is good of you to visit me," replied Turchin laconically. Now that his two friends were present he sensed a curious easing of his feelings. Since he and Nadine had come back to Chicago, he had avoided all contact with acquaintances or places where they frequented; he wished like a wounded woodland creature, to be alone to nurse his wounds, to turn over in his perplexed mind the details of his persecution, for in no other light could he explain General Buell's displeasure. He was all the more grieved since Buell, above all commanders had complimented him for his drill manual, had approved the splendid condition of the troops and of the camp in general.

Naturally, he was led to speak of this to his friends, to implore Nadine to confirm his statements, which she did at once; Nadine indicated that she too, though not blindly overlooking instances when the colonel might have been liable to misunderstanding, was confounded by the unexpected and summary dismissal.

"I remember Senator Vallandigham remarking, Henrietta suddenly recalled, that "General Buell was intimately acquainted with General McClellan. Is not General McClellan an erstwhile friend of yours, colonel?"

She asked the question hopefully, but recognized in Turchin's frowning assent that he should not welcome any suggestions she might have made relative to securing McClellan's intervention on his behalf.

"Why should I fear anything General Buell instigates against me?" he asked rhetorically. "Truth does not have to expound reasons for its being! As for General McClellan, friend though he is, I cannot say that it pleases me to hear he is Buell's friend! I am ready to account for myself to my superiors! Yes! That I am ready to do! But appeal to them! Never! I take an oath to do my duty. That duty I perform as God gives me sense and heart to see it. If I have a brain as well, if I can see what is as plain as my nose, that not our enemies but our leaders deter us in the speedy execution of justice, am I to apologize for this? Am I to turn to McClellan, who ought to be driving the rebels into the sea and ask him to plead for me? Me, who is but one small American."

This reply to her unspoken thoughts caused Mrs. Morrison to blush guiltily, to feel blameworthy and remiss as a friend. She remained only a short while, then, putting her hand tremulously into his, she took her departure. Mihalotzy saw her to her carriage and thereafter returned to prolong his visit with the Turchins.

These few moments with his friends had restored to Turchin something of his normal self. And now with the Captain, he accomplished his duties as host which, to his surprise at first, had caused him to neglect Nadine. She, understanding the perturbation to his friends that his discord had occasioned him, now became happy in the sight of his recovered good humor. The friendship of man for man transcended at times any feminine compassion, she reasoned and she therefore left the two men together while she discreetly occupied herself in another part of the house.

"So!" Turchin remarked pleasantly, as soon as his wife had absented herself. "It is Mrs. Morrison who claims you first of all when you come to Chicago!" He grinned broadly and received the confirming smile of Mihalotzy. "She is a wonderful woman," he praised her unstintingly. "She is not afraid to think like a man!" with which ultimate encomium he acquitted himself admirably. In a matter of moments he was ready to discuss other matters, particularly the progress of the war now in its second year and the growing possibility of European intervention. "I am told that the South is secretly importing war vessels out of British ports," he informed Mihalotzy.

"We shall completely blockade the South before long," was the young captain's answer, delivered assuredly. How could anyone help admiring Colonel Turchin, who had thoughts ever for matters other than his own?

"I am thinking," Turchin said seriously, "that a blockade may play into the hands of our enemies."

"How is that?" Mihalotzy asked, though his thoughts were rather on Henrietta, how sweet and womanly she was, how far above him, how much beyond his wildest dreams. These feelings were not violent, having in them the blandness of the summer day itself. A depth and calmness within himself prevented the stormy turbulences another man than he might have suffered, carrying for two years now a consciousness of his own boldness and unworthiness to aspire to such a woman. Even his aspiration was timid and apologetic, performing only the feat of barring forever any other woman's image from his mind.

"Well, think of it in this light," Turchin explained himself happily, momentarily forgetting the personal troubles he chafed under. "By a successful blockade we can prevent cotton from reaching the mills of Manchester, Cologne and Lyons. Very well. This would mean that large populaces in Europe would naturally become unemployed. Unemployment means hunger, Mihalotzy. Hunger and destitution and these terrible trials of poor people, make them easy prey to unscrupulous politicians. An evil man may arise who will inflame a hungry people against us; they will be too hungry to care that a blockade around the South is a measure we employ to ensure a subsequent greater freedom and welfare. They will hear their scheming politicians declaim against Mr. Lincoln as being the direct cause of their misery; they will not rise to prevent England or France from helping the South, as we want them to. Do you find a blockade then such a reasonable thing, Mihalotzy? Think what it would mean to the rebel government to receive international recognition as a nation? Credit, that's what it means. It means credit and goods and even worse; corroboration in their insufferable arrogance."

"Cotton is undoubtedly the chief product of the South's economy," Mihalotzy said, drawn to pay closer attention to Turchin's words.

"We shall change all that someday," the other prognosticated cheerfully. "When we abolish the slave system we shall make a great garden of plenty out of this Southland. Slavery is like an insurmountable fence shutting one part of the people away from the other."

"It is, Colonel Turchin, remarks like that which, having come to Buell's attention, makes him deal hard with you." Mihalotzy leaned back in his chair and met his friend's bridling truculence unfearingly. "The general perhaps may not resent the truth of what you say, but only the time and occasion of your saying it which does not synchronize with his immediate ends and purposes."

"Nonsense!" Turchin retorted. "There is no right time for truth saying. The peddlers of lies are not ashamed to cry their wares continually; why shall we not cry the truth, sell decency and honor as zealously as our enemies sell lies? No, Buell may not apportion the time for honest action."

Mihalotzy shrugged his shoulders resignedly. "No one, Colonel Turchin, is likely to relish the choice such an attitude as yours imposes upon him. One has to believe himself either the purveyor of truths, which office is open to anyone's questioning, or the recipient of truth which might easily suppose that an absence of it had obtained until then."

"That is an absurd line of reasoning," was Turchin's rejoinder. "I have then nothing but to agree with Buell; that I am a pretender; that I am incompetent to know my duty or to do it either. In that case, I ought to be grateful that my superiors, because they are my superiors, deem me rash and ignorant. Am I to conclude, because of your logic, that I am a pretender? That I am rash and ignorant: that I know nothing?"

By this time Mihalotzy was pained to see the nervous irritation his ill chosen words had thrown his friend into. He was not fond of strife, be it only verbal, and now essayed placatingly to make what restitution he could. He was wiser than to insist upon logic which, to be effective at all must be welcomed and not endured. Had he been able, without suffering the taxations imposed upon the teacher, to give his friend some portion of his own equanimity, he should have done so gladly. Had he known how to comfort him, he would have spared no pains to do so. It did not occur to him to mitigate a friend's trouble by burdening him with the like load he carried himself. Thus he took his leave eventually without informing Turchin that the same onus of disgrace hovered over him that had driven his friend to Chicago. It was left to Baron Trofimov to disclose this to Turchin. Mihalotzy learned this from Brewster, who was another of the friends Mihalotzy called upon in Chicago as Brewster was one of the patrons of the Lincoln Riflemen, which was now incorporated into the 24th Illinois.

Brewster was not slow to learn of Turchin's return. Better than they who were the chief actors in the situation, he understood the intricate connections between the military and the political functions that year, and might have, had he chosen, clarified much of Turchin's doubts and perplexities. However, he was now fully engaged in furthering the nefarious schemes of Senator Vallandigham whose arrogance had attained gigantic proportions over the past year. And this summer, preceding two gubernatorial and county elections, he had had the satisfaction of further increasing his influence and prestige at the polls, not to mention Democratic political headquarters where he was already being groomed for the election in the fall. This promised ample returns for his unmitigated labors expended in the secret war fomented against the Union army and government.

As Vallandigham grew bold and more daring, as he toured his State and neighboring ones as well, Brewster, seeing the goal they fought over more clearly, grew correspondingly bold and daring, more insolent and outspoken. He took but little notice of Turchins' ignominious return to Chicago when informed of it by his son-in-law elect. Trofimov had made tentative suggestions to Brewster in order to enlist his aid in clearing Turchin, a desire he only newly entertained without much passion. Casually, he ventured to express pity for Turchin and was met by Brewster's scornful mirth. "Help that insufferable fool! Do you know what you ask? It is precisely men like that whom Clement and I work diligently to eradicate from public office and military rank." He became angry with Trofimov and showed his wrath unmistakably. "I have admired you, baron," he said distinctly, "primarily because you display unusual character and clarity, not charity. Then, when we really begin to get some action, you turn about and want this nobody or that nobody spared! A clean sweep, that's what we want. We want this country rid of alien influences. We don't want Russia or Russians! For this reason alone, we have good cause to censure that rail-splitter in the White House who insists on opening doors we have the right to keep closed."

"Then why not start on top," Trofimov persisted. "Turchin is far from dishonorable. He ought not to be suffered to face the indignity of a court-martial and that is undoubtedly what he has to expect. After all, he is not a prominent figure. Why pick on him?"

"We shall get to the top in time," Brewster replied. Then remembering a recent incident not widely known, he smiled broadly. "I did not believe men like McClellan would fall in with us so neatly," he said companionably to the baron. "Curious how stray ends rather fit into a single fabric when one knows how to inspect it."

"McClellan is in with you?" Trofimov was not quite ready to believe the campaign successful enough to receive the support of McClellan.

"Perhaps not knowingly," Brewster laughed, "but it comes to the same thing. He has great ambitions and we hold out equally great expectations to him." He grinned slyly. "These bright young men all want to be President by hook or by crook and Vallandigham will one day be powerful enough to make even Presidents. He may even decide to make himself President!"

"McClellan!" Trofimov repeated disdainfully. He recalled how Turchin had lauded this same man, how Turchin had defended him in spite of his radical difference in political opinion. "Poor old fool," he thought of Turchin. "His own patron, one with Vallandigham" and Turchin had never given McClellan's perfidy a thought.

"But we don't count on the mere outer similitudes," Brewster continued. "We rely on the subtler qualities of men like McClellan. These we study and know and that's what makes Clement such a sterling leader. He knows how to exploit these and the accompanying weaknesses and limitations. McClellan is caught neatly in our trap. His own ambitious temperament has trapped him for us. He's been the idol of the entire army and has prematurely grown too big for his breeches."

"Meaning what?"

"That he is now, in his own opinion, cock of the roost. He takes it upon himself to run things as he chooses. He knows better than Lincoln what must be done and he can back up whatever he says with indisputable military science. There, you see, he has Lincoln and there we have him." Brewster was enjoying his disquisition, enjoying the changing expressions he read on the younger man's face.

"He actually believes as we do, that a long drawn out war is a fatal catastrophe for the country, for business, for progress. He has thwarted Lincoln's every wild attempt to force him to attack Lee. Why?" Here he leaned forward intimately. "He snubbed Lincoln right in front of his servants! Snubbed the President of the United States! Now that's the kind of democracy we need!"

"Is it?" Trofimov was amused and contemptuous.

"Certainly. Would you have a sincere man like General McClellan yield to the demands of a demented dictator, who knows the tide is going against him?" He went on to tell his choice story. He left nothing to the imagination of the baron who could easily picture to himself the scene which had reputedly taken place in McClellan's house. General McClellan had hosted a wedding party - incidentally, the wedding of one of General Buell's young officers - when his butler had summoned him, telling him the President had called in person to discuss urgent business.

To this the general was said to have replied that he was currently otherwise engaged and not free at the moment to attend the President. Whereupon Mr. Lincoln had decided humbly to wait in the drawing room of his general and had thusly been waiting some three hours before the over-confident McClellan had had his fill of Washington Society and thereupon inclined to put in his appearance. Upon entering the drawing rooms he had been addressed familiarly by Mr. Lincoln, but instead of acknowledging his Superior's friendly words, he was said to have marched past as though oblivious of him and went upstairs to his chambers. His butler had shamefacedly informed the President that the general had calmly gone to bed!

From this tale and from the rest of Brewster's conversation, Trofimov realized there was nothing to be done for Colonel Turchin by any application in this quarter. There might have been one thing he could have done, were he inclined to impair in the least the careful relationship he had been almost two years establishing; he could have gone to Medill or McCormick of the Tribune and placed certain facts before them. However, the entire dilemma of his friend did not warrant this self-sacrifice, which, he reasoned, would affect nothing appreciably and only tend to endanger him. He finally concluded to do as he had always done, sit back and watch. "If he does not get the axe this way", he thought, "he will find some other. He's always borrowing trouble anyway!" With these consoling platitudes to sustain him, he promised himself to make an early call upon his compatriots and felt immensely relieved.

It was Mihalotzy, however, who called again before the baron found time from his demanding fiancée to fulfill his obligations to Turchin. The baron had the legitimate excuse that his wedding was scheduled for the late summer and that he found little time or desire to visit what he imagined was the saddened atmosphere of the house on Division Street. There was always the disconcerting fact of Nadine. He did not wish to see her, months out of her sight had enabled him to place the quiveringly frail enchantment, which linked them, safely in the back of his mind. He desired no entanglements at this stage of his career and wanted none of the contagious gloom and discredit that was certain to attach to his friends during this period.

Mihalotzy, tactfully, waited until he could come the Turchins with encouraging tidings, something to hearten the colonel. On his former visit he had found no opportunity to interrupt him in order to deliver the kindly good wishes and regards with which he had come delegated from the 19th Illinois to repeat. All the men in the regiment's companies had united their small gifts of money in order to have manufactured for Turchin a token sword. Mihalotzy had imparted this information to Mrs. Morrison who had cautioned silence until the sword was ready for presentation. The gift was now ready and it gave Mihalotzy a happy incentive for speeding to Division Street in the benign early morning coolness of a July day. He found his friends sitting in their small garden where they were trying to find some respite and strength before the extreme heat of the hot forenoon should descend unmitigatingly upon the whole city. They eschewed the park in the neighborhood lest they encounter people they knew. Turchin's one object was to avoid anyone who might question him, who might wonder to see him in Chicago when his country's prospects for winning the war seemed at its nadir.

"You have heard nothing yet?" Mihalotzy began at once, taking a seat on the lawn where Nadine was sitting, her fingers busy winding cotton strips into bandages for the wounded. Despite their isolation, she kept up a steady contact with the hospital.

"Oh, I am a most important person!" Turchin growled bitterly. "They have to have special drums to beat me out with. That takes time!"

"At any rate, Colonel Turchin, the men feel differently, no matter what General Buell thinks. Sir!" He spoke rapidly, as though he could not contain the cheerful news a moment longer. "I am come today to tell you that we all hope and pray that you shall be completely exonerated. The men of your regiment have appointed another sort of tribunal for you. They selected the finest artists to be procured, that they might design and decorate a symbol of your and their unbroken faith. Two days from now, Colonel Turchin, it shall be my privilege to present you with this special sword and its appendages. The friends and relatives of your men decreed this, for they know, as we all do who serve the same cause, that this sword goes into the hands of a man who will not let it rust; neither will he tarnish its blade by any unsoldierly act. It is their opinion, those who have fought, suffered and frozen with you, that a more sagacious and skillful officer never lived, nor a more gallant and humane one."

At the conclusion of these words, Nadine burst into grateful tears and fled the garden into the house. The colonel sat motionless, tremendously moved, his fists clenched until the knuckles showed white, tears streaming down his face, into his beard. In his heart there waxed a fervid devotion.

For two days he remained in this devotional mood, changing from righteous wrath against the enemies of his men - for he saw indictment of him as a mere subterfuge representing an indictment of every fighting man - to ardent patriotism that, in his mind, was conjoined with wrath. Then, a kind of calm came upon him and he prepared himself for the presentation and his first public address. He was like the crusader marching in the name of Right.

Inside the designated hall, he ascended the platform alone, Nadine having preferred to seat herself inconspicuously to one side. Many Chicago dignitaries were already on the stage and from each Turchin received a cordial smile and handshake. He took his seat among them and concentrated his attention upon the huge crowd of auditors convened this evening. They were of various sorts and conditions ranging from the elegantly gowned and coiffured ladies, in their bright colored summer frocks, to the somber and earnest women of the common people, whose white faces stared up at him with fearful intensity; from the young children to the aged and infirm; from the curious to the glowingly interested, like Mrs. Morrison who sat well concealed from public view, though she could see Turchin and all that happened on the stage.

Mihalotzy was the first to speak. He stepped forth from the wings of the stage and proceeded forward until he stood before the men assembled behind the speaker's stand. He first made them a salute, then turned and performed a duplicate for the audience, which applauded loudly, being well pleased by and instantly attracted to his winning and handsome person. He spoke low and earnestly, his white teeth gleaming with every smile and every gesture to his audience. At last he made his final statements and stepped to the stand where lay the gleaming sword.

He lifted it high so that all could see the regimental colors. Then he held it forward, as though to present it first to the people, as their colonel would have wished, as if in the people's trust was the true dedication of the sword.

So eloquent and simple was this tribute to them, that not a man or woman in that meeting hall failed to grasp its meaning. A spontaneous "Hurrah" sounded as the band struck up the national anthem, which was sung by a standing and honoring, congregation.

When Turchin stepped to the front of the stage at last, a hush fell upon the listeners. Every face turned up to him and every face grew dear to him as he saw them all blended together in an agglomeration which was America. Mihalotzy without another word placed the beautiful sword in his friend's outstretched arms where it lay cradled for a long minute before Turchin placed it gently on the speaker's stand. With his hands solemnly folded over it, he began to speak: "Friends, Americans! Captain Mihalotzy has said everything I feel. It is, as he says, a moment of pride for me to stand here and receive from all of you, the parents and sweethearts and relatives of my boys, this signal honor, your confidence, when all of you know I stand suspected of heinous crimes against my country! But today I stand justly proud because in your sight I am the representative of those boys who deserve all your confidence. I am happy that it is so. This sword attains significance because it is the symbol of all their swords, which they are ready to wield in our country's behalf as long as God grants them life and limb."

He felt the audience alive to his every word and their interest was a mandate he could not resist. Carefully he began to narrate the events which had led to his impending court-martial. He began with full descriptions of his regiment's duties, pointing out that though they were not in the more glorious first line of attack against the enemy, it was never the less their constant, unremitting hounding of the Southern lines, menacing the rebel lines of communications and supplies, which tactics were forcing a wily foe to come from behind his ambush and into the open.

"It is not our hardships that try us: It is the shameful dark maneuverings of our unknown enemies hiding behind the guise of friends! There are some who would rather we never fought wars of liberation! Such people had much rather we kill a few thousand, assuage what they think is a mere lust for blood and then join hands with our enemies! And this irrationality is what they want us to believe is the American Way!"

He paused until the stirring murmur his words had roused subsided. Then, lifting his hand in an unconscious signal for attention, he pursued his thoughts further. "Some there are who call me and others like me, if not disloyal men, then deluded and irrational men. It is as though they wish to prove, that what brings men from over the seas to seek haven and refuge here, is a base delusion. That there are no elements of pristine goodness or greatness in the human soul; that we who believe the contrary to be true, are not good men, are only Cossacks and dissidents, not gentlemen.

To find favor with our enemies, I have only to assume that slaves enjoy their slave status and that the defenders of slavery are waging a war to prove a constitutional point of law! Should I agree to this, then I must indeed merit promotions, not castigations! Then I could understand the sense in preserving rebel property intact! If I did that, fellow Americans, how neatly should I prove their contention; for they look upon a black man as so much property; and each man is entitled to have his property respected! Do you not see this insidious logic? I am sure you do and our generals, who espouse this gentle handling of our enemies, see it too. Therefore, what are we to think? What are we to believe when Americans are derided for being Americans?"

Behind him there was heard a shuffling of feet. The city worthies were heard clearing their throats uneasily, besides making other signs and noises to mark their disapproval of such immoderate self-justification, this being the light in which they largely viewed the colonel's analysis of what had befallen him and why.

But their affronted restlessness in no way halted Turchin who continued to speak in the above manner until he had said what had lain grievously upon his heart for weeks. When he was done, he paused, looked squarely out upon his audience and met its concerted gaze openly. A silence ensued after his last word had been uttered. Suddenly, however, even before the chairman could step forward, a spontaneous ripple of applause began. It ruffled over the men and women and then burst into wild acclaim over the wounded spirit of Turchin.

In her obscure corner, Mrs. Morrison wiped the tears from her eyes. Mihalotzy, with his own eyes shining genially, gripped his friend's hand and wrung it repeatedly. Nadine, seated to one side of the audience, nodded her head imperceptibly when her husband's eyes strained in her direction. As he resumed his seat on the stage, she gave him a little smile of approbation. That was compliment enough for him; and with a gallant smile he prepared to give courteous attention to the several other speakers of the day.

By clarifying his position to his audience, he had gained a measure of interior calmness which, until this moment, had with Nadine's best attempts and exhortations, been academic. Sitting on the platform, he knew at last that he had obtained to true calmness and the calm was no harbinger of future storm. It was indeed the calm which a righteous man can create for himself when faced with the need to preserve his honor. Of a sudden, he seemed to possess a complete indifference to the trial being arranged for him at that very moment in Alabama. True, he had not as yet had word or summons to appear for trial, but he knew from his knowledge of military procedure, having already served on courts-martial himself, that the extensive period of questioning and arraigning was currently underway.

"I shall support no fears," he told himself. "It is these people before me who are the forward-looking. They do not back reluctantly into the future. They, who are my true peers, are my true judges. I have appealed to the people. It is their verdict and not that of Buell's underlings, which shall redeem me!"

CHAPTER XIX

Shortly after the ceremony, Turchin returned to Alabama. The initial preparations had been completed and the time was on hand for his trial. But before the trial began, a week of boring examination of witnesses had to be suffered. During this period, Turchin had leisure to study his judges who, for the most part, were colonels from Kentucky. Presiding over those colonels was Brigadier-General James A. Garfield from Ohio. In him Turchin found an interest that stemmed, not from the manners or behavior of the young general, nor from the fortitude with which he attended the preliminary hearings. These he might easily have avoided on plea of the illness which confined him to his cot. Nevertheless, each morning, he had his lieutenants wheel him and his cot into the courtroom from which he performed his duty. The general's interest appeared to stem rather from the strength and beneficence shining in his deep, kind eyes. Of all the men in the courtroom, Garfield alone had, without injury to his dignity, the qualities of humaneness to which Turchin had an immediate affinity, as though they were tangible elements remarkable more for their presence than absence. The non-beneficent faces of the military court judges he took for granted; he was prepared to expect it of them. But the intelligent compassion with which once or twice he thought to see General Garfield inspect him, almost unmanned him.

No word passed between these two men in the first week of the investigation. There was no need for words. Instinctively Turchin gained confidence because General Garfield presided, yet daily he grew more troubled as he fancied discerning in the general's face a pity for him thusly subjected to the humility of trial. He alternated between lifted hopes, elation and crushing despairs made no lighter by the intense loneliness he felt.

He had taken rooms in a small hostelry in Athens. Garfield had not imposed confinement upon him, but of his own accord he chose to remain close to the premises, refraining even from seeking by word or letter the boon of companionship otherwise accessible; the encampment of his regiment being but a few miles distant. Actuated by a fine consideration, he wished to avoid any connections with his men lest through their intimacy with him they might incur Buell's wrath.

Deep summer had transformed the visage of the countryside since he and Nadine had last been present in Athens. The regiment had pushed several miles further south leaving the town comparatively free of Union soldiers save such as were stationed here for routine duty, or directly involved in the trials, of which, Turchin ascertained, his was but one. Several other officers of high rank were to be tried as well as a number of lesser officers. The entire town lay dusty and heavy with the heat and presented an outer aspect of such peacefulness, that it was difficult for the colonel to remember the now placid square filled with rioting men and panic-stricken females, black and white.

One afternoon he walked leisurely down the main road leading away from the city and passed a square field, brown with burnt stubble. It had been a field of potatoes last spring, when he and his men had come down from Tennessee. "Each potato," he thought with rare good humor, "will send up its little ghost to testify against me!"

The ghostly potato figure he conjured up wryly amused him for its aptness and ludicrousness and he recalled an incident concerning the potato patch which he did not doubt would be brought up as evidence proving his Tartar instinct to pillage. This field of potatoes had been one of the properties ordered to be guarded. Men had been stationed to perform this duty which continued peacefully until one day the indignant owner reported infringements on his property rights and demanded action and redress. Turchin himself had ridden out with the irate owner to inspect how the vandals were tearing up the rebel's field.

He had found his men dutifully picketing the field; but within the picket line he saw a miniature army of his boys gleefully pulling up armloads of the vegetables, which, to them, starved for the taste of this homely food, was a succulent prize, irresistible and tempting.

"See! See!" The Southerner shouted. "Vandals! That's what your men are! You order them off my property instantly!"

Upon the approach of the colonel those mischievous lads in the potato field had stopped stock-still where they stood, their arms laden with potatoes, their faces betraying both consternation and fun. "We are only borrowing the gentlemen's spuds," one brave lad volunteered.

"Whose brilliant idea for this despicable crime is this?" Turchin roared out while the rebel stood vengefully beside him.

"Is this the way an honorable soldier conducts himself? Is the army to be mocked by striplings too fond of potatoes?"

When, with a sideways glance at the fuming rebel sympathizer, he roared even more loudly. "This pillage! This rapine! Who is responsible for it?" And when every boy stepped forward to take to himself the whole blame, Turchin's smile was hard to conceal. Pride for his boys welled up in him so that he had all he could do to keep up the pretense of reprimand he was enacting. "I give you two hours to evacuate the enemy premises!" he roared. "In two hours any men caught stealing potatoes will be summarily punished!"

On the face of it, the rebel could not say the colonel had condoned the robbing of his miserable potatoes; yet should the incident be introduced as evidence against him, Turchin vowed he should own his true sentiments. He determined to tell the court bluntly that according to all precedents in the prosecution of a war, the army should subsist on the land it occupied. He was walking firmly as he elaborated arguments to place before the military tribunals and amused himself by imagining their several reactions, when a voice called his name in greeting.

Turning about, he recognized the senior adviser of the Court-martial, Garfield, who at this time was assigned to serve on a series of courts-martial that General Buell had designated. Garfield was a man somewhat younger, perhaps, than Turchin, though the illness from which he was suffering that year and the irksome duties which the courts-marital entailed, had indelibly marked and aged his otherwise attractive, strong face. On this afternoon of his encounter with the Russian, he had felt strong enough to take an airing in the fragrance of the unexpected freshness that some vagrant winds, wandering past the firs and hemlocks of distant hills, had brought with them. He had curiously been thinking of this same Russian when he met him by chance on the country lane.

Thus far, Garfield had no definite proofs of the strong character he later came to respect in Turchin. As to many officers of the army of the Tennessee, rumors of the Russian's high handed methods had reached him, often causing him secretive smiles. Something likable and admirable he thought, must be in the constitution of a man so oblivious of the benefits to be derived from adaptability to what existed, that he braved the active antipathy of General Buell. Not that it required much deviation to bring that haughty general vengefully to the fore at the slightest infringement of his rules. Garfield knew Buell well enough by repute to ascertain what it was that a man like Turchin had failed to do; that Buell had expected of officers and men under his command more than a little reverence for himself and the rank he boasted. Garfield knew, too, that if the strong disciplinary methods that he utilized to secure his own stellar position in the army irked his junior officers, they actually erected impassable barriers in the execution of serious work incumbent upon the more responsible ranks. Quickly he had guessed upon the first sight of Colonel Turchin that General Buell, with his unappeasable disdain had been offended in more than just his habitual pride. Consequently, during the interval preparatory to the review of the case, he found himself giving to the Russian much thought and to the intentions of General Buell something stronger than mere thought.

Ordinarily, a mild and not overwhelmingly aggressive personality, Garfield was naturally reticent in his own thoughts. Always, with a strict sense of fairness, with a respect for truth and justice, regardless of the men involved in the cases that he heard, he made it a point not to consort with the officers on trial. Scrupulous to remain impartial, he hardly knew what sudden attraction caused him to address Colonel Turchin.

He had come up behind him and when he had called out his name and seen the colonel stop and turn about, he exchanged salutes with him, made as much haste as his physical condition allowed, to join him. "I hope, colonel, I do not intrude upon your private reflections," he spoke pleasantly. Then he went on to comment on the unexpected coolness of the breeze, the untoward weather generally at this time of year, the condition of the sandy roads and his embarrassment with his own weakness, which currently excluded him from a more effectual participation in his country's struggle than that of presiding at courts-martial.

Turchin was made painfully self-conscious by the friendly words and stood irresolute and silent. He had come to that bruised state of mind where it seems essential in maintaining the integrity of his personality to shun everything friendly, lest it prove inimical or deceptive. As though sentient of Turchin's hesitancy, General Garfield perceived the deep mortification under which the proud soldier felt obliged to stand trial to acquit himself and as though to make him amends, he held out his hand fraternally. "Come, Sir," he said sincerely, "we are not all your enemies, colonel. We are sometimes put into situations where we are bound to examine one another. I am certain that in your case there will be no less truth or justice applied than we can bring to bear on all." He was gropingly attempting to put the colonel at ease.

His affability produced no immediate response from Turchin. The general's friendliness, as determined as Turchin was not to heed friendly offers, was like fine old wine and gave warmth to his sore spirit. Gruffly he cleared his throat and made answer stiffly. He said that he was honored to be addressed by his superior on such familiar terms and that he was not morbid about the trial. Furthermore, that he feared no more than was consistent with the honor and trust reposed in him by the land he loved and the rightful government which dignified it.

They stood in the road and talked for some time, until General Garfield plainly evinced the fatigue his undue exertion was causing him and suggested on this account that they seat themselves in a deserted, straggling garden which was reaching the road. A trellised arbor of roses, growing wild, offered them a charming seclusion, shutting out the accusing and sinister somberness of the abandoned house behind it and the rutted road in front of it. "They," Garfield waved the cane that he rested heavily upon, "run as before the plague. They clamor for protection and are assured it by McClellan and Buell, but still, they no sooner see us over the edge of the horizon than they scatter like locusts in all directions."

Turchin followed the direction of Garfield's cane which indicated the uninhabited rebel mansion. His glance travelled beyond the house itself and he fancied to see, far across the intervening fields, the jagged outlines of slave huts. "The slaves have not run," he remarked. And as Garfield looked keenly into his face, he laughed mirthlessly. "I recognize slave huts, general. I am ashamed to admit that ours, on my father's land, were not superior to the shacks I have seen in this region - not fit for pigs!" He fell into a thoughtful retrospection which did not annoy Garfield whose eyes also filled with inner speculations. Himself, a hater of slavery, the colonel's words had revived his own discontent with his function in a war against slave owners. His most ardent wish at that time was to be assigned active duty in the field where he knew, without self-praise intended, that every officer of ability was urgently needed. From the few words Turchin had spoken, from the preliminary inspection of the records he had carefully studied, he saw that General Buell's limited perspective was by way of preventing more than one worthy man from doing what his heart and mind urged.

"I myself," Turchin went on feelingly, "would tolerate no slaves, not even a slavish beast!"

"It is strange, colonel," the general wondered musingly, "that you are so opposite to all reports upon you!" He laughed apologetically, already convinced that the entire fabric of confusion, of accusations and vindictive reports on this man, was a tissue of lies begot of malice and prejudiced resentments. So quickly did he come to this, that he failed to allow for an equal certitude on the colonel's part respecting him, though were it otherwise, this would not have weighed too much with Garfield. Once convinced, he was an easy mark for those who had won his initial respect. "I admit to you that when first I heard of you and saw you among us, we who presume to judge you, I could easily conceive you the fierce Muscovite you were said to be by repute." He paused, watching the emotion filled face of the colonel. "I think, now, colonel, that by any name you are described, you must be the sort of man your country would be proud of."

"If you refer to Russia, you err," Turchin boldly replied. "In Russia I have lost status; for in an autocracy my mind is an enemy of the State; a man who could not be trusted to carry out the plans of his Czar. But

Russia is not my country! This is my country! In Russia, because of my lucky birth, I was perforce honored and respected. Here, where it should be obvious, my allegiance owes nothing to birth or chance and my loyalty is impugned!"

"Consider then," General Garfield hastened to assure him, moved to a strong compassion, "that every man's loyalty is impugned when a traitor's gun threatens him! No! Not your loyalty is impugned, colonel!" And his tone said clearly whose loyalty would be on trial during the hearing. "Look upon incidents like this investigation as part of the casualties of war. I am convinced that if you give us a chance, Colonel Turchin, we shall not fail you!" But the kind general knew not whereof he spoke; for well as he understood the necessarily uneven course of events, as far as civil and military conflicts revealed them, he could not conceive of the violent forces moving to still, not only Turchin's voice, but other more significant voices as well.

These words from the president of the impending court-martial cheered Turchin, revived his bruised ardors so that when they both walked out of the deserted garden he felt a happier man, gave his arm gladly to General Garfield whom the walk and the talk had tired and accepted an offer to play chess with him, which he knew was a kind pretext on General Garfield's part to befriend him.

The initial friendliness soon ripened into a true affinity that was mutually shared and Turchin was grateful for the friendship and respect proffered him. Unlike any other American thus far in Turchin's career, General Garfield listened to the words which seemed to form of themselves whenever they met; so unstudied and deeply honed were they as expressions of a man who knows another and not only listens to him but feels for him. If it was a flaw in the colonel that he sought ever this human audience; that he sensed the true life of a thought only then when another quickened upon its disclosure; it was at any rate no moral flaw, being only a rather naive longing to communicate speedily with the latent good he believed anterior to every other component of mankind. "You, General Garfield, have restored for me my will to communicate the things I feel. It was beginning to seem that whatever I affirmed fell short of the truth. Always I have spoken to men as my conscience and my honor as a man and an officer dictated!"

Garfield nodded understandingly. In truth, he was even more understanding than he was willing for the colonel to guess. He, better than Turchin, was cognizant of the conflicting motives represented in the prosecution of the War. But he could not bring himself to discuss either personalities or differences in political opinions. These, commingled, bred those curious contradictions which were inexplicable to a foreigner, who might be forgiven for not grasping the basic freemasonry of the American way of living and thinking. These would have been too tenuous and long-drawn out for him to attempt to elucidate to Turchin. "You tell me you understand mathematics?" He suddenly thought of a way in which to expound what figuratively might grow clearer than in exposition. "Tell me, Colonel Turchin, if we add intolerance for intolerance endlessly together, what sum do we obtain?"

"I fail to comprehend you, General Garfield."

"I imagine I have not been explicit. Well, to put it another way, if we add to the sum total of hate and spite in the world, our own hate and spite for that which is hateful and spiteful, what have we then?"

"A means by which to demolish an evil thing."

"No, Colonel Turchin, I think not. Throw a stone of hatred into a streamlet, whether angry or placid and the ripples it generates are hate ripples to the end of time. Throw a stone of love into that same streamlet and you get forever ripples of love and sympathy. So, too, is it with life. What we have are encompassing errors of judgment in misguided men and women. These confused people we can beat down, perhaps by the sword and the cannon; but we beat down an angry enemy, not a convinced one. They bring us to war, or maybe we bring ourselves to war. In any case, you will say that war is neither the right time nor the right circumstance to debate this. If this be true, then let us not reason now. Rather let us fight, if fight we must. But let us not hate!"

Turchin stared at him in bewilderment. In his mind occurred the startling, unwelcome thought that this amiable young general was defending General Buell's propitiating program towards the rebels.

"I am not in accord with General Buell," Garfield answered his unspoken doubts. His eyes seemed to contain a curious plea for exactly the sort of understanding Colonel Turchin himself constantly craved. Perhaps I am looking beyond the instant. Perhaps, even these men who will judge you are moved to look beyond the moment, though they may not be aware of the forces that compel them in this direction. I say, perhaps, Colonel Turchin!"

"I am not certain I follow you entirely," the other stated gravely. "I believe you are sympathetic to my case and I am not ashamed to be grateful for that, since I know you preside and do not judge at the court-martial. But I think, Sir, that you entertain the idea that my conception of honor and duty are foreign in character, not American. For that I may not be grateful. I am and act like an American!"

General Garfield was at once contrite. He had not, when he embarked on this topic, been certain that the colonel could glimpse in his images, that pervasive truth to which he alluded. He saw now that he had failed of his purpose and made haste to say: "Colonel Turchin! Honor has no nationality! I think you an eminently honorable soldier. All of us owe you a debt of gratitude!" He twinkled good-humoredly as he added, "I hope we shall one day rise to your standards as ably as you have risen to ours!" He was led to comfort him further by asserting that, on the basis of a common love of country, a regard for common humanity and decencies, every officer must respect him. And when they parted he wished in his heart he might have been authorized to promise him definite exculpation.

In this way the first thirteen days of Turchin's trial began and passed. During the initial hearing of evidence, Turchin sat calmly as did General Garfield and heard the testimony presented against him. After the hours of confinement in the bare gray room used for the court, long conversations of taciturn chess sessions between them ensued, broken at no time by any personal references to the accusations or possible defense. This reticence on the subject was mutually complied with since the first talks between them. In fact, these two soldiers contrived to discuss all manner of subjects saving only the trial, so that in the space of two weeks each knew the other well. Garfield was familiar by this time with Turchin's history, his reasons for fleeing Russia, his hopes and aspirations to help build America. Turchin, for his part, was privy to the happy tidings which General Garfield had received at this time, that with improved health he could hope soon to take his place where he longed to be, in the field with his brigade. One thought Turchin did not voice to his new friend. He would not distress him by his pessimistic conviction that even before his version of the Athens incident was given, the colonels in the Commission had already found him guilty.

Garfield also had a few misgivings which he, equally thoughtful of the colonel's sensibilities, refrained from mentioning. Among these was a sad hearted certainty that the colonel's official record admitted much room for criticism when scrutinized in the light of the army's rigid codes. In addition, Garfield felt that the Commission itself was rather partisan to Buell's views. It was composed of nine colonels, mainly from the Border States, whereas, considering the fact that Turchin was a colonel in the "Army of Ohio" as his department was then named, he should have been tried by a more representative body of his peers.

Observing him covertly during the testimonies of the Southerners and officers bearing witness against him, General Garfield was often lost in sheer admiration of the man's self-control and dignity which betrayed neither abnegation nor rancor. He merely sat relaxed and listened to his traducers. Often he leaned his head upon his hand, but otherwise he exhibited no sign of impatience or anger. Now and then his eyes opened a fraction wider as some young lieutenant, with deliberate coldness, turned privileged back upon him whose favor he might not have disdained six months ago. Or again, he might be seen to raise his head a trifle more erect as some passionately vindictive gentleman stepped forth to defend, not only his honor, but that of the entire South he proudly believed exemplified in his person. Thus, with utter faithfulness, the Judge Advocate took down every plaintiff's malice as though it were some precious revelation from on high.

Several times Turchin was granted permission to interrogate his accusers, but each time he had but one question to ask of anyone and he asked it loudly and challengingly: "Are you a loyal man?" And having delivered himself of these words, he triumphantly sat down, leaving the impression in the courtroom that he had malignantly prodded his minatory finger into the complainant's chest. At length the Commission grew wroth with him and General Garfield had to disallow the question, though he did so with heavy heart. In Turchin's one question, in the reaction it roused from Union officers and Southern sympathizers alike, lay the crux of the matter really on trial. Forced to eradicate the question,

General Garfield smarted under the stigma of acquiescence which he fancied the Russian colonel would label him with. He could see how he might interpret the entire court procedure as an attempt to enjoin upon all Union officers, not to offend the vaunted gentility of traitors. To the impassioned Russian it would appear beyond doubt that in the future any rebel might deem himself a fit and proper judge of Union officers and qualified to appraise the amount of harm which might be honorably inflicted upon them, their property or dignity.

As the dreary recitation of facts and fictions continued, General Garfield more than once found himself thinking that of all present in that court room, not excluding the Judge Advocate or the counsel allotted to Turchin, Turchin, upon unbiased analysis and a regard for the limitations bounding his adaptation to American ways, was perhaps the most unconditionally loyal of them all; the irony of the matter resting in his need to stand as the most important witness in his own defense. The counsel assigned him was technically prepared to defend his position, but what in fact counsel most succeeded in doing was to present without clarification the colonel's own attitude with verbal insistence of his right, in language unvaryingly acceptable to the judges.

From the outset, Turchin found himself repulsed by the formal legal actions and aspect of this counselor, Colonel Gazlay, on whose cold impassive countenance not a flicker of emotion passed hour after hour. His deportment was consciously exemplary under the circumstances, he felt and showed considerateness and courtesy which, though lacking personal warmth, failed in no particular to correspond to the manual of rules for conduct becoming officers and gentlemen. If he took care to point out the mitigating circumstances surrounding the perpetration of the alleged violation of orders, he did so without emphasis and with a seemingly neutral civility and detachment.

To Turchin it was plain that the counsel for his defense was discharging his office honorably and in good faith, even if his lack of vehemence and partiality for his client added nothing to convince the Kentucky colonels of his innocence. Turchin fancied that were he in his place, Turchin would have resorted to every passionate appeal; that he would have burned with such patriotic fire that the most obdurate heart in that room should have softened and yielded to the call of justice. He wanted no mercy. Rather he wanted simply justice, which was the highest attribute of brotherly love. "They weigh and measure and balance a man's soul as if it were a sack of meal, as if it could not hear them and had no feelings, no manhood." Such thoughts made him rather more thoughtful than resentful. He could not accustom himself to this deliberately unemotional examination of details and petty infractions of rules which seemed to him not half as important as the great throbbing values involved in the principles for which men fought and died.

When Colonel Gazlay reached his concluding remarks, he closed his academic defense by a masterful summation which had the dubious merit of clearing the defendant without warming a heart toward him. Turchin allowed a faint grin to spread over his face and a sly wink to become visible to General Garfield who thought momentarily that the indomitable Russian was blinking away a tear. Until, that is, he saw the quirked eyebrows and the sad little humor by which the colonel tried pathetically to sustain himself.

Garfield was extremely distressed. He would rather have seen another sort of emotion than that of hollow and facetious humor, this vain effort to rail at himself. Certainly, it would not have occurred to him to imagine Turchin to be mocking at his examiners. At this point particularly, he could not perceive any stimulus to humor. Gazlay had neatly summed up Turchin's defense which, in view of the fact that Turchin chose not to testify, was amazingly generous. First Gazlay had stated that no testimony had been adduced which showed Colonel Turchin as having given consent to or having previous knowledge of, acts of pillage or rapine. This, of course, Garfield knew to be useless justification. Buell would not permit it as an exonerating excuse if eye witnesses, even Southerners, brought him any reports of vandalism committed.

Gazlay elaborated on this defensive statement. He explained that Turchin was, at the time of the Athens incident, engaged in the fulfillment of important military duties and he was not immediately attached to the business of the occupation of Athens. However, Gazlay was careful to give the colonel credit for accomplishing his duty as a commander by saying that Turchin had early appointed a provost marshal to establish and keep order in Athens. He cited General Order

No. 81 from Division Headquarters, which threw the first and most direct responsibility for the good order and behavior of the troops upon company officers.

This having been perfunctorily stressed, Gazlay repeated the findings of General Mitchel and Colonel Turchin with respect to the depositions obtained from the townspeople themselves. With a barely noticeable emphasis he remarked to the court that General Mitchel's orders gave Colonel Turchin a free hand in the matter of pressing into the army, horses belonging to the town's folk or of using and defending Negroes who helped the brigade.

Upon this, several colonels stared stubbornly at Turchin's face as though in its enigmatic expressions they sought a confirmation of their hostility. With a peculiar relish which, if not to his taste, was at least appealing to his mind, Gazlay finished his summation by quoting in full General Order No. 13, which designated clearly the class of "peaceable citizens" not to be molested. This order stated that such "citizens" did not include those who were in rebellion against the government of the United States and that consequently, testimony of such rebels should be disallowed as evidence against Union Army officers. Nor did Gazlay forget to mention with strict scrupulousness that Colonel Turchin, the above order notwithstanding, had, upon hearing of the alleged outrages, ordered the arrest of such men as were suspected and that these men were punitively removed to prison at Huntsville.

The defense Colonel Gazlay made was more grueling than the whole recitation of Turchin's soldierly remissions. When the court was adjourned, Turchin was a weary man for who little rest or respite was held out in the town or even in General Garfield's company. Turchin met him some time later, following Gazlay's presentation and he consulted him with mute eyes no longer pretending a lightness his spirits denied. "Was it so bad?" Turchin broke his rule and asked of his friend. The reply was a quixotic negative. General Garfield asked, "Would you have wished me to arrange for another officer than Colonel Gazlay to plead your case?"

"Would another have been different from Gazlay? He is apparently honorable enough and fair minded. That seems to be obvious. I cannot make an appeal to his heart if his heart is closed to me and only his brain wishes to treat with me. You can surmise that he has no liking for me."

Garfield was sadly silent for a few minutes. He knew the truth of this last. Finally he said crossly, "Colonel, I do not see what you have gained by refusing to plead for yourself. I have so completely altered my first impressions of you, that I venture to say, that every man on the commission would do so likewise and they would be be well disposed to your views, if not already so, were you to let them all see what manner of soldier you really are. Surely you must believe that your sincerity will weigh in your favor as much as Captain Gilbert's signed charges, even if he is the Inspector General. You are defeated, colonel, if you meet your fellow officers in the assumption that anything you say will be of no avail."

Convinced of General Garfield's wisdom in advising him to take his defense in his own hands, he proceeded to follow his friend's advice and on the following day asked for and gained permission to speak on his own behalf. When the proper moment arrived, he rose with some vestige of ill ease and made the initial mistake of appealing at once to the understanding of the colonels. Earnestly and with ardent paternalism, he undertook to correlate for them the seriousness of the war as a whole and his duties in his command, particularly at the time of the Athens affair. Forgetting the aloof air with which he had been treated by them all, excepting Garfield, he held out his hands to them naturally, in a gesture of unconscious pride like that of a chastised child and unhesitatingly detailed in outline form his excellent arrangements for the defense of the town, where it was hourly expected that their regiments would be surprised by overwhelming superior numbers of the enemy. He had every reason to expect this contingency, he said, and against an enemy able to surround and attack him, he needed to be constantly on guard. "Gentlemen," he cried, you may well imagine that so serious a likelihood required my unremitting personal supervision. How could it be expected of me that I should attend to every minor affair or infraction of rules which rightly belong to the concerns of the military police?"

Reading into every face before him a grave attentiveness which he took to be an opportunity and a willingness to hear him out, he labored this opening until it digressed into a tedious recital concerning the function of the military police at a time of war and of the duties imposed by war upon officers called upon to exercise knowledge of engineering and scouting. "I had," said he, "the honor of being a colonel of the État

Major in the Imperial Guards of Russia and therefore I felt able to see the disadvantages by which our Brigade of Volunteers was handicapped. As things happened, I found myself constrained to perform routine duties which rightly belong to my subordinates. Always, I paid close attention to the difficult job of securing information about the country and the enemy and to the hazards involved in reconnoitering positions for my advance guards and pickets. You may believe me gentlemen that I saw to all of these matters before my troops took their first positions in the town. Thereafter, I felt free to leave the town, which was amply guarded, in order to make necessary arrangements with our 18th Ohio troops near Fayetteville. I had in mind with Colonel Stanley's assistance, to deploy my troops more advantageously in case of attack, so that we could form a coherent line of battle together, should the need arise.

He paused for breath as he challenged with his straightforwardness the impassive faces of the various colonels who met his gaze without minimizing their censure of him, without signifying by the slightest thing that they heard his forthright delivery and impassioned self-defense more receptively than the impersonal summation of his counsel. Unaware of their imperviousness, though he sensed the chill of their politeness, he next pointed out the gravity of the anticipated attack, by describing encounters which had previously given rise to his expectation. He told them about Colonel Kennett's surprise raid upon Colonel Scott's cavalry on the Elk River; he mentioned the laborious business of equipping an expedition to reinforce Colonel White. Then, as though not satisfied with this demonstration, he continued: "As soon as it was brought to my attention that my troops were in illegal possession of articles not regularly allotted to them and originating from a source which I considered questionable, I appointed officers to take strict precautions to prevent any unlawful confiscations, any depredations whatever."

If there had been a note of appeal when he commenced, there was naught discernible, but righteous self-approval of all he had done as he finished. He looked about him for a friendly visage and seeing none, shook his head like a dazed pugilist. With a slow, heavy tread he walked back to his seat, for while he had been addressing the colonels he had stepped to the front of the room from which vantage point he had been able to fully command every man in it.

At length one of the colonels rose to his feet and turned directly to Turchin. "You admit, Colonel Turchin, that despite your avowed injunctions to prevent outrages, they did occur and of such a nature that they are unspeakable. Now, do you presume to deny that said outrages were indubitably committed by your men?"

"I do not deny that," Turchin answered wearily. "I also do not justify outrages in any form," he hastened to add. "But whenever small incidents have in them some measure of truth, they must be submitted to the proper understanding of events leading up to them and not only to them, but to this whole campaign! To do less than that is in my opinion to invalidate the whole spirit by which both General Mitchel and I, myself, have sought to overcome the unnatural restrictions imposed upon our men throughout our entire southward march. It has been established that rebels like Mason and Hollingsworth openly joined the rebel cavalry and fought against our retreating troops, those who were lucky enough to escape the merciless slaughter, which the citizens of Athens thought fit reprisal for the civil occupation we accomplished. The records prove how severely our cavalry was decimated by them. We found Union knapsacks and baggage belonging to our 18th Ohio, scattered all over the town and concealed in private houses. We can prove that some of our men were actually burned by the rebels during their attack upon our train at the Lime Creek Bridge; these soldiers were shown no mercy but instead were suffered to undergo a terrible, horrible, slow death by burning."

As he recalled these things, it seemed to him that the very charnel smells of those dead boys returned to his nose and his nostrils in response. His nose flattened and his mouth tightened with an upsurge of wrath. "Is it not evident gentlemen, that such inhuman cruelties are bound to excite reciprocal vengeance and fury among the fellows and comrades of those martyred boys? Is it to be wondered that when we retook the town, our boys could not help but show their grief in anger? Even angels in heaven would have stormed! Examine the facts and then judge as to who perpetrated outrages on whom!"

He was interrupted by another colonel who showed less patience with his long expostulation than his predecessor. "It was your duty, colonel, as an American officer, to take account of such possibilities.

That you are well able to do so, you yourself clearly describe. All the more are you to be indicted for failing to prevent the consequences of frays you apparently anticipated."

Turchin, plainly seeing that this last colonel had won the assent of the rest, snapped his retort. "Sirs, if these so-called terrible outrages and acts of vengeance, with which you charge my men, were of the indescribable nature you assert, tell me, why did neither the civil authorities nor the influential citizens of Athens come out of their holes and ask me to give them protection? But no! Instead of that, they gathered in groups on the corners, formed inciting mobs which refused to disband when ordered to do so. When we forced them to break up their angry gatherings, when we asked them to go back peaceably to their business, to resume their jobs, they openly sneered at us, perversely shut up their shops and stores and paraded about the streets in a deliberate attempt to provoke my men! Those citizens who obeyed me were not molested, neither they nor their property"

A slight murmur rose among the colonels and several put their heads together as they turned over the next complaint against the Russian colonel. At last one stern officer began; in a coldly sarcastic tone, a harangue which instructed Turchin with this lesson: "You are not the one citizen of the United States to whom it is delegated to mete out justice or punishment, nor to determine guilt or innocence. You have been guilty of overstepping your bounds as an officer of this army. You have taken it upon yourself to officiate in civil matters. You have interfered in matters outside the bounds of conduct prescribed for an officer; your general deportment has been in violation of the principles and ethics proper to an American officer." And everyone understood, including Turchin, that his words implied the corollary - that conduct unbecoming an American officer was reprehensible, even if that same sort of conduct was condoned by the Czar of Russia! A stinging rush of blood suffused Turchin's face and even General Garfield had to lower his eyes to his folded hands, which he intently studied.

Conscious that he had gained a telling point, the prosecuting colonel went on with more directness. "We have ascertained from reliable sources, Colonel Turchin, of your having offended in like manner at other times, in spite of the fact that the rules for procedure in all such matters are well known to you, or should be!"

"I had more than 3,000 loyal lives entrusted to my care," Turchin cried angrily as he emphasized the word loyal. "I am proud to admit it, that I thought but little of the inconveniences of the Secessionists!" He turned brightly wounded eyes upon his fellow officers and superiors. "I, who am a new American, I believe what my eyes have seen and my ears have heard. I ask myself, what am I fighting for? Why are my men jeopardizing their lives; for the comfort and security of flagrant enemies? Am I accused now, found guilty, for looking upon and naming as the traitors to America, those who glory in being traitors? Am I being asked to love mine enemy while he hates me? Am I being asked to kill him the while I must treat his property and estate honorably. He is my enemy; but the thought of him I must not so conceive of!"

His words merely confirmed a suspicion of irreconcilable, intangible differences, which were, in truth, standing trial. Garfield felt that Turchin had not improved his chances for acquittal.

CHAPTER XX

On the day Turchin departed from Chicago, the day after the sword presentation, Nadine, who had been evolving a plan of her own, hastily packed two carpet bags and caught the first east-bound train for Washington. Of this intention she had confided not a word to her husband, or of the determination which had given it first impetus.

To undertake such a long journey alone, to support such a daring plan as that of interviewing Mr. Lincoln on her husband's account, had required strong feelings on her part. What those feelings were, aside from her natural fears for her husband, she couldn't clearly analyze. The forthcoming marriage of Trofimov, for which event she had already received an expensively embossed invitational card; the effect of her husband's warm reception at the hands of the Chicago citizens; the obvious almost reverential respect of Mihalotzy; all helped to implement a zealous ambition to obtain for Turchin exoneration from the President. With feminine intuition, she felt that in no other way was her husband's situation sustainable, even if she still had not abandoned every hope of his ability to make his own clear stand intelligible to his judges. She still had hopes, but outweighing them by far was the fear that he was likely to receive from these judges of the court-martial, no greater approbation than he had on other and less important matters from enlightened men of affairs. She knew with despair that his propensity to argue and declaim must alienate even men of clemency.

Had she been of the caliber of Henrietta Morrison, she might have trusted herself to write the White House, or write General Mitchel who, as she knew, was at present in Washington, where he was arguing his case, presumably the same one as Turchin's before powerful friends of the Union Cause. But she never thought to resort to the medium of written words, choosing rather to trust her husband's fate to the humane kindliness she believed the President would show her if she appealed in person. Nor did it occur to her that in planning to see Mr. Lincoln, she was presuming too much; her plea for her husband resting upon pivotal questions of the day and pertinent to the campaign strategy she herself had witnessed in the making.

These, of course, were her superficial reasons. They were potent enough of themselves, to permit her to obviate the need of defining subtler emotions of which she was ashamed and which were tinged with self-pity and self-loathing. Quite honestly, she believed that she wished to escape the heat of Chicago, as well as to avoid Trofimov's wedding where Turchin's enemies would commiserate falsely with her, where Mr. Brewster's penetrating eye would appraise her and make her uncomfortable with his unkind perspicuities. At the same time she tried defensively to convince herself that she was truly happy about the simple solution and the conclusion of the attachment between her and the baron, which the marriage demanded. His wedding must naturally put an end to his dalliance; his wife would ensure his undeviating loyalty through more direct methods than an appeal to his regard for appearances. She took her seat in the airless coach of the train with a pleasant certainty of reawakened love and affection for Ivan. She recounted, as though she had a need to strengthen herself with their recitation, all the fine virtues which marked him. She saw again the palace in Peterhof, where they had met and recalled the life they had left behind them, when they had made their way to this country. With fleeting interest she occupied herself with the rolling landscape over which she and her husband had come in '58, but immediately banished this memory, for it recalled with faithfulness the companion they had met on that journey. Was ever a woman so plagued, she wondered? If only it were not given her to see continuously her folly and utter recklessness! With her irresistible attraction to the baron, she was ever in danger of rousing her husband's ire; of belittling herself in Trofimov's sight; of shattering her heretofore inexpugnable position as an honorable wife of an honorable man; and above all, she feared the aching loneliness Trofimov's marriage would lend her.

Fretfully she wiped a stealthy tear from her eye and experienced the melancholy satisfaction of an unwanted freedom. She reflected how a high purpose lent moral tone to the unconventional. She fancied General McClellan's surprise, should she venture to approach him in Washington and beg for his intervention in this picayune persecution of Ivan. Would he deign to help his former protégé and employee? Would he, recall perhaps, the distinguished Russian colonel who had shown him every courtesy in 1855 in the Crimea? She thought long about this and almost convinced herself that it would be wise to seek out the famous general.

At that moment, however, she thought of the rumors current in Chicago, to the effect that the general was not so popular with Lincoln this year as he had been at first. It was being said that McClellan was laboring under a mountain of moral scruples that, though endearing him to the men of his own army, were hindering the advance of the other armies of Union men against the enemy. McClellan was being accused of want of daring and of want of initiative in putting to practical use his indisputable organizing ability. It would appear that the general was waiting for a sure thing before striking his foe with his magnificent army. If this was the case, how could she hope to influence him in Turchin's comparatively small affairs, when such a man as Turchin was exemplified by what would be called rashness and precipitate disregard for the cost of men and material? No, McClellan was more apt to exculpate General Buell than a man like Turchin. She sighed wearily and wiped another tear from her face. To herself she said, "We will waste our entire lives to defend some vague droplet of truth and in the end, even that droplet will have had only the importance of dew on a morning petal, which opens more readily to the sun that scorches it than to the water that refreshes it." Eventually, she drifted off into the reveries this flight of her imagination evoked and she grew indifferent to the monotonous grind of the heavy coach wheels pounding out no reassurances. "In the end, what are we to think of it all?" she wondered drowsily. "Perhaps it does not matter in what order we wish to arrange our benefits. The sun is important and the water too. Perhaps it is not meant for us to know which one comes first."

She was unconscious of a pair of adoring dark eyes which were watching her unobserved. She had not seen the baron board the train in Chicago and had been too much given to her own troubled reflections to pay attention to any travelers moving through the coach cars. Only when Trofimov's slender cool palms rested upon her ungloved hands did her eyelids flutter up like excited birds stirred to flight in a meadow.

"Baron Trofimov!" she cried out, with unpretended surprise. Her voice evinced a note of happy accusation as though it pronounced his presence on the train as a dear pursuit.

With a delightful grin he slipped into the seat beside her, keeping his hands entwined with hers. "This is a wonderful and happy coincidence," he said in French. And then they each hurriedly explained their purpose in travelling eastward. Hers, she related somewhat disjointedly, for when she wished to put it into words, the whole object of her errand grew weak and sentimental; almost foolish, she feared. His, as he gave it, seemed loftier and to more purpose. It emanated he said, from the determination of sincere men like Vallandigham to balk the bill of conscription which the Republicans were ardently sponsoring. "It is most important that we prevent such a draft from becoming a law," he said as he mimicked Brewster's tone. "It will upset the economy of the country to give any government the power to levy such tribute from its people." He spoke the words almost as precisely as Brewster had whose injunctions he was following to the letter.

For an instant Nadine wished to oppose him, but refrained only because the matter he mentioned was not important to either of them at the moment and the thing that linked them better manifested itself in the clasp of their hands than the words they spoke. To speak at all was merely an instinctive response to old social habits. Only two other passengers occupied the coach and these two were distant from them by the length of the car. Yet their voices sank into the gentle and slightly thick murmurs of lovers who seek and find everything they wish in one another.

The journey was slow and they made frequent stops along the way. The first night they remained awake, talking until dawn when she laid her head on his shoulder. The second night they stopped at an inn in Ohio. Here they experienced a subtle change in attitude toward one another; the happy casualness of the first day gave way to a somewhat strained diffidence combining both heightened pleasure and guarded wariness. When they boarded a train to resume their trip, the stilled anxieties, with which both of them had wrestled unknown to the other, announced themselves in the baron's unceremonious frankness. Seated close together, no longer minding the stares of the curious, who took them for a pair of lovers on a wedding trip, she waiting, and he impatient, his words fell softly upon her ears. "I have decided," he said abruptly. And when she looked quizzingly, he took her hand and announced: "You and I have been fools long enough! The time has come for something to happen!" Then seeing her small shudder, he soothed her by gripping her hand the harder. "We have a god-given chance. A chance like this comes once in a lifetime."

"What is it you mean, Dimitri?"

"Do not be coy, Nadine," his voice suddenly grew sharp. "You are aware of what I speak. Of us, naturally! Not of riddles. I am not given to speaking in riddles. At this moment I realized we have one god-given chance to snatch at something beautiful, if you are brave enough. Come away with me, Nadine!"

"Are you asking another man's wife to go away with you? Is that meant as impertinence, Dimitri? Are you in this way reminding me that my wayward emotions have betrayed me? Do you wish to humiliate me further, now when you stand on the eve of your marriage with Miss Brewster?"

His eyes were bright shining stars as he looked at her loveliness, all flushed with what she supposed was a just anger but what he knew, man fashion, was excitement. "Ah, Nadine, a man could love you more than the empty tittle-tattle of honor and respectability! I will teach you how to separate the false from the truth, how to live free of these stupid, jejune laws and circumscriptions! Don't you see how it is? This wonderful land of your husband's is breaking its neck to imitate the worn out pettiness, the integrated pettiness of Europe. If that be so, why shall we remain here where we are forever alien? Why shall we suffer ourselves to endure the growing pains of a land which is like an over-stuffed princeling! I tell you I am surfeited with all the fat of this land! To enjoy it one has to grow fat like the burghers who dominate it. I grow sick with longing to be adventurous and free of their little schemes!"

She looked at him in surprise, for she had not suspected him capable of so much vehemence, so much passion and resentment. It pleased her that something had pierced the bland exterior he showed the world. For an instant she wished to believe that he voiced, in his strange words, his passion for her. They told her much that she knew he might never more say; that in their respective circles, there was no hope for them together; that to dispel their loyalties to others, they must abandon the spot where they were. The ugly thing of separation, divorce, scandal, he left unsaid. Her quicker feminine calculations accounted for them in the passionate desire which she discerned in his words.

An uncontrollable trembling seized her and she plainly exhibited her fright.

"Do you not trust me?" he demanded, as he felt the tremor in her hand. "I have no wish to delude you, to seduce you, Nadine. I ask you to come back to Europe, to France, perhaps, or anywhere else you wish. I ask you nothing you have not already in spirit condoned in the past!" He spoke forcefully as he fixed her eyes with his commanding glance. "Tell me the truth, Nadine; you have already avowed your attachment to me!"

"That is cruel and unjust," she answered, as tears collected in her eyes. "You have no right to impute to me..."

"Can I have been so wrong!" he exclaimed angrily. "Have these years you spent in a city of savages, dressed up savages, to be sure, taken the free glow of moonlight out of you? You were like a moon princess that night on the packet boat when I first saw you, Nadine! I never saw a lovelier creature!"

She smiled tearfully, knowing his flattery was artless, the boyish, impetuous expression of a desire which grew stronger as he expounded it. She felt how urgent must indeed be her own desire if she could know his to have risen from the moment and not repudiate it for the passing thing it might be. Too well did she know Baron Trofimov to accept this declaration in other than strict clarity. She knew how he hungered for wealth and power, how he had truckled to Brewster and pampered Susan. She even suspected his activities of late purported more than he told. Amidst the conflicts of war and politics, she had grown sensitive to the raging antagonism that men like Brewster boldly hurled against the government. It was not beyond the credence of a woman schooled in the intricacies of foreign policy, to accept the fact of a secret treachery. And in this hidden warfare, she could well believe Trofimov had a part. Therefore, all the more, did she savor the sweetness his words of love held out to her.

"What your words imply, Baron Trofimov, ought to anger and injure me!"

"But they do not! They cannot! Don't you see, Nadine, they cannot, because all along something powerful has bound us by a law higher than the piddling laws these farmers and shopkeepers hold sacred! Away from all this, you and I will be beyond their caviling! I am asking you to leave Ivan and be mine! I need not to ask you! You are no bourgeois. You know that we are related by something beyond their menial grasp!

That she heard him out quietly, she ascribed to shock. If in her dreams of this man, she had longed to hear such words, she would have called the wish a sin and a horror. Profoundly moved, stunned yet singularly lucid and attentive, she knew she must be as one who, flung into a whirling stream, struggling against dragging waters, suddenly yields to the undertow and is pulled down beyond the realm of struggle. Her state, as she listened, was that of a dead victim with a dead peace. Surging beyond these tides of emotion was a sensation of inordinate gratitude. A high choked laugh broke from her and trilled off into a wavering sob. "I am grateful to you, Dimitri. Not every woman, no longer very young, elicits such a tribute, such a rejuvenation of her self-esteem." With sudden submission she began to weep like a child and he comforted her solicitously, the while he thoughtlessly relished her over-wrought condition and the feel of her pliant form against his. The west was becoming the east and his eyes, as they looked over her head, out onto the summery world whipping past them, had no regret for the carelessness with which he was about to fling from him the success he had striven to gain for years. In a curious passivity he felt himself finally resolved. Perhaps he had always known he must declare himself to Nadine and now, having done so, to his satisfaction, confident of her acceptance, he was calm, more resolute than ever.

"We will not stay in Washington," he said, but continue on to New York. From there, passage to France!"

"But we must stop for a while in Washington," she replied with a sudden vigor. Her words made him smile, for they unwittingly gave him the answer he expected. "You know why I come. I am bound to see Mr. Lincoln. I must help Ivan, I must." He nodded, for he heard the thought she did not voice: that she must help her husband before she was free to take her happiness.

"We shall help him," he promised. "I shall mention him to several people who gain the President's ear easily." He spoke sincerely and was even rather glad, after a fashion, to end his unsavory career with Brewster by some small reparation to the man whose wife he had just won. "For Turchin, honor as such, is more important than anything else. Love, power, money, these things, when taken from most men, they tend to undermine them. I cannot really hurt Turchin if, in taking his wife I restore him his honor!" So he reasoned for the remainder of his trip to Washington.

By the time they reached the city, just then sweltering under its annual heat spell, Nadine was quite willing for them to sleep together. She, too, felt relieved that something more definite than the veiled admiration had now been professed and even more relieved when almost matter-of-factly, they found themselves established in their hotel suite. No sooner were their bags deposited than the baron hurried off to present his cards to various worthies and to arrange for whatever assistance to Colonel Turchin could be vouchsafed. The interval granted this for her inviolate state, Nadine used to good advantage; making herself fresh and lovely in expectation of her lover's return. At last she was quite ready for his praises and addresses, yet he did not return. The afternoon faded into a heavy summer nighttime. Darkness purpled over the city and thousands of gas jets flared alive on streets filled with moving people. From her window, she looked down upon the evening scene; officers jauntily promenading in evening attire; cabs being driven to the lighted entrance of the Ford Theater; beautifully gowned ladies with elegant lace shawls; a scene of life and laughter far removed from the darkly somber reverberations of war.

There flashed over her the contrasting scenes of black nights in Kentucky; she sitting chilled, in heavy army blankets which Ivan had laughingly wrapped about her, until her nose had been almost literally buried in them. Dismal miles of muddy roads, made the more impassable by their rough sheets of icy coating, their shattered rocks, cracked wide by the savage cold. "But now," she hastened to assuage her remorse for what she was about to inflict on Turchin, "It is beautiful in the South. They will perhaps believe him and if Dimitri can further help him, he shall be free of dishonor. Some day he will understand and forgive me." This she thought with true hope, since her respect and affection for Turchin lay deeply ingrained in her life. "It will be good if he hates me at first," she consoled herself. And the fugacious regret which had come over her was dissipated by her rationalization as well as the beckoning warmth and life of the street below her. Soon she would be a part of that animated throng, would be sallying forth on Trofimov's arm. Soon she would be having a taste of the fullness of youth not yet forever lost to her.

It grew later and later without the night's disgorging her Baron. She did not know precisely at what moment the premonition came upon her, at what exact point of time she suddenly knew, by the painful beat of her heart and the sickness in her body, that the baron was not returning at all. But know she did, at first with that dead, unemotional knowledge which enabled her to sit unmoved in her chair and appear outwardly the picture of normal expectancy and finally with the agony of despair that crept like a stealthy thief into her rigid watching stare at the door which did not open to admit him.

Unable to endure the tense strain of waiting for his laggard footsteps, she decided with reckless daring to venture into the street below. Snatching her shawl and bonnet she made her way into the lighted avenue where she timidly skirted groups of soldiers and civilians, as though fearing to be recognized, to be confronted with the shame she now realized she had too optimistically brought upon herself. She felt a discarded, besmirched thing. In her confused suspense and dismay she believed the whole of her intended elopement with Trofimov to be patent on her face, visible to all who chanced to look upon her. She kept her face hidden, kept her eyes downcast more that she had not sinned than because she had agreed to. Suddenly she was startled and discomposed as a hand touched her sleeve and a familiar voice arrested her. "It is Madame Turchin! It must be!"

A faint, startled cry escaped her. The friendly fingers which had halted her aimless wandering, were like iron hasps fixing her in her flight from duty and responsibility. Any other voice than General Mitchel's, would scarcely have sounded the knell to her mad moment of freedom and made escape more sure. General Mitchel's, to have been the voice and hand decreed to deter her in the mad passage, frightened her into a stammering apology that Colonel Turchin's recent commander found attractive. "How I admire you, Madame Turchin!" He complimented her and the purpose of her visit which at once he assumed to be allied to his own. Valorously he had pleaded his own and her husband's cause where it was doing much good. Today Mitchel was sanguine of success and therefore doubly pleased to find the dear lady whom he already had sufficient reason to admire, come these many miles to seek reprisal for the gallant colonel. An old fashioned gentlemen, perhaps devoid of the lightness and brilliance which men like Trofimov possessed to an abundance, he showed himself tolerant indeed, when he found her unescorted upon a city street, her a lady of outstanding quality. There were times when the rigid social code could be infringed upon, he thought and one of these times was when a man's honor and military career were at stake. "It is only what I should expect of a gallant officer's lady," he said approvingly, "that you should move heaven itself for your husband. What good fortune for me, Madame, to have come upon you now! You have, perhaps just arrived?"

Nadine nodded her head and named her hotel which was quite close.

"I have coincidentally today sent a letter to your address in Chicago," he informed her as she took his proffered arm. "I have spoken to Secretary Seward who has the President's complete confidence. I believe the entire situation and General Buell's part in it will receive minute review." His words implied that both he and other officers in the western theater of the war had more to look forward to than the courts-martial which were all the answer Buell made to sincere patriots.

"I had hoped to embolden myself to such a degree that I should dare to seek out the President," said Nadine. "I hear he is a good and a just man. This reputation led me to hope that he would intercede in the colonel's case once all the facts were laid before him."

"I am certain, Madame Turchin, that your personal efforts will not damage Colonel Turchin's chances. Your name not infrequently figures in the documents we have already submitted to Mr. Lincoln." He smiled benevolently, with the privilege of a fatherly soul. Without seeking her consent, he led her to a waiting horse cab which then conveyed them to a popular hotel where visiting foreign ministers and diplomats put up. Here in the magnificent lobby or general reception room, brilliant foreign representatives and such officers who were fortunate enough to be near Washington, mingled in good comradeship. Here, too, the fashionable belles of the city were privileged to be entertained.

Nadine was not in a fair mood to respond to the gaiety and the lighted splendor of the huge room, though she was grateful for the diversion which, if it could not allay her inner fears and suspense, at any rate distracted her attention. The sight of men in small and large clusters, engaged in talking and smiling, bowing and moving; the heavy aroma of imported cigars; the occasional splash of color, like the passing scintillation of an opal's fire, which was made by the pert appearance of some fortunate lady privileged to witness these masculine doings; these were what might have compensated her at another time for much of the loneliness and strangeness her American life had brought her.

"You may see therefore, dear Madame Turchin," General Mitchel was continuing a train of thought entirely lost upon his companion, "that my resignation, handed to Buell, was not what he expected. I may inform you that, not only will his high-handed and dictatorial mannerisms be dealt with critically, but that he will find himself in the near future less able to defend himself than either Colonel Turchin or I."

While he thus was conversing, enjoying the lovely lady's uncommunicative company, little aware that her polite attention was merely on the surface, her eyes suddenly beheld entering the great lounge, none other than the baron. He was not alone, she saw at once, for in his wake were several gentlemen whom she took to be his Washington acquaintances until General Mitchel, following her glance, exclaimed indignantly, "That is the infamous Senator Vallandigham from Ohio! Far be it from me to cast aspersions upon any man, but that gentleman's activities remove him from the respect of all Americans. I have heard how brazenly he decries our efforts to hold this country together. I have heard that he has frequently promulgated the wish and intention that the enemy succeeds."

Following behind Vallandigham's taller person, came Brewster, who had on his arm his resplendently arrayed daughter, while his wife trailed after him on the arm of an extremely stout gentleman with the portly bearing of a congressman and with a congressman's eye to public notice as well.

Were it possible to hide herself in her seat, to screen herself by leaning forward toward General Mitchel more than she was then attempting to do, Nadine would have been glad to escape the incoming party's notice. As it was, she fixed a rigid unseeing glance on General Mitchel who startled, stared at her with some anxiety. Before he could remark at her state, Susan Brewster, whose sharp eyes had scoured the full length of the room and had quickly passed over its occupants with her haughtily selective scrutiny, caught sight of Madame Turchin and fixed her, even as a harpooner might fix a struggling flounder in the sea, by spearing her with determination.

Quickly the young lady's discovery of Madame Turchin was made known to the rest of her party, who instantly glanced toward General Mitchel and Nadine. Mr. Brewster was the first to make a move in their direction. He was not loath to inform himself of the Russian lady's distinguished escort, felt indeed that it behooved him at all times to stand in well with the military caste, to which august deportment and General Mitchel's insignia proclaimed him a party. Vallandigham, who like Trofimov, was in Washington to lobby against the pending conscription bill, glanced hostilely towards them and then bent toward Trofimov to inquire of their identity. Being satisfied, when he learned the lady's, he made a biting allusion to her presence in the gay Capital while her husband was being drummed out of the army. "Washington will not be so safe for federal officers in the future," he predicted warningly to his party as all of them moved forward to address Nadine and General Mitchel. "I dare say they," meaning the Colonel and Mrs. Turchin, "will find Chicago too hot for them when General Buell sends him home with his tail between his legs."

When they approached, Nadine, with one swift questioning glance into Baron Trofimov's correctly pleasant face, made the introductions and had the doubtful satisfaction of seeing the Senator from Ohio start and flush with annoyance as she explained General Mitchel's connection to herself and her husband.

"What a coincidence that we should here encounter you." The baron was just remarking that you were probably in the deep south by now," Susan opened the conversation.

"Why, they might almost have been travelling companions in coming here!" Mrs. Brewster exclaimed.

"Nonsense!" Susan answered. "We followed the baron on the very next train and we have only this afternoon got here. How long have you been in Washington, Madame Turchin?"

Not paying heed to her daughter's words, Mrs. Brewster persisted. "The dear Baron left two days before we did. I am sure he did. Mr. Brewster," she addressed her husband, "was it not two days before we set out that you sent the baron to Washington?"

"Oh, it scarcely matters," Susan interrupted pettishly. "Are you staying here in this hotel?" she demanded bluntly. Nadine, pink with embarrassment, looked at Trofimov, who stood unmoved and not a bit ill at ease. In fact, at this juncture, he took Susan's arm with a sign of familiar indulgence which was both ostentatious and vulgarly possessive. Nadine shook her head in denial. Susan, with a victorious smile, said she regretted the fact and informed her that, except they had to accommodate the baron, they should have been happy to include her in their party.

"Under the circumstances, you know, Madame Turchin," Mrs. Brewster took up her daughter's regrets, "how it is with impatient lovers!" as she laughed condescendingly and began a running banter on the theme of young and impatient lovers, until Nadine was ready to burst into tears. She was more than ready to take General Mitchel's arm when he finally made his cold bows to Brewster and Vallandigham who, he later said, were like hungry vultures or other carrion seekers, ready to pounce on any morsel a man might drop from his lips. "I don't trust those men," he said as he deposited her in her hotel, which was nothing more than a converted house for lodgers and tourist trade. "You seem to be on intimate terms with them." His tone was tactfully reproachful.

She was, however, too mortified, too tensely drawn now, to make any but a weary response and this fatigue he noticed and was concerned about, being a kind-hearted man who thereupon left her with a promise to conduct her to the White House on the morrow.

Quickly she escaped to her rooms where, before she even removed her outer garments, she turned the key in the lock, as though with that short and angry motion she had barricaded herself against the shamed thoughts pursuing her into the apartment. It was as if in a peevish moment she hoped to show Dimitri she was capable of shutting him out. He might come from the arms of Susan Brewster, from the embrace of a woman he did not love and he could knock on this door until Gabriel blew his horn, but she would not open it!

She flung herself upon the horse hair settle and surrendered herself utterly to the fierce hatred swelling in her bosom, a passionate conflagration able to drive other more painful memories out of her head. For how long she lay on the sofa with satisfaction over her mighty anger and plans for revenge, she did not know. Gradually, the steady tick-tock of the room clock on the mantel became audible to her and the futility of her rage told her she was well able to lock him out who wished not to enter; that if he never entered it would not minimize the glow of conquest he might forever retain; that he not she, had commanded the situation! Not he, but she, had courted dishonor! He, on the face of it was exculpated, could appear in a light of bright virtue, in the guise of Galahad himself! "Oh, Dimitri, you had far better have seduced me, told me your lies, than strip me of my soul like this, humble me before her, for her, for what her father can give you!"

When General Mitchel called for her in the morning he found a changed woman from the bewildered one of the previous evening. The nervous tension he had sensed in her the day before was replaced by an alert and calmness not unlike such qualities as had been hers on the march to Kentucky. She was brisk and determined. Nothing of her torturous night showed in the clear blue of her eyes. Rather, her smoothly combed hair and the severe collar of her gown, lent her the air of a Puritan maid, along with the dignity expected of one. She did not speak much, though her quiet was not without charm. Stripped of her vanity as she now was, she was instead the veritable embodiment of her mission. In no better spiritual garments could she have entered the White House for her audience with Mr. Lincoln.

Soon afterwards, she was informed that Mr. Lincoln would receive her. General Mitchel, who had been so advised, assured her of the President's vast kindness, even pointing out the signal honor conferred on her, since this very day he was to depart for Harrison's Landing, General McClellan's headquarters. Only a great man with such heavy responsibilities could waive or suspend his own interest in order to set at peace the tender concerns of a wife.

"As a matter of fact, dear lady," he told her cheerfully, "I am certain Mr. Lincoln's consent to see you has its provenance in other sources than your husband's situation; that has been fairly well settled already, Secretary Seward told me."

"Settled how? Will the court-martial not find Colonel Turchin guilty?"

General Mitchel smiled secretively. "It will not matter, I think, whether General Buell's sycophants find Colonel Turchin guilty or not! I may not say more. The President is awaiting you!"

That Mitchel had taken many pains to gain for her this interview she had no doubts. And so much kindness after last night's humiliating rebuff made her suffer great remorse. Now she felt acutely what her husband must have endured at the hands of his enemies. He stood so willing and eager to give and his giving was derided and upbraided. From him whom she had known only as the commanding general, who had never spoken ten sentences to her, she freely received courtesy and understanding. There were tears glistening in her eyes as she followed the porter into a darkened room, enhanced in its gloom by the drawn drapes and high, dark furniture.

A simply clad figure separated itself from the dimness of the room and she thusly found herself in the presence of President Lincoln. A sudden sound of childish laughter drifted in to them. "That is my boy," Mr. Lincoln said. "He does not realize that the White House is not for childish laughter." His words were so sad that she almost dared to look at him. He waved her to a seat while he pulled the drape cords which parted the heavy curtains and admitted the July sunlight. "You know I am Abe Lincoln?" he inquired whimsically, and when she nodded, unable to say a word, he laughed self consciously. "You'd be surprised how many times I'm taken for the porter."

"Mr. President," she tried to speak.

Lincoln had taken a seat before the table that was quite dwarfed against his towering height. He ruffled several papers lying before him, and seemed when he spoke, to be addressing himself to them instead of to her. Only once did he look up, and then his tired eyes shone out of his lined face as though they existed in a life apart from the man, "I know Colonel Turchin's story," he said kindly. "I would that the whole country could know it as it is. Then all the people could see exemplified in him an honest and loyal citizen! They would have learned the lesson of undisguised, unashamed loyalty - loyalty to one another.

When she did not interrupt him with her thanks, or make a single movement, he sighed, and spoke further. "Miscarriage of justice is to be expected, Madame Turchin. Now tell me how the facts appear to you."

Bidden to do so, she bravely told Turchin's story, his aims, his ideals, ever since he had tried to volunteer as a regular. As she spoke, she felt the release of a great weight. It mattered less what she said than that he, the great-hearted man, was hearing it. When she had finished the entire story she rose from her chair with an imploring gesture to which Lincoln responded by taking her two hands in his, and comforting her with reassuring words. "Thank you for speaking with me," he said, "and thank you for having faith in me. You and the colonel are brave, unselfish Americans. I wish that there were more of you. I believe the colonel and I would understand how, sometimes to serve God, we must defy his ministers! They are the learned counselors for the Lord! They have so much to do with reading the law, Madame Turchin, that they are not to be too severely blamed for skipping a page here and there."

He had spoken no promises, added nothing to what General Mitchel had said, but still she was convinced that, come what might at the court-martial, Ivan would be vindicated. She left the White House just as Mr. Lincoln was seen to emerge from its portals to enter the carriage awaiting him. General Mitchel assisted Mrs. Turchin into his carriage, beamed at her, and motioned respectfully toward the president's vehicle now being driven rapidly out of the grounds. "He is going to see McClellan," he explained with a grim disapprobation written on his face. How much longer his patience will suffer that man's opprobrious arrogance, I cannot guess."

CHAPTER XXI

In Alabama, Turchin's trial was nearing its end. The last few days were harrowing both to him and to General Garfield. The General was unable to support the colonel's stand with respect to the violations which, he was forced to concede, made dark marks against his record. Still he could not condone the pointed literalness that the adjudicating Colonels managed to skillfully turn against Turchin, regardless of his defenses to the accusations. The close room became intolerable to everyone in it and the angry passions rose unbridled in all. Back and forth the charges were hurled, with the colonel roused to an outspokenness that added no grain of tempering leniency to his case. Driven to overflowing scorn, at last he turned on them all and cried: "You think I have defied the code of gentlemanly conduct, do you? Well, that depends on the definition for that flexible term! Perhaps, I am not a gentleman! I would rather be an American, and if the two terms are mutually exclusive, as they seem here to be here, well then, name me no high sounding name of gentleman! If Mr. Donnell, who has the colossal effrontery to stand in this room and denounce an American – if he is a gentleman, then I beg of you, denominate me his opposite!"

An angry, consternate murmur buzzed through the room, and General Garfield, who could not wholly suppress the lurking smile these words had produced, turned his face towards the dusty window pane where summer bugs were dying on the glass and kept his eyes fixed thereon as though glued. He heard a retaliatory voice make denunciatory charges, but he barely listened. When Turchin made answer, his attention was again caught and held by the defiant exasperated Russian.

"I am well aware that Mr. Donnell's property suffered on account of the camp we located on his ground. But just who is Mr. Donnell? Is he not the man who, by his own admission, and proudly at that, sided and abetted the rebellion? Did he not pay for the uniforms of rebel soldiers? Did he not admit in this court that he sent 70 bales of cotton to Decatur so that they could be used to build fortifications against us there? The boys of the 24th, the same which camped on this man's grounds, took those fortifications and took them without asking whose life was to be laid down in the endeavor!" Saying this, he turned sternly about, and confronted with his eyes the same Mr. Donnell then present in the court room. Confronted is an understatement, for he fairly glared at him, so that the rebel sympathizer turned uncomfortably to face General Garfield who gave him no comfort or ease.

Pointing at Mr. Donnell, Turchin accused: "That is the man who hates every Union soldier, and openly glories in his defiance of them. He states without the blush of shame, in this very court, that he will never take the oath of allegiance to the United States Government, and that all his sympathies are with the Southern Confederacy! Such a person dared to come to me and insist, mind you, that I must give him guards in order for him to keep his plantation protected! Would you have had me comply with such a demand?" Deep sarcasm colored his next words, though he accompanied them by a beatific smile of such pure anticipation, that General Garfield had to cover his laughing mouth with his palm, lest it be observed how thoroughly he applauded the colonel. Turchin continued thus: "How quickly I should have provided him with a guard. A guard of honor, indeed; to march him off to jail as a pestilential traitor!"

More than once the trying and tried colonels concluded that Colonel Turchin was little better than a lunatic, and the consensus of the court's opinion was that General Buell had the worst of it if he had to rely on such men; that what had been educed in this trial proved fully the wisdom of astute and sensible generals like McClellan, who looked upon human beings as something more than objects for blood and thunder tactics. With various shrugs and opposition, all decided that Turchin's real failing lay in his inability to comprehend the nature of the American tradition. This was a fact that in no way mitigated his soldierly faults but rather enhanced them, for he was looked upon as a sort of Turk, and as such, one unwelcome in their midst.

Garfield, somewhat disgusted with the turn of events in this test case, as he viewed it from start to finish, had little to say to these gentlemen. "He is guilty, yes, of thinking we are in this war to fight our enemies!" he said to himself. Without a single word, he strode out of the room at the close of the day, and was profoundly thankful that the trial was nearly over.

There were still a few details for the records, to be disposed of with dispatch before Turchin was free to quit Alabama. The scrupulous colonels had still to adduce further evidence of his defection. One asked him the next day, "Is it not true that you permitted the depredation of Mr. David's and Mr. Brook's fields and that fences were destroyed wantonly?"

"That was an inevitable result due to military necessity," Turchin replied laconically. Another day and another tedious, repetitious recital was not a pleasure he yearned for. He had practically spent himself on the previous day and was thereafter absolutely convinced that it profited him less than nothing to state and restate his good faith before eyes that would not see and ears premeditatingly deaf. "He who knows how to defend towns would not be surprised to see every brick building turned into a fort, pierced with loop holes and embrasures all through, the trees in front yards cut down, and every street barricaded, if the circumstances were such that only by these means could the place be held."

Having said this, he sat back with undisguised boredom, and contemptuously closed his eyes against the prosecuting colonels as he waited for further interrogation. A slow sardonic humor played about his mouth that told General Garfield the true state of his feelings. Nor could that amiable general help but second his contempt of the mock justice that the questions plainly indicated. Such an attempt on the colonels' part to prove to one another that they were seriously seeking explanations, while all knew that it was only the semblance of justice that was required to still what small qualms they may have had, disgusted him. It would appear, even, that had Turchin been sentient of the basic ingredients comprising the prejudices of these peers of his; had he been willing to cower to some extent, to plead ignorance and so commend himself to their good graces, thereby imbuing them with gracious virtues, he could not have surmounted their fixed determination to get rid of him. "He is too much a man to stoop to such a travesty of justice," was the general's verdict, and he was happy when Turchin's next words proved him correct in his estimate of him. It had just been asked of him to explain the horrible, disgraceful and shameful incident of the two yellow servant girls.

"How can a gentleman explain such outrages? I tried at once to ascertain their truth! While I investigated the rumors, I had every suspected man apprehended! Whoever declares me indifferent to the treatment of any females, speaks other than the truth!" He stood up excitedly as he forced his accusers to attend: "But it matters not what I say! You record religiously what a professed enemy prefers against me, while I must repeat myself, like a cuckoo clock until I am led as you probably wish, to feel that I am the defendant! Not I, Gentlemen, stand here being indicted! It is not necessary for me to defend the truth!"

"But you did harbor a Negro run-away slave, did you not? And your wife was present during the campaigns, was she not?" These were the final trump factors about which there could be no question of interpretation. The judge advocate was now almost as angry as Turchin. The two men stared hostilely at each other and the accustomed military courtesy was lamentably wanting in the sultry atmosphere of the courtroom.

"I have proved already," he shouted, "by reputable witnesses, and would also by the boy himself, would you accept his testimony, that he was with me of his own accord. He has a right to wish to escape. He was willing to risk his life for his freedom, for us! By coming to us, by rendering valuable service, by giving me information about the enemy, by guiding us in vital scouting expeditions, he was entitled to our protection, against our mutual enemy, his and ours! I consider my safeguarding him not only proper, but decent and human! If we had been at war with England and had sent an expedition against that country, we should have landed our forces in Ireland, because we know that the people of Ireland hate their oppressors, the English, and would have readily joined us. For a similar reason did Garibaldi, before he moved on Naples, invade Sicily. We invade the Southern states, where, with few exceptions, the white population is against us, and from them we can get no information concerning the enemy. In our hearts, we know that our only friends here are Negroes. But steeped in prejudices, we are ashamed manfully to acknowledge it. As a matter of necessity, we use Negroes for our purposes. They are willing to communicate with us about their masters, and about the movements of the enemy troops. And after we thus put them in a position hostile to the mass of the white population, are we basely and meanly to surrender them to their sworn enemies?"

"An irrelevant digression from the subject!" was the curt rebuttal he received for his pains. "You speak, Sir, out of bounds!" the judge advocate informed him.

Turchin was beyond caring now what he said. He instinctively trusted himself to speak honestly. He had to speak honestly, and it did not matter a whit that he wasted his words. "Yes! No! Those are the solitary words you would have me speak! The simple words! Simple because they tell nothing of the true nature of my decision to do or not to do what seemed right to me. Yes, I kept a Negro lad in my camp! I wish I could have put a uniform proudly upon him! Upon two million of them! Perhaps I do speak out of bounds! It is the truth in this court which is out of bounds, gentlemen! Very well! I may be dismissed from the service of my country, yet, I shall speak and you shall, as officers and gentlemen, hear me out! I am, have always been and shall always remain, a loyal man to my country! I am not inexperienced in the ways of war. I offer my experience to you. I see that our military policy varies with the generals; there is no unity of action. One general gives Negroes a temporary protection, promises them freedom, then moves on; the next general, superseding the first, drives the Negroes out of our lines. He does not care what happens to them after that. And what happens is that their enemies, and ours, hang them to trees at the first convenient opportunity, that is, when we turn our backs. In fact, the day after we retreated from Tuscumbia, I heard that as soon as our silent guns gave them amnesty, four or five black boys were hanged! Humanity cries out against us for permitting this great travesty to happen."

Circumlocution! Evasion! These were how his impassioned words were dubbed. General Garfield was powerless to intervene in what was now a definite fact, that by his harangue, this sincere officer had roused in his judges an unreserved dislike. There could hardly be any doubt as to the verdict they must eventually pronounce upon him. His own private verdict did the Russian officer more than justice. "What nobility of soul that man has," he muttered. "What a strange selflessness and magnanimity of heart! He would not hesitate to pour forth his rich and varied mind that his very critics in their animadversion might benefit. What a remarkable man!"

As he was pondering these thoughts, he caught one of the last ringing proclamations Turchin made. "I have everywhere in Missouri, in Kentucky, in Tennessee and in Alabama, been hated by Secessionists. I deem it my best recommendation as a loyal officer. But I defy anyone to find a single loyal Union man who has ever been in connection with me, that will make a complaint against me!"

Standing in a pool of shocked silence, he now impulsively extended his arms in an embracing gesture which struck Garfield as both pathetic and beautiful, as indicative of the vast vulnerability of the man. "Gentlemen, beware! The more lenient we are with Secessionists, the more insolent they become. If we do not prosecute this war with vigor, using all the means we can bring to bear against the enemy, including even the emancipation of the slaves, the ruin of this country is inevitable."

He heaved a resigned, defeated sigh; he was weary; deeply and sorely weary. "The problem before us all is great. Do not think I plead for myself. I do not count. Once I strip this uniform from my back, I shall pass into a stream of obscurity, even as I came from obscurity when humanity called me. I came out of a great spiritual darkness to seek light and freedom here in America. I believe freedom less shackled here than in Russia! But Russia has loosened her chains. Here, lies the greater darkness, because of the greater potentialities for light! You, gentlemen, put Freedom on trial today and decry those who lift their swords in her defense! Not I, sirs, stand trial, but human liberty! All America stands trial. As an American I dare to plead with you; condemn our real enemies!"

After this there was an end of the discussions, pro and con. Turchin was at liberty to return to Chicago, which he promptly did, having no heart to linger until the verdict. But before he left Athens, he called on General Garfield once more. He saluted him with the same initial formality that existed at their first meeting. About to leave, being already at the door, he heard the general call his name. Turning, he strode back to his grieving friend who reproached him in these words: "You leave like this; with a formal salute? Between us must be more than a salute, Colonel Turchin! We part not as officers only, but as friends. Your hand, sir," and gripping Turchin's hand, he wished him luck. "I shall always be honored to call you friend," the generous-hearted Garfield exclaimed with genuine feeling.

"The honor is mine!" Turchin answered simply. Two tears rolled down the several new lines in his face.

They did not meet again until several months later. Turchin, having nothing to detain him now, set out at once for his home where he arrived late one evening toward the close of July. The verdict of guilty had been quickly passed upon him, but the news thereof had not yet officially reached him. Nor had the more auspicious decision, from Washington, which not only countervailed the decree of General Buell's more or less arbitrary court-martial, but made the findings of the Colonels invalid with respect to an officer higher in rank than they. This was now the case, for Colonel Turchin by the President's order, had been promoted to the rank of brigadier general, a status higher than that of his judges who were no longer his lawful peers.

All this time Turchin had been unaware of his wife's journey to Washington. She had kept the purpose and the result carefully from him, uncertain as she was of the outcome and too sickly certain of it for herself. For a week now she had been home and had scarcely ventured to leave the house. Yet, she had news of the Brewsters' and Trofimov's return from Mrs. Morrison who had chanced to call the very day scheduled for Turchin's arrival.

Mrs. Morrison had found a distraught Nadine and had concluded that she had apprised herself of something unfavorable to the colonel. During the trial, Henrietta had followed such accounts of it as had reached the newspapers. Several times she had anxiously called while Nadine was absent, but of this she did not now speak. This day when she found her in, she was made acutely uncomfortable by Nadine's cool attitude, though she was convinced that the only reason for her possible pique, for so she read it - was safely repressed in her own bosom, betrayed to no one. She learned from the over sensitive Nadine that Turchin was to arrive in the evening, and instantly offered to call for her, and convey her to the station.

"You are kind," Nadine spoke thickly, in a voice Mrs. Morrison's self-consciousness mistook for angry suspicion or jealousy. "I am not well, Mrs. Morrison." And indeed she did look pinched and ill, so that Henrietta's heart stirred with pity for what must be her wifely grief and suffering over Turchin's impending dismissal from the army, as she suspected was the case. "I do not believe myself capable of meeting the colonel!"

So it was hastily and in some confusion, decided between them that Mrs. Morrison was to stand watch alone for the colonel until he should descend from the train. And the two women who loved John Basil Turchin parted.

When Mrs. Morrison had taken her leave of Nadine, the long withheld tears, which had choked her through the painful moments she had been forced to dally in conversation with the widow, were free to flow at will. The tension and expectancy of crisis had been long storing in her heart, and now riotously tore free of her, and quickly reduced her to a state of trembling weakness not made the easier to bear, with the knowledge that Ivan was arriving that night. Ivan would have his own onus of suffering and expect of his wife comfort and cheer in the face of the misfortunes, he believed threatening him. Shame and repudiation were no light whiplashes for a man of his convictions and pride.

Thinking of her husband subdued Nadine's turbulent emotions temporarily. She had just wiped her eyes determinately, when the knocker clapped at her front door. She thought the knock was Mrs. Morrison's; that she was returning with smelling salts or a strong cordial brought from her own cellar. An involuntary admiration for her relaxed her mouth into a more friendly smile, though in it, for all to see, lay a telltale new intelligence of pain. Suddenly she pitied Henrietta for her devotion to Ivan. Not that she compared that feeble liking of the widow and the new acumen with which she sensed the widow's pain to her own shame and humiliation. But she fancied without conceit that her husband was even more unresponsive to the strictly controlled affections of the widow than Trofimov had been to hers. She hastened to acknowledge that more womanly dignity operated in Henrietta's case than in hers and resolved on a friendlier course in the future as she made her way to answer the door. She paid a silent tribute to the salve of the salutary conventions hitherto protective of her in the same way as they shielded her husband's more circumspect admirer.

To her astonishment none other than the unpredictable baron stood in the sunlight before her. Tall and handsome, his hat in his hand, his eyes slight with eagerness, he was the picture of anything but remorse or regret. He grasped her limp hand and manifested no shamed remembrance of the entire Washington occurrence. "Let us go inside, Nadine," he insisted, pushing her gently backward. "It is not a ghost you see, nor a wicked changeling. It is I! You know you are happy to see me!"

She made no reply, but did not offer him resistance as he led her into the house. The twinkle lay still sparkling and salutatory in his eyes as he minutely inspected her visage. Then he shook his head in mock reproof as he gazed upon the ravages of her grief. The evidence of misery, for whose being he was happily responsible, and knew it, made this woman perversely the lovelier in his sight. Giving way to the impulse of the moment, he pulled her to him and acted the part of the indulgent lover, more with the air of forgiving than of asking forgiveness. With his long strong finger he lifted up her head by the chin, and most deliberately prevented her from uttering anything save a gasping sigh of anger mingled with delight.

But words between these two were inevitable and he was prepared for them much better than she. The sight of him had unnerved her and reduced her again to such a frenzied emotional state that when she tried to call upon pride, it only served to mock her. "You never came back that night," she whispered.

"It was not meant to be," he defended himself. "I meant what I then said, Nadya, every word. I still mean every word. But what was I to do when I found Mr. Brewster and his entire family waiting for me that afternoon at the apartments of Vallandigham? Was I to betray the woman I loved to the tender mercies of our friends? Would you have preferred that I do that rather than use good taste and good sense? Was I not to count on your fine understanding? Was I to believe you had rather shame us both fruitlessly than draw the natural conclusion; namely that only insuperable obstacles could have seduced me from your side?"

"But you sent no word! You were so casual when we later met!"

"Send you word and admit thereby that I was so much as aware of your presence in Washington? Would you have wished me thusly to destroy any chance of helping Ivan?" This he queried deliberately in the sanguine hope that the inherent untruthfulness must escape her. He counted on her feelings, not her intellect, in substantiating his feeble claim that he had in fact sought aid for Turchin. If she believed him, he had a good defense. He remembered that he had in fact, mentioned the court-martial once to Vallandigham when they were in Washington, only to be refused point-blank. Vallandigham would lift not a finger in the colonel's defense, even had he the power to do so. But the fact was that on his own recommendations he could not hope to affect anything for anyone in the White House, where he dared not show himself at this time. These murky dealings she could not suspect. She was happy to find some excuse for the baron and knew any excuse was sufficient save a change of heart. "You did concern yourself over poor Ivan!" said she, much relieved. "I am so glad." Then, in a curious contrariness, she stepped away from his encircling arms and tried to compose herself. "I should hate you. You have behaved, in spite of everything, abominably to me! You have shown yourself to be callous of my feelings and shameless in your faithlessness. But I know my mind now. Someday I shall thank you for sparing me greater callousness and shame!"

Trofimov's white teeth gleamed as his laughter rang through the small house. "But you foolish little goose, you cannot hate me; that too is written. Do you not know as much as that by now?" He again tried to kiss her and received a smart blow on his smooth cheek. "I like you all the better for being angry. I am not like your stupid clouts, those who need prescribed rituals of devotion to guarantee them their masculine pride. I like your knowing now that though I might appear to have failed you, I was in reality being sensible of our mutual good. What are all the dreams we fancy if we are without money, Nadya? In effect I love you more than lightly, else I might have indulged myself," he added, cruelly superior. Brewster has the right idea. Why should not both of us profit from his excellent example?"

"You are horrible!" she breathed. She was moved to revulsion by the implications his words clearly revealed.

"Not horrible. Words like that are for children, to frighten them from aspiring to those things you wish to keep from them. They are words of foolish warning and ambiguous meaning. I am not horrible; I am honest and realistic. This is a cruel world, my sweet, and I know to the fullest extent the cruelty you and Ivan have decried theoretically. Once I worked for pennies per day. I heaved coal into a stupid merchant's stove while he suffered me to serve him! I know the corruption in men's souls. I know what debasement means in cities bursting with wealth for the chosen few. I dreamed short-lived dreams with deluded artists and poets who, to live, sang their plaintive melodies hopefully into the muffled ears of dyspeptic princes. But how long do you suppose a man can live on the fringe of things when he is young and has something to sell which men will buy - and women, too!"

She was appalled by these words, and found none of her own with which to halt the rush of his irrefutable reasoning. "What I feel for you is a kind of madness, perhaps no more substantial than the moonlight which first showed you to me. I should have plunged headlong into that madness in Washington, that is the truth, but for the sheer accident of Brewster's whim which brought him unexpectedly to Washington at my heels. But it happened, so, and I have had time to reconsider. Why should we not have our cake and eat it, too? Why should we move backward instead of forward? Answer me that, Nadya!"

"I do not understand you," she whispered hoarsely. "What you say is monstrous, without conscience."

"What do I care about conscience or petty standards of morality? They tell us that theft and deceit are execrable; but are not their fruits, in time, sanctified by long tenure? The facts of life corroborate me wholly."

"Then what will you of me? How must I meet this unveiled self you show me?" Nadine asked.

"We shall go on, no differently from before. I shall marry Miss Brewster. We adjust ourselves to the propriety of the future moments. Let us not be martyrs. We shall give to one another only what is delightful to give when we are disposed to give it."

"Go away now, Dimitri," she begged him faintly. "Ivan comes home this day."

He took her two hands in his. They lay in his, cold and unresisting.

Gently he kissed first the one and then the other. "Understand me!" he murmured. "Forgive me! Do not abandon me!"

"Egoist!" she cried between laughter and tears. "You abandon me, scourge me and then presume to request that I shall not abandon you!"

On this note they parted. Not once did he turn his head as he stepped into the small carriage allotted to his use these days by Brewster. She remained for a long while staring out after him. With his going the daylight seemed about to dwindle also, and a group of passing clouds stopped in tumbled clusters along the edge of the sky where a few tall masts of lake freighters appeared to support them.

A sudden wish to meet her husband at the station moved her to an abrupt resolve. She turned from the window, and went to don her prettiest gown and loveliest collar. Soon she was knocking upon Mrs. Morrison's door where, to that surprised lady, she announced her intention to meet Turchin's train with her. "If you are still interested in waiting for him, will it not be less tedious to wait together?" she asked lamely, hardly interested in what words she spoke.

"If I had so noble a man to wait for, Madame Turchin, waiting could under no circumstances be tedious for me." Henrietta's tone was tinged with an icy aloofness that Nadine vaguely felt. She turned a swiftly startled look upon the widow, but found on that patrician face no excoriation, only the same restrained smile she had always associated with her. "I shall consider it gracious of you to permit me to be present when Colonel Turchin arrives." So carefully were her inflections modulated that she conveyed to Nadine the impression of delicate concern for the tender feelings of a man who just received his conge from the army. "Here at home he will see that citizens honor him for his trials. Here, he will find friends who love him."

"Thank you, Mrs. Morrison. You have been among our most loyal friends, here or anywhere."

They conversed politely for some time and then proceeded to the railroad station where they had a short wait until Turchin's train pulled into the yard. His was the only figure to be deposited from the train. It was quite dark with the dusk and the smoke, and he did not notice Mrs. Morrison's carriage which he would in any case not have recognized. He had but little luggage with him, and what little he had, he carried firmly in his hands. He dropped his bags in joyous surprise when his wife's voice greeted him, when her soft arms clung to him, when her salt tears fell into his mouth. He did not see his friend, Mrs. Morrison, who had discreetly stepped behind her carriage during the homecoming embrace, and only emerged when his voice happily summoned her forth from her hiding place. "Where are you, Mrs. Morrison. What a good friend you are to hasten our reunion, Nadya's and mine! She has told me all. Only a good friend with the understanding heart could think to please a poor old soldier in this way!" Heartily he wrung her hand till the bones almost cracked under the strain. "You must come home with us, dear Mrs. Morrison. Tonight, I want the dearest people in my life near me!" and with that he shamelessly put his arms about his friend and kissed her affectionately on the cheek. If that cheek grew hot and flushed, the deepening dark of the sky and his own unconsciousness spared her the mortification of having her blushes seen.

All this time Nadine had refrained from mentioning General Mitchel's letter. She might at least have relieved Mrs. Morrison's worries had she told her of that friend and his letter hinting the promotion. But as yet, the promotion was not official. So now she gave little thought to Mrs. Morrison, and would not have observed her flushed face even if the summer darkness had not obligingly obscured it, any more than she would have attributed undue concern for Turchin to it. However, while driving together to the house on Division Street, she thought it meet to mention the good general's letter, its contents and its grounds for good hope. Warmly she praised General Mitchel for his tireless intercession, and echoed his congratulations to our overwhelmed, utterly dumbfounded colonel.

"Are you certain of this?" Mrs. Morrison cried excitedly. "This is wonderful! This is an honor indeed, Colonel Turchin - to have the President sign your promotion as Mrs. Turchin says General Mitchel reports."

"It is a kind hope of my commander," said Turchin, finding words at last, though still hesitant to accept the veracity of such a miracle. "Poor Mitchel! He knows what I have to cope with! Such blindness! Such willful blindness! Such costly willfulness! Mrs. Morrison, only a writer could do justice to the lack of such military justice! What a farce. More and more I begin to see how we lack proper, truthful voices. In Russia I used to lament the silence of the enslaved masses. But what we have here is just as bad, if not worse! A deep silence at least gives a man hope and inclination to dream that out of the depths of that stillness some great and convulsive true intelligence will sprout. But to have clamoring voices which tell lies! We get a terrible confusion, a... a..."

"A cacophony of half truths," Mrs. Morrison put in quietly. "I have often felt exactly like that. That is why, when I might have contented myself with the comfortable life Mr. Morrison provided for me, I sought to put into words what I knew so many people would otherwise never hear!" There was no pride or ostentation in her, no bragging, only simple feelings, simply said.

"It is not always so certain that we know the truth from the half truth," Nadine softly argued. "If I were a public servant I should hesitate to denounce a man's words for half truths. I should rather feel that if so many people will heed the half truth, it may come closer to their identification of it with themselves; more so than that purer quality of truth which is loftily in the mouths of the philosophers but leaves ordinary mortals unconvinced." She smiled wearily. She recalled her afternoon interview with Trofimov, the unvarnished "truth" he had delivered himself of. "He was telling me his truths," she realized. "And I was telling him my sort of truths when I let myself believe him." Her smile was for the interval of peace her conversational remarks to her husband and Mrs. Morrison now granted her. She cared too little for Mrs. Morrison's opinions to take notice of the peculiar glance that young woman directed sidewise to her. As for Turchin, he had paid but brief notice to the words of the ladies. His mind was too busy imagining the true purport of his former commander's letter which he was most anxious to read for himself. Mitchel was not a man likely to indulge in vain flatteries and surmises. If he was certain President Lincoln had promoted him, then perhaps it was so. But not yet would the entire significance of this grace envelop him. He was as yet too much stunned, too tired, too much frustrated by the agents of the past weeks to dare this moment; to close his hand upon the favor almost come to rest within his grasp. "Mrs. Morrison," he cried. "Do you for one believe such good fortune is possible? Can it be that in Washington they have taken notice of such an unknown and obscure man as me? You know," he added earnestly, "that even that fine General Garfield held out no hopes of my acquittal in Alabama."

"Yes, I believe what your commanding general wrote. I can well imagine that men like our President have seen how your cause is just. It means, colonel - nay, general!, that there is right in the world after all, if there are sincere believers in right to bring it forward, to sponsor it with their own lives! It means that we who admire the honest and upright man need not feel our efforts futile or hopelessly remote!" She inhaled deeply, unevenly. "I am happy for you. I am happy to believe the truth of what must ultimately appear to everyone – namely, that you are a wonderful example to all of us!"

In this way they arrived at the Turchin's house where Mrs. Morrison and the new general, at least, spent a memorable evening. Nadine, full of her curious sentience today, thought, "How odd! This day make them happy, these two good friends. She is delighted that her hero, Mr. Lincoln promotes poor Ivan. He is happy because a sad and dark affair has a delightfully bright ending. Yet, the same day that brings them these things brings me the reverse of pleasure. It has brought me a kind of painful peace." Softly she went near her husband's chair, and let his fingers wind tightly about hers. This was happiness indeed for him - to have his wife, his home, his redeemed honor and a good friend.

CHAPTER XXII

Among Mrs. Morrison's numerous friends was a young newspaper man named William Bross. The young man, effeminate in appearance, ambitious in nature, sentimental with lambent sympathies, had an honest wish to serve his fellow citizens, and had lately become immensely interested in Turchin's career. He had been assigned the early reportorial tasks of relating the personal and trivial activities of camp life during the 19th Illinois training period. He had an instinct for the human interest angles, and moreover possessed a turn for a fine phrase which compared well with the best writer on the staff. He added to his qualifications as a newspaperman and writer's of short pieces, certain humble qualities so that he was seldom anything save a welcome audience for his more verbose and assertive friends. His habits were sedate and often furnished his rougher colleagues much amusement, which Bross took in such dignified good humor, that he was a general favorite with all.

Turchin, too, had enjoyed the few minutes' conversation he always allowed to Bross after leaving Mrs. Morrison's office, a small cubbyhole, adjoining the larger room where Bross and several city clerks worked. With no thought to oblige Mrs. Morrison, William Bross really felt drawn to the unsubtle and robust Turchin, who never laughed at him, never preached and always listened to his current problems. Turchin had even dealt gently with his understandable consternation when at the outbreak of the war, during the period of enlistment, he had been refused for military duty. Bross had sustained a severe injury in childhood, and was left subsequently lamed, so that he had a bad limp in addition to periodic attacks of rheumatism in his hips. Bross' most persistent dream was to learn telegraphy. Regardless of the derogation it invited, he was always to be seen with strange papers, odd parcels and all manner of contraptions relative to his dream and he constantly engaged the interest of both Mrs. Morrison and Turchin with inventive devices to improve telegraphy.

When Chicago had first heard the news of Colonel Turchin's trial in Alabama, Bross had personally asked Editor Medill to send him to the spot. In this he had been seconded by Mrs. Morrison, who would have gone herself, except that Medill sternly forbade it. "We will do all we can here, and some day we will really deal the rebels a blow they won't recover from," he said. "Sorry as I am to hear a friend of yours is in trouble, Henrietta, but I need Bross here."

But now, when Mrs. Morrison came rushing into the Tribune building to announce the happy tidings, that conscientious editor was most attentive. When she had urged Medill to play up the resultant unimpeachable inspiring account of Colonel Turchin's promotion, his position in the army as far as his court-martial was concerned, its potential verdict having no power over Turchin now that President Lincoln had raised him to a higher rank than that of the members of the court-martial commission, he avidly consented. He and Bross scurried about until all manner of appropriate activities were arranged whereby the city, or at least, the loyal elements of it, might benevolently pay tribute to the hero of the day, as Turchin was popularly described.

Not insensitive to the honor that the entire staff of the Tribune paid him, allowably proud of the applausive recognition the Chicago Board of Trade gave him, Turchin was indeed a truly vindicated man; his happiness exhibiting itself in no mean gloating, but rather in a new gravity which stood in character with the new responsibilities the President had placed upon him as brigadier-general. Lincoln and America, Lincoln and the people of America, Lincoln and humanity, merged into a unified concept for him. If this state of mind broached on a sort of hero-worship, he would have defended it stoutly, none the less, though ordinarily averse to the theme that any one man, be he even a President, was significantly the embodiment of a period's or an age's progress. He made of Abraham Lincoln a sweeping exception and under the circumstances, he could be pardoned for this sort of adulation.

When he was informed that the civic leaders of Chicago were planning to give him a public ovation, that the large and magnificent auditorium, Byrne Hall, was to be the scene of it, he agreed to speak, and decided to use the occasion to commend the President, to hearten the people so that they could continue to have faith in Mr. Lincoln. This he felt necessary for an army man to express; for Mr. Lincoln's direction of the war was being sharply criticized even by papers and people not openly unfriendly to the Union Cause. The nearly eighteen months of warfare and rebellion had not added confidence or glory to the Government.

Mrs. Morrison and William Bross were instrumental in arranging the agenda for the huge public convention, and for securing some of the worthiest citizens of the city as speakers to share the platform with Turchin. On the evening of the event, Mrs. Morrison posted herself helpfully behind the scenes, so that she could be on hand to encourage Turchin should the sight of the unusual crowd or its inflated enthusiasm touch him with a sudden reticence. "Enjoy this night, General Turchin," she said graciously. "You, above all present, deserve the gratitude and love of these people. "They are the relations of all your men. You are not to fear them, you are a famous general!" She laughed as she spoke, and sent Nadine, who was standing quietly nearby, a hurried glance in which she seemed to apologize for her familiarity with Turchin.

"The general will be fortified when he steps out there upon the platform," his wife calmly opined. "He believes in the innate good of people. He is like one of the ancient patriarchs; alternating between a sternness that frightens them as easily as it awes them, and a facetiousness that only his good friends understand." She meant more than she said, but the widow mistook her meaning, and saw only unjust criticism of her favorite.

"It demands a large nature to be so lavish of itself as General Turchin is," she commented tartly while she wondered what the wife's purport might be; why Ivan continued to look fondly to her.

"General Turchin is lavish; there is no doubt of that. It is that very thing which frightens me," said Nadine. "He believes in all those people sitting out there. And yet because he believes them good, when they fail or falter, it is he who is brutally wounded."

"It is she who has good sense," he said as he went out to the front of the stage.

The two women were left behind the stage. Each knew that she espoused a way of life contradictory to the other and each was prepared to be amiable, although a true intimacy was impossible. Nadine, at the moment, was convinced that all the flattery and adulation, to which Ivan was now subjected, was like the ephemeral ignis fatuus; that the men and women who lauded him today, who pressed and cloyed at him insistently, did so to increase their proximity and identification with him; because they sought to drain off from him the essence of his glory in order to shine by his reflected splendor. In the end he must be disenchanted, and the pursuant disillusionment would crush him utterly.

Mrs. Morrison, on the other hand, was nettled by Nadine's deprecatory attitude. She saw in the Russian woman an unwarranted cynicism. She too was aware of the transitory nature of grandeur or glory, whether it be the glory of a moment or the glory of a life. It was all a matter of time to her. But this constant petulance in judging the transitory, this unwillingness to see the permanent in the impermanent, to see the sparkles of passing lights as an augur for something brighter in the future; all this annoyed her, made her glimpse willy-nilly into the harsh callousness to which men like Brewster were forever appealing in ceaseless and cynical clarity. "It is as if she arrogates to herself the privilege of seeing farther than the rest of us, who are willing to hope and wait - and work!" She was indeed dissatisfied with Turchin's wife, and politely lapsed into a silence which did not anger either lady. Soon both were peeping out of the wings, onto the stage where Turchin had taken a seat. Several eminent judges were speaking their praises of General Turchin, and both waited for Turchin's turn.

Sitting in front with the notables of Chicago, he was far from feeling what either of the ladies behind the curtains imagined. He felt neither the signal honor of the occasion nor the impressive homage of the city judges and merchants who surrounded him, and he preserved a respectful deference as the introductory addresses were delivered. He himself was in deep, meditative thought concerning the nature of the war and the passion of a free people at war. The people, he decided, were the final arbiters of a man's greatness. He viewed the activities on the platform with a great detachment. All the speakers eulogized him and his defense of himself in Athens. All spoke with awe of his promotion. Not one remembered to mention that the promotion, which was here publicly to be awarded in ceremony, was the reward for soldierly skill in devising a plan to take Huntsville with a minimum of bloodshed. Obviously the tribute and acclaim were not for the soldier. They were for the man, the American. Orators performed and the audience accepted everything without demur, applauding everybody who encouraged the flouting of their enemies. "It must be like that," Turchin thought, even as his name was mentioned and greeted by a wild uproar. They prove that I have no personal enemies. They see in my fight against rebel sympathizers, their own fight against their country's enemies."

When he stood up and walked to the front of the platform, he seemed troubled by the quantity of facts he was prepared to submit to them. He knew not how to begin and merely stood before them with beseeching eyes. Sensing this, the audience clapped steadily, encouragingly until his lifted arm brought a ready eager silence. This silence lasted a long minute, and had the heightened effect of knitting all the auditors together in their attention and receptiveness. As though he were a trained speaker, Turchin seemed to know the perfect moment of unbroken unanimity and let his first words drop into the hushed stillness softly. "Americans! Soldiers of freedom! Thank you for coming here tonight. You come to pay me homage? Nay, but I say to you that it is I who come to pay back more than homage. I am here to speak for all of those you have sent to the colors and together we pay you a debt of devotion! Were it not for the artifices of rebels parading as loyal men, I should not be here today without my regiment! I should have been with them where they need me, and I should have been content to wait for that day when we could together face you, our friends, and receive from your hands the noble tribute I must tonight receive alone on their behalf."

"I look upon your presence as the best refutation of the malice to which our enemies, our unseen enemies, too, expose us. We go gladly into deprivations and danger, even death if necessary, to save the instrument and the purpose behind the instrument of our liberty. We are determined to save our Union, which pro-slavery is equally determined to split asunder."

The crowd stirred like an undulating surge. Arms were upflung and hoarse voices muttered loud words. A young man in the rear of the auditorium suddenly shouted: "Down with the rebels," and his cry was roundly taken up by a crowd of cheering and zealous veterans who had come from the hospital.

Turchin again begged for silence, and at last the crowd good-naturedly granted it. The nervous stamping of boots ceased.

"All of you are intelligent citizens," he continued with uplifted hands. "There is no wanting in any of you the full knowledge of the underlying principles of which every mother's son of my regiment is prepared to give his life. Is there one of you fathers or mothers or wives or sweethearts who would countenance less than this in his son? Would any free American, free of prejudice and hate, wish for other than a vigorous prosecution of this war against those who dare to declare publicly, that they defy humanity, and would, like the antichrist, strive to continue the enslavement of humanity forever?" He paused dramatically, as though waiting for an answer, then answered for the entire body. "No! You, good people as you are, have the same credo that I have - to live and, if called upon, to die for this land where freedom has her fairest temples, her most ardent votaries! You, like me, are the unflinching enemy of all traitors. Therefore, would you be less willing than I, to stand trial for your convictions, for the convictions which your sons share with me? And if my tribunals should find me guilty, which is very likely, by the same token they find our boys guilty. But will that nullify the truth; can you gag and stifle the militant spirit of a free people? I say no! I am a small droplet in the great mass of Americans. But it is, in this case, given to me to be representative of us all - and it is given to our great and good leader, Mr. President Lincoln, that he shall be a representative of all your true sentiments; that in his name, yours is implied when appended to my promotion."

The audience to a man rose to its feet, and filled the hall with ringing cheers. In the rear someone began to shout a Huzzah and Hurrah for the Red, White and Blue. Nadine and Mrs. Morrison, out of sight, were individually thrilled by the tremendous demonstration. For different reasons, each moved closer to the platform. They saw Turchin standing, solemn and subdued, in the midst of this spirited reaction to his words. He made no motion to control the crowd this time. Of its own accord it subsided gradually into respectful attention, signifying thereby that they wished General Turchin to continue. He acceded to the will of his people.

"No unblushing traitor, selfish, perfidious soul, who would rather proclaim his attachment to property than to God shall daunt me or the boys of the 19th! We have passed unscathed through the ordeal of fire and death so far. We have proved beyond doubt that we are able to retain our faith even when human hate and spite unite against us." His voice was almost tender with the paternal pride it evinced.

"There is little more to say in appreciation for your loyalty and friendship," he summed up his address. "Noble-hearted friends, united in their adherence to a noble cause, are the best compliments to the leaders of men, whether in political or military action. Today you have here encouraged me to hope that sooner or later our men will meet with an equally heartening approbation wherever we shall go. And this encouragement will extend to my boys, who are now doing the work of slaves at the bidding of General Don Carlos Buell. But my boys and yours are true soldiers, and perform whatever their duty in rectitude and without repining. It will please them to know that in Chicago there is little sympathy for traitors!"

When he was done, he reseated himself among the judges and civil leaders. His mind had emptied itself of all thoughts and emotions, and was like a closed book accessible to no one. Later, when he and Nadine were returning to their home, he found little to say. Mrs. Morrison had tactfully departed before the meeting had been adjourned. "More and more I see the need for effectual distribution of the facts," he said to Nadine wearily. "It is one thing to stand up and tell friends your story, but how much wider would be the influence we could exert if we reached millions instead of hundreds! When we have beaten the rebels to their knees," he said suddenly becoming sententious, I shall turn to letters. The real trouble in this world full of men's blindness and hatefulness is a lack of the poetic sentiment, Nadya! The poetic sentiment is fundamentally a sort of love sentiment. Even the search for things that are beautiful implies a love sentiment! You love a thing of itself that is right and good and want every man to value it for its grandeur. But you have first the need to love your fellow men even more than the thing, if you desire to bring the admirable thing to his attention!" Having delivered himself thusly, he closed his eyes as he lent himself to the rhythmic trot of the horse.

There followed on this memorable civic award of his promotion, long weeks of restless waiting for military confirmation and reassignment. These were not easy weeks for him or Nadine to endure. He, at least, had the comfort of Mrs. Morrison's brilliant company on the days he frequented the Tribune's offices. She, however, was left to her own resources, now circumscribed, to her small chores at home, or brief shopping trips into the heart of the city, with uneventful walks in the nearby park to vary the monotony.

Since her last meeting with the baron, he had not driven by once. In the "Times" she had read a detailed report of his wedding, and a description of the romantic wedding tour, customary for the fashionable at that time. The best people made wedding tours, and sometimes these trips extended over a long period. However, thought she, in an attempt to explain the marked absence, even if the wedding tour were of necessity curtailed, he being new in town, she had no expectations where the baron was concerned. That she admitted the negative proposition angered her; for it unquestionably, proposed to her the presence of the opposite.

Often she envied Ivan his ability to find continual interests in which to use his superfluous energies. Not for long could his health and sanity be repressively contained. It mattered not that he often owned the shortness of his impatience at this time; he was, none the less, not above stopping for long chats with the newsmen and office workers at the Tribune. From these friendly workers on the paper, from the obliging editor, from the publisher himself, Cyrus McCormick, he found sufficient stimulus to save him from a sense of frustration until he could rejoin his men. From these people he first learned that General Buell had been quietly removed, and that a new commander was placed in charge of the western department of the army.

His informant, specifically on this point, was William Bross. Bross was himself disposed to a conservative religious deportment, and was consequently impressed not so much with the new commander's reputed military ability, as with the renown he had gained as a man singularly pious. This new general was William Rosecrans, an exemplary man of the times. He had no supercilious regard for the trumperies of tradition and prestige so pronounced in his predecessor, Buell. He was not given to posturing and posing, choosing rather to base his claims to respect on the performance of deeds. He was an old soldier and a good one, not lacking imagination and fertility of ideas. Added to this was the sincere piety of the man. It was said of him, Bross repeated to Turchin, that he never used profane language, always deplored cursing and any manner of rough language whatever. "They say he won't send a man out to fight on the Sabbath!" Bross was enthusiastic in his praise.

"That interests me less than what he will do on the other days of the week!" Turchin retorted. "I am indeed anxious to return to my duties, I should like to participate on the march to Nashville. I hope General Rosecrans strengthens our lines along that sector; they are thin, too thin."

He had yet another informant about regimental affairs, and this was Colonel Scott who wrote as soon as the news became public about Turchin's good fortune. This friendly young colonel had now resumed the command he had so gallantly relinquished to Turchin the year before. He wrote that General Mitchell had not yet returned to this department of the army, that the new General, Rosecrans, was making radical changes in army, organization, in order to expedite their advance into the rebel country. The center division of the new "Army of Tennessee" was to be commanded by the able General George H. Thomas, and he was the sectional head under whom it was rumored, General Turchin would serve.

This intelligence pleased Turchin who had heard much of the famed General Thomas, already highly esteemed for his exploits, especially his victory over General Zollicoffer, on whom, the year before, the Confederacy had greatly relied. General Thomas had defeated General Zollicoffer in the battle of Mill Springs, where for the first time, the pride of the Southerners was laid low.

There were other sources of information, too, particularly the warm letters from his friend Mihalotzy, whose tribulations had not been so painful as Turchin's and who had fared much better at his court-martial than had his friend. Mihalotzy was re-instated and now urged the speedy return of his friend; for it seemed to him, that with what was becoming symptomatic of all leaders of the North, Rosecrans, too, was reluctant to budge out of Nashville, once they were firmly entrenched. "He wants two million rations first," he wrote, "and perhaps he is to be praised rather than blamed for his solicitations. In that light the men view the matter. They are already vastly fond of him."

"You see how it is!" Turchin cried to Mrs. Morrison and Nadine one evening. They were all drinking tea together. "If I say we ought to smash forward, and think not of the cost; that by striking hard and forcing a hard fight, we stand to lose less men than by a long, drawn-out dawdling, which kills our boys in driblets; then they say I am bloodthirsty and a savage! As if there is any other sort of war than a savage one!"

"They wish to be reasonably certain of success, I dare say," Mrs. Morrison hazarded a guess, and received for it Nadine's mocking glance.

"Battles, even wars, have been lost for lack of daring and impulse. All military men plan for victory, and all military minds know that victory is a state of mind almost as much as a fact of war. Victory often depends on the character of the men as much as on their boots!" This Nadine said with an arch look at her husband, who beamed approval.

"There is the true wife and daughter of a soldier!" he applauded. "What do you think, dear Mrs. Morrison? Would she not make a fine general?"

"She makes a fine general's wife," she returned with an imperceptible note of defeat to Nadine.

By September the pleasant evenings which Mrs. Morrison shared with the Turchins came to an end. The new general was to be soon recalled to active duty, but the definite date was not set. He had still to wait some weeks for his exact assignment, and in the meantime he busied himself following the turn of events in other theatres of operations.

At no time during his troubles had General Turchin lost interest in the doings of his erstwhile friend, McClellan, and he, like the whole of the country, was profoundly shocked when the first news came of the bloody battle at Dunker Church, which came to be known as Antietam. This was a battle which General McClellan tactically won but had he acted differently, a battle which he might have won gloriously. A few days before the actual battle, Union soldiers had fortuitously come upon an envelope containing a piece of paper wrapped around three cigars. The paper turned out to be a copy of the Confederate operational plan for the upcoming battle at Antietam. The paper, entitled "Special Order No. 191, Headquarters, Army of Northern Virginia", was verified as being authentic, quite by chance, as the Union Division adjutant general, Samuel Pittman, had recognized the handwriting on the order as that of Robert Chilton, the Confederate adjutant general to Robert E. Lee. Pittman had taken the "Lost Order" to McClellan, but unfortunately, McClellan, through an excess of cautious procrastination, squandered the unique opportunity, allowing General Lee time to realign his troops and prevent what would have been a devastating massacre. In addition, Turchin was also cognizant of McClellan's reluctance, at the conclusion of the battle, to pursue General Lee into his own territory, despite the President's frank, urgent request. Had Turchin known of the many slurs and insults McClellan had been guilty of committing against Mr. Lincoln, he might have done more than commiserate with his friend; he would have detested him. As it was, he was sad for him, sad for the Cause he believed McClellan was also defending and sad for Mr. Lincoln, whom a rousing victory would have heartened as nothing else could. With grief Turchin read the full descriptive accounts of those reporters who had afterwards visited the field of death and carnage, where the Union Army had sustained the greatest loss of the war. The dead were said to be lying in heaps, their lifeless faces upturned, their broken bodies smeared with their blood and tears; the trees, riddled with shot, now sheltering them when they needed no earthly shelter. This "victory" had come a few days after the Federal defeat at Harper's Ferry and weighed heavily upon the North.

And Turchin feared that with this Pyrrhic victory, the South's chances to gain the recognition she sought abroad, were definitely improved. "It is a good thing the Russian minister Edouard de Stoeckl is still in

Washington", he said. He hoped that this indicated Russia's undeviating support and friendliness. Russia was indeed a powerful friend.

That the President had entertained the same idea was apparent. He had sanguine hopes of obviating Southern gains in European courts by a rousing victory he believed possible had McClellan moved into Virginia to go after Lee as ordered. There, that eminent Southern general had entrenched himself with a mobility of action which was well calculated to outdistance McClellan. After that terrible day of fighting and losses, McClellan had permitted Lee to escape over the Potomac; an opportunity General Lee took full advantage of, and thus turned what ought to have been a telling defeat for Lee into a negative victory for McClellan. When the battle toll was known, the staggering losses in men and material could be viewed as nothing but a defeat for the Union forces. One saving grace the battle had was that the observers in Europe realized once and for all that stout men and mighty means were still available and ready to be unleashed in the defense of the Union. Thereafter, Jefferson Davis was to find more adamant resistance to his wooing. With this show of mettle at Antietam, the Russian Ambassador's minister in Washington took on more meaning to men like Brewster and Vallandigham. Russia might now be a fearsome weight on Lincoln's side.

It was late in the fall when General Turchin, unable to stay away longer, unofficially arrived in his camp which was preparing to dig in for the winter. The army of Tennessee was loosely located about Nashville where General Rosecrans was determined to hold against the rebel strength of General Bragg, the most outstanding southern general in this western arena of the war, and whose name was a by-word in the border sections, where sentiment ran high for both factions.

His coming was unexpected by his officers and men, for as a matter of fact, headquarters had not yet decided where General Turchin was to be stationed. In coming thus to his old regiment, he was, perhaps, violating rules and regulations, but when he explained to Rosecrans his inability to abide idly in Chicago, that good general understood how his feelings had been tried and incensed, how the progress of the war elsewhere must have made him restless to take part in the fight. Therefore, for the time being, he was a general without a command, but was so dearly beloved and welcomed by his old comrades, that, on the whole, he preferred his status here to his inactivity at home.

"Until I am fully assigned," he declared to General Rosecrans and Colonel Scott, "I wish to be allowed to do whatever random duties can be performed usefully by me. I belong here! I care nothing for the niceties of my title! It does not matter to me in what capacity I may serve my country!"

"You are a general now, and yet you ask my permission to do whatever is needed! What a strange man you are, General Turchin!" So spoke General Rosecrans as he gave his ready permission for Turchin's presence. "We shall be happy to have you, general," he said gravely. "Ours is the task, as you know, of pushing General Bragg out of Tennessee. It will not be an easy task. He is a good man."

"So, indeed are we good men!" was the Russian's retort. And soon the two generals were informally discussing a nut-cracker technique which might prove satisfactory.

This indeed came to be the case when General Bragg advanced toward them from Chattanooga, and made his camp on the turnpike near Murfreesboro. Bragg moved north, and Rosecrans moved south, taking his position three miles west of Murfreesboro. It was blustering weather, scourged by ruthless winds armed with sleet and snow. The terrain was difficult, Stone River vicious and impassable, forming a menacing boundary to the battleground within which the two opposing armies would meet. With the armies facing one another, with the Union lines being intersected at right angles by the railroad and the turnpike, the Cumberland army tensed itself to expect a general of Bragg's acumen to try a flanking movement. To counteract such a contingency, General Rosecrans worked out a strategy of equally effective flanking tactics upon which Turchin looked skeptically.

A few preliminary skirmishes, daringly carried out by Colonel Scott, presaged the real battle which occurred on the last day of the year. The night before the battle of Stone River, Turchin bedded down with the men on the icy field, which was to be the scene of the battle. Screeching winds swept derisively through the thick cedar brush all around them. But only laughter and cheerfulness were apparent among the men, who lighted camp fires in defiance of the wind, and ate their supper of roasted horsemeat as if the tough flesh were the tenderest of roast pigs.

Rosecrans planned to attack Bragg's left, and Bragg with the same intention, planned to attack Rosecrans's left. Who would gain the initial advantage by attacking first was left to pure luck. It was General Bragg who succeeded in striking first, and almost won the day. At the close of the first day's raging fighting, only a miracle could have saved Rosecrans's entire army from complete annihilation.

This miracle occurred in the persons of Scott and Turchin. They, by a daring maneuver, cut their way to the aid of the badly damaged left, but not before the fallen dead and the exhausted living were as one fatally entangled mass. Even this desperate attempt to save the left would have been of no avail but for the departure of the short wintery light, which put an end to the decimation of the Cumberland army. But it took only a night's respite to reorganize the Union Lines, and with dauntless courage the following day, they met and rebuffed Bragg's best field commander, Breckenridge, who had to withdraw to whatever refuge Stone River could offer, which was meager in the face of the furious pursuit Colonel Scott and Turchin led after them. Breckenridge's men escaped across the stream, and assumed a favorable position from which to open their fierce batteries against Scott's men.

The gallant Scott, already midstream in his dauntless charge after Breckenridge, was felled by a cannon ball in the chest. His horse stumbled and he reeled from his seat, causing his men to falter in their onward rush; but only for a moment, for Turchin, snatching up Scott's sword, brandishing it aloft, spearing at its tip the fallen colonel's cap, yelled at the top of his voice: "Get up off your bellies! Fix your bayonets! After them, charge the rebels!"

Recklessly he himself dashed forward, unmindful of the shot which rained upon him. A bullet tore his shoulder, but did not stop him, nor did it stop the men who took courage and example from him, and followed him across the river and up the slippery river's banks.

The cost was staggering in men, but the battle was won, and the object gained. Bragg was forced to withdraw. That the South claimed this battle on the basis of the 10,000 lives the Union suffered only roused General Turchin's scorn. "If they were wise, these rebels, they would have seen the handwriting on the wall in this battle. No enemy can defeat such men as fought and died at Stone River!"

He spoke to Rosecrans, but his eyes were turned with pity and love upon the prostrate body of Colonel Scott. "You will not die, boy!" he vowed fiercely. "You will live to see the Red, White and Blue floating from every Southern capitol!"

Walking away from the sick bed of the colonel, he addressed General Rosecrans once more. "This battle will give Mr. Lincoln a fine New Year's greeting! It will prove to him that his faith in us is only a little less than our faith in him!"

CHAPTER XXIII

If the Union armies gave Lincoln a glorious Stone River to round out the year 1862, Lincoln gave the entire country the Emancipation Proclamation, which was issued the first day of 1863.

Intimate friends of the President had long been cognizant that this measure was maturing on President Lincoln's program. As early as September of '62 the original draft of it had been submitted to his cabinet, but was withheld from public promulgation until the turn of the year, when it burst over an amazed country with attendant variations of reception.

In Chicago, stronghold of the Union fervor, but also the seat of much of Copperheadism rampant at the time, the news burst with an impact which rocked the town. In his Times, Wilber Storey was as indignant over this new "effrontery" of the President's as was Vallandigham, who viewed the 'offensive' document as a challenge which he could not pass by. "He wants action, does he? Very well! He shall have it!" He thundered in Brewster's library, shortly after the news of the Emancipation Proclamation reached the streets. Vallandigham, Storey, Brewster and Trofimov were seated before the fire place, and each was unwontedly demonstrative.

"Well may the people blush with shame at having such a President," Storey growled. "I shall tell the whole world as much!"

"At any rate, we shall have to give that man Lincoln credit for a certain low cunning," Brewster stamped angrily. "I don't wonder he pushed inferior talents so far! This slave measure is undoubtedly the work of a wily lawyer, not a first rate one, mind you; so to use the Constitution as grounds on which to violate it!"

Trofimov, who was smoking leisurely, a curious pleasure on his face, glanced at his father-in-law speculatively. Without addressing himself to him, however, he spoke to Storey, who had begun to pace the rug furiously when he was not dejectedly slumped in his chair. "By the way, Mr. Storey, I hear McCormick's sheet has offered a thousand dollars to anyone able to find a constitutional provision against Mr. Lincoln's using his powers as Chief of the Army and Navy. Apparently, he chooses to think that whatever he does strengthens his government and weakens the enemy."

"A pestilential sheet!" roared Vallandigham. "An outrage against decent citizens! Only a godless crew could call this disgraceful abuse of democratic privileges, which Lincoln has perpetrated in this infamous Proclamation, the gratifying recognition of the 'finger of God'!"

"Come now, gentlemen, let us be realistic!" Trofimov laughed. He faced his companions fearlessly. His status as son-in-law to Brewster had obviated the need to oblige or propitiate these men, for now he was on an equal footing with them, and rather superior to them, since he imbibed no elusive draughts of their ambition. His passing opinion was that ambition played the very devil with a man now. To aim for and achieve money as such was infinitely simpler and, on the whole, a less murky business.

The men fixed their attention upon him belligerently, as though daring him to portray them as less than realistic. "Why gnash our teeth melodramatically?" said he, shrugging his beautifully tailored shoulders. "Why rant and rave? If we recognize that our friends in the South have broken with the established government, we have to recognize also that by so doing they have forfeited some measure of their constitutional rights! Any empty threats they make now against Lincoln's new measure, is both futile and stupid!"

"Those are treasonable words!" Vallandigham shouted. He had never taken kindly to the Russian aristocrat, and now hurled dislike into the handsome face which did not alter a fraction of the amused smile it wore.

"I am not impressed with your usage of popular cant!" Trofimov replied. "I suggest we plan action, not stupid debates which amount to nothing!"

"I believe you have something there," Storey said sagaciously. "I for one shall not cease to inform my public of the facts!"

"We would do better to burn that damnable Tribune building!" Vallandigham snapped. The others laughed sourly.

Others in Chicago were, if not so vindictive to the Government, at least as unconvinced that the startling Emancipation would gain anything momentous. McClellan had been the favorite son in this city, and his failure to follow Lee to Richmond dampened weak enthusiasm to such an extent that even the Proclamation was not hailed with much more than faint applause, except by the abolitionist elements, whose influence was seen to grow powerfully among the President's advisers. Thus, doubtful sentiment papers like the Times exploited to the full, losing no opportunity to turn and trim their insinuations in such a manner that they clearly accused the President, by his Proclamation, of weakly admitting his failure to control the situation. They suggested that the President was concealing his inadequacy by empty sensationalism; that he was taking a low recourse in unethical and unmilitary measures to undo a gallant foe, not otherwise to be vanquished.

Storey, true to his promise, was largely instrumental in distributing quantities of literature among the fighting forces on the Western Theater and through his colleagues in New York, and even in the Army of the Potomac. Since fabrications with their detrimental embellishments were told and retold, dissension and fear were successfully sown among the rank and file. Many were their lurid prognostications of exploitive change, such as the charge that Lincoln wished to be king and that the object of the new measure was to free the Blacks in order to enslave the Whites.

These rumors, these descriptive legends were not slow to reach General Turchin, who took it upon himself to forbid the distribution of this propaganda among his companies. Nor was he hindered or reprimanded by his superiors, who were amply in accord with him, though perhaps at first not so fiery and obstreperous in the suppression of insidious statements.

"I believe in freedom of speech," he declaimed to a new friend, one

Alexander Smirnow, who had joined the regiment after its reorganization the year before. "But I am not of the opinion that the motives of the seekers of freedom of speech must go unquestioned. If we are to avoid a repetition of the whole fabric of evils you and I knew in Europe, this point must be carefully considered."

Smirnow, a dreamy poetic man, nodded and agreed with him. He was also a Russian by birth, but of a temperament entirely unlike General Turchin's, being more inclined to philosophy and mysticism than to action and being constantly unprepared for the brutal realities of the war.

Turchin continued, "Freedom of speech which directs itself to destroy the people's freedom, either of speech or person, is the work of the devil; it smacks of a cleverness which ought to be exposed! Take this violation of freedom of speech, exemplified in scurrilous papers like this." He waved the highly illustrated journal which had roused his anger. "They pretend to peddle their lies as a symbol of American rights! Where is the reverence and respect due their elected leaders? Where is the vaunted democratic sportsmanship that inures to the man who wins by the will of the people, that he shall have the loyalty even of his opponents?"

"When men are in a passion, General Turchin, there is no appealing to their sense of right and wrong. But there is an operative force in history, and it is this which makes a people have almost a racial memory of its rights, of its needs for survival; and it is this which predisposes the feelings of a generation, in spite of the shouting of its divided and selfish leaders. I prefer to trust to this deep instinct in the people themselves. It is just a matter of time before their will must emerge to crystallize the solution of confused issues." He spoke unemotionally. No obsequiousness in him led to the belief that he was unduly flattered by the familiarity permitted him by Turchin. Smirnow was not an egotistical man. Without any great tragic experiences to darken his mind, he nevertheless had a dark brooding cast over his whole personality. Whenever pressed by an insistent Turchin to explain what was in him, whether cynicism or optimism, his answer was invariably a curious shake of his head, or an unintelligible shrug of the shoulders.

"I have no great love of life," he said once, "yet no great desire to depart life; all is indifferent to me. I try to avoid pain, to examine pleasure; it does not sadden me that I reach no depth nor yet any heights. For me it is better so!"

"I have no patience with this generalization," Turchin now announced, returning to the subject of violent distortions of truth in the newspapers making a Roman holiday of Lincoln's Emancipation Proclamation. "Men like Horace Greely are all the more to be castigated for articles like this one," he said as he held out the item. If traitors like this New York mayor, Fernando Wood, fail to understand Mr. Lincoln, their deficiency can be explained by their willful, wicked and blind selfishness. He even proposed to take New York City out of the Union and make a free city of it. But what is so hard for a sensible man to understand about the necessity forcing a harried leader to be first a public servant and only second a personal man?"

Even as he uttered these words he recalled Mrs. Morrison and the gentle lessons she had propounded to him a summer ago.

Smirnow, supposedly acting sentry duty for General Turchin, made no reply. He had an admiration for his compatriot, but being much younger than he, being, moreover, better adjusted to the differences in a people he never sought to identify as his own, he often found it peculiar that Turchin so consciously tried to affect a cure for all problems. Despite affection for him, he looked askance upon this and the general's tendency to verbalize. He liked his brisk company much more when they stood a lonely watch together in the night; when the spring heralded itself in a profusion of night essences which an awakening earth exhaled from beneath its crust.

"Here are the exact words of Mr. Lincoln before he issued the Proclamation," Turchin got ready to read. 'My paramount purpose in this struggle is to save the Union,' "Fine," he commented approvingly. "We agree there. 'And is not either to save or destroy slavery'. You see, Smirnow, how distinctly and plainly Mr. Lincoln appeals even to whatever minds the traitors have! If I could save the Union without freeing any slave, I would do it; and if I could save it by freeing all the slaves, I would do it; and if I could save it by freeing some and leaving others alone, I would also do that'."

"There is a sane man," Smirnow remarked. "I personally mistrust your enthusiasts. Enthusiasm can so easily wreak havoc in its passing, and when it passes, it leaves such a dead thing behind - disillusion."

"There is a true patriot!" Turchin glowed, his mind full of Mr. Lincoln. "Does he not portray himself so in every utterance? He loves the idea of this country more than the sticks and stones of it, the rivers and hills, the living things which are transient upon it while the ideal is eternal in it, - everlasting! Look at the great soul of the man, and you can believe he resorts to words for those who can be reached in no other way; but that the inner meaning of them stands crystal clear if you want to see it!" He crumpled the paper violently. "When a man feels as deeply and sincerely as he; when what he defends and embraces is the smallest cry for freedom as well as the greatest; we who are soldiers find in him our highest moral standards!"

He rummaged among his papers and drew forth another periodical in which he had marked a transcript of Lincoln's words on the matter of slavery. "This proclamation comes as a war measure. I as a soldier approve it. 'First comes the Cause we fight for, and whatever emotions we must either endure or contend with, must rest upon the success or failure of our efforts to save the Union.' Mr. Lincoln believes that. I believe it, too. But whatever we do to save the Union, whatever results are obtained from efforts so employed, must carry with them their own permanence. Right now the Emancipation Proclamation is a war measure; tomorrow, in all the tomorrows, it will stand forth in its more fundamental meanings, as a proclamation of human rights." With a moving voice he read the article to Smirnow.

Meanwhile, back in Chicago, the defenders of the Union were rallying to Mr. Lincoln's support perhaps in the same active mood as marked the vilification of its enemies. The secret warfare was disclosing itself. The first shock of the Proclamation was over, and the two warring camps among the political leaders were readying themselves for unconcealed civic struggle. Chicago was not the only, but merely the largest nucleus for the Copperheads of the Western Theater. New York had been just as long in conspiratorial rebellion to Lincoln, so much so that Lincoln had quaintly summed up Mayor Wood's ambition by comparing his efforts to separate New York City from the Northern adherents to Unionism, to the homely figure of a front door of a house trying to set up housekeeping for itself.

Among the diligent supporters of Mr. Lincoln the Tribune was distinguished by its prominence and its unswerving loyalty, which characterized its whole-hearted support of Mr. Lincoln for several years. In 1862 when the bill for federal conscription was pending, the entire newspaper's facilities were strained to further the understanding and expediency of such a measure. Not only was national conscription clarified in the light of its current validity, but also in relation to the welfare of the country at all times. At the same time Mr. Medill was loud in decrying the iniquitous bounty system under which a prospective soldier could buy his release from military service by paying the sum of three hundred dollars. Medill was faced by the formidable spread and sway of Copperheadism and defeatism, but with the help of such staunch Unionists as Mrs. Morrison, he turned his devotion to the Cause into more than just journalistic polemics.

Mrs. Morrison was not the only citizen in 1862 who grew gradually sentient of the devastating moral effects of the campaign Senator Vallandigham carried on. She had begun to suspect her cousin, Brewster's southern sympathies long before she had any precise knowledge of the functional connection between him and Vallandigham outside their friendly intercourse. In former years her husband had also been closely associated with both men in a business way and the association had proved remunerative, indeed. In the spread of sedition she could not imagine what gains Brewster or Vallandigham, men already well placed socially and financially, could hope to make by betraying their country; for in no other light than outright treason could she adjudge their public and private abuse of the President and the Cause.

She and Medill apprised themselves of the feverish activities of the Knights of the Golden Order, her cousin's chief avenue of operations, when several of the inconspicuous clerks of the office reported receiving invitations to attend initial meetings. Also, both these clear-sighted people had lately observed with what cold, proud arrogance the identifying buttons were being worn on coat lapels of men boasting the insignia of the American Indian Head. The emblems were pointedly reminiscent of the copper pennies of the day, and were prominently displayed by wearers of them as though they were pledges of deliverance. Medill furiously sneered at this badge of allegiance, and the name

"Copperhead", by which the "men of peace" felt themselves honored. "Copperhead refers not only to the penny but also to the snake; the snake would be more apt," he told Henrietta. "For shame that these 'Copperheads' go unchallenged among us!"

"We should organize an order to counteract their influence!" she had said on that occasion. And her idea, which she had thrown out on an impulse, fired Medill's imagination.

"That's the very thing! That's precisely what we shall do! Bless you Henrietta, for the fine soul you are!"

And he was as good as his word, following up his inspiration with immediate action. His counter-movement to "Copperheadism" was the Union League, which by 1863 became a state-wide organization, extending into every township of Illinois. It occupied itself mainly in listing known and suspected Copperheads, as were called all pacifists, appeasers, and southern sympathizers, and in watching carefully their every activity designed to interfere with the successful prosecution of the war.

In this undercover work Henrietta proved herself of no little assistance. She became, in fact, Medill's first lieutenant in the extraordinary amount of work that the organization and operating of this Union League entailed. For the first time in her life, she was carried outside herself completely, and provided with a project which enlisted all her abilities, all her resources and all her convictions. More than that, the contacts her work brought her absorbed her so completely that she had little time to nourish into a robust flourishing existence the pure, almost chaste flame of her affections for Turchin. Not that her respect and affection as a friend were feeble, let it be understood, but only her degree of yielding her strong mind to the sweeter longings that those of friendship which she now admitted stirred in her bosom.

She carried no searing secret in her heart, and was of too stern a moral fiber to fan into healthy life a passion she could not respect for itself alone. If her tireless work for Medill at this time served as a sublimation of her growing emotionalism, she was past caring about the causes; for it was enough that the work she did was valuable on behalf of the country she loved no less fervidly than on behalf of Turchin. Sometimes, when fatigue and a sense of endless work yet to be done reduced her to nerves or headache, she dared to give the charming Russian general a longing thought. But no further than that would she go. As to not visiting with Nadine, she offered work as her excuse, but offered it so sincerely and sweetly, that Nadine was ready to believe her completely.

What was her surprise one day in March therefore when her office door opened at the Tribune to admit none other than General Turchin, who had come home for a brief rest and to visit Colonel Scott who had been removed to the hospital in Chicago, his native home.

"General Turchin!" She was too surprised to move, and remained sitting at her desk to which Turchin strode with outstretched hand.

"How tired you look, dear Mrs. Morrison! How white your face is! Is it not security enough for you that your men fight this war on the field; must you fight it in your own person as well? Could anything but concern for our country bring that worn expression to a face made for laughter and beauty?"

She was nearly overcome by surprise and delight in his undisguised solicitude for her. "How uncommonly well he expresses himself," were her chaotic thoughts, "and how fit he looks, and handsome." As she thought this last, she blushed, becomingly, and looked embarrassedly into his serious face as he took her hand and mechanically and rigorously shook it.

"I have stopped here before going home," he told her. "I hoped to persuade you to accompany me. I am here on business and pleasure and you are part of my pleasure." With this gallant speech, he won her heart.

He was in fact supervising the details of enlistments in the Fourth Division of which he was now to command several Kentucky and Ohio companies in the Eight Brigade. There preyed on his mind in addition to the enlistments, the welfare of the young wounded Scott, and he was as anxious to cheer and hearten him with whatever bright prospects the Cumberland Army had in view. The army was coming out of its winter quarters and a new activity stirred new ambitions in every soldier's heart; new hope that this year would be the decisive year, the year to see the end of the war. Before movements began for the contemplated southward march, Turchin had felt the need to revisit his home city, to see his wife, whom he sorely missed, and would miss even more in the months to come. Since the Athens incident, when her presence had been frowned upon; when he had heard her character callously reviewed; when her valuable contribution had not been accorded the respectful appreciation that he felt it merited; when the colonels had called his defense of her as a nurse, officious, despite the lamentable lack of nurses and ambulances; he had determined to leave his wife behind in future campaigns.

Thus he spent a cheerful week in which his friend, Mrs. Morrison figured noticeably, and his old friend, Trofimov conspicuously by his absence. "So you, dear Mrs. Morrison, have been sound in your estimate of Mr. Lincoln. And your abolitionist friends have been more perspicacious than many of our generals. I have for a long time advocated the use of Negroes in the army, as fighting men; for why should they not have the privilege and opportunity to fight for their freedom; to prove they are men, not beasts of burden? Let them fraternize with our boys. In the army, among men fighting for their lives and their country, a true equality levels all conditions and stations."

"Ivan wants everything accomplished with one stroke!" Nadine laughed.

"Perhaps he is wiser than the more cautious men," Henrietta supposed. "I for one am not quite so optimistic of the cogency inherent in Mr. Lincoln's Emancipation Proclamation. For I think it is so liable to misunderstanding, to false hopes. How our enemies could misconstrue its purpose, as well as its meaning!"

"Neither the one nor the other," Turchin defended the document. "It is the drastic, final weapon, yes, but in essence it is only potent because it embodies a great truth, the anticipation of a universal truth. Sooner or later, won't the freedom of the slaves be proclaimed as the underlying reason for this war?"

Mrs. Morrison looked sadly thoughtful. "Yet Mr. Lincoln's stand on slavery has been so moderate and conciliatory, that he has earned rebuke and calumny from his friends along with scorn from his enemies." She leaned forward towards Turchin so that Nadine's gleaming samovar served as a mirror for her pretty seriousness. "You see, general, Mr. Lincoln sought not to precipitate violent social changes. He felt that emancipation should be voluntary and gradual; that where owners freed slaves, they should be compensated as much as possible; that afterward the Negroes should be somewhat in the position of wards of the government."

"That would have been an enlightened method of procedure," he averred, nodding his head. "In other words, Lincoln in his great wisdom, recommended a means to move with the times, without resorting to war!"

"It might so seem," she agreed. "But people do not trust one another to fulfill promises. It would be difficult to expect them to trust to time, therefore! And a moderate advance into the future is a matter of trusting to time."

"A man has to trust something! And if everything is excluded but himself, he has to trust himself! That reduces him to a state of mind like our mutual friend, Baron Trofimov who exhibits crass selfishness, in so gleaming and shell-like a surface that nothing can penetrate to his unreceptive heart. In such a time such a surface becomes such a part of the man, that to detach it from him is to destroy his whole being."

"Surfaces are often good, protective devices," was Nadine's interpolation at this point. "Preserving an impermeable, smooth surface often enables us to go through life without resorting to hate; for we are then made invulnerable to the attacks of spiteful people upon us!"

"I see nothing wrong with hating!" her husband maintained stubbornly. "To hate what is destructive of human progress is no hate to my mind! What do you say, Mrs. Morrison? Do you not think expressions like 'hate' and 'love' are devoid of real meaning unless related to concrete circumstances? If your adversaries seek to destroy you, lest you speak what displeases them, are you not to hate them? When I lead my boys on a charge, can I do so effectively unless I hate with all my soul the bigotry which forces the conflict? I am proud to be unashamed of hating that which brings retrogression and pain!"

They all laughed and applauded when he finished, and Nadine lifted her hands in mock benediction. "Both of you," she included their guest and her husband with one slow nod of her head, "are such fierce people!" She believed in that fierceness with a touch of fright. People like Turchin and Henrietta were difficult people to deceive. And she wished to deceive them, not seriously, only about the softer and less rigid stuff of her own being. "How like I am to Dimitri," she thought with a guilty glance at the other two. "They are without weakness. We are weak, so weak, Dimitri and I."

When Turchin returned to his men, she dropped all pretence of friendship with Mrs. Morrison, and nursed in solitude, without fear of detection from the widow, her longing to see the baron. This she was doubly careful to conceal from Ivan to whom she wrote religiously all during the spring and the summer, when the Cumberland Army slowly and relentlessly plodded its way down into Tennessee until all the land between the Ohio and Tennessee rivers was in General Rosecrans's possession. By the time the Battle of Gettysburg in Pennsylvania was history, the Cumberland Army, or the Army of Tennessee as it came to be called, was preparing to lure General Bragg out of his stronghold, Chattanooga and to force him into an open battle which would, it was hoped, end the Southern grip on the western line of the vast battleground.

This campaign began with a new note of confidence among the officers and men throughout this sector of the army. Gettysburg and Grant's great victory at Vicksburg, the almost free control of the Mississippi and New Orleans, were excellent antidotes to the gloom and defeatism the previous year had bequeathed them. Moreover, at least to officers like Turchin and Rosecrans, there was beginning to be visible some sort of general over-all policy of direct action and strategy which gave point and momentum to the scattered battles and skirmishes which until now had seemed haphazard, and had lent some body to the acrimonious complaint that unity of action seemed entirely lacking among the top generals responsible for the organizational factors in the prosecution of the war.

The super-pattern, which was unfolding itself at last, was simply a vast nut-cracker movement, the left and right wings of which were the army of the Potomac and the Tennessee army respectively. At last General Turchin was convinced of the excellent strategy employed in the Right wing of this pincer, and could throw himself wholeheartedly into the accelerated movement of his men and material with renewed vigor. Until then it had been his dearest wish to join the Army of the Potomac. He now dismissed all personal desires, and saw all theaters of the war as equally vital and interdependent, all converging on the same end-victory. Convinced that wherever he was, was the vital spot to be in, he grew efficient to an extreme. "Ours is not the glamorous theatre of war," he told his friend Garfield one night, "but after all, it is often the unglamorous that makes possible the glamourous. The important thing is to win; not who of us is the first over the line."

Garfield had rejoined his brigade and was now serving as chief of staff for Rosecrans. This position was ideally suited to him, for no man could win and hold the respect and confidence of the brigade commanders and colonels better than he, a comfortable man to trust. But after all the officers in the Tennessee Army, not one was so overjoyed to see him as General Turchin, who almost embarrassed himself by the rush of emotion to which he gave vent when they met again. After that, on every occasion the two men could meet, they deepened the admiration and affection they felt for one another. On one evening of their reunion, the two officers were riding side by side in the summer dusk. "Still a stickler for details and hard work, I hear, General Turchin!" said General Garfield and his fine dark eyes made no attempt to disguise the respect and friendliness they entertained for General Turchin. "By God, general, there is a blessed destiny which watches over our fortunes, that men like you are here when hard dirty work is to be done! It is up to us to invade this hostile country, and to hold all important points of communications. In that way, what General Grant achieved at Vicksburg gains power and purpose. We here are, as an army, like a pot of glue, out of which has come the stuff to make insignificant little pieces of mosaic stick together. Don't you agree, General Turchin?"

Not only did Turchin agree, but thought long about Garfield's remarks that night. The lines of his men's tents, now tolerable in the summer nights; the happy camp fires, over which the men cooked game or pots of rice; the wealth of heavy virginal woods, which spread in untainted innocence on every side of them; the happy indifference of small creatures to the object of marching feet; the natural, unhurried flight of birds into the hills, whose perfumes a kind wind brought down nightly; all strengthened the general and made the Chattanooga campaign, which lay ahead of him, an inviting and purposeful adventure.

Alone in his tent, he often played his muted violin far into the night. While he played mechanically, he did not cease to think of the approaching campaign. He was too good a soldier to separate himself for long from a problem which was unavoidable until solved. As he thought each concise thought, he twanged his violin vigorously so that its meaningless tones created for him an unintrusive accompaniment. "We have moved in the right direction," was the first definite fact he posed himself. "We have retaken all the land Buell evacuated last year," was the second. "We shall have to outwit General Bragg, lure him out of Shelbyville and Tullahooma first and occupy Chattanooga; for he will imagine we are attempting a straight march into Georgia."

He was quite happy as he pictured General Bragg's anticipated movements, the direction of which must be ineluctable, since the South would move heaven and earth to protect Georgia. "That is it! The Army of the Potomac got Gettysburg; Grant got Vicksburg; and we will get Chattanooga by maneuvering General Bragg into the field to fight."

One other cheerful factor Garfield and Turchin discussed in the forthcoming campaign, since to both these men the subject had many personal connotations. This was the evident change in policy with respect to the sterner attitude of the Government towards the rebels, their sensitivities or their claims to property protection. "We can look upon the lessons Mr. Lincoln learned from the past as duly noted this year," Garfield observed. "It cheers a man to see for himself that at least we do not reason and plead in vain."

"Necessity, not reason, argues for a stiff attitude towards the South," Turchin said. "Leniency, as it was practiced last year, gave rise to, nay, invited the notion of impending compromise. It authored the absurd story Mrs. Morrison told me, that the South had offered us a negotiated peace! She is a dear friend of mine," he explained, "and for a woman, she has a remarkable insight and grasp of facts. It seems from her reports, that we have powerful subversive enemies at home as well as in the field." He laughed as he recalled Mrs. Morrison, who was dear to him because the thought of her was always like clean fresh winds, like a sky freshly cleansed by rain. "What a little abolitionist she is! A patient abolitionist, Garfield! I believe all women are patient Griseldas, so to speak."

"They may laugh at us yet, general," Garfield joined him in his laughter. "It's not new with them, or at least, it's not new as a theory. The slow waiting game has its points. The ladies always have the knack of picking out, with a fine instinct, the salient facts of a matter. A wise man ought to have a care with the women!"

At any rate, by the time the army was on the march toward Shelbyville, Turchin knew that he had a free hand to use his own discretion in buying or commandeering fodder for man or beast; that he would not be hampered nor constrained to a policy inconsistent with his beliefs. It was a good frame of mind with which to enter upon the events now lying ahead of him.

CHAPTER XXIV

Withal that Nadine was a faithful correspondent, her life was in such retirement after Turchin had returned to the army, that her letters lacked that quality of intellectual alertness which made Mrs. Morrison's letters such welcome events in Turchin's life. Yet neither lady had written him of the nefarious uprisings which occurred in the late spring and summer.

Nadine, for some perverse reason known only to herself, had eschewed newspapers since the day she read about Trofimov's wedding, and was consequently ignorant of the small drama which had taken place in Mt. Vernon, Ohio.

Mrs. Morrison, directly involved in the grim work of tracking down the sources for such uprisings, was in the East, on a private mission for Medill, and also to attend a conference of women that she was attempting to interest in nursing. In this latter matter she might have had the useful help of Mrs. Turchin, but for her own reasons she refrained from soliciting assistance or instruction. Not that this restraint on her part had not cost her many qualms, for she was too honest not to recognize in her reluctance to treat with Turchin's wife, a form of envious dislike for her, and a measure of other personal feelings which were petty indeed when great national issues were at stake. But the best of women sometimes make small exceptions to the normally fine tendencies of their lives. In any case, she had not written Turchin at all during this time.

The uprisings were engineered by the Copperheads and other such persons as the clever tongue and pen of Trofimov and Vallandigham could deceive into participating. The inflammatory occasion warranting the growing influence of the Knights of the Golden Order was the enforcement of the conscription law, recently passed. With deceptive sincerity they bruited about the devastating losses incurred at the bloody battle of Gettysburg. Nor did they forget to enumerate the equally costly battles of Shiloh, Stone River, Antietam and Vicksburg. In May, when only the reports on the earlier battles were on hand, they spent themselves with spite upon the alleged ambitions of Lincoln. They whipped the imagination of the rural sections into such hysteria that at Mt. Vernon they could marshal together a parade four miles long and a noisy rally of murmuring, angry citizens which Vallandigham addressed with rare savagery. "No man worthy of freedom," yelled he, "would submit to conscription, nor feed the greedy maw of a dictator!"

It was high time that suppressive action was taken, and to this end General Burnside, incensed by the report of this open treason, at Mt. Vernon, Ohio, sent soldiers from Cincinnati, where he happened then to be, with orders to arrest and apprehend Clement Laird Vallandigham. Vallandigham and his neophytes promptly resisted the militia, and had therefore to be seized by force, and taken back to Cincinnati, leaving an infuriated mob at Mt. Vernon to riot and storm and burn the plant of the Republican Dayton Journal, as well as several other buildings. The riot was ostensibly a protest against the undignified arrest of their leader, but it availed them little; Vallandigham was quickly tried by a military Commission, and sentenced to prison for the duration of the war. Moreover, the writ of Habeas Corpus had been suspended under the President's war powers, and the courts could not or would not do anything for him. Lincoln, at the last moment, commuted his sentence to exile beyond the Union lines.

"A miserable miscarriage of justice! A desecration of our civil liberties, cried Mr. Brewster in a veritable passion when he heard of the arrest. "An honorable man has the courage to defy the gullible sheep of this country, and see to what ignominy he is immediately subjected!"

The entire family was gathered in the large sitting room where Mrs. Brewster reigned composedly. Wilber Storey was also present, and he was almost as outraged as his friend. Brewster's son-in-law was seated in the embrasure of the window, where he was languidly reading a book, and only half listening to the others.

"Did you not hear what papa said about Uncle Clement?" Susan called peevishly. "I should think you would show a little more interest in him. You were not loath to interest yourself for your stupid Russian friend last summer when you and Madame Turchin arrived in Washington simultaneously!"

"It's all Medill's doing at the Tribune!" Storey interrupted. "That man is worse than a regiment of riflemen! He has been a thorn in our side ever since he organized the Union League."

"I could never see the need for more than one paper," Mrs. Brewster remarked. "I can hardly bear to read even yours, dear Mr. Storey, and I am sure no one bothers to read all the unimportant doings." No one bothered to comment upon this, and Mrs. Brewster with a pert nod contented scolding her daughter who was in no condition, she said, to weaken herself at this time, by the excitement of politics.

"I think Mr. Lincoln is quite foolish," Trofimov spoke up without removing himself from the window seat. "Now in England or France, Vallandigham would not be merely banished, he would be made to vanish completely; or is high treason a word only your side - pardon me, our side can employ?"

To this Mr. Brewster caustically rejoined in general terms that now when the goal was attained, the prize secured, some fools imagined it safe to play in any way they chose.

Baron Trofimov rose and strolled casually to his wife's side. With one arm carelessly flung about her shoulders, he addressed his father-in-law. "I see no sense in mincing matters. With that Emancipation order Mr. Lincoln has finished us. We might as well leave Vallandigham to his own resources, and turn our attention to other matters - like keeping the wolf from our own door!"

Brewster was somewhat mollified, and spent the remainder of the hour admiring his son-in-law whose meaning he had speedily grasped.

"We ought to stand by Clement now!" Storey demurred. "We are in as deeply as he. Banishment behind the lines will not be pleasant."

"But not as conspicuously, sir," Trofimov retorted. "That makes a difference. I see no reason for mock heroics." He patted Susan's little hand. "I still think Mr. Lincoln extremely generous to his enemy!"

"Why nothing has really happened," Mrs. Brewster interjected herself again. "The south is such a lovely place, and he has many friends in the south. He will go south, won't he, Roger?"

As a matter of fact it was later learned that Senator Vallandigham had received a polite but singularly cool treatment in the warm South, which no more loved a traitor than the North. He therefore subsequently journeyed to Canada, the land of his exile until it was expedient for him to return to Ohio.

Later in the year, in July, the Conscription law was used as the goading spear to incite even more serious riots than those in Ohio or in Chicago where an attempt to storm the Tribune building was happily averted. The more serious riots occurred in New York City were Vallandigham's colleagues had gained more acceptance than in the Northwest. In New York huge mobs were organized which burned down draft offices and adjoining buildings, raided the state arsenals, armed themselves with muskets, and prepared grimly to use them against city officials. To mark their mood they immediately caught and hanged thirty Negroes as a warning to Washington, and then put emphasis to this deed by lynching a number of white guards as well. Before they had finished their murderous work, four hundred citizens lay dead among them, and ravages to city property amounted to five million dollars.

It was the last violent flaring up of rebellious energy, and like its parent source in Ohio and Illinois, it proclaimed the sputtering end to the treacherous business of Copperheadism.

That there had been occurring a well organized insurrectionary movement behind the lines, Turchin would readily have believed; but he would not have believed his friend Trofimov was involved unless he was presented proof; fortunately he was never to have it. The only person likely to prejudice Trofimov in this respect was Mrs. Morrison, but she was not the type to malign anyone. When, after the publication of the Emancipation Proclamation, and the succeeding victories of the Federals at Gettysburg and Vicksburg, Vallandigham arrested and the New York rioters forced to disband, it was altogether pointless for her to review the baron's part in the Knights of the Golden Order, even had she had more substantial proof than mere suspicion.

Turchin meanwhile, had his own problems. They revolved mainly around military matters and the prospective march against Bragg in Tennessee. Unfortunately, this was preluded by the appointment of a departmental head, one General Halleck who was designated it seemed by Mr. Lincoln to supersede McClellan in his advisory capacity. This selection surprised and affected every general in the army, especially Turchin, who had so personally identified himself with the war as a whole. Halleck was not unknown among many officers. It was said that he lacked the best soldierly abilities, the directional skill of his predecessor, McClellan. However, he made up for this deficiency with his finer diplomatic skill, notwithstanding his known irascibility, arrogance and his utter lack of democratic behavior toward men of lesser rank than his own. He had to his credit one battle of some importance, and a fine record at West Point, plus the fact that he could or would be amenable to the President. Certain highly placed individuals were prone to consider him a brilliant military scientist and tactician on the basis of his translation of the French strategist, Jomini.

Turchin, Garfield and Rosecrans had good cause to be rather apprehensive of the selection of Halleck as chief commander at this time. Halleck's first act of his command was to order General Rosecrans to march directly forward, carrying out an order to divide the Cumberland Army into independently functioning parts. This turned out to be both reckless and short-sighted as Turchin, for one, had foreseen.

"What absurd tactics, dividing the Cumberland army!", he complained to Garfield, who looked none too happy over the revised plans that Rosecrans, perforce was compelled to adopt. "General Grant in Mississippi shall have nothing to do with Rosecrans in Tennessee; General Burnside shall be deaf and dumb and blind to Rosecrans! Why he ought to be flanking us and siding us in every way! What we have left, by this sort of tactics, is a balky team!"

"I know," Garfield sighed. "It will be like an orchestra where neither harmony nor music is possible."

The divided army began to move. But the obvious march toward Georgia had in any case, the hoped for result of dislodging General

Bragg from his entrenched position, causing him to leave Shelbyville in his march toward Chattanooga, at which place he proposed to give Rosecrans a fight.

On the eve of the battle of Chickamauga, by which name the bloody struggle for Chattanooga was latter known, Turchin, first with Garfield and latter with his humble friend Smirnow, spent many fitful hours of uneasiness. Always, he had had a sort of Slavic prescience before grave dangers. What General Halleck had done with the Cumberland Army in preparing for this encounter with Bragg, easily induced ominous anxiety in Turchin as he rode among his men, inspecting them, their weapons, their equipment and their morale. "I tell you, General Garfield," he confided to his friend, who was riding from company commander to company commander with Rosecrans' latest instructions. "If Bragg attacks us now, we may all have to fight piecemeal for our very lives! What idiocy to divide our combined forces now! What can he hope to gain by it? Does he think Bragg an ostrich with his head in the sand?"

Since Garfield was constrained to obey orders, and moreover not given like the Russian to sharp criticism of his superiors, Turchin got little corroboration in words from him, but had to resort to his humbler friend, Smirnow for that quieting and comforting audience, which must listen without venturing to comment. "Smirnow!" he hauled the sergeant out of his tent, "I want to see you!"

Smirnow was glad to oblige him. The magnetic qualities which attracted him to his general operated on him as they did on all the men who served under him. With a fine discernment he had discovered how to be fraternal with his superior without calling down upon either of them the resentment of jealous petty officers. Usually they talked at night, when the men lay asleep or when the camp guards stood their distant watches on the lonely outskirts of the cantonment. Especially during this balmy spring and early summer, these two men had drawn closer. Both felt the enchanting unity of still nights under unfamiliar heavens strangely peopled by familiar stars. Often the general and the sergeant walked to the horse sheds, and smoked their cigars in companionable silence. At other times they talked of Russia, war, death, freedom or slavery.

Tonight they talked of trivial things, as men often will when they are particularly sentient of tremendous forces impending. "Our horses are well blooded," Turchin began.

"They are restless, need a little blood-letting to quiet them." There was a tinge of bitterness in Smirnow.

"I don't hold with that theory of bloodletting," Turchin said, not referring to their horses. He knew that Smirnow, addicted to his own habits of allegorical allusion, would understand the unspoken thought.

"It has its points," Smirnow insisted with curious perverseness. "Cool an animal's humors and you have a saner beast." He spoke in swift, guttural Russian.

"It does me good to speak in Russian," Turchin suddenly cried. "Tonight it especially does me good. Somehow, I feel that I round out my day by this touch of the old, which conversation in my first tongue effects."

With that homely thought in his mind, he left his sergeant and retired to his own quarters, where he sought to allay his fears and apprehensions by reading for some time. He read by the light of a field lantern, which cast a fuscescent glow on the pages of his book, not a clear white light, and suggested the random thought that things are not always as they appear. He tried to conceive of a successful unfolding of Halleck's plans which at first appeared to have accomplished Bragg's withdrawal and retreat from the towns he had held securely for months. "God!" he cried aloud. "It is clear to me now! Bragg has outmaneuvered us! The retreating soldiers from Shelbyville and Knoxville are preparing to reinforce him against us!" He groaned audibly. "We ought to have a concerted army to meet Bragg! Alone, we are not strong enough, if what I now suspect is true! We are walking into a neat trap!"

Not familiar with the topography of the region, he could not know further facts which would have made his night even more restless. He did not know with what stealth and purpose Bragg had deployed his men about the mountain passes through which, in order to reach him, Rosecrans would have to debouch his men. Nor did he know that Burnside, with the best intentions, but following out previous orders, was safely ensconced in Knoxville whence he would not be enticed save by a confederate victory and recapture of the town.

What he did know was that both armies were in that deadly quiet of expectant listening and waiting. The men on either side were in battle position, with the Union troops on the west side of the river, and the rebel troops on the east. The forced marches through the rugged mountain were already made, the troops stationed in readiness for attack or defense. The Union troops commanded a view of the only passable road leading to Chattanooga, and had in fact a desirable advantage in commanding the heights. "But they have to descend from their heights," he thought, and restlessly tossed and turned. At length, unable to sleep, Turchin rose and stalked into the night. He stopped before darkened tents, and listened to the noises anxious men make in their sleep; sudden cries, groans, some muffled dream of home and love. The mountain chill hung over them and seeped into their huddled warmth as it did into the rough comfort of Turchin's cloak.

Garfield, whom sleep also eluded him, was on his charger, and had come riding with a minor dispatch to General Reynolds, as a pretext, in hopes of finding, as he had expected, some fellow spirit still awake. He consecutively encountered Reynolds, Baird and Turchin. The officers met with one another, and whispered in hurried colloquy. "There are twenty thousand men in each of the three corps," Reynolds said to General Baird, who had ridden up at this moment. "Ours stands to take the brunt of the fight if Rosecrans attacks tomorrow."

"He realizes Bragg may be fooling," Garfield replied. "He knows we are in a tough spot if we have to defend Chickamauga Valley alone. It will take time for the rest of our men to join us, and Bragg is said to have 50,000 ready to meet us." He was grave and anxious, and had but one message to give all officers and division commanders: to stand by in readiness, to have the men prepared; that reinforcements had been called for.

"The men are jumpy," General Turchin said. "They have a feeling that it is close, the battle for Chattanooga."

"We are all a little jumpy," Reynolds replied gruffly. "We have good cause to be." With which the Generals went their separate ways, Turchin riding with Garfield half way down the slope of the mountain.

A wooden, minatory hush settled heavily over the thick forests and deadened all sounds. Before dawn Turchin had his men up and moving into battle stations. The stealthy creeping noises of heavy boots on mossy hillsides and through impenetrable thickets evidenced none of the taut anxiety with which each moving man was loaded in addition to his battle gear. They knew that the order to charge was soon to come, perhaps at the break of dawn, and every man's eyes furtively scanned the brightening patches of sky to be discerned through the dark lattice-work of leaves and branches. As the light increased and an autumnal sun began to rise in deliberate stateliness, Generals Thomas, Reynolds and Baird gave the prescribed signal. The 14th Army Corps in which Turchin served took up arms and charged down the hillsides. At their head rode Turchin indifferent to the ethics demanded on such an occasion. With a skill unsurpassed by any cavalry officer he guided his horse down the slants of the mountain and rode with his footmen into the first fire of Bragg's furious cannoneers and riflemen.

A swaying, bending, mass of Blue hurtled itself against a wavering, surging mass of gray. Men advanced and men retreated on either side. Lines cleaved and opened in gaps, and swiftly a stream of Blue or a stream of Gray flowed in like living fluids to fill the rents in the gaping lines. Batteries shook the mountain sides, and death-dealing missiles of grape and canister rained upon the howling, bleeding men, cursing as they fell, macerated by the dread shower. By the end of the first day's struggle, the Union lines had been forced to retreat to the low line of hills behind them, and here they reformed their decimated ranks as the endless summer day drew to its close and thereby offered them the first respite since dawn.

As soon as the rebel fire was withdrawn from the field, when the Gray took advantage of the night and the lull to recoup somewhat and count their losses, the Union generals met on the silvered crest of the low hill, and conferred together. They stood some distance from the living and the dead, who were indistinguishable amid the lingering smoke and the dusky gloom embracing the whole scene. A figure was seen ascending to them from a crude pathway cut into the side of the hill. It was Garfield braving all dangers to bring communications from Rosecrans, who had already apprised himself of the woeful infliction which Thomas's Center had received. As Chief of staff he had no easy task, being forced constantly to ride back and forth from field commanders to Rosecrans' headquarters, enduring the petulancies of the first and the furious anger of the second, as the case might be. Now he had come with orders from Rosecrans, all too soon discouraged that the generals on the spot were to decide what further course of action to follow; whether to try to beat back the Grays or retire to the road they commanded in the rear and leave to General Bragg the glory of Chickamauga.

The council of war was duly called. Garfield particularly singled out Turchin for consultation, which honor moved that general almost as much as the untoward events of the day. He strode to Garfield's side, and gripped his hand hard, as though seeking and imparting encouragement concurrently. "Our lines are all hacked to pieces," he said, and received ample corroboration from Baird and Reynolds, who stood by biting their lips.

"Does it look altogether hopeless to you, Reynolds?" Garfield inquired.

"Very bad, sir, I'm sorry to report."

"We could not stem the rebel break-through this afternoon!" Baird, who seemed the most discouraged of all, added to Reynolds's report.

At this moment General Thomas, one of the most beloved men in the army of Tennessee, joined his fellow officers. His face was grave and scarred with worry. His jacket was dusty with powder from the day's battle. He had stood his ground immovably, in the center of his men, fighting alongside them with a disregard of rank. "Have you brought us the general's orders for the morrow?" he wanted to know, looking directly at Garfield?

"No orders, sir, save to hold out as long as you deem it feasible. He has implicit faith in your wisdom, General Thomas."

"And you, General Garfield, what is your opinion?" Thomas asked frankly, with sincere willingness to respect another's opinions, which added to his fiery mettle and made him the idol of his army.

"I too have faith in you," General Garfield responded.

"We are in a bad spot," Thomas stated. He turned to the other corps officers and addressed them severally, obtaining various opinions as to the wisdom of pursuing an enemy which seemed invincible. All were of the opinion that unless reinforcements were available, and soon, the fight was an unequal one; all except Turchin, who stood forth alone with a contrary opinion.

"We cannot afford to let this battle fall into the laps of our enemies," he argued belligerently. "As for the fight being unequal, the inequalities in numbers is more than balanced off by the superiority of spirit and the preponderance of right on our side! I say General Burnside must be sent for; I say let us stick it out until help comes! It is true our right wing is almost gone. We have a terrible rent in our middle. We are virtually surrounded on three sides, and it is true we could retreat through the back door! But I say, let us cut our way out the front door, like honorable men!"

He had turned truculently upon Thomas whose face had somewhat relaxed while he spoke. Only hours ago, Turchin had come raging to his rescue and his readied saber had hewed an opening for him and his men, averting a complete collapse of the center. Thomas had not forgotten, but his tired smile was one of pity for the indefatigable Turchin who must be exhausted as any man; he had certainly fought as ferociously as the best.

"You are a gallant officer," he complimented Turchin, but the enemy has the advantage. Victory is within their grasp. They will not slacken their speeds, their rage or their determination." He turned away with a sudden flare of anger. It seemed unfair to him that General Rosecrans should have put the responsibility of final decisions upon him. He thusly interrupted Garfield's words that he was to hold out as long as possible; they connoted but one thing, that Rosecrans was already convinced of ultimate defeat, and concerned only that the defeat be not an ignominious rout. He shook his head in answer to his unspoken cogitations and his officers guessed the extent to which he was being taxed. They too had lived through harrowing hours of the uncertain day, with the unremitting fears of annihilation. The howling rebels; their mockery followed by raucous burst of cannon; their rapid diminution of shells and shooters, cast a foreboding gloom over them. Each of them could still hear the derisive mockery: "How many rounds you got left Yankee?" How that vicious taunt rang in Thomas' ears. How it recalled the hard-bitten report: "But the rounds, general; only five rounds a-piece now; only two rounds, general!"

"Even the enemy knows we are low in ammunition, men!" He remarked to the heavy-laden officers, who awaited his decision. He seemed unwilling to act without their approval. They agreed that retreat was the wiser source.

"Let us fight on, and when our fire is low, when we have shot our last rounds, we shall give them bayonets!" So spoke Turchin in fierce dissension to the others' rueful resolve to retreat. "In memory and honor to those already cut down; to avenge the hell we have known this day; to give sanction and meaning to flesh grinding on flesh, and rapiers thrust into bellies, let us fight on!" As he spoke he wiped the perspiration from his face. A cool wind was chilling it on his skin. He had a stubble of beard on his chin, and his eyes were blood-shot and watery with the sleeplessness of the night before and the travail of the past hours.

"Same old Turchin!" General Garfield gripped his shoulder affectionately. Then, pausing to think, thinking how much this campaign meant to them all, to him in particular, who was soon to retire from the service, he gave momentary hopeful credence to Turchin's stubborn insistence. "There is always the chance that we might hold them off for a day until help comes. If we pursue them across the valley - for they have sustained as grievous losses as we - if we are after them tonight, if we do not give them a chance to reform their lines; if we hammer away until the Rossville Road is ours beyond doubt, the battle on the field will be ours too." This was Turchin's idea exactly, and Garfield gave it in a tentative tone.

But the generals shook their heads negatively. No word of reinforcements was had, said they. Rather, Rosecrans had moved back some miles, and had already conceded defeat in a dispatch to Halleck. To continue further was a needless slaughter of the men. They finally agreed to retreat the best way they could, which was through a mountain pass behind them, McFarland Gap.

On the morrow the enemy showed no more desire to recommence hostilities than the battered 14th Corps. Nor did they dispute heavily the retention of the ridge where Turchin and his men had slept under the cold moon. A few desultory exchanges of shot and shell were the fare of the second day until late afternoon when a sort of major conflict showed signs of developing. Toward dusk, in General Turchin's sector, where some 600 men suddenly found themselves confronted with a raiding force of 2000 rebels, a great blaze of bursting fire and blinding human passion flared up, and might have accomplished the destruction of the Union center which the rebels had failed to do on the previous day.

But where the valiant men alone might have faltered in opposing this sudden horde, not so the fiery Russian, who, again this day, did as much as his guns in putting the fear of God into the enemy's bosom. Before his cursing rush upon them, before his flashing eyes, the gray-clad lads reeled backwards. "Hold them boys!" he shouted, and indeed, they held the sector until help arrived, which it fortunately did, soon enough to defeat this extreme attempt of the rebels to gain a telling victory.

The men who came to relieve General Thomas were not of General Burnside's division but of rather of General Granger's; and this courageous soldier had come of his own accord, without orders from General Rosecrans. Together, Granger's and Thomas' men pushed back the rebel lines sufficiently causing the Blue-coats to remove from the battle field.

Soon the orderly retreat of the 14th Corps was underway, and Bragg's men were left in undisputed possession of all the strategic positions in Look-out Valley, on Missionary Ridge, and in the plateau about Chattanooga. These positions gave them the complete command of the river in either direction, as well as the means to threaten and harass the Union railroad communications to Bridgeport, which was the Federal base of supplies for this theater of the war.

The defeat at Chickamauga cost General Rosecrans his command of the Cumberland Army, able though he was. In his place General Thomas, head of the 14th Corps was placed by the High Command, perhaps in a meritorious acknowledgement that his men had virtually out-fought General Bragg's. Of this forthcoming promotion Thomas could have no inkling when he marched his men sadly in retreat from Chickamauga. He, like his men, was unashamedly downcast and grieved; every soldier smarted in anger, no matter what his rank or capacity. General Garfield rode moodily with Thomas for a while, and then slowed his horse until Turchin, with his men, met him. They were a sorry looking lot, those men who retreated from Chickamauga. Mules and horses were as weary and bedraggled as the men in their soiled and crumpled uniforms. The cooking wagons trailed slowly behind them with their load of wounded and dead. Giving General Garfield a friendly nod, Turchin grimly promised: "We will come back! If we must die, we shall sell ourselves dearly!"

Garfield made no reply, only guided his horse steadily onward.

"General," Turchin said, "the way our men fought yesterday must redeem us to some extent. We may lose a battlefield. That is sorry enough. But the country that can boast such men as ours at Chickamauga must triumph in the end."

Garfield nodded with a sad smile.

CHAPTER XXV

The disastrous losses and unavoidable set-back received at Chickamauga seemed to generate prompt action of a definite sort from Washington, for a complete reorganization of the fighting forces along the western section took place, with General Grant now raised to full command of three armies, linked together in what was called the Mississippi Department. General Bragg was still confidently entrenched in Chattanooga, and the purpose of the High Command continued resolutely to be one of forcing him out of this citadel in order to clear the way for an unobstructed advance into the heart of the Confederacy.

Turchin and his companies were part of the huge besieging forces detailed to surround the strategic valley and hold Bragg. As it turned out, they, not General Bragg became the besieged; they found themselves hemmed in by unscalable crags on three sides, and an indomitable foe on the fourth. Their lines of communication were in the enemy's hands. The river and railroad became virtually ineffectual for Union use, and starvation was the grim prospect ahead of them, as a bleak winter was ushered in on the heels of a fruitless autumn.

The men in the Cumberland Army were short in supplies, short in food stuffs and woefully lacking in medical supplies, not to mention doctors and cooks. They were cut off from their home folks by the inability of the mail wagons to make the extremely arduous upward climb through the mountains. This left the stranded men encamped in the valley, this side of Chattanooga, in desperate straits.

Of their indescribable trials the people back home had no knowledge, and knew naught of the gallant struggle, made in the face of every inclemency, to withstand the concerted might of the South; a savage strength now shifted from other confederate fronts, lest the growing splendor of General Grant's prowess succeed in splitting open the hitherto impregnable back door to Richmond, Jefferson Davis' seat of government.

Nadine had written meanwhile of the tragic death of young Colonel Scott, who had successfully recovered from the wound he received at Stone River the year before, only to die less gloriously in a commonplace accident. He had been thrown from his carriage a few weeks after dismissal from the hospital. General Turchin however, did not receive this intelligence until much later. To have learned of his young friend's untimely death would have saddened him doubly, since he was still mourning the loss of Sergeant Smirnow, who had been struck down at Chickamauga.

Weeks of enforced idleness reduced him and his men to irascibility and distemper the cause for which only the successful demolition of Bragg's siege could have eradicated. In the meantime the suffering grew acute. When rations had to be cut first in half and then in quarters, Turchin grew glaringly angry and resolved: something had to be done to at least open the river, lest his men die like rats in a trap. "Bragg shall not starve us," he swore, and he passionately concentrated upon a plan to seize the opposite side of the Tennessee River, whose shore, if once cleared of enemy batteries, would enable river boats and crafts to ride clear for the few vital miles to the Union depot.

He sought for and gained General Palmer's consent to attempt a daring raid of desperation, and with the help of a bridge of pontoon boats, in the use of which he was already expert, he and a task force of 1,300 men crossed in the dead of the night, and seized the rebel guns, thereby forcing the enemy pickets and scouts to flee, and creating a life-saving spiracle. Bragg did not feel that this meager vent in the blockade he had affected would be a sufficient relief and he relied on his best ally, starvation, to challenge Turchin's possession of it.

Thus, while a small aperture was gained, through which a bare minimum of food could be dribbled in, nothing really remedial against the long siege was effected; the men starved, the beasts starved, the rebels gloated and waited for surrender, and Turchin fumed and steamed until even his fellow sufferers laughed at the picture of impotent rage he presented.

Not alone their situation, not the hunger and cold and inadequate ammunition nourished the perpetual wrath constricting the bosom of the fiery Turchin. Unable to do more, having done everything possible, he fretted in impotence and indignity. Moreover, he had the deep loneliness to endure, which deprivation of friends imposes on a nature like his, essentially gregarious, and happy only when in easy contact with his fellow creatures. At home there had been Nadine and Mrs. Morrison. Even Trofimov had served some kindly end now and then. There had been Colonel Scott and Mihalotzy, whom he had seen only infrequently since the commencement of their march south. And there had lately been General Garfield and the dreamy Smirnow; but all these persons had either died or were removed by other agencies. This left him with his companion sufferers who were not prepared to discuss aught but food and with the cold comfort of communicating only with himself, through his journal, in which he wrote only desultory.

With General Palmer, a man he admired greatly, he struck up a sort of friendship, but after Garfield, he was a poor substitute. General Palmer was the man who had been assigned the role so ably performed by Thomas, and was now the divisional head of the 14th Army Corps. At first he had been received condescendingly by the younger officers in this division, who were rather nettled that a man not of West Point should have attained such a high rank. It was Turchin who had made the first welcome gesture to him, and Palmer consequently conceived a proper respect for his brigade commander. He often invited him diffidently to play chess or discuss small matters pertinent to the maintenance of morale among the men, who had been put to such a terrific strain of deprivation and hunger. Generously he referred Turchin to Grant's notice, and was lavish in his praise for Turchin's brilliant plan and his exploit in having taken Brown's Ferry, the name by which the formidable enemy beachhead on the opposite shore of the river came to be known.

The long siege dragged on into November. Everyone looked to General Grant to do something. But still he waited and watched, rode among his men, scanned the fearful crags of the mountains looming ahead of him, frowned and rode away with little encouragement to the harassed men fretting in their confinement.

Another man of responsibility had ridden into this region at the same time on the opposite side, and had mounted the towering cliffs from which he could look down upon the encampment of Grant's army. This man was none other than the confederate President, Jefferson Davis. Here, atop Missionary Ridge, whose steep slopes dipped into the ice-laden stream below, he delivered a rousing speech to his own men who camped on all the escarpments of the mountain, and crowned its summit with their colors and their cheering fires. Grant's men had during the day, heard the booming of welcoming guns, and at night, seen at a distance the nests of glowing flames from camp fires burning like clusters of prismatic jewels set in the frosty folds of Missionary Ridge.

Late in November began a slow and inconspicuous movement of troops. Reinforcements from the Army of the Potomac arrived daily, the fear of an attack upon the Capitol at last allayed - a fear under which Mr. Lincoln and many other officials in Washington labored constantly during the first year of the war, when it seemed General Lee might choose to contend for Washington, and take the treacherous and dangerous climb into the mountains. The men took heart, and resumed more actively the intensive drills and maneuvers which General Bragg was free to witness often from his secure, elevated vantage point. Generals Sherman and Hooker, appearing on the scene, added to the growing confidence. The days grew clearer in the cleansing frost to which the interminable rains of October at last yielded.

But these trials and travails, hopes and despairs, Turchin's wife could not guess. The same dark fall months which had witnessed the ill-fated contest at Chickamauga, had ushered in for her, a renewed social life and pleasure, and for Chicago, of which she wrote, an auspicious season crowned by news of Grant's success.

The fall of Vallandigham had been greeted by shouts of glee from such loyal sources as the Tribune, and the city was aglow with feverish and kindly efforts to speed the victories it now hoped would follow one after another. The toll in lives was tremendous, but an increased optimism in the air made the mounting losses in men and material less gruesome to bear than the deadly stalemate which had existed when McClellan commanded the Army of the Potomac. The mass of the people in the North, well typified by the populace of Chicago, was sensitive to the juggernaut drive attendant upon the will of General Grant.

Thousands of women were canning vegetables and fruit to give to the Armies. Henrietta Morrison, relieved now of her office in connection with the Union League, supervised hospital activities, spending her strength and energy in ceaseless solicitation, from door to door for the urgently needed articles of nursing. Overcoming her feminine resentment of Nadine, she had earnestly sought her out and detailed to her a conspicuous part of the training schedule for nurse's aides. In addition to teaching what skills she possessed, Nadine came faithfully to the hospital each day to nurse the sick and wounded, whose numbers were now growing to alarming proportions, and who overflowed the inadequate space of the hospitals, until Henrietta suggested the removal of several to private homes where comfort and space could accommodate them. In this humane work the two women drew closer together than either one had ever wished.

Busied at last, Nadine scarcely gave the baron a thought. The more was she surprised, one fine day, as she was starting out for her duties in the hospital to find herself accosted by a servant of the Brewsters. This smiling old coachman related his present errand, which consisted of a plea for help. The Trofimov's had acquired a son since the year before, and the child, a tiny infant, was dying, the man declared; and it was his mistress while in her hysteria and grief had remembered Nadine's nursing skill. "There ain't no doctor they can get, what with all the lame boys in the hospital, Maam," the servant said. And with that he led Nadine to the carriage, which took her once again into Trofimov's life.

With her kind office toward the little child, Nadine ingratiated herself with the entire Brewster family, including Brewster himself, who had grown crusty and bad tempered since her last encounter with him. Upon arriving at the house she had been led directly to the child's nursery, and there, with hardly a moment's delay, began to attend to the child who was suffering of a pustule she immediately punctured.

In a silken wrapper, frothy with colored laces and ribbons, Susan stood by, wringing her hands. She exclaimed first over the dreadful lack of doctors. Every one of them were so busy trying to get recognition and cheap glory from the city officials, that they cared nothing for the life of a helpless babe. And then over the heartlessness of a father, meaning the baron, who was more interested in running off to New York than to worrying about his son.

Mrs. Brewster, who had come in during the small operation, now stood near Nadine and gave her sharp orders and advice, when she was not joining her daughter in denouncing the heartless baron. "The minute he heard that the Muscovites had sent their fleet into the harbor at New York, off he was! Mr. Brewster told him the names of the ships that anchored, and the baron suddenly remembered a relation of his was on one of these ships!" In her voice was a hint of doubt as to the purpose of the baron's trip to New York.

"The Russian Fleet anchored in New York? Are you quite sure, Mrs. Brewster?" Nadine felt a strange excitement. More than mere excitement over this information, she felt elation because no pang stirred her heart over Dimitri's absence. "I can be even glad that he is not here today," she said to herself.

"Of course I'm sure," Mrs. Brewster answered petulantly. "He pretended to have a relation, that's what I say. Did you ever hear of anyone having a name like Rimsky - something or other? That's the outlandish name he would have us believe his relation bears! Fiddlesticks! I say."

"Rimsky-Korsakov!" Susan scowlingly corrected her mother. "I remember that name very well. The baron has frequently mentioned it, said he was a distant relation, and since he is a commissioned imperial officer, I believe it."

"A fiddler, the baron said he was, or a pianoforte player! Mrs. Turchin, can you imagine an officer of the Czar's fleet playing the fiddle or the pianoforte?" She appealed to Nadine who made her smiling escape, but not without accepting a pressing invitation from the two ladies, who were quite bored with each other's company, to visit them on the morrow. Gradually Nadine became a familiar visitor, and indeed, for some perverse reason, a veritable favorite with Mr. Brewster who seemed quite willing to heap upon her a quantity of flattering he had in bygone times reserved for his cousin by marriage, Mrs. Morrison.

That lady had not entered his drawing room since the banishment of Senator Vallandigham, though she had given no explicit reason for thus denying them her company. Without ceremony the head of the house often invaded the upper story where the ladies had their private rooms, to avail himself of Nadine's conversation. Truthfully to say, she waxed, animated and brilliant, under his clever guidance, to the delight of Trofimov, recently returned. He joined them whenever he could escape from the vigilance of his wife and mother-in-law, not to mention the absorbing interests which now devolved upon him - for he was amassing a fortune in his own right by means he would not have chosen to confide to Nadine. The new interest rested for the main part on substantial dollars paid him by the Confederate Government, in return for which he did sundry offices for its agents, including his recent surveillance of the Russian Fleet so mysteriously arrived in New York.

It was quite true that he could have proved a formal relationship to a young midshipman on the Russian clipper, Almaz, by the name of Rimsky-Korsakov, had it become necessary or convenient to do so. His interest in the fleet, however, was not certainly derived from this. Now that the reigning leaders of the Copperhead movement were apprehended, men of persistence like Brewster and his myrmidons were concerning themselves with whatever material aid in arms, money and goods they could muster for the rebels. A bit of reconnaissance was part of this service, and the presence of the Russian Fleet at no one's behest or request, puzzled and frightened Southern sympathizers. Trofimov had gone to New York to feel out the sentiments of the Russians. He had essayed to apprise himself of the nature of this visit, but had succeeded in nothing save the acquisition of a permit to visit his "cousin," which fact netted him only one interesting result: he had been aboard the flagship of the fleet at the time Mrs. Lincoln was escorted on an inspection tour of the ship, and had the dubious privilege, as Brewster said, of bending over her hand, and attending a ship's concert of Russian music provided by the officers themselves.

Why the fleet was anchoring in those waters during these critical months of the conflict; why there were five other Russian vessels in the Pacific harbor; what the intentions of Russia might be in case England should come to Davis' help, these he could not discover. Russia's continued friendship to Mr. Lincoln and the United States required no observation of his for authenticity. Brewster was quite glum.

"I know one thing," he said to him, "Russia means business, and is standing guard over Mr. Lincoln; that is obvious from the full equipment of the vessels, festooned and gala as they appear. Believe me the guns and the men are in readiness for any emergency. They are here to prevent British ships from steaming into the port!"

"Shameful!" Brewster cried. "Absolutely what you would expect of a government of savages! What in the world is there in it for them, to protect Lincoln! It costs millions to equip, man and dispatch a fleet! You can see for yourself how this will work. All of Europe will turn a cold shoulder to Davis for fear of antagonizing the Czar! It actually prolongs this war endlessly! The President's lady gives them her blessing, and a sincere patriot like Vallandigham is banished out of sight!" After a moment's angry thoughtfulness, he said, "I never gave anything for nothing. No one can tell me Russia simply loves us. It doesn't add up."

But of these doings, the coming of the Russian Fleet, the sharp criticism it instigated in the press, the men of the Cumberland Army had no knowledge; nor would knowledge thereof have meant much to many of these weary men, with the exception of Turchin, to whom such data would have brought a cheer. He would have seen at once the political and military significance of this candid expression of good will from Russia. He would have been the first to point to it as proof positive of the benefices which an unshackled people were capable of. He would have given old Herzen in London a silent bow of acknowledgement, and he would have forgiven his native country much of its past stultified stupidity.

Only, of course, he would not know these things then. He, like the rest in that beleaguered army, had to wait until General Grant was ready to make a break for freedom out of the fearsome prison of the three mighty mountains around the plains of Chattanooga.

The coming of Grant to direct the operations against Chattanooga was looked upon as an omen for successful action; so legendary was his renown. This general was much more energetic than Rosecrans, gave more heed to details of reconnaissance. From the beginning he could be seen scouring the countryside fearlessly inspecting and studying the north shore of the Tennessee, facing toward the mouth of the South Chickamauga. Missionary Ridge drew his most intense speculations, and in this direction observant soldiers like Turchin looked for whatever action Grant should decide to take.

The available maps of this region were faulty, and the opportunities to secure complete knowledge of the terrain impossible. General Sherman and Grant had to trust partial information and their own sight, helped by field glasses, to judge the extent of the ridge through which they hoped to attempt a break. Through their scrutiny they ascertained that the North end of the ridge was guarded only by a slim patrol of rebel pickets. This point was General Bragg's weakest link in his ring of excellent defenses including cannon, earthworks and fortifications.

Initial preparation began on the 24th of November, and by the following morning, when the preliminary ferrying back and forth had been accomplished and details of men had been stationed on the opposite side of the river, the order came for all troops to stand attention. Sherman's troops were the first to advance. Their orders were to take the low hills at the foot of Missionary Ridge, whence they must drive the rebel gunners out of their rifle pits.

An unforeseen alteration in their plans caused a momentary panic. Sherman, upon advancing to an expected ledge, found himself trapped by a ravine not noted in the preliminary survey. Immediately Bragg's men fell upon his troops. To relieve Sherman and save his isolated regiment from annihilation, the brigade commanders gave the agreed signal to charge across the open valley of Look-out Mountain. General Grant undoubtedly meant this frontal attack as an effort to draw off the rebels from General Sherman's flank, and it was successful in that. Bragg's siege cannons boomed, light artillery and muskets rolled, a great roar filled the air as the rebel guns blazed from their rifle pits at the base of Missionary Ridge, and from the bristling brow of the mountain top. Four Union divisions of men yelled and dashed forward into the hail of bullets. A curious transformation came suddenly over the men now dashing across the open plain. Flags were held aloft; the sun beat down in a clear white light, the conflict of long patience with slow hunger meshed in a fury like a torrent rushing towards a dam. No ordinary Yankees from the towns and villages of Ohio, Tennessee and

Illinois rushed over that desiccating wind of fury. With blasts of rage and ancient instincts, the object of which no man could dream as he ran forward, each kept close to his fellow, stepping automatically into the vacant place when a screaming bullet felled a companion.

Only four of Thomas' divisions were engaged in this lightning rush to smash the gunners at the base of the mountain. Other divisions of the army had made a stealthy and secret crossing some half mile down the river, and were preparing to move to assist once the rifle pits were taken. But those four divisions came rushing forward in double quick time, indifferent to the sheet of flame which burst upon them in searing flood, enveloping them like an evil cloud, which, when it lifted for seconds at a time, showed gaping holes in the lines of blue. But it failed to halt the panting pace and served rather to increase it.

As a single body these divisions moved on, and yet not a wildness inflamed them or pushed their feet over their dead and dying horses and men. No wild disorder, but instead, a steady, driving inhuman logic appeared to impel them onward until even their officers lost control of the men, and had to follow rather than lead them.

What this undaunted forward rush must have presented to the Confederate soldiers can only be imagined. The rebel boys occupying the rifle pits yelled in screaming terror as the first Union men reached them. Blue-glad soldiers flung themselves upon those who crumpled, or tried to precipitously flee upward to their own lines. Like living beetles the rebels began to scale up the side of Missionary Ridge and scramble hysterically over their breast works on top.

In an instant, hordes of Union soldiers pursued the frantic gunners up the slope. In their midst, with sword uplifted and possessed of the same rushing impulse as his men, was Turchin, unmindful of rank and orders, filled only with the instinctive compulsion to scale that mountain slope and destroy his enemies at its crest.

What had actually given rise to the spontaneous pursuit, no one knew. Not only Turchin uttered the wild cry of retaliation. Every soldier took up the blood-curdling roar of men beside themselves. They fought, clawed and dug their way upward. Between gasps, they hooted and imitated the rebel revilement which came fulminating down upon them along with the shells. When the cannons were unable to continue their deadly work, due to the rigid angle their construction imposed upon their movements, the shells were ignited and rolled down the side of the slope so that they would explode under the legs and bellies of the climbing soldiers.

These burning, dismembering shells only served to further infuriate Turchin. "Butchers, cannibals, swine," he roared. "Swine, god-forsaken mocking howling swine!"

Mihalotzy, who was in the mad rush, now reached his friend who was a third of the distance up by now. "Stop it, general! It is against orders, and it is suicide!"

"Out of my way!" He tried to push away from him. "Up after them; it is now or never!" And with one hard shove he sent Mihalotzy sliding downward as he rushed on until he could see the earthworks plainly. "Up boys," he cried to those swarming about him. "Up and at them! We have come this far, now up! The rolling rocks and lighted shells cannot stop us! Their cannons cannot stop us! Hell cannot stop us!"

In a matter of minutes the towering line of the trees in their wintry aloofness and solemnity reared into view. A final terrific spurt brought the men in blue to Bragg's breastworks, to the smoking mouths of the cannons, swiftly captured as panicky gray-clad figures yelled, threw up their arms, and ran for their lives, more awed and terrified by the ferocity in the attackers than their numbers or incredible agility in scaling the slope. A triumphant, jubilant roar went up, mingled with curses and weeping. Flaying bayonets gleamed in the frosty clarity, and slumped bodies piled up under stampeding feet. Turchin stood on the earthworks and laughed like a mad man. His tears coursed down his cheeks and his heart almost burst in pride as his men wrought confusion among the rebels racing away, crying and dying among the tall trees on the ridge. Here Mihalotzy found him, and at his side fought off the fiercest onslaughts. Soon thousands of Union men were sweeping the ridge, now clear of rebel resistance. By late afternoon, under the masterly direction of General Hardie, the rebels had become completely disorganized and routed. "Justice was done this day," said Turchin, unaware that his cheek bled profusely. "For this day have I lived."

"Did you give the order to ascend?" Captain Mihalotzy demanded. "If you did, general, I am immensely surprised. The end cannot justify the risk; to race into the mouth of the cannon directly trained on you; perhaps to deliver these countless dead to a premature fate!" He had never been so outspoken before.

"I gave no order!" Turchin replied crossly. He was limping from the bruises acquired in scaling the slope. "The men responded to the genius of the moment. All at once it seized them; and what is my duty but to go along and direct them to exploit this genius, this vision that orders them forward because the moment no general can foresee dictates advance!"

He had a curiously satisfied gleam on his taut and smudged face. Mud and blood and dust clung to him from head to toe. None the less, the smile on his lips was beatific. Mihalotzy said no more.

"Besides," Turchin added to his former remarks, "I saw immediately that in scaling the hill our boys were safer than they could be while remaining in a direct line of fire. I knew if we got past the first few feet we would be beyond reach of the cannon. The guns can be inclined only so much, and cannot depress sufficiently after that to do much damage. In fact they form a sort of area of safety within their angle." He laughed aloud. "Mihalotzy, we got them this time! This will wipe out the shame of Chickamauga. They had to scamper like rats over the other side and we are free to move forward. The siege is broken!"

If there was a ring of joyfulness in General Turchin, something perhaps less applausive though not less pleased shone in General Thomas' face. He had been observing the fantastic rush across the valley and up Missionary Ridge from the observation platform on Knob Hill, where he had stood beside General Grant throughout the charge. How Grant was receiving the visible miracle before their eyes, was plain from the heavy frown on his face. Suddenly he threw his glasses down angrily. "General Thomas. Who gave the order for that ascent? Am I not to be obeyed when I give an order? I said to take the rifle pits! It was too dangerous to attempt the ridge!"

"No one gave any orders to the contrary, general," Thomas replied. But his face showed an uncommon approval of the valorous action of his boys. "They are the men who retreated from Chickamauga," he explained quietly. "They suffered since September in the siege Bragg laid upon us. They are men, general, and they gave themselves their orders when the time for reprisals came. No one needs to give such men orders!"

The pursuit of the last of Bragg's army on the ridge continued until nightfall. Six brigades participated in the last struggles to push the rebels off the ridge entirely, and they almost succeeded in capturing the noted southern general himself. Grant, soon reconciled to the change in his plans, was able before the day was out, to wire his Commander in Chief: "The day is ours!" Others expatiated more rapturously on the unprecedented assault of the Ridge, which they gladly accredited to "the magnificent charge of Thomas's troops."

"It will please Mr. Lincoln," was all Turchin would say to General Palmer when late at night these two officers were free to pause for a moment.

"But some of us, General Turchin, stand to be charged with disobedience. As officers we committed a breach of discipline." He was a quiet and dignified sort of a man whose emotions were always so well checked that his face had a perpetual cast of inscrutability upon it. If he joked, his words were couched in such a laconic and often solemn voice that only if one looked directly into his twinkling eyes could the suggestion of humor be discernible.

"We have routed a stubborn army! That is all Lincoln wants to know! That is all we need to justify us! What are orders in the face of accomplished facts? I have given orders enough in my life to know that all orders must be predicated upon a passion for success, a high determination to achieve it at any cost and by any means. We have done precisely that this day. Our rank and file answered a higher duty than that imposed by their generals. Today they have out-generaled their generals."

General Palmer had to laugh outright at this, and hoped there would be no inglorious aftermaths of this historic charge and this sweeping victory. Later on, when it was estimated that 6,000 men had been captured along with nearly sixty pieces of artillery; that the menacing obstacle of Bragg's forces in Tennessee to all intents and purposes had been liquidated, no recrimination for breach of etiquette or violation of orders occurred.

Late in the night, after the excitement of the momentous charge up the slope was somewhat modulated, Turchin joined the men in their open camps where, despite the biting cold and the incongruous drizzle of rain, and hail, the men joyously built roaring fires and lolled out in a forgotten leisure. No more would they have to peer shiveringly over the valley and into the slope where the enemy camp fires burned like beacon lights while their own were non-existent. No longer would they be constrained to silence, darkness and concealment. The night now was no harbinger of death and sudden attack; it was a light and protective thing, a delicate instrument for concealing and containing the tenderest emotions which get shuffled and thrown to the surface during a crisis. Only a purposeless laughter fluttered about them, only a vast gratitude that life demanded nothing further of them for the nonce; no thoughts, no discussion, no fears, hopes or plans. For the time being a magnificent equanimity obtained in them all.

The next morning ushered in Thanksgiving. Turchin, an early riser, was the first man to stand awake in the dawn of the new day. The crispness, the clearness, the holy calm of the slumbering valley upon which he could look as though he were lord of the universe, filled him with an awe so moving that irrepressible tears stood in his eyes. Long he stood devoutly on a ledge, and filled his heart and sight with the glory of Thanksgiving, picturing to himself the rugged gray simplicity of those first immigrants, washed to the shores of this land. Then he walked slowly to the river bank, down to the edge of the thin sheet of ice polished smooth by an industrious north wind. The darkly looming ridges of the mountains were still watchfully reposeful after the extermination of the invaders of the day before. A flock of large screaming birds wheeled over head, and passed by in perfect formation. "Thanksgiving!" he muttered, and dipped his hands into a hole he made with the heel of his boot. He sloshed the icy water on his face. "Clean in the sight of the Lord," he murmured.

He had but a short time in which to enjoy the feeling of piety which gripped him; only until the sun mounted into the sky and signaled the stirring of life all over the valley. A fine, almost imperceptible mist began to rise toward the mountain slopes, making the silvered brush and pine bluish and vague. A group of out riders moved across the open plain, just when the big guns at Chattanooga began their victory boom. The guns at Fort Hood took up thundering strains of Thanksgiving, and soon called forth the men, who flocked into the valley in droves. There they grouped themselves with caps in hand, heads bent in voiceless prayer. The color sergeants reverently lifted bullet-riddled standards and regimental colors so dearly preserved on that impossible ascent of yesterday. "It is no mere rag they hold up," Turchin mumbled, and his throat ached with choking sweetness and pride. This pride was a diffuse emotion in him attesting to the glory of life and of God, for whose worship on Thanksgiving Day there was no fitter temple than this valley; no more splendid dome to vault across a widening future than a brightening heaven, radiant with sunlight. The siege cannons continued to boom and to enhance for him the illusion of nature in a mood of devotion. He seemed a boy again, lost in the interior of a magnificent cathedral, amid the anthem which the young voices, still raw and hoarse from the weeping and yelling of yesterday, spilled into the freshness of day, the most mystic of hymns. The hills gave back the song the young men sang, and Turchin's heart, like the hills about them, made no oral response, only a faithful echo.

CHAPTER XXVI

A gradual change came over Nadine during the long months of the Chattanooga campaign. A curious unwanted bitterness reflected itself in her bearing, in the assiduity with which she worked at the hospital, in the brittle smiles she habitually wore when visiting with her reinstated friend, Trofimov. Even in her relation with Mrs. Morrison, which seemed of late to take on warmer aspects, there was an alteration. She began to notice her closely, take note of her unassuming airs, her simple costumes and her utter departure from the fashionable accoutrements which had at first impressed her. Now the young woman garbed herself grimly and soberly. She affected a plain appearance which was oddly at variance with her pretty face. Sadness in her eyes lent her a premature gravity and dignity.

There was at that time a certain lady in Chicago, who was largely responsible for this increased seriousness in Henrietta's manner which, as Susan Trofimov acidly opined, was the appropriate attire for a woman who should never have been a wife. In her own status as a baroness and the mother of a son, she was freed of many verbal reticences propriety prescribed for an unmarried lady. Now she freely mixed a natural asperity with an unnatural flutter which irritated the baron and amused the sick boys at the hospital, where, not to be outdone by other social matrons, she visited once a week, with her retinue of servants bringing good things from the Brewster kitchen.

The lady who so profoundly influenced Henrietta was a Mrs. Mary Livermore, whose kindliness and good sense had provided the genius and organization to the excellent system of nursing care Chicago was installing. On this great-hearted woman, Henrietta wished now to pattern herself and to Mrs. Livermore she offered not only her personal services without limit, but every access to her wealth.

"You are troubled, my child," that good lady had frankly remarked upon first inspecting the young widow, who wished to be of help in the organization of the Soldier's Home.

"We are all troubled in some fashion," Mrs. Morrison had responded.

"Work is the best anodyne for trouble. Work for others," Mrs. Livermore had kindly advised. Her intelligent and motherly eyes held a sternness which was not unacceptable to Henrietta, who read in the controlled sympathies lying behind her eyes, a pledge for gracious respect. She wanted a friendly personality to whom she might attach herself for a while.

"I want to work for others," Henrietta cried with swift passion. "I want to learn how. I want to give more than my money!"

"You have great love to give, my child," the older lady remarked, noting the flushed and hectic cheeks of her young friend. "Work first of all, at the task which meets your eye. Give as you can, and love your fellow creatures, where you will find rich rewards in love. You are a widow," her voice had dropped, for too well she knew the pain and agony of these new war widows. In her arms she had comforted many a young wife these terrible months of 1863.

She was not amazed when Henrietta burst into uncontrollable sobs, and shook her head to refute the understandable mistake Mrs. Livermore had made. "My husband did not die for his country," she corrected, wiping her eyes. And then Mrs. Livermore guessed that the widow hopelessly loved someone. She shook her head commiseratingly. In her work she had come close to the profound truths of life, among which she knew the problems of love to be a vital ingredient; but it was a healthy ingredient, and her main concern was with death and pain. Therefore, she asked no questions, and assigned many tasks to Henrietta which would have taxed the endurance of Nadine or Susan.

These three acquaintances attained a new level of understanding, one with the other. Subtlety the ties had been shifted and it was Henrietta who now stood aloof. She was excluded, though generally by her own wish, from the whirl of small social affairs in which Nadine took part. These were generally sponsored by Susan and her mother, who mysteriously managed to attach, by her husband's prestige, if not her own charms, the most prominent matrons in the city. Since the day Nadine had cured the baby of its indisposition, she had been accorded cordiality as genuine as any the Brewsters were capable of. If Susan took a malicious pleasure watching her new friend in the society of her husband, she betrayed none of her spite or pique except by an occasional pouting reference to his warm eulogy of her. "I do believe he measures every woman by standards, Mrs. Turchin! I tell him it is most undemocratic in Chicago! After all, we can't all have the honor of being born countesses. You were a countess, do not deny it!" Yet her tone held a small barb. She was much too secure of Trofimov to do aught but play with Nadine's attraction to him, a fact she shrewdly suspected but in no way resented; for having instantly appraised Nadine as a fastidious creature unable to do more than flirt mildly, and having fathomed Trofimov's mercenary cautiousness, she felt haughtily superior to jealousy.

Irresistibly, Nadine was drawn into the Brewster circle of acquaintances, and consequently drew further away from Mrs. Morrison, who had become, as was generally said, utterly devoid of taste and common sense. "Henrietta's constant companions were common people she collected indiscriminately," said Mrs. Brewster," and her unwise expenditure of the fortune her husband had left her, was senseless." Suspecting that her behavior had become degenerate and really quite ostentatious, what with her affections and mannerism in eschewing the decent apparel of a lady of her position, Mrs. Brewster could not abide Henrietta's mannish garments. Had Henrietta been poor, she would have approved.

"Perhaps she suffers of unrequited love." Trofimov contributed this generous analysis of Mrs. Morrison, and as he spoke he directed a meaningful glance at Nadine, who flushed uncomfortably.

"Unrequited love, indeed!" Susan scoffed. "Who would refuse to wed as much money as she has?"

"One who was already wed to honor, my love. It might be the dear lady's lot to meet with one who loves honor more than money. I believe some such do exist."

Nadine did not take note of the baron's harsh allusions. She had for months accustomed herself to such a demure casualness that it admitted of no familiarities, though this did not diminish the attraction the baron still exerted upon her. She had come to what she believed was a safe level in her feelings for him. The humiliation was held in abeyance, the warming of her blood in check, the glance of her eye in reserve… she hoped. She did everything but deny herself what small secret comforts the sight of him rendered possible. If he handed her his hand, in or out of his carriage, if he took her in to dinner on his arm, if he dropped by to spend half an hour with her in her home, she was satisfied; and for those little offices she returned him more thought than she gave General Turchin, wintering in loneliness and longing in Chattanooga.

This last winter assumed a grave importance in the course of the war. The Gateway to the South, having been broken open, had to be thrown back to admit a decisive march to Richmond. The groundwork for the spring campaign meanwhile, had to be carefully laid. Entrenchments had to be dug and roadwork built. Huts for the men had to be constructed, and more than that, instruction for such a building project had to be taught. These things occupied General Turchin completely for they were the only assuagements he knew for his growing homesickness. He worked like a beaver, and recommended a like cure for the others as lonely and homesick as he.

Letters were again available; Nadine's and Mrs. Morrison's, and curiously enough, even a few from Dimitri Trofimov. These last were penned in such a friendly vein, so patently frank and unassuming, that often he was led to revise his opinion with respect to the baron's disloyal sentiments. He became prone to judge him more gently, to see in the baron's bewildering casuistic tries nothing more than poor attempts to supplant with a facile tongue his recognized deficiency of talents and morals. So much death and havoc, so much deprivation and anxiety had he recently passed through, that he allowed his general kindliness to extend to the baron. Never a lover of money, he felt pity over the baron's passion in this matter. If a man chose the accumulation of money as an end in life, he concluded, that man manifested a deep lack of appreciation for life's truly beautiful and creative elements. He had no love, no inspiration, and no grand conceptions. At very best, he might have a diseased ambition for power.

They were routine weeks, those weeks of winter entrenchment, but he lived them with a singular tolerance. He began to work on a series of articles on the general nature of warfare, and on the events of the battle of Chickamauga, the loss of which he was never resigned. It was his intention one day to amass sufficient material to compose a full book on the subject and with that initial work to launch into the literary field. This resolve rose in a spontaneous refutation of the reiterated theme in all Trofimov's correspondence. With an utter disregard for any reflective consistency, Trofimov now openly denied the validity or strength of the South's cause, and this despite his partisanship of the year before, even boldly admitting it. Now he wrote callously that there was no sense in siding with the loser, which was the role fortune was delegating to the rebels. There was no point, moreover, he wrote in spending one's time with presumptive concerns better adjudicated on the battlefields. In his present opinion, Davis had already lost politically and militarily and the subsequent procedure of the war no longer interested him. In his words, "Not being an American allows me this liberty."

One of his letters began, "This futile contest is nearing its end. I have always been a reasonable creature and I know how to adjust myself to the times in which I find myself. I am your friend, Turchin and I don't mind telling you that I am ready to do you a good turn; without laboring the point let me inform you that I am in a position to do it. I have done a little speculating on the side, and I tell you that fortunes are to be made hereafter in railroading and in land. And with your ability in this line, I am sure we can advance ourselves profitably..."

Each day, Turchin's growing lack of respect for the baron was becoming more self-evident. "I like better my meanest lad here; I trust him more, and I value any affection he has for me more than the avowed friendship of so unprincipled a man as Trofimov," he exclaimed one day to Chaplin Conant on whom fell the privilege of substituting his cheerful talents for the spirited friendship of General Garfield, Mitchel, Smirnov and the rest of the comrades who were now either dead or gone.

"What do you make of such a fellow, Chaplin?" Turchin inquired impatiently, tossing him Dimitri's letter to read in its entirety.

"There are many kinds of men, general. All have a place in the divine scheme of things. A man comes along who merely crosses your path for a moment, and yet his influence may affect the entire pattern of your life. There is a kind of honesty in your friend. It is obvious he believes in nothing. Some men like to proclaim their villainy because it is the only way in which to extend themselves out of the oblivion they detest. Their passage is rough and may bruise us, even kill us, yet they teach us the deeper significance of their opposites. Your friend may be one of these."

"By such a doctrine, Reverend Conant, we can be easily misguided, led to countenance what is destructive of general good," said Turchin.

"Who is to judge?" the minister shrugged his shoulders. "I find it simpler and sounder, in the case of individuals, to seek a man's good than to sit in adamant judgment of his failings. I am content that he suffers his burden of disaffection without the cruelty of exposure to public censure. Let us expose the generality of folly and wickedness. Let us unite in defense of the good, and the fruits of the union we establish will demonstrate and teach by exemplification."

"The union we have fought hard to save is the kind of union I believe in!" Turchin answered heatedly. "It is concrete and requires no pious promises. It is clear, and sets definite limits a man can understand. The other is too vague. Who is to unite to defend what good? Good for whom?"

They involved themselves in constant friendly altercations of this sort which always ended in a forgiving handclasp. Conant was incapable of harboring anger except toward abstract evils. But in spite of an underlying harmony of intellect, these two failed to achieve a complete understanding of one another, each concluding at various times that only in their combined efforts to enliven and cheer the men under their supervision, did they really see eye to eye.

In this way the year came to an end. A more hopeful Christmas and New Year's Day passed with but a few hard skirmishes to prepare the Cumberland Army for the job which lay ahead of them, once the roads became passable and the rivers navigable in the spring.

One small battle was fought with General Bragg's reformed army.

Bragg had retired to Dalton, some miles south of Chattanooga, which was in the path of the Cumberland Army should it begin to move southward again. Bragg, in spite of his defeat on Missionary Ridge, was still in high favor with Jefferson Davis, a fact which was said to be remarkable in view of the temperamental nature of Davis's relationship to his generals. Bragg, no mean soldier, easily recognized that the next objective Grant would attempt to gain was Atlanta, and consequently had entrenched himself in Grant's path. If Bragg was not repulsed at Dalton, he might reestablish his former great prestige, before the Missionary Ridge debacle and it was fair to assume, might even rival General Joe Johnston.

As it was, since it was unlikely that Bragg could hamper Grant at Dalton; Hardee was given the defense of Atlanta. Hardee had been one of the chief defenders at Missionary Ridge. In fact, he was the last general to abandon his position. But his tenure was brief and was followed by General Joe Johnston's. General Johnston was more highly rated by his opponents than he was by his chief, Jefferson Davis. He was noted for his shrewd judgments, his keen intuition, and his lightning strokes from which many a Union officer had suffered in the past.

It was against this wily foe that Generals Grant and Sherman coached the Cumberland Army in the spring of 1864. All officers were strictly advised of their duties. Regiments were carefully reorganized, and it fell to Turchin's lot to have his old 19th, Illinois reattached to his brigade. His brigade was still under General Thomas' command, but their guiding spirit was General Sherman who was a man of Turchin's own heart, at least as far as his attitude toward army quartering was concerned.

Sherman's command covered more than 100,000 men and Sherman insisted that every one of them be properly fed, clothed, and equipped with guns and ammunition before they attacked Atlanta. He was a man who was receptive to advice and gladly consulted the experience of able generals under him. He gave special heed to General Turchin who boldly suggested a thorough reconnaissance of the entire area, a thinly populated terrain stacked for the most part with picturesque woodlands offering little opportunity for forage and sustenance to a moving army.

The difficult, crude roads, slow to thaw, worried Turchin excessively.

He intimated his fears to Mihalotzy, who responded with a loud laugh. "Friend," he declared wryly, "if you continue to worry much more about the roads, the ruts you will cut in your face will do for our wagons."

"It is no laughing matter, my friend," Turchin grumbled. "When we finally get enough wagons and animals, we get no roads."

"Then we will travel light," Mihalotzy continued laughing. He had ridden over to see Turchin, but could not bring himself to discuss what lay uppermost in his mind. He had come for encouragement and advice on a delicate matter. He had composed a letter to Henrietta, in which he had hesitatingly, apologetically declared his love and hopes, but he still lacked the courage to send it. He hoped that her good friend Turchin would confer a tacit permission to do so. He had only to find a good moment to reveal his intention. "Hmm!" Turchin growled. "I don't like this idea of travelling as though we were without bellies! Speed is important, I grant you, and travelling lightly argues for speed, but how far and how fast can we go if we have no decent food, no proper cook wagons. It's such items we will have to dispense with if we travel light. It's bad enough we have only one ambulance, but only a single mule to the regiment for carrying pots and pans! Impossible. I hear General Sherman will insist on this!"

"I think, Turchin," Mihalotzy exclaimed, "that if we fail to take Atlanta by storm, you will blast it down by your faith! I never did think the walls of Jericho crumpled by the blast of the horn. It was the mighty faith of those old Hebrews. You are like one of those ancient patriarchs." He was silent for a long while. They watched the stars and clouds overhead without comment. "A woman could love you, general," Mihalotzy said irrelevantly, and Turchin looked at him in surprise.

"One woman does, the only one I wish so," he answered, showing in his quizzical expression the curiosity roused by the other's remark. But Mihalotzy became embarrassed, and bit his lips. He said nothing of his letter.

A few days later the order to break camp came, and Turchin's brigade led the vanguard of the march. "Our corps is like the biting edge of the knife," he proudly boasted to General Palmer.

"I believe you!" Palmer smiled as he rode by. "We shall need a sharp blade to cut our way to Atlanta."

In a matter of days the entire army had reached Resaca, where a pitched battle ensued. For a time it seemed that circumstances had gone against the plans of Sherman. Certainly the army was not prepared for the clever and daring defense the Southerners obtruded here. At their first sight of the admirable defenses which met them, blocking their rapid approach to Atlanta, Turchin with a small force of men advanced upon the front lines of the enemy. These he hoped to surprise by a rush attack, by dealing them a staggering blow with his divisions. For the first few minutes he succeeded in beating back the foe, causing them to sway and bend. But immediately thereafter, reinforcements were thrown in which surrounded the Union men. Desperately leading his men with flashing bayonet, Turchin commenced to hew an opening in the encirclement, hoping against hope, to rescue his boys who, since no aid had been sent to them, had been forced to a fighting retreat. It was a bloody retreat and went only as far as the creek at their backs. Meanwhile, from the low hills nearby, rebel guns were splattering them with lead. Turchin's horse was shot from under him. A young sergeant sprang to assist him, but he was spurned by the general. "Fool! Never mind me! Mind the rebels!"

The creek was intractable, deep and slippery at its banks. Here the harassed brigade was forced to a stop. Turning to the smoking hills the general shook his fist: "Not you up there, but only nature can stop us! Fire away!"

Turning to his officers he gave rapid orders for a stratagem of cross firing and enfilading which tactics kept their enemies at bay until Sherman's reinforcements arrived and pushed back General Johnston's forces across the Oostanaula River. The road was opened by this Confederate retreat and was clear for the Cumberland Army which could now advance from Resaca to Lost Mountain, Raccoon Ford and eventually Atlanta.

From then on the march was vigorous, and the army indeed travelled light. Everything superfluous for lightning maneuver was discarded. Each man carried only three days rations in his haversack and on his belt only a half canteen and a small tin pot in which to boil his coffee. This pot and the half of his canteen were the sole utensils Sherman permitted the soldiers on the march to Atlanta. The half canteen served for every conceivable purpose in the life of the soldier on the march: he cooked in it, fried meat, washed himself from it, and even used it to scoop out shallow trenches or rifle pits.

For all this, the march was less forced than those the troops had experienced in Tennessee and Kentucky. Summer was approaching and the country which they were traversing was deep in its beauty. Now and then, when forced to make camp for the night in an open field which invited stealthy attack, Turchin would strip his coat and work along with his men in erecting field fortifications. He taught his men how to throw up fortifications out of stacked arms, piled up axes and crowded wagons.

Inflated hopes animated every man's bosom. Atlanta loomed incitingly ahead of them, and when they reached Jonesboro, where all the commands were to converge for the concerted drive, it seemed reasonable to expect success. "We are almost over the hump," Turchin exclaimed happily to General Palmer, with whom he was chatting in the noon-day sun. "Once Atlanta falls to us, the way will be open to the sea, then Richmond and victory!"

General Palmer, less sanguine than his brigadier-general, was shading his eyes as he scanned the azure sky. The sun was beating down with extraordinary force, presaging a scorching day. White puffs of harmless clouds drifted by, and melted into the heightened brilliance of the sky. "Sherman is right," he said, "when he declares we must literally rip out the heart of this rebellion as we proceed. We'll have to destroy the land where it will hurt most. This region just ahead of us, is the bread basket of Davis's ambitions." He spoke meditatively. "It is hard for one American to treat other Americans like this." Regret tinged his matter-of-fact speech. "But I am afraid there is no other recourse."

"You think a traitor is none the less an American?" Turchin was incredulous.

"Is an incorrigible child less one's child?" Palmer chided. "The lads in Gray are kin to ours in Blue; never forget that, General Turchin. From what rumors we hear down here, some of those ladies are beginning to grumble, sure enough. I hear that in Charleston the new slogan is 'It's a rich man's war and a poor man's fight'. Perhaps Mr. Lincoln's emancipation measure is having far more effect than we thought it would at first." He lapsed into silence, and again contemplated the augur of a scorching day's event.

Turchin's mare was beginning to paw the ground restively. The Russian was seemingly attentive to General Palmer's remarks which apparently required no replies.

"How man will fight for his freedom!" Palmer concluded. "These men, whom we shoot and who shoot us, view Lincoln and the Republicans to be tyrants. We call Secessionists traitors, but they call us..."

He never finished his sentence, for at that moment Turchin went limp in the saddle, his horse shied, neighed loudly, reared on its hind legs, and flung Turchin off his back as easily as though he were a loose saddle bag.

"General Turchin!" Palmer cried, and in an instant was on the ground beside the fallen man. Suddenly half a dozen officers and men leapt to his aid, and together they lifted the prostrate general who had turned a sickly white. "A sun stroke!" General Palmer believed. "Get him to a tent."

Thus at the threshold of Atlanta, General Turchin ended his military career; for after the severe stroke which had come upon him unannounced, he was rendered not only unfit for duty, but because of paralysis, almost senseless and hopeless. He was removed to a military hospital in Chattanooga from where he was sent back to Chicago.

His arrival in his home city was unheralded. Intelligence had been immediately forwarded to his wife, but due to the delay of communications, she had not as yet been apprised of the misfortune, and at the very time her husband's pain-racked limbs were being carefully lifted onto the hospital stretcher in Chicago, she was dining with the Trofimov's and the Brewster's.

Henrietta was working in the hospital at the time of Turchin's admittance. One glance at the unconscious man who she was told, had an intermittent delirium, and she began to tremble violently. Her face turned first extremely pink and then contrastingly pallid. With her own hands she bathed his fevered forehead, and refused to leave his bedside until the fever abated and he regained a lucid moment.

"Is that you, Nadine?" his voice weakly asked while his big limp hand made an effort to reach for Henrietta's.

"It is I," she whispered. It did not matter to her that he believed her to be Nadine. She would have been willing for him to be thusly comforted.

"It is not Nadine!" he fretfully cried, his eyes opening wide, and looking straight into the widow's face. Recognizing his beloved colleague and friend, he managed to bring a faint smile to his eyes and voice. "It is you, dear Mrs. Morrison! It is you, when I am weak and helpless! How good you are." He closed his eyes and fell again into the uneasy slumber from which he had been unexpectedly roused.

As soon as she was certain he had sunk into a beneficent sleep, which the doctor assured her might continue for an indefinite time, she hastened to Division Street in search of Nadine. For long minutes she knocked at the door, until she was convinced Nadine was absent. "Where can she have gone," she wondered anxiously. "He needs her now. I must find her."

She thought of Susan and Trofimov, of their recent close society, and thither she hurried. It had been a long time since she had voluntarily entered her cousin's house. She was too kind to refuse the Brewster's or Trofimov's her company on the grounds of her suspicion of their disloyalty, and preferred that they construe her aloofness on any basis they found convenient. She was not insensitive of the criticism which they were instrumental in spreading concerning her and the activities she sponsored. But these considerations vanished in the light of the urgency which brought her now.

She found the family entertaining at dinner. The house was more sumptuously furnished than the year before. In the dining room where she appeared, the faces before her all seemed to have become obesely larded since her last visit. Susan was bursting with ruddy opulence. Mrs. Brewster was stuffed tightly into her stays. Nadine was aglow with a fulgent radiance of her ribbons and laces, while Turchin lay ill, perhaps dying. The gentlemen were all prosperous-looking and pompous, even Trofimov, in whom the married state had produced a kind of repose in spirits which allowed him ample margin for indulging his wit which flowed evenly as Mrs. Morrison was shown in.

"Mrs. Morrison is the very symbol of the country's pinched condition," he greeted her, easily including her in the stream of table-talk. "Forgive me, Mrs. Morrison, but it startles me to see you personally embodying the nuisances of this war in your strange manner and dress. I regret the alteration I see from a beautiful woman of whom there are lamentably few," smiling his exception of her to Nadine, "to a fiercely social-minded uplifter."

"I shall take that as a compliment, Baron Trofimov," she answered coldly, refusing a seat at the board. "Beauty is as beauty does. But I came to summon Mrs. Turchin, not to engage in fruitless palaver. May I have a private word with you?" she addressed herself directly to Nadine, who sensing something untoward which the company missed, rose and followed her out of the room.

In a matter of moments Henrietta conveyed her message to Nadine as gently as she could. Nadine turned deathly pale at the news. Without another word, and without a farewell to her hosts and hostesses, she departed the house.

"Henrietta becomes more uncouth daily," Mrs. Brewster scolded.

"At least we have one attraction which draws her here," Brewster snapped. "I wonder what is in the wind. Have you heard anything baron?" The collapse of his venture with Vallandigham did not sweeten his temper, and grudgingly prepared him for the defeat of the South as well.

Trofimov was perplexed. Quietly he rose from his seat and excused himself. Without further ado, merely following a sudden hunch, he hurried to the stables, and mounted his horse. He gave himself no time in which to reason his impulsive action. He knew with a sharp clarity that something was amiss, and knowing Henrietta's recent absorption at the hospital, thither he made his way. Too well he understood human nature not to have read an inkling of some trouble involving Nadine in Mrs. Morrison's tense face, and restrained manner. That the trouble concerned itself with Turchin he did not for a moment doubt, nor did he propose to scruple in offering assistance which he reasoned Nadine might be prevailed upon to accept. The possession of means enabled a man to be quite generous to a friend and this one he comfortably imagined not too seriously wounded. "Now he would be a hero," he thought.

He was in the hospital before Nadine and Henrietta, and was

admitted to Turchin's darkened chamber. Turchin had not yet roused from his sleep, though his inarticulate murmurs suggested an early awakening. Stepping close to the sick man, Trofimov took his lax hand and held it hard. "You may not believe it, you old fool," he said under his breath, "but I am your friend. You actually got it at last?" He was more moved than he cared to show, especially when Nadine and Henrietta, conducted by Mrs. Livermore herself, were ushered in.

He met Mrs. Morrison's startled glance with a mocking bow, but to Nadine he gave his hand in genuine sympathy. She gripped it as though to hold on to something firm. Her eyes were staring, full of tears, upon her husband.

Her stricken silence was unbearable to the baron who broke it by a fillip: "There's the answer to your high ideals! A man follows his honor, and gets for his pains a silly thing like a sun stroke. The doctor has told me it is that!"

Mrs. Morrison's mouth tightened in anger, but she uttered no word.

"A sun stroke!" Nadine weakly echoed, and fell on her knees beside the bed.

"Is that you Nadine?" Ivan's voice asked weakly. Again his hand reached out for hers, and this time her fingers folded into his.

"It is I, Vanya," she murmured into his ear. He did not open his eyes, but he smiled peacefully.

CHAPTER XXVII

It was many months before General Turchin would have the use of his legs. He had sustained a back injury when his limp body had fallen from his horse, and that, plus the shock of the stroke, rendered him helpless until October. After that he began gradually to revive and mend, but the recuperation was ineffably slow, even after the New Year advanced. He had a return of his feverish illness when he received his discharge from the army in the late fall, and endured further grief when Mrs. Morrison, whose company he begged for plaintively, relayed the sad news of Mihalotzy's death during the Atlanta campaign.

"He was one of my most promising pupils," she said the night they all sat together, waiting to hear the newsboy cry the outcome of the election regarding Lincoln's second term. Lincoln's opponent was none other than his recalcitrant general, George McClellan, making his bid on the Democratic ticket. Trofimov and Susan had remained visiting late into the night. Though Susan showed signs of restlessness, they were indifferent to the news. It didn't matter who should win, both candidates were odious to Susan.

"All we hear about these days," she complained, "is the death of people. As for me, I'm quite used to hearing about death now. Papa says each time there is a war, more people die."

"Each time there is a war, my dear, there are more people to die," said her husband.

"People like Scott and Mihalotzy never really die!" Turchin cried, raising himself in his comfortable easy chair. "What they lived for goes on as long as humanity lasts!"

"A doubtful boon!" sneered Trofimov good naturedly. Now that the first anxiety over Turchin was dispelled and the general was on the way to recovery, he naturally again resumed the role of verbal antagonist; not because he disliked Turchin, but rather because the gruff atmosphere thereby established between them offered a sort of protection against the unknown. He had never actually harmed Turchin, he assured himself, and stood rather to help him once the war was over. Already, he was mulling over plans in his mind with a view to outdistance Brewster, to escape altogether his smarting dependence upon his father-in-law, by making a bold and profitable stroke in a new business venture. More than his father-in-law suspected, he had busied himself lately with secret scouts and informers who had slipped through the enemy lines and had come back with fulsome details of what the weakening armies of General Lee were permitting and causing by way of panic and confusion. The fortunes in land and speculation, to be made by quick-acting men of foresight, were prodigious.

"When men like Colonel Mihalotzy offer their lives, they seek no thanks from citizens like you, baron," Henrietta interrupted. In her bosom laid a small folded scrap of paper. As she looked into Turchin's face that moment they both knew what private memory of the dead Mihalotzy moved her to blink her eyes in order to shake away the tears. It was a crumpled sheet of paper, very much soiled and spattered with mud, which had been found upon the gallant Slav. Since it was generally known that he and Turchin had been fast friends and since his men were under Turchin's command, General Palmer had thoughtfully forwarded to Turchin, this scrap of paper which was part of an unfinished letter.

The letter read, "To my dear friend and teacher, my dearly respected Mrs. Morrison! For very long I have borne in my heart the wish to speak to you, not as a friend, but as a man hoping to have the honor of loving you, of asking you to be...." There it ended.

With a sudden insight into Mihalotzy's secrets, Turchin had felt it the task and duty of a friend to hand this unfinished love letter to Henrietta. With dismay and an overwhelming grief she read it and wept her patent and secret sorrow. She could imagine what Colonel Mihalotzy had intended to write. A suppressed emotion of love was no strange experience to her sensitive being. "The pity of it, General Turchin. The pity of it!" she wept unrestrainedly.

Today with her veiled contempt for Trofimov struggling against her regard for Turchin, she sat quietly among these queerly assorted friends. She had grown remarkably thin. Dark shadows encircled her eyes and gave to her face a perpetual gloom that her unsmiling lips made no effort to contradict.

"Well, Mrs. Morrison, do you think your favorite Mr. Lincoln will be re-elected?" Trofimov baited her in retaliation.

She merely looked at him without altering her expression.

"And to think General McClellan is his political rival!" Susan cried. Turning to Nadine, who was unduly quiet, she continued. "Once I knew his wife; she was always a most distant self-opinionated person, and she treated us quite coolly in Cincinnati. It will make her simply unbearably proud now if General McClellan should win over Mr. Lincoln."

Their words and opinions weighed little with General Turchin, who had with great effort, gone to the polls just as he had on that other Election Day in 1860. He and Henrietta, at any rate, knew a happy satisfaction when Lincoln was re-elected. For them Lincoln was still the idol and emblem of all the things they believed America still stood for. It was for him, the humane man in the White House, that Turchin had striven impatiently to re-enlist before his second test at the polls. He had been politely refused and gently discouraged. Late at night they heard the good news of Lincoln's success. It came like the report of a great battle won.

In the following spring, but a few weeks after his second inauguration, and only a few weeks after Grant accepted Lee's sword at Appomattox, President Lincoln was assassinated. The war had been concluded by Lee's surrender to Grant, immediately after Lincoln's inauguration, almost four years to a day since the first shell was fired into the side of Fort Sumter. The assassin's bullet ended Lincoln's life while yet the spirit of the new Easter was green in the land. A continent wept his loss with a lone, sick brigadier-general in Chicago, who mourned as for a father. Turchin was like a man broken. At times he flew into a violent rage, which tore out of him in loud blasphemy and imprecation against the merciless assassin responsible for the calamity. "Always the evil ones want first of all to silence the voices which have dared to lift themselves against slavery and crime! Silence! How they, the oppressors, wish for silence! Eternal silence in their victims! They do not mind seeing the horrible grimaces of pain, the broken bodies – only and let there be silence. To speak is to commit an offense greater than the damnation of their own mothers! But Mr. Lincoln will never be silenced by death. We who have fought for his God and our God, we shall not be silent." At other times he submerged himself to the lowest depths of despair. These emotions, Nadine could not understand, unable to see what identifications he had made during the long years between the life of Lincoln and the life of his dreams.

Mrs. Morrison, who was more the recipient of this fury and grief, rather than Nadine, who was plainly troubled by its expression, nodded her head sadly. "It is a true challenge, general," she said. "I feel it too, this greater responsibility which now devolves upon all who really mourn Mr. Lincoln." She was serene with her new, stately quietness. "There is a funeral cortege following him to his final resting place. It will stop here in Chicago. You, general, should be among those who honor him by a last service."

"I will be. Nothing could stop my offering to a great man the last earthly service any of us can render him."

Shortly thereafter, General Turchin was visited by a delegation of his old friends from the Tribune, not the least among whom was William Bross, still eager, still enthusiastic, still turning every occasion into a matter for his fertile pen and inclusive imagination. They invited General Turchin to form part of an Honor Guard to watch the coffin of the President while it lay in state for all of a mourning city to view, which invitation Turchin accepted enthusiastically.

Although Trofimov detested the funeral and the leering mobs equally, he felt that it behooved him to make an appearance. His father-in-law, with a more ruthless individualism, flatly refused his wife's pleading request to attend. "I disliked him living; I dislike him dead; I shall never cease thinking he made a mess of this country!" was his final dictum.

The city was draped in black when the long train of mourners paraded to Lincoln's bier. Shops and saloons closed appropriately for the occasion and almost all the citizens were garbed in black, as though for the loss of a personal friend. Friends and foes came alike to pay their respects, and for that one day it appeared to Turchin that a spiritual intactness had descended upon every one. He stood erect and stiff, albeit that his legs felt shaky and his head throbbed with a thousand incidents of the past four years. And as he stood, he wept openly and shamelessly.

"You are making an exhibition of yourself, Turchin," Trofimov hissed in his ear as he passed him. But Turchin was indifferent to Trofimov's rebuke, and gave himself freely to the rending emotions which filled his heart. Today, standing long hours at his post, he felt himself the old man he considered himself to be. He was forty-three, poor, wrecked in health, and beaten in spirit. Lincoln lay dead; his face as it was visible in the coffin was at peace. This fact Nadine had adduced as a sort of comfort for him, though she would not reveal that she had a basis for comparison; that in his own study in the White House, she had actually talked with him for a few memorable moments. This was to be her everlasting secret, bound up with that other, that deep, searing shame, which now lay like a paralyzed thing in her heart, unable to prevent her from following where Dimitri led. That gentleman led nowhere, and yet he freed her in no way. He had for nearly two years played the casual friend of her and her husband, but his eyes still sent her eloquent messages, and his fingers, wandering lazily over her arm when a chance moment favored the dalliance, were warm and inviting.

At last the ceremonies of sorrow were over. The friends met together at the house on Division Street.

"I think there is something so vulgar and common in making a public display of Mr. Lincoln," Susan began as soon as they were seated and Nadine had hurried off into the kitchen to prepare tea.

"It is neither vulgar nor common, I suppose, baroness," Turchin retorted, "to make a public display of the ridicule heaped on all a great man held sacred - the loyalty to one's country, which is the pledge citizens make to one another. Yes, to one another! This is a democracy, baroness." He made no effort to hide the sarcasm with which he stressed the title.

Trofimov, plainly enjoying his wife's wrath and discomfiture, laughed aloud. "Turchin, how you can hate," he declared. "Why don't you take to heart the kindliness of your favorite's last words? He said 'malice toward none', not even little goslings like my precious Susan."

"I shall take them to heart," Mrs. Morrison stated softly. "I may as well inform you, my good friends, that I shall leave Chicago soon."

"But where will you go?" Susan inquired curiously. "You are not a married woman, and it is not meet for you to be traipsing alone, all over the country. You are forever disgracing us, Henrietta." She spoke in a lofty tone, relying on her marital perquisites to lend weight to her admonitions.

"But she is a rich unmarried woman, my love. Money makes an excellent duenna, eh, Mrs. Morrison?" remarked the baron.

Mrs. Morrison was speaking to Turchin who seemed strangely wounded by her change of plans; as if she rejected him, and proved the innate separation he had always hoped friendship would efface. "I shall travel a bit, and give up my house, which is up for sale now, and the money from which will continue my workingmen's clubs for a while. Then I shall start a school in Carolina. Or perhaps I shall go back to Massachusetts - my folk come from there originally, you know - and open a school for those who can afford to go to no other." How breathless she was as she elaborated her intentions.

"You should get married again," said Nadine, coming in just as Henrietta had finished speaking. "Is she not still a young and lovely woman?" addressing herself to the whole room. Curiously she felt for Turchin, for the vacancy in his heart so often lacerated by the loss of friends.

"Down South!" Turchin mused. "That is not a life for you, Mrs. Morrison. That is work for a man. There is an entire country to reconstruct if all of General Sherman's plans are to be carried out. The country is being occupied by troops. You will see much hate and backwardness in an occupied country. It will be like beginning at the very start of society."

"All the more reason for my going," she responded. "I want to help. There are displaced slaves. They are ignorant, in want of the most elemental essentials."

"Ha!" Trofimov cried. "What a Roman holiday it will be for those who can take advantage of the primal chaos. A few hundred will buy abandoned plantations. Labor is cheap. Turchin, why don't you go down and make yourself some money? I shall invest in you!"

"Not in me you won't," Turchin retorted brusquely. "It will take at least fifty years to industrialize the South, and it must be industrialized. Why should I go backwards? I have no love for the South. My place is among those already advanced enough to appreciate progress and industry! Here, right here, where no long healing from brutal whips is necessary, we can progressively push ahead. Those people down south, who aided and abetted traitors, are a lost generation. I want none of them. And as for the free men, let them come north! Only here will they feel the absence of chains and tethers which, though broken in fact, are still binding upon them in their souls."

"You try my patience," Trofimov snapped. They had all forgotten Mrs. Morrison's quiet words, and she made no second reference to her plans. Soon she made all her arrangements, and left Chicago, but not before disposing of her books and fine china to the Turchins. Her staid old mansion she sold to Susan's father, who, for once in his life, paid a price without quibbling.

Trofimov was one of those fortunate men against whom, it seemed, fortune never turns away. By the time the war came to an end he had his clever fingers in many enterprises, and his attention always on the alert for new ones. Nothing was too small to engage his speculating eye. He was gracious without being kind and ruthless without being cruel. It pleased him to retain as thankful friends men whom he had fleeced without compunction in business transaction.

"Soon, Nadine, I shall be able to buy anything I wish, anything! Lord, what a sense of freedom knowledge like that gives a man! That is real freedom!" He and she were strolling in Humboldt Park while Turchin had gone ahead to make a round of visits among his friends in the city.

"And what is it you would buy when you are able to buy anything?"

"The moon and the silver it sheds! Remember the moon on the ocean the night we met?"

She was silent. "You were so beautiful. To touch you was like grasping a fistful of moonbeams. You dare not try lest you perish with the disillusionment."

She bit her lips. "You never brave that one thing, do you, Dimitri?"

"Disillusionment? Of course not! Defeat I expect. That's in the fight. Success, I expect because I think myself capable of grasping it or bargaining for it. But disillusionment - ha! That would imply a maudlin belief in the impossible, and once the impossible is believed to have been reached, disillusionment is the result! No, my lovely Nadine, I find the sure thing marvelously exciting."

Wishing to change the subject, which made her uneasy and sore at heart, she asked him about his projected trip to Washington.

"It is a city of great decisions," he answered cruelly, for his eyes held no regret for that other Washington trip, not even a shade of repentance. "I shall enjoy the fancy victory parade, the jejune posturing of the conquering heroes. I have secured a good view from an upper story of a hotel, the one you stopped in. I want to enjoy the privilege of gazing down upon great generals marching on parade, about whom I shall know this, my dear; that their guns will boom when men like me want them to."

Turchin at this juncture, rejoined them, and was made acquainted with the baron's intention to attend the Grand Review in Washington. A dark flush of quick anger spread over his face, and for an instant he looked full and furiously into his friend's eyes with a barely restrained animosity which said clearly how unjust it was, that he whom he suspected to have leaned heavily toward the traitors, was possessed of the means to attend a glorious Review to which he had no honest right, even as an innocent spectator, while he, for want of the money, must remain in Chicago!

"I was thinking, my friend," Trofimov said with a bland smile, guessing fully the emotions with which the other contended, "that you might care to make one of our party. There is room to accommodate you. We go on our own private coach."

"Who goes?" Turchin demanded with some truculence, though he was suddenly bereft of all harsh feelings toward the baron.

"Brewster and some friends of his."

"I do not go with Brewster!"

"The war is over, remember," Trofimov coaxed in just the properly persuasive tone.

Therefore, it transpired that on the 19th of May in 1865, Turchin made the long journey to Washington in the company of Brewster and Trofimov. He was not an affable travelling companion and irritated Brewster who made no effort to include him in his conversations. "One can't open his mouth to say a word on the most trivial topic without eliciting oration from the Muscovite," he growled. Turchin had gone to smoke on the observation platform, and Trofimov was Brewster's confidant. "For a man as poor as a church mouse, with a miserable pittance from the army, if that, I think him remarkably insolent."

"His wealth is of another coin than ours," Trofimov replied.

"You must refer to his charming lady," said Brewster. "I admit she is a rare creature." He was pretending to stare out of the window. "I fancied at first you were unseasonably attached to Madame Turchin."

Trofimov met his glance with mockery when at length he turned to confound him. "A man has many attachments," he said, "but the contract alone is binding. That's what essentially counts, the contract."

"You are certainly gallant these days," was Brewster's final comment, with a snort.

In Washington Turchin became so agitated over the gay spectacle and scenery, that Trofimov was embarrassed with his childishness, and feared he might have a relapse. He watched him covertly, somewhat dismayed at the unfeigned reverence which lit up his eyes, and gave him a fanatical character. The streets were full of pedestrians and horsemen. Carriages ran so close to one another that wheels were likely to scrape, people to scream, men to argue. But such life color and bustle Turchin had not seen before, not even in Moscow when the Easter Festival convoked the people from every part of the land.

On the day of the Grand Review, he was barely restrained by the baron from racing pell-mell into the street in order to join the members of the Cumberland Army, the men who had marched through Georgia to the sea. As it was, he sat fidgety and overwrought at the wide window. "They are all there; Sherman, Grant, Thomas, Logan and Palmer, besides many, many more unknown; they are on foot and on horse and walk with the thousands who will never march again." He spoke loudly like a man conscious of his deafness, trying therefore to make his companions hear.

"See, see them all; the boys from Shiloh and Stone River and Chickamauga. Their spirits march with their comrades!" And standing up as he shook off Trofimov's restraining hand, he made a salute and he would not reseat himself while his comrades were marching below.

"You see how glorious a people's victory is!" he cried still more loudly. "It is an everlasting testament of democratic superiority. Mark it well, Mr. Brewster! There, before you are the living and the dead. They give you the lie if you think this republic can live divided, half free and half slave."

No other of the party shared his sentiments. He gained nothing but sour looks from all who were near him, but he was impervious to these, as he was to anything save the Grand Review and the memories it evoked. From it he drew new life, new purpose, it seemed, and when at last they were ready to make the return journey, he felt he had been cured of all his physical and psychic ills. He spoke most cheerfully of his future prospects, lent himself charmingly to the general discussion, and frequently lost himself obligingly in his own voiceless reminiscence, which permitted Brewster to hold the floor at his will. So far was he pleased with the changed mood that Turchin carried away with him from Washington, that Brewster allowed himself to remember that he had held, if not an admiration for the man previously, at least a healthy respect. "What great inspiration do you take away with you, General Turchin," he was prompted to inquire. To that Turchin made a ready reply, that a long entertained resolution was now concretized; that he aspired to authorship. Not penny-a-line fiction, but serious workmanship for serious minds; that the reverence paid to the recent victors proved conclusively that his fellow Americans had come of age; that they were prepared, by the agony they had lived through, to hear such voices as dared to tell the truth plainly.

"You mean to say you wish to write books?" This was extremely amusing to Brewster, and even the baron hid a smile.

"I consider writing the truth in any form, the highest duty of a citizen who knows whereof he speaks. I know about war. I know that by analyzing wars we can abolish them, by knowing a weakness we can therefore fashion a strength."

And this labor of love he set himself to do as soon as he was again settled in Chicago. Fervently he worked on his book, which he entitled "Military Rambles" and in which he set forth the problems of the War of Rebellion, clearly and succinctly. He took time to solicit for its publication with persistency, finally securing a publisher through the kind intervention of his friends and a few of Mrs. Morrison's. John B. Turchin had become an author.

The book was not however a success. At any rate, it was not a substitute for remunerative employment, and consequently after two issues of it in pamphlet form, the entire project had to be abandoned in favor of a more immediate and profitable source of revenue.

Just about that time, they received a short note from Mrs. Morrison who was in the East lamenting the prevalent lack of all facilities to encourage new talent which, she prophesied was the most promising material to be looked to for a speedy recovery from the ills of war. This letter from his friend gave Turchin the idea of establishing experienced engineers like himself to make advantageous contacts between inventor and manufacturer. He worked energetically at this venture, and managed to earn for some time a meager livelihood which for his simple tastes seemed adequate, but for his wife, it was a beggarly stipend on which they could neither keep up appearances nor enjoy the common decencies. Poor Nadine told herself that she expected no fortune, that she had no wish to emulate Mrs. Trofimov nor the fine ladies who constantly filled her upstairs sitting room. But the last fleeting years of her early life were declining rapidly. Her youth seemed spent. In the gold of her hair she often detected faded strands which, without the adornments of fashion, seemed pitiless reminders of the evanescent desires she now wished to forget.

As kindly and persistently as she could, Nadine urged Turchin to avail himself of Dimitri's proffers of financial help, but he stubbornly refused assistance. He continued to be a solicitor of patents for several years, and always with undepleted, resurgent enthusiasm whenever he furthered some young fellow's dreams.

"We will get nowhere," she often remonstrated with him. What gratitude is there ever in the bosom of one of these young inventors? What do you gain for yourself by pushing another's ambitions?"

"Happiness and self respect. This land is great and new skills are needed. A man must lend his talents where they are most needed. That's why I do this work. If these children succeed, in like measure do I."

In despair she appealed one day to Trofimov, that he use his influence, to persuade Turchin out of his idealistic foolishness. "It is not that I do not appreciate his motives," she said, "but for years now he has frittered away his real abilities in fostering amateurs and pretenders."

So distraught and pressed for money was she at the time, that she departed from her usual dignity and proud independence and allowed herself to plead in the presence of Susan and Susan's parents.

"Your husband is a fool," was Mr. Brewster's response to this.

"For a man who seems to know some of our best people," Susan sneered, "he certainly fails to profit by them." She had never overcome her disaffection at the mere mention of General Turchin. All manner of personal spite she found convenient to vent on him; his greatest fault being a simplicity she interpreted as an affront to her aristocracy.

"He was formerly very friendly with General McClellan, was he not," Mrs. Brewster remembered. "Why, General McClellan aimed to be president." Satisfied that she had described the ultimate elevation of Turchin's friends, she sat back solemnly.

"Well, Madame, the general's aim was bad," Trofimov put it acidly.

"General Turchin might take advantage of his noble title. He has a title in Russia, has he not? I should think a real title is superior to a military title." Susan uttered these words with bright malice in her eyes, directed fully upon Nadine, but including her husband as well.

"Madame Turchin is fully aware of the value attached to titles," Trofimov silenced his wife. He made no effort to disguise the contempt for her which he brought to his words.

"Well," Brewster said with nice punctilio, "I see no sense, when one needs money in not taking advantage of the opportunities available to one claiming aristocratic heritage. It did not hurt you, my boy, to sound your own horn."

"Sometimes I do believe his is a tin one, papa," Susan cried.

The subject was carried to exhaustion, and the purport of Madame Turchin's request and concern forgotten. In astonishment over the vulgar squabble she was privileged to witness, in a sort of shame for Dimitri's relations, and in hurt pride for her summary dismissal from the minds of all, she took her leave, scarcely missed even by Trofimov who was busy in rebuttal.

After that Nadine made no second appeal. Proudly she received the baron and his lady as cordially as heretofore; proudly she offered them her plain fare; just as proudly she forced herself to accept their few invitations to join the bevy of newly acquired friends fluttering and flattering about the wealthy baron. With her regal dignity she made up for the lack of jewels. With her steady forbearance she shamed those who, by signs or words, impugned her husband. Her loyalty was fiercely defensive.

Turchin's business went from bad to worse through 1867 and 1868. In 1869, a small break in the monotony of their spartan existence occurred. They received an invitation to attend the wedding of one of Turchin's former young lieutenants. This was a forthright, intelligent young man named Joseph Benson Foraker. Foraker had been one of the first officers to follow Colonel Scott's example in extolling and defending the Russian against adverse criticism. Though there had never sprung up between them an intimacy comparable to that existing between Turchin and Scott, the young lieutenant had, none the less, maintained through the years an abiding affection for his crusty old commander. With sincerity, he requested the honor of Turchin's presence at his wedding in Cincinnati, and thither the Turchins betook themselves for a holiday they could ill afford. The office was accordingly closed during the period of their absence. He tacked up on the door, a carefully printed, neat card, underscored with the information of his departure for all to read, and the date of his return in heavy black crayon as if to punctuate his optimistic turn of mind. However, to Nadine he wryly confided that his clients, being such rare birds, would in all probability barely notice his absence, be it ever so prolonged.

In Foraker's home, he and Nadine were received with graciousness and kindness and here they remained as guests until after the wedding ceremony. All would have passed as a pleasant experience to Nadine had not one of the house-guests inadvertently mentioned a piece of old political gossip to the effect that while still Secretary of State, under Johnson, Seward, fulfilling a promise made by Lincoln, had negotiated and closed a deal whereby the United States had purchased Alaska from Russia. "It is no wonder Johnson nearly got himself impeached!" the narrator ended. "Such a piece of deviltry to be perpetrated upon an unsuspecting public. It was his duty to prevent it. As for me, I should not hesitate, though I have no proof to substantiate me, to state that this is all tied to that other business of the Russian fleet in '63. Five million dollars for an icebox of no use even to the Eskimos! What earthly good is a frozen wasteland to the taxpayers?"

Turchin made haste to inquire the details of this rumor, and the gentleman, an Ohio congressman, freely, and with peppery relish recounted everything he knew about the matter.

"Why, sir," the narrator said pompously, "that land went a-begging in all the courts of Europe - and for only two million! Does it not strike any sensible man as a piece of skullduggery for us to pay five million for the same article?"

Turchin was in a brown study. Naturally he was familiar with the incident of the Russian fleet mysteriously arrived and ostensibly unsolicited. Since then it had been common knowledge that four more war vessels of the Czar's had also anchored in the Pacific. He had taken it as an omen of good will, and had felt with many others, that Russia was giving an earnest display of her good intentions by thusly protecting the American coastline against foreign invasion in case of European help to the Confederacy.

"It is my opinion that poor old Seward was committed by Lincoln to buy Alaska," the narrator continued. "He was compelled to it! Yes sir! I have no doubts that in secrecy our late Mr. Lincoln contracted for that very fleet. I imagine that it would cost about five million, to furnish and keep a fleet of nine or ten vessels in our waters for as long as they stayed. And it is my opinion Mr. Lincoln is to be severely criticized for that, and for other duplicities. He was not king to act with our money in that arbitrary fashion."

Hearing Mr. Lincoln's name used in that tone, Turchin took instant umbrage. "Is it the part of a congressman of the United States to vilify the intention of our great, martyred leader?"

"Vilify, sir!" the congressman shouted. "Vilify Mr. Lincoln, indeed! Is it not poor Mr. Johnson who is being vilified, for Mr. Lincoln's secretiveness? Poor Johnson has to honor a debt the late President assumed for us to pay. This purchase of a useless hunk of ice will be to Lincoln's undying discredit, let me assure you. It is all a feint to throw dust in our eyes. Honest Abe, indeed! Alaska is what we are saddled with in order to pay for a fleet which did no one any good, unless it was Mrs. Lincoln, who was said to be quite a belle among the officers, visiting the ships at her will."

Unable to control his wrath any longer, Turchin drew himself up like a fighting cock, readying to strike. "I am Russian by birth," he began calmly and coldly, "but I am a loyal American by choice and inclination. I do not defend Russia, though in fairness to her I see nothing to castigate in a gracious friendliness on her part. Is it not just as reasonable, and much more courteous to the memory of a great man, to believe that the Russian Fleet, passing this way, merely stopped to make a courtesy call? Is that so unheard of? I tell you it is not. You are not well informed of these practices, if you contend otherwise. And what if it is as you say? Is it a wrong Russia did us, to post herself here when we were weak, when our ships were all pressed in the task of blockading our enemy? If you are as receptive as you show yourself to be today, how readily then, in a crisis would you have approved our President's need to act quickly? We had no time for persuasive arts when the rebels were mowing us down in our tracks!"

"How dare you, sir!" The old gentleman was sputtering with rage. "What impertinence is this, Foraker, from your - your guest?" Turning and churning, the esteemed politician stalked out of the room as twenty pairs of eyes turned obliquely from Turchin, who could not mistake, but yet failed to understand, how he had affronted Foraker's friend. Foraker, a rising lawyer and politician, was involving himself heavily in delicate state matters, which he was required to attend, and properly evaluated his friend and adviser, who found himself mortally offended by the fervid general.

"Softly, sir," he cautioned Turchin nervously. "He lost two sons at Gettysburg."

Nadine during this exchange of words, was mortified, but dared make no allusions afterward to this unfortunate and necessary curtailment of their otherwise pleasant visit. Foraker had no need to press Turchin to be circumspect. He was firmly determined to depart on the following day. He was prevailed upon to stay long enough to attend the marriage service, but not a moment longer. "I am sorry young Foraker is playing in politics," he complained to his wife. "Politicians, the ruthless, selfish sort, will contaminate him. He will forget the lessons we taught him at Chickamauga and Missionary Ridge.

CHAPTER XXVIII

"I cannot understand," said Turchin one day to Baron Trofimov, "why, with the whole country booming, my business should be steadily declining. I myself do not mind declining with the years. I expect that, sometimes in a man's life, the time comes for him to realize that the crest has been reached, and that it is time for him to move downwards. It is even good like that. But a business, which has a life apart from the man, ought not to be like that."

"You are obviously in the wrong business," said the baron. "No one will thank you for minding their business which is precisely what your business seems to be. I have tried as a friend these many years to tell you as much. A man with your talents should have utilized them - for himself. I have discovered that people like being used, providing you flatter them in the process. They find their purpose for being in serving you, and thank you into the bargain."

The two men were sitting in Trofimov's office. It was early in the evening, and neither man showed a desire to terminate the conversation. It was not often that Turchin sought out this old friend for advice. Today he showed a nice respect for him, and Trofimov was enjoying the novelty; it proved his theory that nothing was so successful as success. For a long time he had been aware of Turchin's bad luck in the patent-soliciting business, and of his own accord had discreetly discussed with the officials at the Illinois Central the possibility of re-instating Turchin in his old work. He wielded considerable influence, coupled as his own name and untold resources were with his father-in-law's. But for all his good offices, there seemed to be no place for a man nearly fifty years old in an organization filled gradually with the young and vigorous talent of the country. Surveying and engineering in those days still entailed hard physical labor, and the general's health would not warrant the strain, Trofimov was told.

He was turning over in his mind some scheme whereby he might offer the proud Turchin for Nadine's sake at least, a sort of suitable employment in his own far-reaching enterprises. A two-fold delicacy prevented his candor; first he was not willing to disclose to him the exact nature of his business, which, if that irascible patriot suspected it, would bring down the torrent of his reproaches and scorn; and secondly, he honestly hoped to spare him the humility of patronage. "Why should I be so tender of his sensibilities?" he asked himself irritably. "It is as hard to do something for that old fool as to gain a difficult end for one's self."

Suddenly a burst of clamoring voices was heard on the pavement below. Police whistles were blowing madly, and fire bells made a deafening din above which neither man could hear the other. Both leapt to the window from which they could see, shooting across the sky, heavy black clouds spiraling around and unfurled by tongues of flame.

"My God! Turchin yelled. "A fire, a scourge from heaven!" They dashed out of the room, and disappeared in the confusion of the crowds already densely massed along the avenues. The human congestion caused a traffic jam, which in turn caused a panic to tear through the hysterical crowds. A scream pierced through the uproar, and was at once caught up and amplified by a thousand throats. With elbows and legs they forced their way through the crowds which carried them willy-nilly towards the center of the city where a terrifying fire of gigantic proportions was lighting the evening sky. Corps of policemen and firemen were trying frantically, but in vain, to thrust the surging crowds back from the burning sector, already blazing like an inferno. As though they were made of paper, instead of wood and stone, one building after another dissolved in the blinding glare, only periodically obscured by fuliginous oily clouds, also immediately swallowed up by the consuming fire. Water mains exploded and gas pipes burst. The wail of onlookers, who knew that hundreds of men, women and children were trapped in the holocaust which could not be abated and the indescribable horror of tumbling walls and a disintegrating world, charged Turchin and

Trofimov with the strength of two teutons. They fought the fire for hours while its havoc was strewn over city blocks.

In the very heart of the conflagration was Turchin's own modest little office where for five years he had been patiently building up a business which gave him more righteousness than income. Washington Street was a shambles when at last, in the dismal grayness of another day, he inspected the ashes which were all that remained to him of his equipment and belongings. But it was not the destruction of millions of dollars worth of property which made him stand grief stricken; only the thought of the wanton destruction of human life.

While Trofimov had long ago left the fire to the firemen, Nadine had continued giving tireless aid during the period of the fire. She had not slept for thirty-six hours, and had torn her best linens into bandages which she soaked in linseed oil to soothe the grievous wounds of the victims. In the breaking dawn she stood beside her husband and like him was covered with gray ash from head to foot. "This is a land of calamities, Vanya!" she said droopingly.

Instantly he bristled. "Nonsense! Things like this are likely to happen when men act the fools and cram into the suffocating confines of a city. All of them come with their packs on their backs to the city! Why don't they stay on the land, and leave the city for those who are traders and thieves! I see in this fire a portentous warning to myself! I have been too long away from the land. Already I feel myself caught like a fly in amber, in the shapeless mass that flows into the city, and so destroys the symmetry of nature itself." He paused and wiped his face, which was rough and dirty, distorted with his inner anger, and fatigued with his arduous labors.

"I believe it is not meant for people to crowd with one another like pigs in a trough. They have a great and green land. What need is there for them to pile their residences in cooped up brick squares, layer upon layer five and six times over? In the city they resemble the madmen who built in their blindness and egotism, the Tower of Babel. God became displeased that arrogant man should think to climb sooner to heaven than the slow way virtue ordained; so he created confusion and agony to illustrate their futile efforts."

Nadine sighed and sat down on a pile of bricks and mortar nearby.

Out of sheer fatigue she began to cry, then laugh, then both to cry and laugh simultaneously, upon which reaction her husband frowned in annoyance, not departing from the train of thought he was pursuing. "People ought to be taught to use the great green fields and meadows, the rivers of plenty which water the lands. They should be taught how to help nature herself fructify the land. They should learn to live in the joy of creation!"

She remembered, irrelevantly, a phrase Mr. Lincoln had spoken to her. She repeated it now to herself, "Counselor for the Lord". Then her broken laughter became shrill, until several people, digging industriously among the ruins, their diligence prompted by a scavenger instinct to salvage some miserable stick or stone from the debris, turned irately toward her. Their anger was fierce and disdainful, as if eager to find an object for its bite. In its radiations Turchin would not remain a moment longer than necessary.

Slowly they trudged homeward as the day increased. Near their house he suddenly took her hand in his. "Nadya", said he with a renewed enthusiasm which always seemed to rise out of his misfortunes like a brave defiance of folly and error, "I have an idea, a wonderful idea. We belong on the land. So many people are flocking to the United States, and so much land is lying idle and neglected, that it occurs to me we can do a real service to the country. We can help new citizens orientate themselves as we have."

She met his assertions and new hopes with no leaping cooperation. Her mind was too tired to brook further problems. Not as quickly as he, did she throw off the creeping fears of poverty and destitution. The one they had surely reached some time ago and the other stared her in the face with brutal frankness. Their home was miserably poor now. Their exiguous purse admitted no entertainment. Even the samovar was only infrequently used, for tea was expensive since the war.

Not only the interior of their house displayed marks of decay; their persons too, were reduced to the unelaborated simplicity which satisfies itself with a requisite comfort, and is grateful for that without hoping for the appurtenances of fashion and style. Only Trofimov, of all their former acquaintances frequented the small house these days. His wife, grown haughtier and more forbidding, as the baron grew richer, neither sent invitations nor came with her husband. Whether the baron resented his wife's manner or not, Nadine never inquired. Often, indeed, she found herself voicing a gratitude toward him for his indulgence, for the secret kindness he often showed; the appearance of an uncalled-for grocer's cart with all manner of viands that the Turchins had almost forgotten existed; the delivery of a bolt of silk which she instantly secreted, afraid to make it up into a gown which could not be worn anywhere; once, even a stack of books for Ivan, which she casually explained, in an effort to shield the donor, to be a bargain she had picked up in a book stall.

Between the baron and Susan there had indeed risen an unbridgeable rift, the worse for manifesting itself in nothing concrete. Susan's mother had recently died and left her personal fortune to her grand-son, a gesture which was meant to show the baron his function in the family. Susan, as though taking a clue from her mother, after a proper display of daughterly grief at her passing, became callously indifferent to the handsome baron, whose charms had long since palled upon her. Vanity and an unmeasurable pride forbade any public exposure of the change, so that even Mr. Brewster, who was growing gouty and quarrelsome, did not wholly perceive the true state of affairs, and even if he had, would have found it enjoyable. He still had a cynical liking for his son-in-law, who, in these attractive middle years of his life, looked more distinguished then when he had pressed youth to his service.

Thus it was to Trofimov that Turchin gladly confided the hopes of a new work in life. "There is a need of such a service that I can render my country", he stated happily. "The more I think about it, the more I'm confident that it's the right thing to do. Surely I can convince influential people to invest in a project to settle waste lands, to turn the barren into the fertile."

"I am willing to give you money, Turchin," Trofimov said, carelessly. "I shall give it to you as an outright gift. But I think your project of a piece with your other follies. Don't ask me to subscribe to it."

At this Turchin grew furious. "I ask for no charity. I would not touch your money given in such a spirit. I might have known that for a man like you it is more savory and delightful to make money by devilish means than to make it by helping other people. I shall borrow money elsewhere."

Not disheartened by this first rebuff, Turchin spent the next few weeks making complicated charts and computations. To the minutest detail he worked out his plans to reconvert the waste lands owned by the railroads, grants of land which could be built into green gardens of plenty, and then he marched with his plans to the head of the land department of the Illinois Central.

Moreover, he prepared a masterly argument which was well received by Mr. Daggy, the land agent of the Railroad. Other railroads were already beginning to utilize the vast grants of land through which their lines ran, and Mr. Daggy was willing to listen to a man who had specific ideas and calculations as well as a keen, well informed mind. "I think it a fine thing to open the land and the country to new settlers, or to people from other sections who would be willing, if the inducement were good enough, to come here and sink their roots. I am especially interested in establishing a colony which will attract people from backward lands like Poland. I believe I know such men. I am sure I know my Slavic peoples particularly. I believe I am fitted to inspire in them the ideals on which this land was founded. In their own language I can convince them, and in the American language, I can prove all that I say."

The land agent listened attentively. The general had much more to say on the subject; how he could discipline men; how personal contact was more effectual than impersonal land sales; how together a community could prosper and create plenty for everyone, investors and agents alike.

A week after his several interviews with the railroad official, he was granted a commission as agent for the Illinois Central, which he received as proudly as a citation. The terms were fairly generous. He was to receive for his share a five percent commission on sales made to persons whom he introduced as customers, providing they resided, at the time of the purchase either outside the state, or north of the Alton Railroad. If the purchaser lived south of the Alton Railroad, he was to receive fifteen percent on every acre sold. The contract ran for a year, and if within that year he had sold four thousand acres, it was subject to renewal.

The first thing he did was to sell his house on Division Street, and with the money realized by the sale he purchased a parcel of land in the area of his operations. His own land he determined to use for the erection of a primitive depot in order to facilitate the movements of families into the colony whose existence he already visualized.

Having assured himself of so much, he next badgered Mr. Daggy, and the whole of the Land Sales Department, until he and it acceded to his demands for their financial assistance in the matter of transportation. His argument was reasonable, and Mr. Daggy saw increased possibilities for attracting many people into the colony, half fares, for a period of six months, besides greatly reduced freight rates for their household goods and livestock.

All this transformed Turchin from the aging man, scarred by disappointments, to a man with a semblance of the sprightly spirit which had been his, fifteen years before.

He felt he had reasons to rejoice in the favorable turn his affairs had taken, for in addition to the cooperation he had gained from Daggy, he had made the acquaintance of a Pole who professed the same colonizing interest in foreign settlements that he had himself. This was a happy coincidence, and offered him the needed impetus of a strong friendship, an ingredient in life which, if present, lent savor to his undertakings.

Soon Michael Michalski and he were constant companions, working and talking and arguing as though they had known each other all their lives. Michalski was gabby, with a curious habit of finishing other people's sentences before they were half uttered. At first Turchin had politely ignored this bad habit until it threatened to create a lasting irritation in the new companionship. Finally, in a serious and fatherly tone, he admonished the Pole. Michalski, with some pique, made an awkward apology and continued to apologize whenever he cut the other off. Eventually his sour apologies became more offensive than his bad manners.

As garrulous as Michalski was, he avoided all direct questions pertinent to the affairs of the new colony. A few facts escaped his guard occasionally and of these Turchin, in a kindly mood, made the most. The man had served his country; he was clean of person and speech; he was amiable at times; and had money to invest in the colony, a prime ameliorative in a partner's character.

At last the time came for them to leave Chicago and begin the new life in Radom, Illinois. Turchin was fortified in his new business by several prospects acquired in Chicago itself, and with these would be tenants he was conferring with eagerly even on the last day of their residence in the city. His wife had methodically packed their belongings, and was awaiting the wagons which would deliver them to the freight yard for shipping. She felt sadly resigned; even a little resentful of the encroachment another summer would inexorably mark on her years: it meant another year of petty economics and exalted hopes in a husband who did not notice the gray in her hair. He would worry about the next President to sit in the White House, instead of worrying about the cruel wasted passage of time. Impersonally, for this of late had become her habit, she envisaged the years lying ahead - she and he farming, tilling, living, dying.

There was no one whom she wished to say her farewells to. There was nothing which held so tender a sentiment for her that she would be loath to part with it, not even the little house, grown like themselves, older and shabbier with the years. Seated during the past hour on a stack of books, she was mindful of Mrs. Morrison who also had fled the city without any fanfare. "I never did justice to her," she said aloud.

At that moment she heard a carriage drive up before the house. Thinking the wheels to be those of the wagon she expected, she rose and went to the door. Flinging it open she almost fell into Dimitri Trofimov's arms. Instantly she retreated, a bright flush staining her cheeks. Her hand automatically went to her disheveled hair which she continued for an awkward moment to smooth. She was at a complete loss for words. It had been many months since they had spoken without his wife or Turchin in the background. Their solitude now, made her immensely embarrassed. But Trofimov, in an angry mood, did not notice.

"I hear you are leaving Chicago," he began at once, crossing the threshold into the house. "This is a mad thing! How can you permit that crazy Cossack to take you away like this from civilized life?"

"He is my husband," she answered, and then reddened in the confusion of her quick realization that by making him this answer she was admitting her lack of enthusiasm. She became suddenly cold and proud. Her unlovely house wrapper and her graying hair notwithstanding, she was lovely in her Junoesque wrath.

Still not noticing her emotional turbulence, he moved familiarly into the next room and laid his stick and hat on the table. He began to pace the bare floor, which stripped of its carpets, rang hollow under his tread. "Nadine," he called her attention. "Nadine, do you realize we are both getting on in years?"

"Look at me!" she retorted. "I am almost an old woman! How could I forget it?"

"You are never an old woman to me, and never will be, even if you live to be eighty!"

"Save your pretty speeches," she replied, though her voice was gentler.

"I am now a rich man, Nadine." As he spoke he wondered at his own weakness in being upset by the news and signs of their leaving. He hardly knew what his next words would be.

"That is good. You wanted that above everything else." Scorn was in her voice.

"I wanted something more once, but you know how things happened!"

"Yes, I know."

"Today, I ask you what once before I asked; perhaps I failed you that other time, but this time I will not. I am able to defy anything now. Come away with me. Stay here, rather, and let me take care of you. With Turchin you will starve."

She looked at him with the first compassion she had known for this man. Passion she had felt; anger and disdain; grief and remorse; but, never compassion. Until now. She shook her head, no anger burning in her cheeks.

"Will you, Nadine? We still have many years ahead of us. We do not need that bright madness of youth. I need what you have for me, the deep tones, the subdued colors, the sweet accent, the touch of home."

"How poetic you have become; you a man of nearly fifty years."

"Flaming youth is not the only time for love, Nadine! The need for love is stronger now. We can afford to take life by the tail!"

"Curious, how you fail to convince me, yet I believe you. I somehow always believe you," she continued, "but it is too late. I go with Ivan. He needs me."

"I need you also! You are an indelible tracing in my being!"

"Yes. I am for you a pattern of strange markings. For you, you have gone far out of yourself, Dimitri, to admit this. But you see, my friend,

I have long ago discovered that you are able to survive my loss. How lucky you are; you can survive almost anything, while Ivan..."

"Who speaks my name?" Turchin laughed, coming in through the open door. And seeing the baron, he shook his hand joyously. "So you came in time to see us leave? For all your dire predictions, you see I am able to fend for myself. Other businessmen, as astute as yourself, did not find my proposed project such a fool's vision! But let us forget all that. Come and see us at Radom. You will, eh?"

In this manner these old friends parted, not to see each other for several years. Turchin was too radiant with his success to remark about the acid congratulations of the baron or the unsmiling gravity of his wife, who scarcely made a remark during all the hours of their journey to their new home at Radom. Once or twice, she confidingly placed her small hand in his, but if security or comfort was what she sought in that warm, safe palm she was disappointed. "Nothing is really changed," she brooded. "I feel the same cold emptiness as before. I feel no pride, no gladness, not even shame, that Dimitri should still offer me degradation which he knows not by that name. Ah, poor deluded man."

Happily for both of them, the new activities, which demanded energy and ingenuity, soon put a convenient cloak about their sore memories - his disappointments and her attachment for Dimitri. In the bracing outdoor life to which they newly accustomed themselves, they found a modicum of peacefulness. She had long hours to herself, for Turchin and Michalski were often on trips to distant parts of the state where they zealously solicited tenants to join the steadily expanding colony. They even went as far as the Appalachians in an effort to persuade miners to become tenant farmers in Radom.

"How is it, friend Turchin," Michalski once asked him after a hard month of travelling and talking, "that you possess so much energy? At your age most men are content to sit still."

"It takes something to believe in, in order to remain young!" was the pleased and confident answer.

"If only a man could know what to believe in these days," the other said cynically. "As far as I have observed men, I find it impossible to believe in anything they say. I don't have your faith in people."

"Words are of little importance. One has to see beyond words.

Many good people are limited because they lack the exact words to say what is in their hearts."

"People have no hearts, friend Turchin. Stomachs and gonads, that's all they have. To satisfy one they call it ambition. To satisfy the other they call it love. Bah! The only thing a man can believe in is the dollar in his pocket and anything or anyone who puts it there!"

Turchin was thoroughly angered by Michalski's words. They sounded much like those that Trofimov had been saying these many years. In Michalski, he had hoped to find one of his own people, sharing with him a dream to do good for people, not a hardened, worldly man like the baron, who spouted the backwash of all dismal sinners. These sinners, having flung everything sacred from them, and finding themselves rudely naked, held that nakedness or realism as they called it was better than clothing, comfort and health of the spirit.

He could not abide a mocking spirit in his co-worker and sought to infuse something of his own ardency into his partner. "There is a more lasting thing to believe in than the dollar. There is love, for example. When a man is young he believes in the love of a God who will bless his endeavors and fulfill his desires; later, in the love of a woman who will be his complete self; still later, he knows these objects of his love are but one, a divine unity begetting his love for mankind. If man loves his fellow man, he makes sensible and honorable his love for all other things."

"I am afraid, friend Turchin, I love but one thing - pleasure. What gives me pleasure is good; what does not is bad and I am at liberty morally to destroy it. I came to this country to get pleasure sooner than I could at home. When I have enough money I shall be able to get more pleasure at home in Poland than here at the same price."

These words, callously spoken, sank like leaden weights into Turchin's heart. This then was the sort of man he had chosen unwisely for his partner. This man could at will flout his dearest wishes, and would not hesitate to do so when and if the project failed to enrich him sufficiently. He was not a kindred soul, not a man who would be a friend, who would stand with him shoulder to shoulder, and share the sacrifices, if called upon to make them, as he would share the profits.

A deep dislike suddenly sprouted between them. Out of the

generality of their speech had arisen the infrangible wall which was to separate them thereafter. Bound by their mutual interest in the financial end of the project, they daily felt the creeping animosity which colored their every other relationship. A year passed without qualifying this disaffection.

What might have come of this tug o' war between two strong minded men, one can only guess, but fortunately for the project and the hundreds of tenants now resident at Radom, a newcomer appeared whose beneficent presence made Turchin's disposition more amenable to the necessity of his association. This newcomer was a young man, Mikhail Vladimirov, who had chanced on the Chicago office where Turchin's agent received foreigners. He had been directed to Radom where he arrived one fine day with three hundred rubles in his pocket, two strong young arms, and as fine a figure of a man as could be found anywhere. He was like a younger edition of Turchin himself, having Turchin's light coloring and the same sort of bright blue eyes. He lacked the aggressive self-assurance which had characterized Turchin as a younger man, but he compensated for the lack with a winning smile no one could resist, not even Michalski, who resisted everything rather successfully. In him Turchin found a well of refreshing candor and unspoiled simplicity, which was all the more remarkable since the man was not unlettered, though born under serfdom. He was in fact a writer in search of materials.

"I do not come to America to become a citizen," he explained simply. "I come because we in Russia must know what the outer world is like. I shall stay here one, two, maybe three years, and then I shall go back."

"Go back! Why should you wish to return?"

"Because I love my country, and if I bring back knowledge, it is my greatest gift to my people!"

"You see," Nadine smilingly addressed Turchin, "he is content to limit his horizons. His own people are enough; he does not seek to embrace all of humanity."

Vladimirov was patently in the dark concerning her words. He looked from husband to wife, and grasped none of the feelings each of these two was seeking to voice.

"Madame Turchin thinks because I see in this country the best face of humanity, that I am perhaps sentimental. Well, perhaps I am. I love progress, and progress is a universal thing no matter at what stage one envisages it. In Russia I thought progress was too slow to be worth waiting for, and in our own Southland, at this moment, progress is too slow. The most advanced expression of citizenship is what challenges my mettle.

"It is the becoming which intrigues me," Vladimirov said. "I like you, I see your ideal as the highest, but I would wish to be a part in the conversion of an illiterate people into an enlightened citizenry." He smiled good-naturedly. "However, sir, it comes to the same thing, if the spirit is right. You probably feel that to reach for a higher state of living denotes an eagerness for a better life. I believe the eagerness is there in all people, and shows itself as opportunity affords - that is, when the time for progress has come." He rose from his seat and came to stand opposite Nadine, who was twinkling her approval. "If I were an American, it is the Southland, where the freedman lives, that I would choose for my field of operation."

Michalski, who arrived at this juncture, and took the seat Vladimirov had left vacant, immediately followed the drift of the discussion. "Yes, friend Turchin, tell our young Russian comrade why it is we interest ourselves in the peasantry of Poland and Russia instead of the freed Negroes." Turning his eyes full upon Vladimirov whom he liked as much as he did Turchin, he laughed harshly. "For two years now people have asked him that same question. I really wonder what his answer to you will be."

"The same as it has always been. It is no secret. I know the people of Europe. They know the land. Land is what we have to deal with. We have no time to waste on a problem which will take years to solve with people who have never been farmers, only menials. Moreover, I think beyond the few of a land. I think of the entire people! We have an entire continent to cultivate, not merely a few unfortunates. By furthering the development of this area, where railroads already run like living nerves through our body, we store an energy which the whole country can use. It is the building of that national energy which interests me!"

"As far as I am concerned," Michalski said, "I am content to colonize Poles. They are problem enough for me. At least I know I am not interested in them personally, but in selling land. I'd sell it to the Negroes if they could buy it. But, even if we could get them here, they would not be tolerated, despite the fact that friend Turchin will not believe that. He won't admit that people with railroads and industry are capable of prejudices. He thinks a pianoforte in a drawing room means that people love music!"

The atmosphere grew strained as Turchin's features clouded with hard repressed anger. Every time the Pole opened his mouth, as though with a veritable genius for saying exactly what would annoy him, he felt the constriction of dislike and animosity. In this third year of their partnership, he felt more than ever that they were like two horses of unequal strength and inclination, yoked in an unhappy alliance. Now he contained himself, for speaking would make him appear undignified before the young Russian. To Vladimirov it would have been an insult to explain that Michalski operated on the premise that a colony of foreigners would be looked upon with dislike by the neighboring citizens. Michalski had fiercely opposed his efforts to hire an agent in the city, one who would induce native stock to come and mingle with the foreigners. Therefore, he now remained silent, and trusted Vladimirov to discern the state of affairs for himself.

This, the young man readily did, once he began to mingle familiarly with the ruddy men and matrons who were fast building the Radom colony into something exemplary. He found, among other things, for the people talked freely with him, that two camps actually existed. One camp consisted of persons who liked and admired the direct and non-haranguing Michalski; this group looked to him for leadership and sympathy. The other camp followed Turchin blindly, not because they understood him, but because he bullied them, scolded them, taught them, and understood their yearning religious and emotional needs. The one man was God-less, and attracted those elements of the tenants who agreed with him that life was a mean, hard business. Turchin for all his shouting and peremptory discipline, was God-loving, if not God-fearing, and he taught his people a rich satisfaction, which was an adornment to the primitive life they perforce had to endure while the basic necessities were being built and instituted.

Vladimirov threw in his lot with Turchin. He did not alienate Michalski however, and in time formed an indispensable link between the two partners, and later, between Turchin and a newly arrived priest, who at Turchin's invitation, joined the Radom tenants soon after his own advent into the colony.

CHAPTER XXIX

For three or four years, with Turchin, Michalski, Vladimirov, and Father Jan Wollovski as leaders, the Radom colony prospered. The land along the rail line was reclaimed for arable purposes. Verdant meadows stretched far into the flowering river lands. Houses were built and roads were cut and laid. Wild woods became cultivated orchards with slender new saplings to delight Turchin each spring. A communal center was established, and a small school house was erected where Nadine supervised social activities, and instructed both the adults and children in English lessons. The Polish priest became increasingly bitter that English had supplemented the native tongue, and as time went on, his resentment was further aggravated since the church he was promised by Turchin never materialized.

The priest, a small, thin man with a perpetual complaint on his face, was the same type Turchin remembered well from Russia. He was not an old man, yet his ideas were ancient and dogmatic. Not with love and intelligence did he seek to maintain his influence with the tenants of Radom; not by teaching the American spirit of amalgamation and Freemasonry; but by the time-worn methods of prayer, ritual and unquestioning subjection to the church and to himself as a representative of the church. It was inevitable that he and Turchin would soon be at odds. Not a day passed without friction and antagonism between them.

"I am teaching these people the ways of America!" Turchin brusquely reminded him one day. "I invited you to join us because I feel a practice of religion softens a man's heart, so that he can live happily with other men. These people are religious. It is right for them to mitigate these hard first years by the help of your intelligent guidance; but not your insufferable mumbo-jumbo of ingrained narrowness! What do you teach my people? To think they owe nothing to anyone save the church? You, should teach them love and tolerance instead of dissension and strife!"

The priest scorned and defied him. "Not you, Mr. Turchin, called me to my people. God called me. These people who are torn from their old moorings need me to have the entire burden of keeping them faithful without the aid of the church you promised to build. You have a hall for making music and merriment. You have a schoolhouse where the children are taught to look above themselves. But where is the church you promised? I can only think you are an impious doubter whose word is the word of a worldly recusant!"

This promise of a church, for which there was neither time nor money, led to innumerable arguments between the priest and Turchin, a fact which did not add to the harmony of the colony, but indeed further divided its many men and women. Orthodox followers of the priest began to abet his efforts to expel Turchin. Once having opened the way for the church, Turchin could not easily rid himself of Father Wollowski or his insidious influence.

There were countless other problems and Turchin received little assistance in solving them. From the first, the priest was admittedly a third factor in the management of the colony. Michalski manipulated the cash interests, and Turchin the loans, credits, land sales, and such outside activities as pertained to the marketing of the surplus food stuffs raised by the colonists.

For another five years, though beset by difficulties, Turchin realized both profit and satisfaction in the project. Then the tiny cracks and fissures which had been developing, widened dramatically; the factions began to war among themselves, joining only long enough to war upon Turchin, whom they now accused of selfishness and tyranny. Disgruntled tenants threatened open rupture. Many actually moved, leaving behind unpaid debts which Turchin, having given personal guarantees, had to assume. The priest declared his secession, and stealthily gave Turchin's competitors his conniving ear with Michalski's consent. In lofty verbiage they plotted to save the souls of Radom from their uncompromising founder and leader. This required patience which Michalski unfortunately lacked.

One day Michalski disappeared, taking a good portion of the available money with him, a catastrophe that threw the tenants into rage and disorder, resulting finally in irreconcilable conflict which Vladimirov's best efforts could not alleviate or pacify. Vladimirov, with saddened heart, was soon to return to Russia and would have wished to leave untroubled waters behind him. But things had gone too far. Reconciliation between Wollowski and Turchin was impossible. The priest sneered at Turchin's financial difficulties and obligations, besides making every effort to inflame the tenants. He promised them that allegiance to Turchin meant their utter ruin, not to mention their spiritual damnation. Eventually, Turchin discovered his machinations.

"I shall whip him out like a dog!" he cried enraged and indignant. "He is a disgrace to the cloth he wears! He has not been a softening and purifying influence! He has been an abrasive, a harsh abrasive rubbing everyone the wrong way!"

"Your reasons for ordering him away," Nadine said heavily, "will be misunderstood. He has many loyal adherents. You will antagonize all your people."

Vladimirov, a party to their discussion, had an inspiration. "Let us put the matter of the priest to the vote," he exclaimed. "Let the people vote him out. He must obey the will of the people!"

So it was eventually decided. With pride and humble gratefulness Turchin discovered that the majority of his tenants voted for the dismissal of the priest, who thereupon left in high dudgeon and with violent maledictions. His departure left Turchin at last in complete control of the colony's affairs, which was no blessing, as he shortly learned. The vengeful Wollovski and the absconding Michalski, as well, soon joined forces with Turchin's competitors from other railroads wishing to establish colonies on their idle land-grants. They conspired together to draw off many colonists already residing at Radom, and to outmaneuver Turchin in acquiring new ones. In addition, the chief rival Turchin had in land sales, a bright but ruthless young man with an industrious zeal for gain, began a malicious whispering campaign among the neighboring farmer folk of the area. As a result, within a year, Radom found little market for its crops and cattle, but instead faced hostile aversion whenever they ventured into the nearby villages and towns. The whole colony suffered in gloomy isolation and ostracism.

Meanwhile, Turchin's debts grew enormous, and might have snowed him under, had not Trofimov, at this time, made a visit to Radom and offered him a five thousand dollar loan with Turchin's house as security. In his pocket now reposed Trofimov's bank draft for five thousand dollars. This all came about so casually that Turchin was under the impression that the baron in coming to them, had availed himself of his old invitation. He did not suspect that Nadine had written of their troubles to her old friend. He thankfully accepted the loan and plunged into his problems with renewed vigor.

The years at Radom had affected Nadine markedly. Her youthful beauty, which had lingered long upon her, was starkly absent, the more noticeable so since the outlines of it testified to its former existence. Her hair was now as beautifully gray as it had once been beautifully golden. The baron's own head was also handsomely gray at the temples. His former luxuriant dark curls now receded far from the brow, but added rather than detracted from his personal charms.

The baron and she met, spoke, touched hands and were silent. Her blue eyes were the only remnant of her beauty, still bright with undimmed youthfulness. His dark eyes were still glowing alive, brilliant and more inviting than ever; in spite of the habitual mockery which now lived in their depths.

"Well, my country cousins," he began, "I have interested myself at last in your nonsense. How could I resist the glowing description of your acolyte, Vladimirov? Did you know, Turchin, that your disciple came calling on me in Chicago? A convert, that's what you have in him! He will return to Russia and deport half the peasants to this country!"

"A fine young man, fine young man," Turchin beamed. He listened with pleasure as Trofimov continued. He explained how Vladimirov had praised Radom, and predicted great profits. He had come personally, therefore, to invest in Radom, he said. Boldly he looked at Nadine, as he spoke. The first shock of her appearance soon yielded to the subtle spell he could never escape, once in her presence. Not a middle-aged woman stood before him. Not a thin figure with pale cheeks and roughened hands. He looked at her as she was, and the image of what she had been, superimposed itself upon her present form. In his eyes lay the miracle of his illusion. And she, reading it rightly, felt an unwonted warmth steal over her, into her bosom, into her slim hard fingers, into her lips where the blood charged with sudden willfulness.

"You see us reduced, Dimitri," she said quietly. "We are now poor and old people! We might even have been grandparents!"

"Old people!" Turchin scoffed indulgently. "Women are always afraid of age. What is wrong with old age? Are we to remain always young and competitive with those coming after us? We have had our great moments. We have the fruits, the happiness of steadfast loyalties. We have something young people only hope to achieve - experience."

"Still rhapsodizing, Turchin?" Dimitri sneered. "You are the modern version of Don Quixote."

"Ah, Trofimov, today you cannot annoy me. I see past your jibes. You are, at bottom, in your own way, a good man. I am ashamed to think I once almost believed you disloyal. You are what you are, and I must learn to accept all people on that basis. Yes, I have been wrong about you."

"It's the money which makes him so tolerant all of a sudden, "the baron laughed to Nadine. "It never fails, this thing you dear people abhor so much, when it is honest and open and without fancy appendages; money - it is the best leveler, the best appeaser, the most eloquent counsel, the most intelligible partisan."

"Come with me," Turchin was jollity itself. The burden of debt being lifted momentarily from his shoulders, he found even the sly taunts of Trofimov not unkindly. "Come out and see the lands," suggested Turchin. "You have a stake in them now." Trofimov accepted and the two men strolled into the spring sunshine, into the greenness and blueness, the youth of the land.

Trofimov returned alone an hour later. He found Nadine clothed somewhat more becomingly in one of her outmoded gowns whose laces she had freshened in honor of Dimitri's presence. Her hair was brushed and softly braided over her head. Her person exuded a reminiscent, faint odor of wood-violets. The skin on her face seemed still fine and tender, and she had rubbed lard over her hands to make them appear smoother and younger. Her cheeks had a fleeting color of their own.

"Tell me, Nadine, are you not satiated with this rustic existence?"

"Even if I were not, Dimitri, what then is there for me?"

"I am for you," he answered doggedly. "The years only prove it more and more. Listen, Nadine; I, who can buy the youngest and prettiest face, who may have every diversion invented by man, who can afford everything, find all I have to be tasteless, because I cannot rid my mind of you."

"You need the remembrance of my folly to uphold your ego, Dimitri," she replied with quick moisture springing up in her eyes. "But I do not mind that. It is all so long ago. I have curiously little pride now."

"I ask you again. Look at me Nadine! When your letter came, when you appealed to me, did I fail you? Did I not receive your Vladimirov as you suggested? Have I not gone to all lengths to preserve your precious Ivan's neck?"

"Five thousand is not such a great length to you."

"I came here myself. I express an interest in this fantastic dream of his. I walk with him, and pretend to see great new cities rising around with a cathedral and towers where only bull frogs croak. Why do I do this? Do you imagine it is easy to oppose Susan? She is a whip which lashes me without a blow. I need you. You calm me. Leave this insanity here. Leave Turchin to his frogs and farmers."

She shook her head. She was not even angry at these impulsive words. "We are not young people to think in such terms. I shall not make any reply to your fantastic suggestions. Suffice it to know that it was never love between us, Dimitri. It is Ivan that I really love, have always loved. Likewise for you, it must be Susan. Our lawful passions are the only real and proper ones.

"You were not always so conventional."

"I have attained to wisdom."

"Or defeat, Nadine!"

At this, they left the subject. Trofimov lingered for a few days in Radom, and then returned to Chicago. Before he left he dropped the news casually to his friends that Henrietta Morrison had returned to the city and that she was a changed person. He said that she chose to live in the slums among the workers in the growing meat-packing industries; that Susan had snubbed her publicly because of her conspicuous costume, which was mannish and austere and also because she had been seen lecturing on a platform in a public park before a mixed audience.

Turchin, upon hearing the name of his highly valued friend, heard nothing of the baron's implied derogations. "She is back! God, Trofimov, that alone would induce me to make a day's journey to see her. If only we could get people like her to come and settle here!"

"I dare say you could," Trofimov replied with a cryptic glance at Nadine. "She is an uplifter, like you. Only in her, reprehensible as it is, it is not half as ridiculous as in you. No matter what she says about universal suffrage and eight hour a day programs for the workers, she adds charm to her arguments with her indisputable wealth. Even the odd garments she affects, the curious company she keeps, take on a gleam from the thought of her gold."

With this cynical observation he left his friends, who were of the opinion that all that they heard of the new career Mrs. Morrison was following lent proof of her admirable personality. In Nadine's mind there was a slight envy. Not the widow's wealth occasioned it, but the knowledge that she was vitally active amidst the excitements of the city for which she herself longed without cease. Turchin hardly knew how Henrietta's return to Chicago could afford him such pleasure as it did. He had a deep liking for the good tenants to whom he sacrificed every moment of his life; yet he missed the stirring bustle of city life as much as his wife did, and associated it unconsciously with Mrs. Morrison. Moreover, not indifferent to the outside world which came to them through old periodicals and journals, he too had for some years interested himself in the growing problem of the laboring masses.

In his reckoning, the people who fifteen years before had marched off to the wars were always destined to be the masses. These people as a body were his own people. He loved them as he continued to love the land that nourished them. Gradually he had come to see how, in the name of progress, the conditions of the laborers must become a part of progress. Industry he believed was not like the life of the land, where no prescribed hours for toil could be ascertained. But apart from farm work, he readily agreed that the men who fought black slavery must now voice their combined protests against white enslavement; must sue for more liberty in which to live apart from the environment of their toil.

These thoughts, quickly revolving in his mind, converged in the thought of Mrs. Morrison. To Nadine he said: "Is it not like that noble woman to take up a just cause? In her, Nadine, the things we fought for become concrete evidence that we do not fight any evil in vain. We shall have to invite her to visit with us, or better still, we will make a trip to Chicago."

This was a wish they clung to for the next several years, but which they could not realize. The good that Turchin had expected from Trofimov's loan was a transitory good, and the money was but a drop in the bottomless crater of his obligations and debts. In his great zeal he had consistently overreached himself and overtaxed his resources on behalf of tenants to whom, wishing to expedite their complete ownership of title, he gave personal loans which were never repaid. Ever more burdensome grew his own indebtedness until the fatal day arrived when the banks refused him more credit. He was forced to reluctantly liquidate his Radom holdings.

This untoward event came at a time when he hadn't the will to resist the downrushing current. He had just learned the shocking news of President Garfield's assassination; a crime which was the direct outcome of the nefarious spoils system introduced into politics and allowed to flourish during the incumbency of President Grant. A disappointed office seeker had shot President Garfield in July of 1881 and the President had succumbed to the grim reaper some 11 weeks later. The day he learned of his old friend's death was one of the few times Turchin gave himself wholly over to unassuagable, inconsolable grief. "Ah, Nadine," he choked, "I have but to love and honor a man for calamity to overtake him! All the friends of my life yield to an evil fate! I honor Mr. Lincoln and he dies. I love Scott like a son and he dies. I respect and admire Mihalotzy and he dies, too. The best and truest gentleman of them all, Garfield, is murdered. I find one who is not fortune's child, that fine Smirnov I told you about; and he, so harmless and good, dies at Chickamauga!" He became so wrought up by his own recital that agonizing tears streamed over his face.

Nadine was nonplused by his outburst. It was true, she had not known Garfield. Therefore, his loss and the means of his death, deplorable as they were, did not evoke such a storm of grief in her breast.

"Take hold of yourself, Vanya," she cautioned with a shade of coldness. "Neither you nor any man is so important in the universe! You invite madness with such superstition and prostration."

Not listening to her, having in fact not heard a word she said, he swung from grief to passion, from tempest to fury. He raged and swore with a gusto that ripped through the building and brought several of his neighbors anxiously to the windows at the side of the house. They peered into the room where he wept, and on their honest, frightened faces came a pity for their tempestuous leader who looked mad with his flailing arms and wild cries.

When the city banks soon afterwards forced foreclosure upon him, he took the dismal termination of his colonizing venture as a sort of anti-climax. It even seemed to him somehow appropriate that in this unequal measure, he should suffer in the name and memory of those that had been dear to him, and who had died through the malice and predaciousness of mankind's enemies. The evils of the times were emendations of his and Garfield's foes as they had been in Lincoln's. America's old enemies stalked the streets in new attire; that was the only difference between them and those honestly in Gray, or the more cowardly ones with the copperhead buttons on their lapels. In view of such emotion he scarcely felt his own collapse of fortune; although he lost everything.

The house was left them; this because Trofimov held the mortgage on it. If he had heard in Chicago of his friend's failure in Radom, he was tactful in his silence concerning it. No word came from him which revealed this knowledge. Certainly, he made no claims for his money, nor did Turchin expect him to make any. "He may be callous and hard, but he is no carrion bird," Turchin said. He is not of the disposition to rub salt in a man's wounds."

Wearily he spent the next three years in Radom where his small garden and cornfield granted them a bare existence. His visage was always grim these days with the knotty problems of soils and rust which were adequate symbols of those other problems with which he coped inwardly. His sturdy frame grew thickset the way an old man's often does, in spite of the meager table fare. Correspondingly, his wife grew leaner, until she was like a silvery birch beside his gnarled oak. When not busied with the endless chores a bleak existence necessarily imposes, she sat at a small table, and copied her husband's voluminous notes which at this stage he endeavored to transcribe into a rousing book, wherein would be revived the militant, the sound call to unity of a people pushing together for life and liberty. Her fingers often grew cramped and her eyes dim with application to a task made infinitely tedious by his perpetual and peremptory orders, his lengthy digressive explanations of military tactics, and his vituperations upon a generation which realized the benefits of the expended blood and toil without returning an iota of respect or appreciation.

"I shall open their eyes to what my brave boys underwent at Chickamauga. I will take it to them at their breakfast tables; at their dinner tables. They will have it in a book they can read and reread," he declaimed. "There's nothing like the compact form of a book; it is better than my trying to reach limited audiences from a soap box. Poor Mrs. Morrison! I see what her honest heart is essaying. She picks out a certain group, the workingmen, and hopes to aid them. But I am interested in the entire country. I shall appeal to them all! All classes, all groups, all Americans! If necessary, I shall go about and speak to the old veterans. They shall enter into the fight to restore to America, what Mr. Lincoln gave his life for!"

With this in mind he worked assiduously on the book "Chickamauga", which was ready for publication in 1886. Upon its completion, with whatever money they could beg or borrow, Turchin and Nadine took the long wished-for vacation to Chicago where, without much difficulty, they found Mrs. Morrison.

She was residing in an old building not far from the large packing-house whose workers formed the majority of her friends. She was quite unrecognizable to Nadine, who remembered her as a flashing and lovely woman with dark sparkling eyes. Now she stood transformed, seemingly much taller than Nadine remembered her. Her hair had become snowy white and of a fine texture which did not lend itself to attractive dressing. It was sleekly pulled back from the thin face, and tightly secured at the top of her head in an unbecoming bun, fastened with gray metal pins. She wore silver rimmed spectacles on her nose and a long silver chain attached these to her shirtwaist.

Her house was orderly and neat, though it lacked the inviting comforts which had furnished her fine mansion of the past. The entrance hall was dark with the heavy walnut shelves on which were stacked dusty volumes a scholar might have been proud to own. Her drawing room was a virtual office with tables and chairs and utilitarian oil lamps to be seen here and there. Her fingers were stained with ink and nicotine; she had taken to smoking cigarettes and when she had got over her excitement and surprise at the sight of her old friends, she lit one and offered the box containing them to Nadine and Turchin.

"You will find me the worst for wear and tear," she said with a small smile for Nadine whom she scrutinized with shrewd eyes, noting with a real regret the ravages of time visible on the once fine skin and lustrous hair.

"It is not one's exterior a friend sees," Nadine replied gently, experiencing the same sort of regret Henrietta had.

"She is right, dear Mrs. Morrison! You are even lovelier than you ever were." He looked eagerly about, drinking in the bookish atmosphere of the room. "I have it," he exclaimed, turning to his wife. "I know what this room reminds me of! Herzen's house in London! Remember it? There is in the very air of this room, something akin to what I sensed in Herzen's apartment - suppressed excitement, feelings of urgency and valuable time." It made him happy to make this association. "It makes me feel," he continued to Henrietta, who had seated herself and was listening in her uniquely rapt manner, which had first attracted Turchin, "that all struggle toward enlightenment, large or small, is of a similar sort; whether it is to free slaves, to enlighten downtrodden victims of ancient feudalism, or to do this work you are doing."

They warmed to this subject and in a little while the separation of years was safely bridged. Henrietta sympathized with Turchin's aim in publishing his recollection of Chickamauga at this time, and promised assistance. While they talked, she reached into a drawer and extracted a hand-bound copy of his first literary effort, his "Military Rambles." "I think you write beautifully," she said. "Your next will be as good." She had no power to render him any help in advertising his book she explained, for she no longer had connections with the Tribune. "If I had a fraction of the influence with it that once was mine, I would do everything possible for you, general. But because I fight for the poor, I am looked upon with distaste by all except a few old coworkers. Bross - you remember him - is still active, though he is quite elevated now, a popular journalist. Most of my acquaintances, however, eschew me." Her tone fell depressingly. "It will be no advantage to you to consort with me. I am looked upon as though I were personally pulling the cornerstone of democracy from under the White House, whenever I try to get an article published." She shrugged her shoulders in a new gesture, peculiarly resigned at the same time that it was resolved, and left it to her friends to determine for themselves to what extent she could be of help to them.

She did offer them her hospitality and whatever facilities her home offered, for as long as they elected to remain in the city. This kindness they accepted and in return accompanied her wherever she spoke - in meeting halls, in private homes, in public squares and parks; discovering to their astonishment that she was beloved to all the humble folk who knew her.

What Turchin had gleaned from the baron heretofore about her advocacy, now gained clarity and a better perspective. From her succinct, simplified illustrations and analogies, he began to find plausible her proposals for remedies in the welter of social evil that she pointed out. Yet for all her passionate pleading of the cause of organized labor, to take but one example, he was unable to persuade himself that what he considered merely a local and limited struggle was as cogent a medium for his mind as the problems of national progress which were now obsessing him. The logic, the justice of her arguments, he agreed to without reservations, but the immediacy and significance of them as determinants of America's future, he would not concede. "The problems of labor are only a fraction of the problems of America," said he stoutly.

"This is not a new struggle, General Turchin," she pleaded for his comprehension. "Long have the city workers been compelled to exist under conditions which have militated against all progress. The industries of this land have swelled enormously in size and profits. Is it not fair for those who have a great stake in industries, those who are the ultimate consumers, to ask for conditions and hours of work which are just a little more suitable to our age of enlightenment and progress? It is only a demand for the common decencies which prompts us to ask for eight hours to sleep, eight hours to play, eight hours to work and eight bob a day."

"Ten hours are not too much for a man to work if he lives sensibly," he contended, unconvinced either of his stand or hers, and a little impatient of both.

"There's another good reason for an eight-hour day," she urged. "For two years our coal miners have worked but half the time. Two years ago it was estimated that more than a million and a half people were unemployed. On the one hand, we hear the cry that too much wheat has choked the market; yet people cannot buy bread because they have no work and therefore no money." She warmed to her subject, and fell into a pose so like a public speaker that Nadine smiled involuntarily.

"There has already been a wave of strikes to gain this eight hour system. One strike alone cost the Knights of Labor over a million dollars in lost work. That is serious, General Turchin, but by shortening the ten-hour-a-day work week by one fifth, more men could be put to work."

"You mean to tell me that with the tremendous things to be done in this country, men are out of work? They are lazy, these men, else surely they would find something fit and useful to do!"

She smiled at him sadly. "You have been out of the city too long, general. I used to think that in the South, where a whole system had been overturned, my best efforts could be utilized. Now I am firmly convinced that an even greater change has come to us in the cities. It is here we have to guard our liberties, general! Asking for an eight-hour day is only an elementary form of the essential demand we are making, namely that those who labor shall not be deprived of the gratuities an expanding economy can apportion wisely. A great war, heaving changes in our political life, the spoils system and the unprecedented growth of our railroads; you should easily conceive of what inequalities are bound to rise out of all that, general. A period of financial reverses is a mere forerunner. Trofimov can attest to my truth. He is a great stockholder. He can tell you of the suffering of the rich as well as of the poor. Our population increases daily. Immigration is congesting our cities. Labor-saving machinery is the great threat to our economy."

Turchin, quite bewildered by her arguments, caught the last remark as a drowning man reaches for a log floating in a turgid stream. "But, my dear Mrs. Morrison! What are you saying? You have the same intensity we had in '61' when a nation's life was at stake! And now you tell me that labor-saving machinery contributes to the peril of our economy! Why, I spent five years of my life on behalf of young inventors, in an attempt to sell and make more inventions, so that, by the machine, man shall be freed from his endless toil! Nay, I cannot agree with you on that factor as a grievance. I am afraid your observations are distorted by imagination. On a convex mirror, small markings appear exaggeratedly large."

Soon his own partial success in the haranguing groups of veterans, in the publication of his book, "Chickamauga", which for a while seemed to rouse great interest, occupied him away from Mrs. Morrison's influence. Wherever he went he found a glad welcome, even in the drawing room of Mrs. Morrison's cousin, Brewster. He, with a strange perverseness, as though thereby insuring the prolongation of a life he found acidulously exciting as he grew freer of its foibles, heartily welcomed Turchin, the former object of his contumely and derision.

"So you have not forgotten us, eh," he demanded. "I am happy to announce to you that now you must accord me civilities you seemed incapable of twenty years ago. I am an old man. They tell me old men deserve respect. After twenty-some years with my elegant son-in-law I am in sore need of it." With a fierce look at his disapproving daughter, who stood her ground, proud now to be able in her great affluence to condescend to General Turchin, he held out his hand to him. The old gentleman was confined to a chair and, in spite of warm weather, was forced to keep his thin limbs covered by several blankets. Turchin took his hand, and found himself pitying the invalid. Where was the rancor of those by-gone years? Why did he not scorn the hand of a man who was a traitor? He could not answer these questions. He reacted to the moment, and forgave his old antagonist.

"I am a gentleman of wicked upstarts," Brewster complained. "We had more healthy stuff in us twenty years ago. This whining and snapping and striking and bargaining with one another - and my precious cousin by marriage, from all reports, in the middle of things as usual! I am glad to see you take a healthy interest in advising the fools of today to look to our intestinal fortitude to fight for what we believed. We put uniforms on, and took up guns! But this caviling against those of us who won our fortunes by our wits and intrepidity - bah! We disagreed, you and I. You were right. I am glad that, from all I hear now, we see eye to eye. I bought your book."

The approval from his old enemy upset Turchin. He looked to Trofimov (who all this while was coolly staring out of a window) to edify Brewster, to employ his old sarcasms against which he could stand more sincerely than against this dubious praise. But the conversation of the old man with the friend of his youth interested Trofimov in no way. Nadine was not present. She would have interested him, and but for Susan's sharp watchful glances, which he felt on his back, he would have interrupted them to learn about her. As it was, this room, his father-in-law, his fleshly wife, the brocades and the rich decor, had long grown wearisome to him. The conversation in this setting left him irritated.

"I don't agree with Father," Susan said coldly to Turchin, "that your book has any point after all these years. I don't agree that there is any purpose, except childish bragging, in your rehashing to audiences disagreeable things best forgotten. I should have thought by this time, General Turchin, you would have established yourself quite respectably. You cannot hope to earn much money reviving ancient legends!"

"It isn't solely a matter of earning money, Madame Trofimov," he was stung to reply.

"Why I know you have none," she insisted with sharp malice, careless of the crudeness which, all else failing, she knew would force her husband to face about.

Turchin had flushed scarlet. Trofimov indeed did whirl about, incensed by the vulgarity of his wife both in speech and manner. "She refers to the mortgage on your property. She learned about that. She is an Argus. There is nothing Madame Trofimov fails to note!"

"Someone has to look out for the interest of our son!" she snapped. "You don't. Papa enjoys putting up with your insolence, but fortunately neither my son nor I have to!"

Brewster, with his hands in his lap, with his bushy gray eyebrows quirked up in amusement, enjoyed the quarrel which sprang full-bloom between these two wedded partners and only nodded his head with impatience when Turchin, in deep embarrassment for them all walked from the room. "Ah, it has come home to him," Turchin thought compassionately of the baron. "His days, instead of being full and calm, are troubled by a shrewish tongue, from which the last drops of honey dried long ago. That is apparent. I am happy Nadine did not witness this." He shuddered slightly, and felt an impulse to return and to take Trofimov with him to Henrietta's house.

However, he made no further calls upon Trofimov. Instead he sought out his old friends at the Tribune where a few old-timers still remained and remembered him. They were gray and aged men who peered at him with short-sighted eyes and politely pretended he was the same handsome colonel who had exhorted them so long ago to support Mr. Lincoln. Some mentioned querulously the serious labor troubles the country was experiencing. To a man, these old republicans denounced the movement of organized labor to 'extort' privileges from their employers. All were worried over the years of unrest which the labor agitation only accentuated. From them he heard with indignation how political corruption was rampant, how Negroes were unlawfully incarcerated, not in the South where it might have been expected, but in the North, if they attempted to cast a ballot. "These crimes are isolated cases, surely," he cried, but in his heart despondency dwelt all that year.

On May 4 of the year 1886, an incident occurred in Chicago which added more gray hairs to his head, more sorrow to his secret sorrows over his beloved America, more determination than ever to go about the land and preach the lessons of the Civil War, when all men united to fight for human liberties, for a land dedicated to the proposition that all men are equal. "Only education will teach the heart," he declared to the ladies; "Only love for one's fellow men," to the gentlemen.

The incident which so affected him began after a peaceable lecture had been delivered to a vast audience of workers in a building not far from the property of a great meatpacking house, employer of most of the workers attending the lecture. The lecturer, on this occasion, was an editor of one of the Union papers, a man known among his fellow Chicagoans for his outspoken, fearless labor protagonism, especially in the case of the eight-hour day demand that labor was making. During the year's many strikes and labor disputes, he had risen to local eminence and won the respect of people like Mrs. Morrison with whom his charming wife was friendly.

His name was Albert Spies, and on the night of the lecture, he was in excellent form, full of pungent wit which was well received, and full of oratorical fire, also warmly taken. Like almost all the labor orators of his day, he took the occasion and the size of the audience as omens of a general susceptibility and launched forthwith into the history of the unions and the antiquity of their just claims. Among his listeners sat Nadine in her plain dark dress and Mrs. Morrison, who listened gravely, now and then turning to a friend with a meaningful little smile lost upon Nadine. It said nothing, it offered nothing, but it pleased her neighbors, who included Nadine in their affectionate regard of Henrietta. For Nadine this was the breath of life. Insensibly she relaxed. She could not drink enough of the vitality that clung about a city audience. What Mr. Spies said did not matter. It mattered that she was removed from the butter churns, the sheep and goats; that she need not see the Polish women spreading their wide toes on the grass.

She was sorry when the speaker finished and when the people began to surge into the square nearby. Haymarket Square was a pleasant, spacious place for an eager crowd to linger in and exchange comments on the speech just heard.

Several women were clustered about Henrietta, who had just waved her hand to Mrs. Spies. They were all serious women wearing cotton gloves and honest faces. Their husbands worked in the packing house. They loitered to gossip while their men re-enacted the lecture with loud words and gesticulations.

Suddenly out of several side streets leading into the square, a small corps of policemen debouched quietly, quickly, and fiercely. Their clubs, menacingly raised over heads that hardly suspected their presence, came down in a shower of stunning blows. An indignant roar of protest instantly welled up among the men, many of whom crowded together for flimsy protection against an onslaught which had risen without provocation. A few men, after the initial surprise, began to retaliate with ineffectual blows of fists and feet. A woman cried out as a club descended upon her shoulder. Pushing his way through the crowd, a well dressed man rushed to the spot where Henrietta and Nadine stood petrified, near a gas lamp. It was the baron. He had chanced to drive by and had caught sight of Nadine's face.

"Come with me, ladies!" he panted. "I have my carriage nearby. There is going to be trouble! Believe me, I know. These yokels have been begging for reprisals like this for a long time."

"Then go away!" Henrietta advised curtly. "This is no place for fine aristocrats, as you probably know better than we!"

"Do not argue!" he insisted, taking Nadine's arm. "I tell you this is no pleasant picnic!"

"Then go away as Mrs. Morrison advises," Nadine repeated Henrietta's words, though there was not in them the stingy reproach Mrs. Morrison's held.

But neither the ladies nor Trofimov, increasingly pressed by the riotous crowd belabored by the policemen had time for further parley. At that moment a bomb mysteriously exploded in the middle of the square. A deafening roar sounded in everyone's ears. A horrified scream rent the air, and where the bomb had fallen, bedlam broke loose amidst the dismay and surprise which had started the night's work.

Seizing Nadine's arm, Trofimov dragged her from the scene even before the smoke had cleared away, disclosing eleven dead bodies and the maddened people, pushing, mauling and tearing, one against the other, to force an egress out of the horror.

The explosion of the bomb subsequently roused the citizenry as nothing since the war had done. Suspected persons were hunted out and arrested. Albert Spies fled for brief safety to Mrs. Morrison's house. Newspapers assailed and cried down the unions. Workers marched in protest parades at which fashionable Chicago, in unfashionable passion, hooted from their curricles and coaches. Policemen on horseback rode up and down the section. Fear gripped the people most nearly involved, and betrayals and suspicion centered on the one man most sought, Albert Spies. No secret was made of the fact that the security of many of his apprehended friends lay in his speedy submission to the law.

In her house Mrs. Morrison paced angrily back and forth in a frenzy of anxiety. Mrs. Spies sat in a corner and wept, brave though she always had been in the espousal of the principals she upheld as staunchly as Spies himself. "It is madness to give yourself up," cried Henrietta, pursuing the theme under discussion. "In you they will find the dearest object of their hate! They hate us! My own fellow Americans are lusting for the blood of those who threaten their undisputed dominion! We all lived through the horror of an internecine war! This is war, too, friend Spies! You, they will kill if they lay hands on you."

Spies, a short heavy-set man with square-cut features, steady gray eyes and a friendly mouth, stood dejectedly near his sobbing wife. "I cannot permit them to torture innocent men, perhaps send them to death. They are not, any more than I, responsible for that bomb. We know that. Yet, if my person will satisfy our enemies, they may dismiss these others."

Thus, three days after the search was instituted for him, Spies walked into the police station and gave himself up, though innocent of all wrong. Eight anarchist's leaders were convicted as accessories to murder. Four, including Spies were condemned to death and hanged. One committed suicide and three others were sentenced to life imprisonment. In 1893, the Governor of Illinois pardoned the three survivors.

CHAPTER XXX

After the Haymarket affair, Turchin and Nadine returned to Radom. It was she who was almost eager to leave the city this time. The explosion of the bomb had been only the final rent in her dim veil; the weeks preceding it had opened her eyes to the motives which propelled both Mrs. Morrison and Turchin along their separate ways of service. Never an entirely unresponsive person, Nadine now felt an aching desire to relive the past years; to delete the traces of her sick longings for Dimitri; to live inwardly conjoined to Ivan as she had lived outwardly faithful.

The lecture engagements which had occupied much of Turchin's time during their sojourn to Chicago were not renewed for the following year, a fact which disturbed Turchin, who was all the more eager to repeat the satisfactory performances he had given, and to enliven the veteran clubs. They had little money and were too thoughtful of Henrietta to impose on her any longer. That lady made a poor and unapologetic hostess these days. The arrest and trial of her friends had aggravated her so greatly that she took to her bed. After that, in a fury which Turchin understood more than Nadine, she began an intensive campaign among rich and poor to secure counsel and intercession for the victims held incommunicado in jail.

"General," she had begged, just before they departed, "Is there no person with influence on whom you could call in the case of these innocent victims!"

"Ivan!" Nadine cried suddenly, "what chance is there that your friend Foraker might help? He has gone far in politics. You said so yourself."

"I do not know," he answered doubtfully. Turning to Henrietta, he promised, to dispatch a letter, which he did at once. But there was never an answer to his request for intervention. Over a year went by, once they were again at Radom, before they heard either from Mrs. Morrison or from Foraker; yet strangely it was the latter who first wrote. He was now governor of Ohio and personally invited Turchin to come to Columbus to attend the great Civil War Reunion. Gracefully he reminded him of his former, esteemed role as brigadier-general, and of his own insignificant part as a lieutenant. He ended by asking the honor of housing him among his personal guests. He made no mention of Turchin's letter concerning the men tried and convicted for the bombing in Haymarket Square.

"After all," Turchin excused him, "he is a busy man, and perhaps ethics do not consent to his interfering in another state's problems."

The Governor's "ethics" on the subject made Nadine curious. Over and over in her mind she reviewed the entire scene as it had appeared to her, when she had witnessed it. The peacefulness of the crowd; the sudden rush of the armed policemen; the uproar and dismay when the bomb burst among them; the appearance of Trofimov who had dragged her away. "He thought I was as indifferent to those poor slain victims as he," she said to herself. Aloud to Turchin she said, "How odd that the Governor makes no mention of that Haymarket riot. As a public-spirited man, ought he not to take notice of such things and lend his support to the defense of the innocent?"

Turchin replied, "If he says nothing, perhaps those friends of Mrs. Morrison's were not as innocent as she believes. She is an emotional creature, our dear Mrs. Morrison, and women get easily carried away to believe what they want to believe. I tried to tell her that allying herself to local factions and struggles would amount to no good. She's be better off to find a fine husband."

"Still, Ivan, if you go to Columbus, speak for those imprisoned men. I have the feeling that they are innocent. I saw no one hurl that bomb. It was thrown only after the police invaded the scene. It may have been an accident or a plot," she ended vaguely.

He paid little attention to her last words. He was thinking of the Governor's invitation to come to Columbus for the Reunion. It was to be no little affair. All who were able and willing, he thought, would be there from every part of the country, from all the states that had sent their sons to the armies of Grant and Sherman and the others. Grant's son would no doubt be there. Sherman, still hale and hearty, would certainly be there. The memories and evocations of all who had loved and fought for the Union Flag would also be there. "How can I go without money?" he asked sadly. "I am sick of borrowing. I cannot pay my fare on the railroad with a bag of turnips."

"There is yet time, Vanya," she answered resolutely. We shall find the money somehow." She went to his side and comforted him as only she could. "You will certainly go! You deserve to be honored among your old comrades!"

During the few months of anxious preparation for this anticipated event, she contrived to earn money among the tenants at Radom and the farmer folk of the surrounding area. She daily solicited for work and could be found many a morning sewing some young farmer lassie's trousseau linens or pretty petticoats. She still had a fine figure and a reputation for taste and knowledge of former glories which was impressive to the good women of the neighborhood. She was in demand everywhere and bore her servitude with a sweetness and patience everyone admired. In her fallen estate she gained more friendship than in her days of plenty.

At last the money was laboriously accumulated, and in plenty of time, so that Turchin could, with a joyous heart, set forth upon the long journey into Ohio. He carried only a single piece of luggage, but in it were his carefully brushed uniforms, his regimentals and the beautiful sword his men had given him a quarter of a century ago. As the slow old coach car bumped along its route, he rehearsed the speech he intended to make. First there would be the matter of reviewing the results of the war. He would tell them how wonderful it was that among the true patriots the glorious struggle of the War of Rebellion lived forever as a symbol of all struggles for human liberties. Next he would reveal to them how they, the veterans, had fallen below the high level of their achievements in battle, by permitting the fruits of their victory to spoil somewhat. He would cite the many errors of judgment he had noted carefully in a small notebook. He took this out of his coat pocket, and scanned his entries with approval. Among his notes he had especially marked for stress the corruption in politics which resulted in President Garfield's murder. Another asterisk stood beside his notation of the unlawful disfranchisement of Negroes at the polls. He had a tentative reminder to mention the labor disputes, but decided, as he returned the notebook to his pocket, not to embark upon this subject which, he felt uneasily surpassed his facts. Mrs. Morrison's dates and figures he did not accept as reliable. Without being aware of it, he was rather old fashioned in his regard for women's intellectual powers, no matter how well schooled he might consider her. "Ah," said he, "this reunion of old comrades will be something with which to embellish my life, this honor, this privilege of meeting my boys again."

He was still in this happy frame of mind when, two days later, he entered Columbus. The small city, quite cosmopolitan with its state house and official buildings, won his instant liking. To him, Columbus seemed a model city, neither monstrously gross nor yet overly countrified. Its buildings were handsome and decorative without diminishing the natural beauty of the interlocking trees and the pretty flower beds neatly fenced in along the wide avenues. An unusual amount of traffic thronged the squares; horses, coaches, many indicating signs of long and dusty journeys; buggies, and farmers' wagons rolling creakily toward the state house. People in gala dress trooped in couples and groups toward the Governor's mansion. Ladies in brilliant summer dresses and with parasols of silk entered and left the long shaded walks of the many charming houses along the way. All was gaiety and laughter.

Turchin drank in the sight avidly. He believed the beauty to be fitting tribute to the soldiers of the Union. The flocking of the whole city to the scene of the convention was also part of the homage owing to brave men, living and dead. The scores of gray beards, filling out their ancient jackets and sporting their old colors as they waved little banners of red, white and blue, or ribbons of tattered silk, once designating their special regiments, thrilled the old soldier who was making his way on foot.

If he secretly hoped some one of the animated faces his eyes scanned might light up with recognition, he was disappointed. Some few did give the old soldier a passing glance and an impersonal smile. Two stiff old veterans peered out of their spectacles at his brilliantly gleaming buttons which Nadine had carefully polished to a high luster. But no one recognized him who, at sixty-six, was a far cry, as they all were, indeed, from the stalwart officer of those distant days.

Coming at last to the Governor's mansion, he saw the lawns and the porches overflowing with color and life; clusters of old soldiers with their handsome matrons beside them; young men laughing above their high, stiff collars; blooming young women with spots of excitement inflaming their cheeks. Colored lads ran hither and yon as coach after coach rolled onto the grounds, as group after group mounted the wide steps of the mansion where they were welcomed by Governor Foraker. Trailing slowly behind one such group, he mounted the wide steps briskly. He was quite winded, and still carried his carpet bag which he had refused to relinquish to the servants. He walked toward the Governor slowly, unsmilingly, indifferent to the fact that his grimly serious demeanor must be looked upon as a reproach for the gaiety of the others.

When he stood at length before the Governor, he simply stopped and looked him in the eyes. Catching a polite surprise in Foraker's bland geniality, he raised high his head, and made him a salute with such precision that several women nearby applauded merrily. The governor, at a loss for a moment how to respond to this unsmiling military salutation, awkwardly lifted his long unaccustomed hand in return. No recognition lay in his eyes, however, as he did so, and but for the military dress of the old man - Turchin had carefully donned his uniform before leaving the train - he would have been at a loss to account for him among his personal guests. As it was, he believed the somewhat shabby old man in the glittering buttons to have strayed afield from the general body of veterans encamped in a nearby meadow.

Having made the salute and received a response, Turchin next extended his hand in familiar greeting, and this, the Governor perforce was compelled to take, though becoming a bit annoyed at the small farce, he not knowing who the profferer was. His lady, standing next to him, and busying herself with polite smiles and courtesies which the many guests demanded of her, suddenly leaned closer, the behavior of the old soldier having attracted attention, and peered searchingly into his face. She had not seen him since her wedding day nearly twenty years ago, but she knew him now. "It is General Turchin!" she whispered to her husband, and holding out both her hands she welcomed him in a charming fashion instantly emulated by the Governor who with a sudden pleasure repeated his name twice.

"General Turchin! General Turchin, welcome!" Turning to those near him he presented them all to his old commander with a signal deference and respect which Turchin took to encompass the remembrance and appreciation of all that his boys had done for the country he loved. These were his people, the same people who had lived through those memorable war years. Experiences such as they had shared in time of agony and travail bound men together forever. He congratulated himself that he had always judged his fellow soldiers correctly. These men would act again in defense of a Nation's honor, once they fully understood how their country needed them in these trying days; needed, if not their youth and strength, for wielding swords and shooting rifles, then needed for their maturity and wisdom in leadership. His exalted emotion choked off the conventional words he had planned to utter in response to the Governor's flattering sketch of him which he gave uncommonly well amid the smiles and ripples of pleasure from the ladies.

Suddenly, Mrs. Foraker took him in tow, and as they moved from the Governor's side, almost pushing him gently by the arm, she spoke easily and brightly of the happy prospect made possible by this great reunion of all the armies for the Republic. She pointed out to him the supererogatory kindness of the citizens in putting up the overflow of visitors in their own homes, in permitting their lawns to be used for the pitching of tents, and in arranging the complimentary reception that the old soldiers were receiving on all sides. There were thousands of flags, banners, pennants and flowers, not to speak of the grandiose display of arms and of the magnificent bands convening on the outer fields whence came already the sounds of martial music in rehearsal.

Mrs. Foraker conducted him into the house, and personally showed him to his room, which was a handsome large apartment full of stately furniture, now somewhat disarranged with ten incongruous cots placed in the center of it. One of these cots was for him she said, and pointed out the bell he was to ring when he wished anything.

He was the first guest in the room, and sat down at once upon one of the cots. The heat, the trip, the excitement had tired him more than he realized until confronted by the row of inviting beds. Yet, though he stretched himself on his back, he could not relax. His head throbbed annoyingly and all his old wounds, as though they were sentient things, revived their clamor; his shoulder twinged and his legs twitched; a pulse in his wounded cheek beat rapidly. He began to unfasten his military coat, which seemed to have grown out of shape. The sleeves were shorter, and the collar tighter. The buttons strained hard in the button holes, and roughly sprang apart as he released them.

A knock on the door made him start. Quickly he began to refasten the buttons. Opening the door he saw with amazement the Governor's lady herself standing in the doorway; a pitcher of water in her hands, a warming gracious friendliness on her face. "I brought you water, general," she said, holding forth the pitcher. "The servants are so distracted that I fancied it might be some time before one remembered to serve you."

"You, yourself drew that water for me?"

"It is an honor, dear general," she answered. "After all, you were the governor's commander. You are mine today."

Needless to say, he was deeply touched. Perhaps it was because of his age, or because of the weariness of the journey; in any case, he retreated into the room with tears of gratefulness. Above every other emotion he had was the one of familiarity with the intangible excellence these people, he knew, must possess.

In the same mood with which he had closed his eyes that night, he came downstairs in the morning to breakfast with the Governor and his house guests. He found nineteen ladies and gentlemen seated at the table, and places for as many more set. Mrs. Foraker quickly motioned him next to herself. She engaged him frequently in conversation so that, in a short time, the momentary ill ease he had experienced upon descending into this unaccustomed splendor vanished. His blue eyes, a little dimmed, gleamed with a buoyant alertness. Soon he was commanding the entire board and regaling the morning company with delightful anecdotes culled from his various experiences. "But nothing I have ever been part of in my life delights me so much as this reunion today," he declared. "To think that seventy thousand men have come from all over the land! What a telling refutation we are as a body, to the chicaneries of rascals and thieves in politics."

Governor Foraker, a white-haired man of florid face and steady eyes, looked disconcertingly down at his plate. Several ladies rustled like flustered birds, and Mrs. Foraker laughed aloud at the unwitting sally leveled at the lawmakers. "You are indeed a brave man, General Turchin," she applauded nicely, and in such a merry gaiety that others followed her example, and joined in the merriment which the old man accepted as plaudits to himself. "We shall want you to represent your brigade, and to give us a talk, which I am sure we will all enjoy and profit from."

"You have made quite a name for yourself with your recent lectures," the Governor suavely added, regaining his composure and overlooking Turchin's excoriation of his colleagues, as he chose to indulge in his remembered affection for the old man. "It will be an honor to hear our glorious days of youth recalled as eloquently as the newspapers say you have done with Chickamauga and Missionary Ridge."

"Yes," the beaming old general acknowledged the compliment seriously. "I have been gratified, but not surprised, at the enthusiastic reception I have received from my old comrades. We ought to bring up for discussion, the positive obligation for us to place markers where our own boys, especially, made history. It is only right that the Ohio lads shall have the credit they deserve for their gallant part in Missionary Ridge. I have often thought of that oversight. I learned that in recent years individual credits may have been incorrectly marked. Not that I hold with individuals receiving marked distinction where the entire teamwork of the army gained the victory, but in special cases, like the storming of Missionary Ridge, it is only right to commemorate the spot by monuments and markers ascribing the brilliant deeds accomplished there, to the boys directly responsible."

To this Governor Foraker listened interestedly and punctuated Turchin's pauses with vigorous nods which the others repeated up and down the length of the table. All praised the conscientious old soldier and the discussion was ended by a proposal that he be seated next to the Governor on the reviewing stand.

"Thank you, dear friends," he answered to this, "but my place, even now, is with the men I led then. I wish to march with them, the lads who followed me and who wanted nothing more than to save the Union and abolish a degrading institution!" He paused dramatically. "When I march with my old friends, I shall feel that beside me stand those others who have marched the greater glory road." Everyone knew with downcast glances, that he referred to the lamented dead, who were not there to share in the Review, whose bones were crumbling, perhaps, in the fields of Maryland, Alabama, Tennessee and Pennsylvania. No one said another word.

It was the day of the parade. A lovelier, summer day could not have favored the grand spectacle which the thousands of veterans, marching amid brilliant silken pennants and old reverenced standards, presented to a cheering throng. The whole populace of the city moved with them while three huge bands began to play simultaneously. Veterans and onlookers lustily raised their voices in song and the entire city resounded with the glad singing. Along each side of the road, splendid horses pranced in the parade and on them sat the sons and grandsons of famous generals, some living and some dead but none forgotten. The loose lines of veterans, under the stimulus of the stirring music, suddenly tightened their ranks, and the old feet, which had first tramped in their youth, took up a livelier pace, until the lines of faded blue captured the illusion of the past, and carried it proudly with them as they paraded through the cheering city. Five hundred gaily-glad children lifted their shrill, high voices in jubilant song when General Sherman in jovial good spirits, rode by at the head of the men. "Marching Thru Georgia" was their song, and Turchin sang each word with them. In the singing of the song he completed the service to his country that his sun stroke had interrupted. The years dropped from his stocky shoulders, and the scenes of his other years spread before his eyes. In fancy he saw himself marching through Georgia to the sea, to the moment of victory.

For hours the long parade wended its way through the streets of the city and with the passing of hours the military rigidity of the lines slackened. Old soldiers dropped off to the side of the road, where they joined the city folk and cheered the hardier marchers with laughter and pleasant jeers, caps waving high over their heads. Others leisurely occupied the reviewing grounds where the drill exercises were to take place, and also the speeches of eminent statesmen and warriors which were the highlights of the day.

The Governor of Ohio spoke. Other dignitaries and notables made jolly speeches and provocative speeches, and serious ones too. But all spoke to a crowd predisposed to like and admire whatever they said. Brightly colored fans were sold and the odor of cooking meat filled the air. Huge barrels of beer were stacked prominently in view and drew the attention of the old veterans almost as much as the speakers.

Turchin, who had marched all day, late in the afternoon, stationed himself near the kegs of beer. He leaned against one of them in happy fatigue, his eyes scanning the whole field of men. Suddenly a hand fell on his arm. "It is General Turchin!" a voice spoke eagerly. And Turchin looked up into an old man's face. "I fought with you at Chickamauga," the soldier said. "I stood with you when we cut General Thomas free of the encircling rebels. Fellows!" he turned to address several men standing nearby, "this is the Commander of the Eight Brigade. Give him a hand!"

In the small corner of the field Turchin found himself suddenly in the limelight. Half a dozen men with a roar of laughter and goodwill lifted him bodily off his feet and set him on top of one of the beer barrels. "Give us a speech, general," the first speaker implored. "Silence, everyone! A man, who knows why Thomas stood his ground at Chickamauga, wants to say a few words to you!"

All over the field an expectant hush fell momentarily. The scene near the beer barrels had attracted brief notice but as soon as Turchin uttered his first word, the interrupted buzz of conversation and laughter resumed, also the preparations for the succulent feasting. These distractions Turchin did not hear. He heard only the words which were pressing for release in his chest, words he had been rehearsing for just such an occasion all during the weary miles of his journey from Chicago.

"Comrades! He spoke thickly. Comrades!" And then his voice faltered. How could he convey to them, these men who had fought a nation's peril with him, the almost painful tenderness he felt for each and every one of them? How could he explain this strong, aching fraternal love which robbed him of his voice now that he wished most to command it in their behalf? "Comrades!" he began again in a somewhat stronger voice. "All of us know, today perhaps better than twenty-five years ago, that we require a high faith in democracy and a staunch belief in our Republic in order to weld ourselves together indissolubly as a nation. Only by binding ourselves closely with one another can we transcend the conventional terms of legal citizenship, and obtain to a greater unity in friendship as well as law."

He looked down from his beer barrel, and saw his closest audience intently watching the beer keg at which presided a white-aproned brewer with a tilted sergeant's cap sitting ludicrously over one ear.

"We require a swig of beer to whet our whistles, too!" a burly old veteran appealed to the crowd with comical gestures. "There's too much talk. Let's save the love for another time, general!"

"Quiet!" Turchin's advocate roared out. "Go on, general, tell us about Chickamauga! If he calls for beer we'll make him regret it."

"Let's get to the beer first and drink to Chickamauga", several others insisted. They waited for no consent, and made a concerted rush to the beer barrel on which Turchin stood abashed. Friendly hands, with no thought to cut him rudely off, lifted him down, and the ex-sergeant-brewer complying with the will of the many, drew him the first foamy pitcherful.

"Give him three mugs of beer for good earnest!" a voice in the dark urged.

"Over this way, gentlemen!" a crier called. "Roast pork, not salt fat back today, eh, soldiers?"

Upon this the men broke up into little scurrying knots which made for the sizzling meat pits where, on revolving spits, whole sides of young pigs were browning deliciously.

"See how it is, general," someone spoke respectfully. "Give these old fools hot meat and cold beer, and they think they have not fought for nothing!"

Bewildered and dismayed, the words of his speech crowding indignantly in his throat, Turchin almost tottered off to one side, where he sat down alone on the grass. Rising after a few minutes and being unobserved by those who chanced near him, he bent his slow footsteps toward the city and the Governor's mansion. The house was almost as deserted as it had been overflowing the day before. A few servant girls eyed him curiously as he mounted the back stairs and fetched his carpet bag. They made no inquiries of the fiercely frowning old gentleman when he reappeared and left the house without a word.

Nor did he speak to anyone later on when he boarded a homeward-bound train.

Once some miles out of Columbus, he took his notebook and methodically ripped from it the notes he had scribbled earlier. With slow and seemingly calm deliberation he stalked to the platform of the coach and hurled the useless pages into the oblivion of the night. "They will never listen, he muttered, "never, never! They drink their beer, and listen to nugatory politicians flatter and charm them with the tawdry spells and incantations of pleasure. Like stupid children they play on and on while one by one they disappear into darkness and ignorance. "Ah, Nadine, how right you have always been!" he called in fancy to her who remained the one steadfast reality in his crumbling universe. He longed for her desperately.

When he returned to Radom a few days later, his wife saw at a glance that no happiness had accrued to him by this sojourn in Columbus. She looked at him, so weary, downhearted, travel-stained and hopeless, and burst into tears she could not repress; yet her tears were precisely what he needed to give him the will to reassert his creed and heretofore unwavering faith. "The parade was fine, but it was an occasion for light talk and merrymaking," he told her. "The women and children and the bands made serious work impossible. I am an old fool to grow angry over a natural weakness of mankind - to meet together and grow jolly. I am afraid I behaved quite childishly, Nadine," he was able to say as her tears continued to drop over her face. "If a man is truly dedicated to a serious end in life, it should not count overly much with him if others are not as ready as he to listen."

"The goat has died, Vanya," she sniffed, "and I have begun to give music lessons so that we shall soon be able to buy another." This irrelevant digression from the trend of his thoughts did not anger him today. Instead he went out into their barn and inspected what little stock was left to them. An ancient sow slept in the hot sun. She was too lazy to shake off the large bluebottle fly resting on her snout. A few matronly hens pecked unhungrily at the pebbles on the ground. A large dog stood near the water pump, as though waiting until someone should come to draw water. The horse stall was empty and the small wagon disabled; it was like a still-life exemplifying the decadence of the entire farm. His wife had followed him out. "What shall we do now, Vanya? Are you still bent upon transcribing your notes for another book? Maybe the next one will be successful."

"I shall never stop!" he replied. Suddenly he whirled about and encircled his wife's slim waist with one arm. "If you can remember enough of the piano-forte to give lessons, I can still resort to my violin!"

"You will not sell it? I shall not permit that!"

"I had not thought of that," he laughed ruefully, "though we could get a fair price for it. I have never seen its equal anywhere. But I was not thinking of selling it - I was thinking of playing it - for hire."

So it was for these two old people. She went about, either sewing or giving the wealthier farm children lessons on the organ or the piano-forte, while he worked on his notes and sought to earn money in saloons as a musician. The sewing was strenuous, for her eyes were easily tired these days. She had further to tax them with the labor of love her husband's immense writing exacted. He had hundreds of pages, full of data relevant to every phase of those momentous years of the Civil War. He had besides these, a long treatise on surveying, and another on the philosophy of nature, which was in the vein of Rousseau whom he read repeatedly.

In addition to his own work she had to copy his crabbed abstracts of the writers he loved, notably Emerson and Thoreau. He was composing a short paper concerning itself with his criticism of the communal colonies which had but lately been a sort of intellectual fad for the idealists, especially that renowned experiment, "Brook Farm", with which Emerson's name was associated. These kept her busy and forgetful of the pressing problems of money and their waning strength.

Each day, year in and year out, Turchin made his long tramps to the small towns of the area. He carried his beloved violin tucked under one arm while with the other he carried an egg basket with eggs to sell. He applied in all available places for work as a fiddler; the churches, the county fairs, the communal meetings, and lastly the saloons where hire was most frequent and where in time he became a welcome adjunct to the evening's amusements. His eyes, his legs, his back lost something of the fine strength which had been his until Jonesboro; but his fingers, in spite of the expected stiffening of age, lost nothing of the cunning that touched the heart and spoke in trembling cadences of all things human, warm and appealing.

In this manner, bound together with a tenderness similar to that characteristic of their earlier years of marriage, these two continued humbly to cling to their obscurity and self-respect at Radom. The community had developed. It seemed to have literally stretched away in opposite directions from their small abode. The life that leapt and whirled past them left them out of its torrents. They had only one another and the little things that grew on their land. He grew white to the tip of his beard, and she frail and fine like old faintly marked ivory. They dressed in rough country clothes and looked like two strange peasants: he in a dun-colored smock and she in her coarse gray skirts and starched cotton waists.

Later, in 1893 their old friend Trofimov paid them a visit and this broke the threads of their mutual interdependence. No sooner did Nadine set eyes upon this will-o'-the-wisp love of her youth, than the old wasted misery again began to beat its worn-out life feebly against her reason and her age.

It was summertime again. She was absorbed in the kitchen where rows of jars stood ready for the contents of the jelly kettle. Turchin was weeding in the vegetable garden in the rear. The door knocker at the front of the house rose and fell several times before she heard it. All sounds took longer to penetrate except the tick of the metronome when she gave a lesson. At last the knocking became audible. She went slowly to open the door, and found herself gazing into the still whimsical face of the baron. "You!" she said, wiping her hands on her apron. Rather than surprise her tone implied reproach for the long delay.

"I," he said simply. He held out his hands to her.

"After so many years?" She did not take them at first.

"After so many!"

"You have come all this way to see us?"

"No. I have come with all my bag and baggage, Nadine. It is all being sent here in a cart from the station. I have come home!"

She was so startled at this that she failed to hear the back door slam as Turchin came shuffling in, his hands green stained and his face brown and moist from his labors.

"It is! It really is my old friend Trofimov!" he shouted happily, catching sight of him. He strode to him and grasped him by the shoulders with such a grip the baron winced and made some tart observations about a soldier's grip lasting at least in memory longer than the soldier. Nevertheless he was sincerely glad to see him too, and proved it by lapsing into Russian, to the delight of both Nadine and Turchin.

"You see how it is, dear friends. In the end I return to you." He spoke banteringly, but his words held great bitterness, even a touch of querulousness.

"You return to us? You were never of us!" Turchin exclaimed. "What are you talking about?"

"I forgot to mention it, but I have decided to come and rusticate with you and the cabbages. As a matter of fact, I don't have much choice, it would seem. My son has given me my conge, my pension and my just desserts. In short, he has disowned me, the young brat! With Brewster's money, now that mine is gone, he took that esteemed grandfather's name. 'Brewster' looks better on checks."

"Your son's disowned you! That is a calamity!" Nadine was sorry. "Surely Mrs. Trofimov could do something about that."

"She could and she did. She died, and left him her personal fortune. You know, old Brewster did the same five years ago. My son is over thirty. He pitied my gray hairs and bestowed upon me a pension providing I retired from Chicago. So here I am. My son finds me to have been unworthy of his honor. He's so American - you'd like him, Turchin."

"An unnatural son!"

"A chip off his mother's bustle," Trofimov said flippantly. "She died without much regret, I must say; she died to spite me!" Callously he laughed, but Nadine heard nothing except the accent of unhappiness in his recitation. Her imagination pictured in a flash the domestic hostility on which his marriage had floundered and his expectation burst. She gave him a sympathetic smile, and coaxed her husband. "He wishes to stay with us, Ivan. What do you say?"

Turchin was happy to accommodate his old friend. The fact was that he longed for company, even the baron's, and in a short while Trofimov was comfortably established in a pattern of life which went on with almost no break. But he was not a good companion. The years had taken their toll of Trofimov also and each day, with little patience and less humor, he had to undergo hours of headache before he was fit to present himself to his friends. Aside from this and a tendency of chest complaints, he was well preserved in a curious stateliness of dress and manners. He maintained a dandyish elegance which he even accentuated when he saw it irritated Ivan, who considered him a guest in spite of the board money Trofimov discreetly placed on the mantel every week.

"So this is what your worldly ambitions have come to!" Turchin could not help but remark one day in the fall when the seasonal rains and the tinge of an early chill cooped them all close together in the sitting room. "You sport a useless fancy before us, instead of that tinsel world that has ejected you."

"I have done better than you, my friend, "the baron rejoined snappishly. I at least have had everything a man desires! Yes, everything!" He looked over to Nadine who was smiling a secret smile of success.

"And it has all come to nothing! You have no fortune; you have no great enterprises; your son takes his grandfather's name - you say so yourself - and in the end you have only those old things you scorned thirty years ago! In the final analysis there is left to you only the untested glory of what you might have been had you lived for something other than yourself."

"I'd like to know for whom else one can live except oneself. I lived. I didn't dream. It is better to have had all the things I wanted than to end my days unfulfilled. I am old now, my dear ex-general, and at least I have success to look back upon. What do I need power or money for now, at sixty-seven? I have a competence. I have had millions! I have a son, the exact image of his dear mother, one of your exemplary Americans! He has a moral conscience which permits him to do only that which keeps him safe and intact! He has enough integrity for both of us and enough money; I am in debt to your fine Americanism!" His mockery was hollow, and the attempt at levity misfired completely. He did not deceive his old compatriots, who exchanged glances and kindly remained silent.

"Self ambitions," Turchin finally broke the silence - he meant to be kind - "come to nothing. A wise man would have known that in advance."

"Oh, spare me the philosophy, Turchin! I regret few things past or present. Life is given us to enjoy, not to moralize with. I have sampled of nearly every joy a man can know. I do not resent the sour tang at the core of the plum. I tell you I have no regrets! Even the one thing I might have wished added to my sum total of joys is not utterly lost to me. I am able to enjoy it in spite of obstacles!" He turned his eyes boldly on Nadine, who did not lift her silvery head, though her eyes quivered.

Catching the baron's meaningful glance toward his wife Turchin, for the first time in his life, knew an unreasoning jealously and savage, painful suspicion.

"My wife! She is the one thing you would have added to your sum total of joys! And all these years I called you a friend! I gave you every benefit of the doubt! I trusted you to honor me as a man, if not as a mind! Now, sir, I am not too old to whip you to your knees for the dog you are! Pack your things, and go back to the miserable filth that spawned you! Out!"

Nadine rose hastily. The white satin for the doctor's daughter's wedding gown fell in a shimmering heap to the floor. "Stop this stupidity, Vanya," she cried in mortified anger. "Dimitri said nothing of the sort. You are looking for an opportunity to revile him. You are sick!"

"Let him know the truth!" Trofimov said sarcastically. "He is the vaunted lover of the truth. Very well. You shall have the truth, my friend! In the first place, it has always been Nadine. You might have known it thirty years ago had you not been so self-interested! Secondly, what is there to do about it? You order me out of this house? Ha! Ha! Ha! Nadine, has his memory gone with his wits and his sense of decency, not to say gratitude? Turchin, remember the bank draft for five thousand? Do you recall that I hold a mortgage on this property? Does it occur to you that in all these years you practically owe me your life! Your house, indeed! If I choose, this is my house, and not I, but you would have to pack and leave the premises!" He was beside himself with a rage whose origin lay far back in the years. He showed himself without the smooth control that had always been a large factor in his charming mastery of difficult situations. But like Turchin, he was not a young man. Now, in anger, the handsome face gave evidence of the depredations of time. The lines deepened, and the skin was taut and discolored. Moisture clouded his once sparkling eyes.

While Trofimov was giving way to this violence of feelings, Nadine stood stricken. In her mind a strange, harsh laughter sounded like echoes in a tomb. At this time of life, she thought hysterically, after thirty years, to have this scene occur, to escape which she would have damned her soul long ago, transcended irony, became tragic farce. Her transfixed gaze on Dimitri brought him to his senses. His smarting anger turned slowly to shame. They stared mutely and forlornly at one another. They had forgotten Turchin, who had become silent and now sat slumped in his chair. Both of them simultaneously turned to speak to him, and found him in a dead faint. He had had a stroke, a cerebral hemorrhage, the doctor said.

CHAPTER XXXI

From this serious stroke, Turchin gradually recovered to some extent in the body, but never in the spirit. Between him and Nadine, a blank wall had suddenly dropped, cold and stony, through which in spite of her redoubled care of him, she could find no admittance and which shrouded her days and nights with lacerating remorse and repentance. Even the baron showed some remorse for the part he had in provoking and inciting Turchin to the frenzy responsible for the stroke. He tried to make amends but the sick man turned a deaf ear to both the baron and Nadine. Daily, when he was again able, Turchin walked into the nearest towns where he took sundry odd jobs in order to earn his few pennies. These he meticulously placed nightly at his dinner plate without uttering a word. When compelled by weakness to stay at home, he sat by himself in the front parlor, and did nothing but stare out on the deserted road leading from their front lawn toward the station, as if he watched and waited for someone. "Friends, friends," he mumbled inarticulately. Or if a neighbor woman came to offer Nadine work, he turned his back to her and suffered any and all to think what they pleased. He was utterly apathetic, filled with a dead indifference, often pathetically gentle. It was as though he had taken a vow of continual silence. At last the baron was determined to clear up matters and attempted one day to taunt him into retaliatory speech. He succeeded in obtaining only a sad smile and a disconsolate shake of the head; Turchin refused to speak. Hoping to elicit some speech from him by another ruse, he informed him that Mrs. Morrison was arriving to pay them a visit. The answer he got to this was another smile, but a gentle, kind smile which lasted a long musing moment, long enough to stir up anew the voiceless grief. With a low groan he started up and without a backward glance at Trofimov or Nadine, he went out into the grayness of the November day.

But the baron had not told a lie and some days later, upon receiving Nadine's letter, Mrs. Morrison did indeed arrive at Radom. Turchin was at the station to meet her. As she descended from the train she saw him and began to tremble. So stooped and old was he now, that the sight frightened her. She ran to him and clung to his outstretched arms. "Mrs. Morrison! Mrs. Morrison!" he cried with trembling lips.

"Can you not permit yourself the license of naming me Henrietta, my dear friend?" she quavered. And then the two, with a fit of foolish pleasure in one another, embraced and laughed and cried all in one.

"All these years I have wanted to have you here! If only you had been here when this beautiful river valley was flourishing! How often I thought of you!" His voice was clear, and his whole frame straightened up.

"If you had but once called me!" she was about to say, said it to herself in fact, but pressed back the telltale words. Even as an old woman she could not depart from a lifelong habit of reticence and restraint.

She took up her abode in the neighborhood and remained in Radom, until her death, ten years later.

Her coming broke through the icy barrier which Turchin's silence had reared. She had abandoned her austerity of dress, and with a curious contrariness, perhaps that of advanced age, resumed the gracious and fastidious costumes of her youth. They were somewhat gay, but she was grave without false dignity. Her beautiful imported laces were softening and beautifying to the dried parchment-like quality of her face. Her fingers showed stark blue veins running through them, but she added no garish jewelry to attract notice to this defect. Later, she took to a delicate use of the rouge brush.

She spent much time with Trofimov who seemed to draw sustenance from the impersonal friendliness she now bestowed upon him. His old animosity she quite forgot and chose to look upon him as a kinsman.

"How odd, Mrs. Morrison," he said one day in the early spring, that in these wintry years of our lives, we should find ourselves thusly united. You with all your money - I suppose you were not wiped out by the stock market panic last year? - I with my pension - I must tell you how my precious son Robert granted me a stipend out of Susan's money - and the Turchins, who end with nothing, neither money, fame nor honors."

"General Turchin has memories worth more than money," she replied.

"He has your abiding affection and respect! I can see that. Still adamant in his defense, eh?"

"Yes, he has that," she retorted with a faint blush on her yellowish cheeks. "If I could devise a way he would have whatever money is left me!"

Trofimov was skeptical as he dallied with her. He still made an interesting figure of a fine old gentleman. With a curious whim, nature seemed to have brushed his palette with mixed colors so that his hair, streaked with gray at the temples, remained dark though not lustrous, on top while his eyebrows and sideburns were almost startlingly white. This odd coloration lent him a distinction in appearance and a suggestion of the inscrutable; no one could tell whether he was of a benign temperament or a surly one; at various times his demeanor bespoke one or the other and often both.

"No one can help that man," Trofimov growled. "At his age, for the services he had rendered a fantastic cause, he ought at least to have some small compensation. But who is so brave as to suggest that nothing comes to any one of its own accord? One has to push and scratch and claw for it! In other words, go after it!"

"You do not yet understand the noble stuff of this man," she smiled.

Nevertheless, when everyone else might have been timorous to broach the subject, she braved Turchin's displeasure and persuaded him at length to compose several letters to prominent men like William Benson Foraker who might interest themselves to secure the old general a pension from Congress. There were kind responses to these letters and it was these responses in themselves rather than what benefits lay in the power of writers to bestow, which brought Turchin a great happiness. Foraker particularly promised to exercise all his ingenuity in procuring for his old commander at least the small allotment that he felt the country owed Turchin.

Foraker, now a Senator from Ohio, earnestly endeavored to do whatever he could for the good old general and meanwhile entered pleasantly into a desultory correspondence with him.

With the disturbing presence of Trofimov alleviated by Mrs. Morrison, Turchin was regaining a measure of his old enthusiasm, which if not forward pushing, considering his age, was at any rate worthy of him, and served as a reminder of great deeds and acts of the past.

Two years slipped by uneventfully and another election year was approaching. Readying himself to take part in this forthcoming event, he was inevitably brought to think of other years and other issues. Those which were confronting the citizenry at this time, he lost sight of in the recollections of other days, and more stirring times of real conflict. There was talk in the wind of America's bad feeling toward Spain, of possible war looming in the distance, but he discounted these "journalistic rumors" with a high snort of disbelief. "After the War of the Rebellion," he announced to his guests at dinner one evening, "the country has learned the fearful cost of wars. There will be no more. The preciousness of the course of agreement, conciliation and compromise has been learned. This land is intended as a haven for the war weary of the world. It is as is expressed in that poem you read me, Henrietta, the one you said they put on the great statue that France has sent to this country! You see, the poets of this land recognize our country's true function in the world. This talk of war with Spain is nonsense - but it is no nonsense when my country is falsely informed about the valorous deeds of our heroes, defenders of our freedom. At Missionary Ridge we turned the tide of destiny. There is the turning point in our country's history, I tell you, good people! And I hear from Jewett Palmer that my brigade's part in the assault that day has not been duly accredited to us!"

He paused for breath. He had been extremely short of breath lately. "When America forgets its Union heroes - and all those who died at that Ridge are her heroes! - I shall admit I have dreamed a great dream in vain!"

The company laughed and agreed with him on the importance of accurate markers on the historic site. Eagerly, thereafter, he occupied himself with rectifying what he considered a grave error in justice. In 1896 he, accompanied by his old friend Trofimov, attended a convention of the survivors of his old Eighth Brigade, held at Marrietta, Ohio. The long trip left him spent and weary and frankly honest in admitting to Trofimov that he felt his years heavily. "Seventy-four is no travelling time for an old, worn-out soldier," he laughed.

"You will undoubtedly find justification for it, none the less," was the ungracious rejoinder from the other. Trofimov had come with Turchin at Nadine's express wish. That she worried over Turchin, exasperated him. In spite of his own venerable years, in spite of the long years of knowledge and of the pointlessness of whims and frustrations now, he could not quell the pique occasioned by her concern for her husband. The issue of his ownership of the house had never come up a second time, nor the fact that it had all but estranged him from Nadine, so that Mrs. Morrison's presence was in the end the factor which ensured his continuance at Radom. In the past year the atmosphere was more pleasant and the four old people adapted to one another in a generally congenial fashion.

"I may be old, Trofimov, but I am still a man and I still have a sense of right and wrong, something I think you never had."

"I took good care to iron it out of my life before it made the fool of me it has of some others I could name."

"Save your breath, Trofimov. You wheeze at night as it is. You didn't storm that bristling crag at Missionary Ridge. No son of yours lies moldering in forgotten dust. You have no need to wish monuments where you trod! Where you stand and where yours will stand will be eternal wastelands. You will, however, fortunately for you, never realize this; and a little unconsciousness is undoubtedly good for you."

But bluster as he would, he was nevertheless thankful for his companion who attended the Marrietta meetings with him and the other old men, who found a point of communion in their childish clamor for praise, as he scoffingly put it. He sat through the tedious arguments and debates, digressions and reminiscences, until he inwardly groaned; but at length the matter was concluded with very ceremonious details and strict formal rules. A commission was arranged and a brief was drawn up to be presented to the War Department. Charts and drawings were to be submitted as well as actual records and depositions. The claim was duly established, that a certain position marked inaccurately was rightly the point where the Eighth Brigade, under General Turchin, had made its rushing attack upon Bragg's gunners on Missionary Ridge.

At length he and Trofimov made ready to return to Radom. The journey and the work involved in organizing the Commission, the painstaking drawings Turchin, with remembered cleverness, had worked out patiently, were, nevertheless, too much for his battered old frame. Soon after his return, he suffered another severe setback, this time a dire heart attack from which it was not thought he could recover.

Oddly enough, he regained both consciousness and a feeble health, losing however, that which was most deplorable, the even flow of his ideas and his speech. For long months he was confined to his bed or chair. For long months he was barely able to totter into the garden where he always found Mrs. Morrison, red of eye, but ready to smile as soon as she beheld him. Seated near her he was often, for long hours, the complete master of himself, but when she took her leave, he fell into a childish whimpering mood which, while it disgusted Trofimov, brought Nadine kneeling to his side. "I am here, Vanya!" she often cried when his mind wandered painfully into the past, when he became, in his fancy, a fourteen year old lad riding his horse on his father's land.

If he ever heard or understood her passionate devotion, he attended to her words as if he were a stranger listening to a meaningless cry. Sometimes her tears and her pleas for his attention threw him into a clear, recriminating fury. "So! You are here! The wife of my bosom! The beautiful darling of my heart! But by whose grace are you here? By his! Go to him who has graciously left you to succor me now!"

"He is going mad," Trofimov declared, not without some regret, though his temper was often tried to the fullest by Turchin's wild, unbearable accusations. If he is going, I wish he'd have done with it.

Nadine only wept silently.

"Go on, Nadine, be very feminine and ease the intolerable situation by turning into a weeping mortuary! I say he is a demented old man. Old age affects some people like that! We are old too, if not as old as he! If I grow slobbery and insane, please shoot me!"

Nadine would not reconcile herself to the idea that Turchin was on the verge of insanity, if not already there. Tenderly she nursed him with both care and prayer and a love in her heart which now begged for forgiveness of every line in his face, of every breath that came stertorously from his chest.

One night poor Turchin woke as from a trance. A new year had come and almost gone without his being aware of its coming or going. Suddenly, with a lucidness that illuminated his whole mind, he woke from his disturbed sleep and crept through the house. He could hear Trofimov's heavy breathing and Nadine's light tossing and turning. With a sly quietness he crept down into the sitting room where the banked fire in the fire place was burning dully red. Without lighting a lamp he began as though by instinct, to haul down his books, armload after armload. These he stacked neatly along the hearth tiles. Next he withdrew folders of his papers from the desk drawer. These he also piled high before the fireplace. Then he gathered his old violin close to his bosom, stroked it several times longingly, and laid it atop the books.

"Now!" he whispered softly. "Now I shall show them all! I shall give the answer of a loyal American to those who press this great and good land to their dirty work! War with Spain! More blood, more pain, more feeble old mothers screeching when their sons go off! These books! These papers! What good are they? They would not listen. They smiled and patted my back and shook my hand, and told me what a great general I was! Then they wanted to drink beer when the time for action was on hand! They should have put into use the lessons we taught them at Chickamauga! But I shall show them! I shall make a blaze to reach up so high in the sky that they will all see it! I shall make a blaze out of the words they would not hear! Well! They will see them now, in letters of fire!"

Slowly, with very crafty deliberation, he began to place volume after volume in the fireplace. He made no sound save that of a ripping of paper as he tore his manuscripts into bits. For hours he crouched in the increasing heat of the room and burned his books. A pale lightness began to show across the sky. He looked up at it through the window, studied it with angry defiance. "You shall not force me to retreat!" He shook a clenched fist at the dawn. "See", and with one thrust he threw all the remaining books into the blazing fireplace. A great cloud of smoke, rancid with the demolition of old leather and brittle papers, enveloped the room. Hysterically the old general began to cough and choke and at the same time, to laugh. This woke the other two occupants of the house. Smelling the smoke, they came scurrying downstairs just in time to prevent the entire house from catching fire.

At one glance, both Trofimov and Nadine saw the huddled form of Turchin, crouching in the corner beside the book case. In his arms he held his violin with awkward strength, for he was bent double in exalted unconsciousness.

After this third attack he could not be left alone. In truth, his condition left him so weak and will-less that there was little fear of another wild outburst such as this last one which resulted in the destruction of his papers and books. Between periods of listlessness he was subjected to transports of impotent fury. Only with Henrietta was he genuinely calm and able to sink into a gentle slumber under the soothing ministration of her fine reading voice. With Nadine he was usually like a fretful child, wishing nothing so much as her hands to smooth his forehead. Trofimov he appeared not to know, or at best only to accept as a moving shadow across a screen growing ever more crowded with shades.

The last year of his life was calm. The good news that arrived for him as a reward for a life time of love expended, he was unable to appreciate. Senator Foraker and his colleague had at last obtained a hearing for General Turchin and the Congress of that year had granted Turchin a small income effective at once.

The century rounded itself out. Another war had been fought and won. A new generation and a new century marched vigorously forward, unaware of an old American who lay in a mental hospital at Anna, Illinois. His end was near. For some months it had been necessary to keep him in the hospital. Each day, three old, dark-clad figures were to be seen walking side by side on the hospital grounds. These were his last friends. They came with sad hearts to apprise themselves of his condition. The doctors had said his flickering life was a matter of days or weeks.

"If only he will know that his life's efforts have won him recognition," Henrietta said softly.

"He will know, he will," Nadine assured her, believing this last firmly, in spite of Trofimov's assertions to the contrary.

One day when all three people who, each in his own way loved him, stood silently about his bed, Turchin indeed opened intelligent eyes upon them. "You are all come to me!" he tried to smile. "Come nearer, all of you. You too, Trofimov. That is you, is it not, baron?"

They drew closer fearfully. The sick man stretched both his arms out as far as he could with his spent strength. "My right hand I give to you, Nadine," he said reverently. "My left one to you, Henrietta!" Then withdrawing his hands from the shaken women, he held them out forward toward Trofimov. "To you, old friend, false baron, foolish compatriot, I give both my hands in friendship!"

He dropped back exhausted upon his pillow. A smile tried to hold its place but failed.

"Call the doctor, quickly!" Henrietta urged Trofimov who flew to do her bidding.

"She is a true friend," Turchin murmured to Nadine. "Her heart tells her I go now!" And as Nadine burst into heartbroken sobs, he tried to shake his head though it felt rigid and immovable on the pillow. His hands clutched the empty air, and then spread peacefully open.

The doctor and Trofimov returned just in time to witness what seemed the last motion of Turchin. They thought it was all over as a shudder shook his old frame. But he suddenly raised his right hand in salute. "I pledge allegiance to you, Mr. Lincoln and to the Cause we both loved better than life!" Then his arm dropped like a leaden weight.

These were his last words.

Printed in the United States
By Bookmasters